D1436877

TAKING
LEAVE

ALSO BY JANET SHAW

Some of the Things I Did Not Do

TAKING
LEAVE

JANET SHAW

VIKING

VIKING
Viking Penguin Inc., 40 West 23rd Street,
New York, New York 10010, U.S.A.
Penguin Books Ltd, Harmondsworth,
Middlesex, England
Penguin Books Australia Ltd, Ringwood,
Victoria, Australia
Penguin Books Canada Limited, 2801 John Street,
Markham, Ontario, Canada L3R 1B4
Penguin Books (N.Z.) Ltd, 182–190 Wairau Road,
Auckland 10 New Zealand

First published in 1987 by Viking Penguin Inc.
Published simultaneously in Canada

Portions of this book first appeared in slightly different
form as two short stories, "Inventing the Kiss" and
"The Courtship of the Thin Girl" in the author's collection
Some of the Things I Did Not Do published by the University
of Illinois Press. Used with permission of the publisher.

Grateful acknowledgment is made for permission to reprint
excerpts from the following copyrighted material:

"Sweet Baby James" by James Taylor. © 1970 Blackwood Music Inc.
& Country Road Music. All rights controlled and administered
by Blackwood Music Inc. All rights reserved.
International copyright secured. Used by permission.

"Worried Man Blues" by A. P. Carter. Copyright 1930 by
Peer International Corporation. Copyright renewed.
All rights reserved. Used by permission.

"He is more than a god" from *Sappho, A New Translation*,
translated by Mary Barnard. © 1958, 1986 Mary Barnard.
Used by permission of the University of California Press.

LIBRARY OF CONGRESS CATALOGING IN PUBLICATION DATA
Shaw, Janet Beeler, 1937–
Taking leave.
I. Title.
PS3552.E345T3 1987   813'.54   86-40322
ISBN 0-670-80054-6

Printed in the United States of America by
R.R. Donnelley & Sons Company, Harrisonburg, Virginia
Set in Simoncini Garamond
Designed by Ann Gold

Once more, for Bob

I would like to acknowledge the generous help of
C. Michael Curtis on this story, and of Dr. Phillip Dibble,
Geoffrey Black, Kristin Beeler, Mark Beeler, and Laura Beeler
for special information. I owe a great debt to many other
friends, and especially to Jack LaZebnik for his
inspiration and encouragement.

TAKING
LEAVE

1

The late August afternoon had been hot, but now Trawick saw lightning throb through cumulus massing where the sun had set; with a storm, summer would be over. On Kartnerstrasse he hurried by the vendors of chestnuts, cut flowers, ice cream, women lingering at sidewalk tables over last coffees. At the corner of Saint Stephen's Square he stopped to read the name of her new hotel again on the scrap of paper. It was his good luck her tour had missed the plane. He'd been chasing her all over town. In another block he came to her street, but he checked the paper twice again—the back street was almost as narrow as an alley. But there it was, in the curve, the small canopy, Hotel Anna.

An ambulance siren, rising and falling without rhythm, cut across the traffic noises. As he turned into the side street, the wailing and the circling lights sped toward him. He glanced into the hotel entrance—a faded blue rectangle with a fat blue couch in the center—and continued past it to the doorway of a grocery shop. When the ambulance turned the corner in a tumult of lights and noise, silence sucked in at the walls of the apartments and shops, shadows tumbled back into the gutters. The sky dropped lower.

Pressing his thumb against his lower lip, Trawick turned back to the hotel. He knew it was a place popular with students because of its location and cheap rates. The tour had found rooms here because the university wasn't in session. He loped across the street and pushed open the glass door. The lobby was deserted. He saw his reflection in the clouded mirror behind the desk. He wasn't as young as his Levi's and open shirt suggested. The strains of fatigue under his eyes, the deep lines there and at the corners of his mouth where his inch of beard didn't hide them worried him. He didn't like the way the wind had pressed his yellow hair to his forehead. He pushed his fingers through it impatiently.

Instead of ringing the bell for the concierge, he leaned across the desk and turned the room ledger around. Easy to find her name: Hale, *Zimmer 3*. An incredibly cheap rate, so she must be in one of the unoccupied student rooms. But how to find it? He started down the hallway toward the sounds of voices, then saw the narrow staircase. What the hell, just give it a try. The staircase was dark. Without searching for the light switch, he bounded up, two stairs at a time. At the window of the second floor, he paused and looked out into the airshaft. And there she was, directly across from him, opening heavy shutters slowly outward into the dark airshaft, as though pushing them through water. A pigeon beat up from the railing, and she gazed after it, then up at the sky, a half moon disappearing behind the clouds. Lifting her dark hair from her shoulders, she fastened it behind her head with a clasp she opened against her teeth.

He felt he'd chased her for years. He wanted to call out, Hey, wait there, I'm coming. He shoved at the window sash, fumbled for the lock and tried to spring it. It gave but the window wouldn't budge. Painted shut.

"Damn!" He let out a long breath, tasted the grit he'd knocked from the windowframe into his face. But there was no hurry now. And he was so close, no farther from her than the length of a room. He could easily see the shell she wore like a charm on her single hoop earring, her man's waterproof watch flashing when she turned to pull on the water faucet. Steam rose from the small bathtub. He settled down to wait.

Pensively tapping the shell in her earring, she bent over the tub. With her hair skinned back except for her bangs, her face was more quaint than pretty—thick brows, down-slanting eyes, short nose, lips pale and chapped. Even in repose, there was animation in her expression, an alertness, as though something might be about to happen. Though she was slightly plump, there was nothing soft or yielding about her. He thought she still showed that singleness, that independence of spirit a girl has when she hasn't yet begun to try to please a man.

She glanced at herself in the large mirror already misting with steam, then began to unload her backpack, stopping when she came to a red and white Band-Aid tin. She took from it a folder of cigarette papers and a sandwich bag of pot. With her fingertip she gathered the grains from the bag and the bottom of the tin and rolled herself a joint, taking long, hungry draws on it before setting it on the lid of the box. From the backpack she scooped up a handful of underwear, dumped that into the tub, squirted some soap in from a plastic bottle. She unbuttoned her pink shirt as she watched the tub fill. When the waterline was high, she turned the streams off. Stubbing out her joint on the Band-Aid box, she stepped behind the window.

"Jo." He didn't mean to say her name, only to be quiet and to watch. He'd been pressing his hands up against the window sash, the muscles in his chest and arms tensed, like a dancer lifting his partner. Scabs of paint had flaked onto his wrists like gnats settling. He shook his arms, his hands tingling as the blood flowed back. In the close hallway it was still midsummer. The trapped heat smelled of disinfectant, cigarettes, and, unaccountably, oranges. "Jo Hale."

He remembered the names of her sister and brother-in-law, too. On the letter in his jacket pocket he'd written "Dr. and Mrs. William Brenner," a masterpiece of formality. The thin hotel airmail stationery rustled when he touched it. Except for that insect sound, and his breath, the stairwell was quiet. It was the service stairs; no one would use them until the meal downstairs was over. He licked sweat from his upper lip, felt a trail of it down his chest. Even if she looked directly across the airshaft at him, she couldn't see him in the dark hall. That was part of the excitement. Come back, Jo, he willed her.

When she did, she was nude. She was full-breasted, her waist thicker than was popular, her legs short but well-muscled. One foot propped on the other, she leaned against the tub to untangle a braided elastic clothesline. A knot in the line required biting. She gave up, tossed the clothesline onto the chair and climbed into her bath.

A slick of sweat formed where his hand pressed against the windowframe. She rubbed shampoo into her hair, streams of pearly bubbles dripping from her pale nipples. When she rinsed, she gathered her hair in both hands to wring it, then wound a towel into a turban. Propping her feet on the end of the tub, she shaved her legs, hesitating over the sharp bones in her ankles. She soaped her armpits, shaved there, then—he bit his lip—knelt up to shave the dark hair from high inside her thighs. He cursed at the pigeon that stepped stiff-legged along the railing in front of her.

Standing, she tucked the second towel around herself like a sarong. Out of the bathtub, she was behind the window again. He tried by the force of his will: *Come back.* She stepped into the center of the room to take her laundry from the tub.

His chest throbbed—he wanted to pace, to run. Instead, he pressed harder still against the windowframe.

With the corner of her towel she wiped clean the misted glass of the mirror. Almost facing him in it, she appeared to him as she saw herself. She cupped her breasts, a silver ring on her right middle finger catching light. Now she stood taller, pulled in her belly, tensed the muscles in her thighs until they were clearly outlined. The hot water had brought out a rash above the line of her bikini. She must be asking her reflection, *Am I pretty, then?* Her thumbs stroked until her nipples pointed. She was asking herself, Am I sexy? He hadn't thought to wish for this. Nor for what followed, for she arched her back, slipped her hand down to her dark triangle, parted the lips and touched there, too. More and more quickly, light glanced off her silver ring. He held his breath. *Come. Back.* He looked from her fluttering fingers to her face: she'd shut her eyes with the effort of concentration.

Voices in the hallway below. He'd have to get out of here. He stepped back and stumbled into a wire wastebasket. When he tried to swallow his mouth was dry. He looked again at Jo. She rested against the basin, her eyes still closed. Watching her, he took the letter from his jacket pocket, tore the paper across into halves, then into quarters, ripped those, too, and dropped the shreds into the wastebasket. Jo ducked down for her towel and bumped the window closed with her shoulder as she turned for her backpack. The glass was opaque.

Now there were heavy footsteps coming up the stairs. He put his hands in his jacket pockets and ran down, brushing by a thin-faced young man in a blue work jacket, who said something brusque in German, but Trawick didn't stop. He hurried into the lobby, where a few members of the tour were gathering. How could he cut Jo out of this herd? And the last people he wanted to encounter right now were her sister and brother-in-law. At this moment, even more than being with Jo, he wanted to think. He'd been given a gift, and he wasn't sure yet what it meant.

2

Will had managed to run far enough to put an ache in his chest
and a wash of sweat over his body. Vienna was a good city for
running. Although the streets were crowded all day, at dusk the
city emptied out for an hour or more and he had the sidewalks
to himself. Tonight he'd run windsprints, too, though at his age
such conditioning was crazy. Tomorrow he'd be trapped on
planes. Tonight seemed like his last chance. "Last chance" was
an expression he'd begun to use lately about a lot of things.

The hotel lobby was airless and overheated after the cool
wind outside. As soon as he pulled off his headband, sweat slid
down his temples and into his eyes. He scrubbed them with the
back of his hand and saw the concierge through a haze. "The
number of Miss Hale's room, *bitte.*" He wished he'd taken the
trouble to learn a little German, at least enough to ask a simple
question. As he'd run past a pastry shop he'd got the idea of
asking Jo if they could bring her a slice of Sacher torte when
they came back from dinner. Laura told him Jo was in one of
her blue moods.

The concierge peered at him, her glasses casting triangles of
light onto her rouged cheeks. "Hale?" he repeated.

She bent over the book to search, then held up three fingers.
"Drei." She gestured toward the corridor behind her, an open
kitchen door there and another one into a storage room. Surely
she'd misunderstood him.

"Miss Hale?"

"*Ja. Drei.*" She stood and brushed abruptly at the lap of her black skirt, then took three steps down the corridor and pointed. "*Eins, zwei, drei, vier.*" At each number she nodded for emphasis until he understood that there was another wing of the hotel on the far side of the family rooms. He smiled his understanding and she plumped herself back into her swivel chair, the goosenecked lamp pooling yellow onto her stained hands.

He hesitated—maybe he'd just bring Jo a slice of torte and surprise her. But now the concierge watched him as though he must pass her desk before she could return to her account book. So he headed toward the kitchen and the other wing.

The hotel served only the standard breakfast of rolls and coffee; he guessed the kitchen was strictly for the family who ran the place. The scents of pork roasting and onions frying made his stomach moan. He wished he could have a meal right now— meat and potatoes heaped with those onions. On evenings like this one, when he was a kid, he'd run home from football practice, or track, or swimming, as tired and hungry as he was tonight, and as he pounded up the drive, scattering gravel with each stride, he'd smelled the welcome of the onions his mother fried. When she hugged him her hands smelled of them. Even then he was smart enough to guess that the pleasure he felt was more than for the meals she fixed. The scent of the onions signified that the universe was still in order. Nothing bad had happened to him yet.

As he entered the cramped hotel kitchen, a young woman glanced up from her cooking at the dark iron stove. She was round-faced, her red apron stretched tightly across her pregnancy. Three white plates were set on the wooden table. Perhaps she was the daughter of the concierge. Perhaps in a little while her husband would come home to his supper. It would be good to eat here in this bright room. More and more Will hated restaurants, the damned ceremony of restaurant meals. Jo was smart to hide out tonight. He wished he could take a handful of the shredded cabbage mounded on the serving table by the door; instead, he stepped out into the dim courtyard to find Jo's room.

A gray cat jumped away from his feet, sprang into the dark doorway on the far side. Above the doorway and to the right, one window was lighted. As Will looked up, a beam flashed as the double doors opened a foot or two. A nude woman reached to latch the top of the door in place. A flash of tanned skin, white breasts, the dark shadow beneath the taut belly. The thrust of her raised arm lifted her breasts. Then she stepped sideways. As the second door swung into place, he saw it was Jo. Her shadow swayed a moment on the white curtain and then was gone.

He turned as though he'd been shoved and leaned on the wall. The young mother inside turned on a radio, American music, of course. The only surprise was that it was an old James Taylor cut Will liked himself, ". . . let me go down in my dreams, and rockabye sweet baby James." He closed his eyes but the image persisted the way sunlight stings when it reflects off moving water.

His glimpse of her was like one of the first sexual dreams he'd had as a kid—an urgency that he must somehow possess that faceless naked woman. He had responded to Jo before he recognized her. The rush of those feelings, pleasure followed by shock, confused him. Lust, that was all it was, a natural thing, nothing to apologize for. But when he saw it was Jo, the blood rushed to his face. As though he'd done something wrong. He'd seen her in her bikini often enough this summer and noticed only that she was pretty, prettier than she knew. But he'd certainly felt no desire for her. It would have been inappropriate, to say the least. It would have been unthinkable. He'd helped raise her. She was his wife's kid sister, off limits, even for a quicksilver flash of desire.

He walked back through the kitchen, crossed the stuffy lobby, and let himself out into the dusky evening. The wind lifted his sweaty hair from his forehead. The lamps surrounding the small canopy overhead came on with an amber glow. At the rim of the light the first drops of rain appeared, a spatter that brought up the smell of dry leaves. Across the street a woman snapped open her umbrella. At the corner a tall guy yanked up his jacket collar and began to run, head down, as the rain thickened suddenly into a downpour. The street was loud with it.

Will stepped from under the canopy and turned his face up. The torrent pressed on his closed eyes. But Jo's image stayed, like the blinding flare of a flashbulb. Now it seemed that her uptilted chin, the line of her throat, her reaching arm were like Laura's. But all the rest was Jo's own. Anyway, it was just an accident, no more than that. He was hornier than he'd realized; that was the only lesson.

He folded his arms and jammed his hands under his armpits. He was also more tired than he'd guessed. Traveling was the hardest job he knew. In a moment he'd go take a long, hot shower, then he and Laura would get a light supper, and, if he was lucky, he'd fall asleep quickly and manage to sleep through the night. Tomorrow, at last, he'd be back in Chicago, back at the hospital and his office where life was predictable and under his control, the way he liked it.

In the early morning the windows of the airline terminal streaked with rain. People pushed in for the first flights—a stench of wet rubber, perfume, cigarette smoke. Will grabbed a cart for their luggage and sent Jo ahead with Laura to wait in the check-in line. If only there were some way to get home instantly, a time warp, like the ones in science fiction. Zap—the packed terminal would vanish, along with these long flights that lay ahead. They'd be in a limo heading in from O'Hare. He was in a rotten mood, all right. His nerves ached with caffeine and his mouth was sour from the rye rolls they'd been served for breakfast. He'd only had one beer at supper, but he felt hung over. Maneuvering the luggage cart through the crowd, he stared at the soaked black tarmac.

Laura stood at the Lufthansa counter. She wore her white jeans and that baggy black men's cashmere sweater she'd bought in London. Slim, light-haired, she looked good. She rummaged in her shoulder bag, then pushed their tickets across the counter to the attendant. Choosing a spot at the side of the line, he waited with their luggage. Her hands in her Levi's pockets, Jo smiled up at a tall guy who had his back to Will. On this trip she'd got more attention from boys than she'd had yet back home. She complained that she didn't get many dates in high school because she wasn't the cheerleader type. But everywhere in Europe she easily struck up conversations. When Laura felt particularly invaded, she said, "The trouble with Jo is that she thinks everyone is interesting." Will answered, "She likes to ask a lot of questions." But this morning as he watched Jo he was uneasy. He knew that came from his feelings last night in the courtyard. Jo was just a kid again in her striped T-shirt and faded jeans—the woman had gone into hiding and he was glad. But he'd better give her a little advice about asking so many questions of men.

As she spoke with this one, she drew a strand of her hair around her finger and pulled it across her lips. She listened more than she talked. Then the guy turned slightly, and Will saw his sun-streaked hair, his beard. He was the one she spoke to a couple of days ago as they waited in line to watch the practice at the Spanish Riding School. "A perfect example of the Aryan race," she'd said to Will, not even whispering, because the guy looked so undeniably German—his coloring, his hair, his tense military bearing. But damn if he wasn't American after all, had teased Jo about prejudice, about labeling him, about stereotypes. Then he'd discovered they were all from the Chicago area. One big happy family. He'd even insisted on taking a snapshot of Jo and Laura—"The blonde and the brunette, I can't believe you're sisters." The jerk. Jo had enjoyed the whole scene. She'd teased back, nervous, but loving it. She was learning from Laura how to flirt, and Laura was an expert. But what was the guy doing here at the airport at this hour?

Laura waved Will forward. He hefted the bags from the cart onto the scales, watched the attendant snap tags on them, hoped they'd reappear on schedule in that bedlam that O'Hare called customs.

"We've got seats in front of a bulkhead," Laura said. "No smoking, so that's good. But they start boarding in forty minutes or so. We've got to hustle." She liked being in charge; she'd signed them up for this tour. If the choice were entirely his own, he'd stay home. Part of his foul mood, he guessed.

Now he watched Laura's expression shade from businesswoman to hostess. "Who's here with you, Jo?"

"Isn't this a spooky coincidence? Thomas has a flight out of

Vienna this morning, too." Jo played with the collar of her jean jacket.

On cue, Thomas swung toward them, hand at the ready like a drawn gun. "Mrs. Brenner, we meet again!" As though they'd been separated against their will. "And the good doctor."

Jo said quickly, "Will, you remember Thomas. We met him at the Spanish Riding School."

"Thomas Trawick." He released Laura's hand and reached for Will's.

"Yes, I remember." Trawick's palm was dry, his grip more cautious than his smile.

"Looks like we're all being driven out of Eden at the same time. Now we have to take our leave of innocence and face real life back in the States, right?" Trawick winked at Laura. She smiled back at him. She knew all the social graces anyone could need. She could be crying in Will's arms one minute, and the next talking gaily on the phone: How simply grand to hear from you! Will was the only one who knew how real the tears were, or the struggle she had with her disguise. He wasn't so good at disguises, and didn't want to be.

"Don't tell me we're all on the same flight!" Laura tapped the ticket folder.

To Will's relief, Trawick said, "My luck's not that good. My flight doesn't leave for an hour. Then I've got a couple of days in Rome before I see the Windy City again."

"It's so much more fun to travel with friends." Laura was pouring it on, maybe from habit, maybe because the guy seemed so interested in Jo.

"What's our gate number?" Will asked her.

"F seven."

"That sounds mystical," Trawick said.

Will hoisted his carry-on bag to his shoulder. "Let's get going."

"Do you believe numbers can be mystical?" Trawick said to Jo. "Do you believe the number *drei* could be mystical?"

She flushed. She hadn't learned answers to stupid questions yet; she still thought people asked in order to learn something. "Three? Like the trinity, or something?"

Trawick laughed. "How about synchronicity? Do you believe in synchronicity?" He touched her wrist as though that would help explain his question.

"What's that mean?"

"Synchronicity means meeting someone you need to know at exactly the same time that person needs to know you. 'In sync.' Think of it that way."

"And we all believe in Tinker Bell," Laura added.

"Come on!" Will said to her.

Laura and Jo started across the long lobby toward customs. For a moment before he followed them, Trawick looked Will in the eye. A locker-room assessment. It had been late in coming, Will thought. No *way,* buddy. But in a couple of long strides Trawick caught up to Jo and walked beside her.

Laura fell back, gave Will's hand a squeeze that he read as Take it easy. Jo's voice, throatier than usual, and Trawick's baritone drifted back to them.

"So, you're from Chicago, Jo?"

"Highland Park. Right on the lake, almost."

"Nice area. Lots of condos with riparian rights, as the real-estate ads say."

"Ours is a regular neighborhood. We're on a park."

"Sounds charming."

"It's okay. Do you ever come up that way?"

"Sometimes. On business."

"What do you do? What business?"

"I'm in the synchronicity business."

Jo giggled. "Oh, stop."

"I'm self-employed, I guess you'd say. I'm a writer. What did you think of those white horses at the riding school?"

"They were pretty."

"That's all? The great Lippizaners only rate a 'pretty'?"

"I was disappointed, actually. Mostly I thought about how hard on them it must be to keep their heads tucked and their necks arched. I hated the jumps they did like mechanical toys. I wished they'd run flat-out. I'd love to see that, wouldn't you?"

"I would, indeed." Trawick smiled. "I'd like to see us all run flat-out. That could be a good way to live."

She looked up at him. "I think you're teasing me. You're agreeing to be polite. I don't believe you."

"Why would I lie? You can, you know, believe me."

"I guess it's a question of knowing you better."

"Believe me when I tell you that the best part of the Spanish Riding School was waiting in line with you." He touched Jo's chin with his fist and she blushed.

Laura whispered to Will, "He must have learned his routine in singles bars." But the color was up in her cheeks, too.

"I wouldn't know," Will said. He thought Trawick had quick stops and starts as if he were on speed, except his eyes were steady. As if he'd learned the right moves but not the timing. If Will were a coach, he'd kick Trawick's ass off the team.

"Maybe we should get in on this conversation." Laura nudged Will, but he shook his head. She caught Jo and Trawick with a few quick steps. "You two sound like old friends already. Better slow down, Jo."

Jo frowned. "Oh, Laura!"

But Trawick said quickly, "No, no, your sister's right, Jo. She knows you shouldn't trust strangers. If you're a smashing blonde, you learn to be careful with men. Pay attention to her—she *knows*."

Will pushed between Laura and Trawick. His bag bumped Trawick's arm. "Turn here," he said to Jo. "That line on the right."

His body-block wasn't lost on Trawick, who did a backpedaling dance with his hands. "Time to say good-bye, my friends." To Jo he added, "Let's get together when we're both stateside. I'd like that."

"You would?"

"That's an understatement. Your last name's Hale, right?"

"Yes, but I live with Laura and Will. There's just the one phone. It's under William Brenner."

With a quick wave Trawick turned away behind a glass panel that divided the lanes for passport control. He glanced back once, a narrow face, wide-set eyes, unsmiling.

Jo's face was still flushed. "He just showed up, Will. I didn't invite him, if that's what you're thinking."

He hadn't known his anger was that obvious. "Forget it."

"I know he pisses you off."

"I'm in a crummy mood. It's not your fault, or his."

"He comes on strong," Laura said lightly, smoothing her hair on her shoulders as they stepped into line.

"I don't want to talk about him," Will said.

"You wouldn't." He thought she looked smug.

"Meaning?"

She handed him his passport from her shoulder bag. "Meaning you wouldn't want to talk about him, that's all. He's not your type, I know that," she said softly.

Jo smiled and looked in Trawick's direction. "He *is* a fox, don't you think, Laura?"

"I think he's a traveling salesman, babe. He's much too old for you, and you'd better learn not to take chances. With men, it pays to be skeptical."

"I think you liked him," Jo said.

"He has a certain style." She looked up sideways at Will, but he didn't make the effort to acknowledge the apology, if that's what she offered. "Just be careful," she told Jo again.

"I can look after myself."

Though Will was most often the peacemaker, now it was Laura who said, "I think we're all anxious to get home. Time to click your heels together, Dorothy." Their old joke.

Jo's docksiders tapped—once, twice—she wanted to make up, too. She couldn't sustain her anger.

The uniformed guard motioned to Will. With a sigh he handed over his passport. The guard looked up twice from the smiling face in the passport photo to Will: the same prominent brow bone, the same hooked nose, the same dark hair and the same scar below his left eye. Take a good look, fella—it's the real me.

3

When their taxi rounded the commuter station and headed east toward the lake, the familiar streets closed around Laura like an embrace. *Home.* She said the word over and over to herself, savoring its roundness, wholeness, the vowel sound like an egg, smooth and symmetrical. Overhead the oaks and maples blocked the morning sun which streaked through a haze of leaf smoke. The maples were already pink at the tops, the birches edged with yellow. She leaned against the warm taxi window and looked up into the trees that lit their way like paper lanterns. She was glad to be back, no, more than glad—she felt delivered. Rescued. Brought back into her favorite season when mild days still lingered before the long winter came on with its power to shut down even Lake Michigan. "Freeze-dried Illinois," Will called this place then. He compared it to the winters he'd spent in Louisiana and claimed he preferred the heat. Laura was glad he'd gone to the hospital and that just she and Jo were in the taxi. She wanted the place to herself, with no comments from Will about how the streets needed paving and how many leaves they'd have to rake. She rolled down her window so she could breathe in the sweet smoke. Her eyes stung and she didn't wipe them. She'd been raised here. This place was hers. I'll be all right now, she thought. And I'll be all right tomorrow. Oh, please let me be all right.

Their trip had been so much harder than she'd dreamed it

could be. So terribly hard. That it had been so difficult astonished her. She'd hoped for a transformation. *Again.* How many times had she planned a new start, a new life? As though she could shed her old self like a snakeskin, leave it behind and begin again, a shining new being who lived life effortlessly, guiltlessly.

Their flight home was the worst part of it all. Her energy was completely gone. She was too tired to feel anything more than a blank determination to get the trip over with. Will pretended to sleep, and even Jo had nothing left to say to anyone. Laura felt like a trapped vixen, one leg in the irons, chewing on her own flesh. Vomiting it up. How *could* Will love her? How could anyone love a woman who trashed her own life and couldn't stop?

But now they were almost home. Their taxi turned along Sunrise Lane and followed the park. The lake whelmed up blue and vast, as vividly azure as those travel photos of the Pacific. She could breathe again, deep breaths that pushed down into her lungs; she hadn't really breathed for days.

"Stop here," she told the cabbie at the entrance to the park. She paid him and tipped him too much because she was so glad to be back, then handed Jo the house key. "Take your shower. I want to spend a while in the park."

The taxi drove on, weaving around potholes. Laura watched until she was sure Jo was inside their house. Then she walked toward the bluff, smelling the damp, leaf-covered earth and tasting grit and smoke in the air. Her head ached, her throat ached from vomiting, her skin felt raw, as though it barely stretched over her bones. But the view from the bluff eased her. From up here she could see so far in every direction. She always forgot how much sky there was until she stood on the bluff and looked east over the lake.

A long stretch of grass as dark as pine, scattered oaks, some saplings with all their branches bent west because the winds came off the lake, a bench here and there—that was the park. It wasn't much, but even the weathered benches carried a meaning for her. Like this one, where she paused now, by the stairway down to the beach. This was the place she'd got her nickname.

She'd been three and a half, maybe almost four years old. Miss Campbell hunched right here on this bench, hiding a cigarette in her cupped hand, the lighted end toward her. She smiled down at Laura as Laura stood holding Momma's hand. Momma was taking her down to the beach, a place she was never, never to go by herself. Laura was surprised that the white-haired lady in the pink dress was barefooted, like she was. A wavery snake, the smoke from the lady's cigarette curled up out of her hand. "Morning, Ellen," Miss Campbell said to Momma. Then she nodded at Laura. "This little one of yours surely is a peach!"

Laura wasn't sure if she remembered those words, or if she'd been told the story so often that she thought she remembered. Momma began to call her her peach, then Peaches. Laura was round-faced and rosy then. That was long, long before Momma died and Estelle came. Later, Laura understood that Miss Campbell slipped from her house, where her sisters looked after her, and came to this bench to smoke because she'd been ordered off cigarettes by her doctor. She smoked in secret. She couldn't stop even though her life depended on it—the ultimate triumph of addiction. Now Laura stroked the gouged wood of the bench—she understood Miss Campbell.

This bench was also where her father brought her in his arms to watch fireworks—her oldest memory. She was in her crib and he reached down for her. Even though the room was dark, she knew it was Daddy. He picked her up, and took her cuddling blanket, too. Then they were here on the bluff. Lights burst and hissed down all around them into the lake. Daddy smelled sweet. When she was older she knew that sweet smell was whiskey.

Now she pulled off her shoes and rubbed her swollen feet. How strange that the past has so much power. How helpless we are. Will often claimed that there was nothing at all but the present. He said that everyone reworked the past to make it fit the present. He said the past didn't exist: when he was welding, he had hated the heat in Louisiana, but now he remembered it as pleasant, he said—in that way he'd changed the past. But she wasn't like Will. She remembered things just exactly as they were. The truth was that there wasn't any real present. There was only the past that invaded and possessed the moment and the future that might never come. More and more it seemed to her that she had nothing except memory and desire.

She glanced toward their house, where Jo would be showering. Her sister had grown up in a different family—she couldn't care about the past in the same way. Jo could barely remember Daddy. And of course there was no way to explain to her how good life was before Momma died. It wasn't Jo's fault that Momma died, but sometimes, when Laura was especially sickened by herself, and lonely, she blamed Jo. Her mother's death was random, it had to have been, an accident, that's all, like a piece of metal flung from a bridge that just happened to skewer someone walking below. Anything was better than believing Momma's death was ordained—at this time, in this place, this woman will bleed to death giving birth to her child. No, not that.

In her bare feet Laura walked down to the oaks that leaned out over the edge of the bluff. Below, the lake sighed at the base of the bluff. Already the water was less intensely blue, had flattened to a milky green. She was alone in the park. That was one reason she loved living here—there was really no reason for anyone to be in the park, ever. There was nothing to do here, no playground equipment, no picnic tables, no benches except the few old ones. Every so often someone from the west side of town proposed picnic facilities to the City Council and the motion was immediately voted down. If there were things to do, then people would come and do them, and no one on this side of town wanted anyone coming here, especially not those soldiers from Fort Sheridan or those big families from the city with their cases of beer and Weber grills.

The picket fence, put up several years ago to keep kids away from the steepest part of the bluff, had fallen over the eroded edge. When they'd left for Europe, the fence was still upright, but now it was draped in the Queen Anne's lace. Leaning out, she caught a glimpse of the Millets' brick wall that had surrounded the end of their garden until that storm last spring took three feet of earth and the wall down onto the beach. It had rained six days, then there was a windstorm. All night they heard trees falling, the loudest one that old hickory just behind the garage. The wind howled and a pale green light slid from under the black clouds. Laura went down to the kitchen to look. Over the garage a huge new piece of sky hung where the hickory had been. Dressed in their yellow sailing slickers, the Millets stood in their backyard. By the way Cecil held Pat, Laura could tell that Pat was crying. Beyond them, raw space. When it was light Laura put on her own slicker and walked across the marshy grass to look. There was the Millets' garden wall, broken casually, like a child's game of blocks, onto the beach far below. They didn't put up another wall. The bluff's going, little by little. As Will said, we're all going, little by little. After his thirty-fifth birthday he'd begun to talk like that, as though his life were eroding from beneath his feet.

But the largest oak, her favorite, still clung to the edge, some of its roots exposed out over the lake. A storm could take it any time, would take it. Nothing could be done. She leaned against it, shaded her eyes to peer toward the Michigan shore. Heat rose from the beach below in an updraft. It would be lovely down there on the beach, warm and windless. Down there she could sleep.

She rested against the oak to study their house. The window was up in Jo's back bedroom. She'd had her shower, then, and was sleeping. But Laura didn't want to go inside yet. She opened her palms flat against the rough bark, and leaned back as though she was tied to the tree. She'd stood this way for that last snapshot her mother took of her.

"Lean back, Peaches, and try to smile." Momma fiddled with the lens setting of her camera, resting it on her swollen belly. In a day, maybe two or three, the baby would be born. She wanted some snapshots of Laura to have with her in the hospital. Laura had just come home from Girl Scouts and was wearing her uniform. She was cross because Momma said there wasn't time to change into her jeans before the light faded.

"That skirt's getting short. I'll let it down for next year."

"I'm not joining next year. Nobody in seventh wants to be in Scouts." Why didn't her mother know this? She was so wrapped up in having this baby! Laura shifted impatiently and Momma told her to hold still.

Momma's head was bent, a line of gray showing at her part

where her hair color needed touching up. "Do you think you could smile, honey?"

She didn't feel like smiling, she was thinking how horrible seventh was going to be. In seventh girls like boys. She opened her hands against the oak, pretending to be trapped, tied to the mast.

"You're getting to that awkward age," Momma sighed and snapped anyway. It was the last picture on the roll.

Two weeks later a woman called from Walgreen's, told them to come pick up the film. Of course they'd forgotten about it. They'd forgotten about everything. The world had been torn apart. Momma was dead and the baby squalled in the room next to Laura's and Aunt Hattie slept in the sun-room. Aunt Hattie picked up the film when she went for diaper-rash ointment and more formula.

The snapshot of Laura was underexposed, dim. It was a photo a kidnapper might have taken of his victim to send to her parents for ransom. The girl in the picture was clearly in trouble, one foot up on the tree as though pushing at her bonds, hands behind her back, head tilted slightly forward, either from fatigue or in acceptance of her bondage. Laura imagined the photo was a message sent back from Momma: "This is who you are now." As if Momma had guessed that Laura would never again be that round-faced girl called Peaches.

Now she pushed away from the oak and started for their house. Narrow, steep-roofed, one room wide except for the sun porches, it was a summer house her father had bought and converted to a year-round home. It was his one creative impulse, his achievement. A city boy, he'd got a place for his wife and baby where they could live by the lake.

She closed the screen door behind herself and walked down the long porch that encircled the whole front and half the side of the house. Deep shade blinded her. Her eyes ached, grainy and dry from the flight. She eased into the old rope hammock for a moment. Lilacs brushed the screens and a trapped fly buzzed. The hammock swayed, a motion like the waves soughing over the pebble beach below the bluff. Her head felt disconnected from her body, floating. But here she was safe.

In her sleep she heard the phone ringing, far off but insistent.

The damned phone! At night all the calls were for Will, of course. They'd got twin beds so he wouldn't wake her when he had to get up at night, but she woke anyway, always with her mouth dry, her heart pounding. What terrible news did she expect to hear?

In the living room she grabbed the receiver. Too late—the phone was dead. Jo must be in a deep sleep, or she'd have got the call—she usually got them on the first ring.

As Laura lugged the suitcases up the front stairs, a sharp, warning pulse began behind her eyes. The day wasn't going as she'd hoped, needed, wanted it to. She'd given in too much to fatigue. She needed to be very busy in order to stay in control, and now the phone had wakened some anxiety she couldn't account for.

Quick, think of something else. She pulled open the bedroom windows. Lake sounds entered like a rush of wind, and from up the block she heard children's laughter and shouts, the music of a radio. Their bedroom was smaller than she'd remembered, all these rooms were smaller. But it had only been a vacation house before her father put in better plumbing and storm windows. He'd had plans to add a family room off the kitchen, but after Momma died all the plans were forgotten. There was only Estelle, cooking her greasy hillbilly meals in the little kitchen; no reason to remodel the kitchen for a housekeeper.

Laura traced the dust on Will's dresser, a dark maple chest from his mother. Her own dresser needed dusting, too, Momma's mahogany dresser. It was the only thing of Momma's left in the house. When Daddy died and the house became Laura's, she had Goodwill come and take everything except this dresser. Start over. That new life. Again and again, that fantasy, as though the yellow carpet and these yellow bedspreads would change anything.

She stripped off her travel clothes, pulled on shorts and a T-shirt, washed her face, took two aspirin and a Valium. An exhausted but striking blonde looked back at her from the mirror. You're okay, lady, everything is okay. Take it easy. But her hands shook. Get busy, then. She pulled the laundry basket to the bedroom and unpacked their suitcases, flinging their soiled clothes carelessly into piles on the floor around the hamper. She made a bundle of Will's stuff for the dry cleaner, then sorted their toilet articles back into the bathroom cabinets. But the plastic bottles kept tumbling to the floor in her hurry.

Grabbing the stuff for the cleaner's, she hurried down the back stairs into the kitchen. At the counter she scribbled a list: Daisy from the vet's, groceries, mail, call paperboy. As she wrote, her words overlapped, blurred into each other. Get out of here, get out of the kitchen.

Then the phone started in again. The bell made her jump, as though she'd been caught in the act of doing something humiliating. She snatched it off the hook and tried to sound calm. In control. "Brenners' residence."

A woman's voice quivered over the line, high-pitched and impatient, a thick accent. "My party is calling Jo Hale at this number. Person-to-person, please."

Long distance for Jo? "Just a moment, I'll get her." Laura set the phone on the counter and hurried up the back staircase. Upstairs, Jo's door was shut.

Laura let herself into the small room that had once been hers. Over the narrow bed the sloped ceiling reflected light and leaf shadows. Wearing bikini panties and a blue T-shirt, Jo lay spread-eagled on her stomach. Her face was buried in her pillow and her damp hair soaked a ring around her head. She slept the drugged sleep of an exhausted child.

"Jo?"

She didn't stir.

"Hey, Jo, the phone." She touched her shoulder, but Jo's eyelids didn't even tremble. Why force her out of this sleep she needed so badly? Laura closed the door again. She'd take the call for her.

Downstairs, she listened to the shushing on the phone and imagined the cables covering vast distances. "Hello, operator?"

"Jo Hale?"

"She's not here right now. I'll take the call, if you like. I'm her sister."

There was a brief conversation between the operator and a man. He was making a demand, slightly mocking. A Midwestern accent. Then he said, "Mrs. Brenner? This is Thomas Trawick."

She sat on the stool by the counter. "Hello. I thought you were going to Rome."

"I was. I did. I'm calling from Rome. How was your trip back?"

Calling from Rome? His aggressive style, but what was the urgency? "A long flight, two flights, actually, and Jo's so wiped out that I couldn't wake her just now. Do you want to leave a message?"

"So you're back safely. No, no message. Just tell her she's on my mind. I saw this astonishing sunset over the tile roofs outside my room and I just thought I'd tell her about it." He laughed. Laura heard the self-mockery in the laughter, but after all, he had made the call. She imagined him hunched over the phone, concentrating—as she was.

"Thomas, what's up?" she said abruptly.

He laughed again. "I shouldn't have had so much wine with dinner. It's a disgusting European habit. Wagner probably had too much wine and then sat down and wrote *Tristan and Isolde*, right? Just greet the chick for me, will you?" And rang off.

She listened a moment more to the shushing, the cable on the floor of the ocean twisting like a sea serpent in the tides. Then she let her breath out slowly.

Trawick, putting the make on Jo. It didn't make sense, absolutely no sense at all. Maybe he was on drugs. Watching him talk to Jo in the airport, Laura imagined she saw electricity ricocheting through him, as though he'd grabbed a live wire. She'd thought, oddly, He's like me.

As she crossed the backyard to the garage, she paused to look up at Jo's window. The eyelet curtains stirred in the breeze. Why would Trawick chase a kid like Jo? He must have met hundreds of girls like her. What would he want with her? To dazzle, astound, overwhelm a person less experienced than himself? Would that be a turn-on to him?

She tried to bring Jo into focus, to see her as a man might. She was pretty enough, curvy—men liked that, though Laura thought Jo should knock off a few of those pounds. Jo was less honest than she seemed, but she gave the appearance of simplicity. She had all the usual adolescent rebellions going, but maybe Trawick liked that, he seemed the type who enjoyed breaking rules. Jo certainly wasn't threatening. She was without any masks, maybe that was it. She wasn't self-conscious—someone as aware of herself as Laura knew how rare that quality was. It was as though Jo traveled through her life without protection, no makeup, no armor. Okay, that's appealing in a very young person. But would that be enough to inspire this rush Trawick was giving her? It didn't figure. Jo could use some looking after, here, though Will wouldn't see it that way. "Let her make her own mistakes," he always said, as though he thought, You've made yours. Though he never said that.

Laura turned away from the house, scuffing at the few maple leaves that lay like scraps of yellow construction paper on the sidewalk. She wasn't hurrying now. She was enjoying the enigma of Thomas Trawick, his puzzle, his game. Jo might not be able to psych the guy out, but Laura knew she could. She was his match, if anyone was. Already she knew a lot about him, knew he was both impulsive and very determined. Even Will's gruffness hadn't slowed him down or frightened him off. They'd hear from him again, and soon. Good—she could play his games.

As she unlocked the garage door she caught sight of herself in the window. She hadn't realized that she was smiling. She really should be grateful to this Trawick guy—because of his intrusion she was in control again. She was okay, now. She slid into the station wagon. And suddenly it was like that dream she'd had when she first met Will, that wonderful dream that she'd had just that once and never again, though she remembered it so vividly: in the dream she'd been cured of her anorexia, and she drove a sleek red sports car down the narrow streets of an unfamiliar town, but without hesitation, without confusion, finding her own way all by herself to the wonderful new home which awaited her.

4

Without opening her eyes, Jo turned onto her back and stretched her feet down to the maple bedposts. She knew from the sounds below in the kitchen that Laura was prowling around, probably cleaning out the refrigerator. *Her* refrigerator, of course. *Her* kitchen. Her whole damn house. Laura liked to run everything, have it all her own way, and she was such a bitch if you crossed her. Jo would never travel with her again, never. Here, she had her own life to escape to, her own friends—the ones who were left now that everyone was off to college, at least Kit, whom she'd dated last spring.

Sun warmed the foot of the bed, so it must be noon. How many times had she wakened in this exact way? The trip had shown her how confined her life here was—always this house, always this room, always this bed. It was time to move on, but where should she go? Away, that was all she was sure of. She could be going away to college like the others who couldn't wait to split Highland Park. But last spring when it was time to choose a college she'd lost her nerve. She'd decided to be a day student for her first semester.

If she had parents it would be easier to move on—she'd know she had something to come back to. Parents must be almost more a place than people. Laura and Will were only people. Who knows where they'd be in a year or two. Laura was always threatening to sell the house; Will claimed his life would

have an easier pace if he moved his medical practice to the
South. If Jo moved out, what would happen then? But right
now she wished she'd had more courage last spring when she'd
decided to go to Woodcliff. Now she wanted to take some
chances. If Estelle were alive she would have persuaded Jo to let
go, to try new situations; Estelle would have *insisted*.

Estelle had been big on taking chances. When Jo panicked
about going to the Y camp that first time when she was eight,
Estelle grabbed her right up into her lap and told her, "Take a
chance, tootsie! Nothing to lose. Anywhere you go you're gonna
be *you*."

And when Jo broke her nose in soccer scrimmage, three years
ago, and Laura had let her ask Estelle to visit, she sat right here
on the end of the bed and told Jo, "Of course if you don't take
any chances you never get hurt! But who wants to live that
way?" Peering out of the plaster mask, Jo wanted to put her
head in Estelle's lap; *Estelle, come back, stay with me.* That was
impossible, of course. And how queer to have Estelle as a visitor
in a house that had been practically her own. Like a kid asking
for a familiar bedtime story, Jo said, "Tell me about John
Holden again." She meant, tell me about *me,* tell me about you
and me.

Estelle settled back and crossed her plump legs. That day she
wore a man's shirt untucked over a too-tight black skirt, and her
usual load of silver bracelets. Her tinted hair was done in curls
so carefully made Jo thought she could put her finger into one
of them and not touch any side. After her first bout with cancer,
Estelle had switched to more rouge and a redder lipstick. She
was in her late thirties but could have been ten or even twenty
years older. "Oh, that John Holden! Still the same. You fall in
love with the wrong man and your life is doomed!"

Estelle said that with pride; she'd been singled out for a life of
passion. She wasn't like other women, certainly wasn't like
those lumps down there in Missouri who'd never lived for even
a moment in their lives, and never would. "You remember I
told you how I fell for him that summer I turned sixteen? Well,
it's just the same, exactly the same. Older but no wiser." She
smiled as she spoke.

At sixteen she'd fallen in love with the wrong man, John

Holden, who was dark and slim and ran the A&P down in Piedmont. He was wrong because he was way too old for her, he drank too much and screwed around. Though a lot of gals thought he was a catch, her folks hated him, of course. They were Church of the Nazarene people and John Holden was the best example of an unrepentant sinner around there. He not only drank, he gambled most of what he earned. But he knew how to give a gal a time! When they went to Bagnell Dam he bought her a yachting cap and took her out in a speedboat. They bought Kentucky Fried Chicken for picnics at Sam Baker Park, where they danced to the music on his car radio. There was a tavern over on the Mississippi where they got fried catfish and whiskey with beer chasers. And oh, Lord, was he sexy!

Estelle's folks wanted her to marry Russell Clark, who was the county agent and drove a blue pickup to her house on Sunday evenings. He was as flat as stale cola, as much of an old shoe as John Holden was dressy.

Then she got pregnant. John used protection, but she'd known it was only a matter of time—after all, she was doomed. He didn't want anything to do with a kid, and she knew he wouldn't, even though she loved him. He wasn't a family kind of man, but the truth was women didn't always love family men. For example, she would never have loved Russell Clark if he'd wanted ten babies with her. So she stayed with an aunt in Columbia until her baby was born, and when she came up to Chicago to make good she left the baby with her mother, who wanted to raise a Christian child. By that time John Holden was seeing a woman who drove her black Lincoln all the way down from Saint Louis after work every night and didn't care if he was a drinker or a gambler or what else. Before Estelle left Piedmont that time she heard it said John was boozing so bad he might lose his job. It would have been different if he'd married her; she'd have been good for him. Not that she didn't like to have fun, but she'd have settled him down some.

The really sad part of her story was that Estelle had to leave her baby to come to Chicago. Every time she told Jo this story she made sure that was understood. "I cried all the way to Chicago when I came here. Folks on the bus thought I was going to a funeral. Not to brag on Daniel, but you should have seen him then. He had his daddy's hands and feet, real narrow-boned, but he was chubby like me. Perfect strangers would come up to me in the grocery store and ask to hold him, he was so chubby." She got off the bus, bought a newspaper and began to answer ads for live-in housekeepers. When she came here and saw Jo, so tiny and pale in her cradle, and that tight-faced aunt of hers dribbling a bottle into her, Estelle fell in love all over again. "They say you don't have those feelings unless the baby's your own, so I guess you were already my little girl. I felt the milk rush right back into my tits. Of course I'd always had enough for two, even with Daniel going at me like he did. I picked you up and you nuzzled my cheek and that did it. I took the job."

Things here in this house were an unholy mess. Jo's daddy was trying to manage, he did what he was supposed to do, even got himself to work, but at night, every night, he bawled himself to sleep, if he slept at all. Then he started drinking more and didn't cry so much. And there was this little blond twerp, Laura, who wouldn't talk, wouldn't eat unless she was allowed to fix her meals herself, and then only ate the teeniest bits all spread out over her plate. She turned up her nose at good country ham and red-eye gravy, turned up at her nose at twice-baked potatoes and bride's salad with marshmallows. Estelle tried to tame her, but Laura wasn't having any. She wanted to mope, wanted to stay in her room or disappear for hours in the woods. Even if Estelle had had the time to chase her down, what good would it have done? Estelle bought her ankle socks with lace on the cuffs, but Laura threw them in the trash can. Estelle tried sandwiches with the crusts cut off and nothing but tuna inside. No go. Everything she did *offended* that girl. That was Laura's way. She was angry and brokenhearted, and why wouldn't she be? Laura was also a complete pill.

But Jo, now there was a different story! A puny little baby, but all that silky black hair and the prettiest doll face. Not that she made up for Daniel, people aren't like puppies—one gone so just get a new one. But to see Jo growing, eating, smiling— something just bloomed in Estelle to be loving that baby. "You, honey! Look how beautiful you are now. I predicted it."

Jo felt her plastered nose with her fingertip, ran her fingers through her hair that needed washing, sucked on her braces, still on although she was fifteen.

Estelle took her hand in both of hers, her turquoise rings glittering. "You are my shining light, tootsie."

Jo squeezed back. Her head throbbed from the gauze packed inside her nose. "Tell me what John Holden's doing now." She meant, tell me about your life without me.

Estelle said, Oh, that was the oddest thing! After all these years of selfish living, John Holden was remorseful! He hadn't seriously changed his ways much, but one night last summer when Estelle was getting chemotherapy and laid up at her mother's house, here came John up the front porch steps. She barely had time to get her wig on. Her mother let him in, though she wouldn't say hello, of course. That didn't bother John. "I have to see Estelle," he said, and Mother sent him into the downstairs bedroom. He looked good, awful thin, but tan and still had all his dark hair, only a little gray in it and that pretty white hair at the throat of his shirt. She hated to be seen in bed that way, but over the years he'd seen her every way there was to see a woman. She said, "Hi, baby." Right away he went down on his knees by the side of her bed. She thought he was going to propose, though they hadn't seen much of each other since that new cocktail waitress over at the Show Me Bar had taken a liking to him. Still, there was always this *thing* between Estelle and John; when he came looking for her she always let him in, she couldn't help it, he was her fate. There he was down on his knees, looking right into her eyes so tenderly she thought she'd faint. He took her hand and his was shaking. "I got to ask you to forgive me," he said.

After the shock, she thought she'd laugh. John Holden on his knees? And, anyway, there was nothing to forgive, really, she'd always been in it with her eyes open. He'd been good to Daniel, too, taking him fishing and buying him a Ford junker for him to fix up. He wasn't any father, but he was a kind of uncle to the boy. "Does this mean we aren't going to make love any more?" she asked him. He liked her to be bold. He got up, then, and brushed off the knees of his good navy pants. "You are something else, Estelle," he told her. She knew he meant it as a com-

pliment. He came by a couple of weeks later and drove her to
Sikeston just to get her out of the house. He didn't say anything
else about forgiveness, and she hadn't told him she'd forgive
him, either. They'd just dropped that conversation.

"But the cancer's gone away, right?" Jo asked, still squeezing
Estelle's plump hand.

Yes and no, yes and no. But John was paying her more attention. "He picked me up just a couple of weeks ago and took me
to that roadhouse where we liked to boogie. I wasn't too frail to
do a little dancing. Do you remember how to boogie, toots?
Come on, show me." While Jo got up and found her bedroom
slippers, Estelle tuned in some country-and-western music on
the clock radio. "Let's see those little hips of yours moving.
That John, he *invented* hips!"

That day they'd boogied right here in this room, Estelle shaking her shoulders and snapping her fingers, Jo with her face in
bandages but swinging out because Estelle liked it that way, fast
and loose, so what if things shook, they were supposed to. Men
liked to see a little motion.

Estelle had all the answers; passion had made her wise. If Jo
had any problems, Estelle knew one or two solutions, sometimes more. Right now, if Jo were to ask her, "What will happen
to me?" Estelle would say, "Live your life! You don't have a
choice but to follow your heart. That's the way it is, toots."
"Follow your heart" was Estelle's motto. When Jo was a kid
she'd imagined this heart she was to follow to be like a friendly
golden retriever leading her up her own front walk and to her
own front door. *Oh, Estelle.*

Now Jo sat up and scrubbed at her face to get the blood
circulating. In her small bathroom she splashed cool water on
her cheeks and soaked a washcloth, laid it on her eyes. She
wished that Kit would phone her. Right now. She'd wanted to
miss Kit, although she really didn't know him well enough to
miss him very much. Still, he'd kissed her that last evening before he left to be a camp counselor up in Wisconsin. She imagined Kit lying with his head in her lap the way she'd seen some
French students messing around, drinking wine from a wine-
skin. She'd touch Kit's lips with her finger, lean down over him
and he'd kiss her.

She thought about him for a long time before she called his house. After she unpacked her suitcase she even looked up his photo in the yearbook. It was hard to get his image back. She traced his square chin, his unruly red hair down to the collar of his shirt. He was good-looking, not like a man, but like a boy. That's what she wanted. She thought she knew what to expect from Kit. Men like that Thomas guy she'd met in Vienna made her feel dizzy and off-balance. She was eighteen and had never been in love. She didn't love Kit, but she wanted him. Or maybe she just wanted to get laid.

When she called the O'Rourkes', Kit's mother answered. Yes, he was back from camp, but he was subbing for a lifeguard at the Fort Sheridan pool. He'd be home at eight and she'd tell him to call. "Want to leave your number?" she asked Jo. "He knows it," Jo said, wondering if he did.

5

W ill's taxi let him out under the canopy of Saint Mary's Hospital, then pulled away down the circular drive. He took a deep breath, like a diver readying to go under, then huffed it out. What the hell was he doing here? What an illusion medicine was. Once he was back in the operating room again, he'd be comfortable enough—he had good hands and he knew his work. But this business of transition. Coming here before going home was an act of discipline.

He saw himself in the glass doors as they parted for him, a wiry guy in a rumpled tan suit, shoulders slumped, hands in his pants pockets. He straightened as he walked through. Get *on* with it. Still, his gut tightened as he came into the entrance hall.

Sister Therese sat at the front desk. She still wore a full habit, although the other sisters in her order had adopted street clothes. She looked up without smiling, but then he'd never seen her smile. "Welcome back, Dr. Brenner."

Behind her, Sister Annie Riley, who pushed the delivery cart, cried, "We missed you, Dr. Brenner!"

"You *were* missed," Sister Therese said, and let Will take her surprisingly warm hand in his.

"Glad to be back." He wondered if he'd actually been gone at all. Hadn't Sister Annie Riley been wearing this same blue polyester dress when he saw her last? The entrance hall smelled, as always, of carnations and the bitter disinfectant used on the tile floors. And Sister Therese's sober face was like that of the nuns he remembered from childhood.

Arranging roses, Sister Annie Riley asked, "How was your trip, Dr. Brenner?" Careless about herself, runs in her stockings, shoes down at the heels, she reminded him more of the mother of a large family than of a nun.

"Fine. Just fine." He pressed the elevator button, leaned against the stucco wall to wait. "Haven't been home yet. I thought I'd see how things were going here."

"As always," Sister Therese said.

"Fewer broken bones now that school's started, but more sports injuries. We need you." Sister Annie Riley nodded as though agreeing with herself.

Sometimes Laura said, "Damn those nuns! They treat you doctors as if you were priests! You're just *men*." As if he needed to be reminded.

"So it's business as usual?" My God, he thought, I sound like a butcher coming back into his shop.

"The usual." Sister Annie Riley took a white carnation and broke off the stem.

He let her slip the flower into his buttonhole. "Pretty formal when you consider I slept in this suit on the plane." But the flower pleased him. He wished he could lay his face, his whole body in something as fresh and cool—a stream, the lake. He should have showered before coming here, washed off the dirt of the trip. "Is Dr. Perrone in today?" He wanted to see Jerry first, if he could. Jerry steadied everything for him with those same tired jokes, the stock dialogues they'd developed over the years.

"He's in surgery," Sister Annie Riley said. "They've got a full morning scheduled." She smiled down into the bucket of carnations, as though the flowers were faces.

He checked his watch against the wall clock—only ten-forty-five. A full morning meant Jerry wouldn't be free until noon. He'd go to the doctors' lounge, catch Jerry between procedures. The elevator arrived and Will hit four.

Drinking coffee out of cardboard cups, Stuber and Walsh

were the only ones in the lounge. "Hey!" Stuber said. "How was the big trip? You look great."

Will touched the stubble on his chin. He felt gray, aged, as though while he'd slept on the plane ten years had gone by. But he liked Stuber, he was the best anesthetist around. Stuber slugged Will's shoulder, and Will punched back. Locker-room stuff. "I look like hell, but the trip was fine. How're you doing?"

"Great."

"Where did you go again?" Walsh stirred his coffee with a plastic stick. "Everyone on the staff has been somewhere this month."

So Walsh was in one of his foul moods. When he was like this he was hell to work with—absentminded, cross, demanding, impatient. "Germany, Switzerland, Austria," Will recited.

"Yeah?" Walsh peered down into his cup.

"Either Walsh has been there already or he doesn't want to go," Stuber said.

"I was there all right. Second World War. The good one."

"Come on, Walsh. You aren't that old." Stuber winked at Will.

"Fifty-nine. I was a goddamned bomber pilot. A hot-shot kid."

It was impossible for Will to imagine Walsh as a hot-shot kid, although he was unreasonably glad to see his heavy face.

"Why haven't you told us any war stories?" The warmth in his voice surprised him.

Walsh must have noticed, too. He looked up at Will, his bushy eyebrows drawn. "Maybe I will. I've got a few, you know."

Trying to sound more casual, Will asked Stuber, "What's new here?"

"The Cubs had their collective asses kicked in by the Cards yesterday. That means no Series for us again."

"Stuber thinks the only part of the paper is the sports page," Walsh said, and Jerry came in.

Hugging Jerry was like being taken into the embrace of a freight train. His shoulder thudded against Will's. "Hey, old Will!"

"Son of a bitch!" Will found himself grinning. "I hear you're having a big morning up here."

"On the seventh day I rest." Jerry rubbed his dark eyes, propped his glasses up on his balding head. "What's good enough for God is good enough for me."

"I thought you *were* God," Stuber said.

"Sister Therese is God," Jerry said. "Ask her. She'll admit it when closely questioned." He scratched his beard, sank down on the couch in front of Will and looked up, laughing. "Damn, I'm glad you're back!"

"I'm glad, too."

"I've saved myself for you."

Walsh groaned.

Over the loudspeaker a woman intoned, "Dr. Stuber and Dr. Perrone, room eight."

"I'll be right behind you," Jerry said to Stuber. "I'll have to scrub up again now that Brenner's brought in all these European bacteria."

"How's it going?" Will sat down by him. There was a lot more gray in his short, black beard than Will had remembered.

"We're moving them through." He flexed his hands. "The golden fingers at work."

"How about you, Jer?" Will leaned back, arms behind his head. The tension had gone out of his stomach. What he'd guessed was true—things were as they'd always been, no one had missed him except Jerry, and he'd missed Jerry a lot.

"I'm doing fine. Sitting up and taking nourishment. We're making big bucks even without you by my side. I hope you'll do the same for me when I make good my escape. Listen, I'll be through in an hour or so. Do you have your car?"

"I took a cab from the airport."

"Let me give you a lift home, then. I'll tell you case histories and all the gossip you need to know. Okay?"

"Right. Just tell me quickly what the word is on Marks." Smashed up in a car accident, Mr. Marks threatened to sue when his face was scarred. Jerry said he'd saved the man's life.

"Turns out his son is an attorney."

"Shit."

"Exactly. They are suing. But I will defend my honor."

Lowering his glasses into place, he smiled at Will. He looked tired—a man who hated to sleep because there was so much else that he wanted to do, or so he claimed.

"Worried?"

Jerry shrugged. "I did my best. The emergency-room staff did its best. What else is there?" He glanced up when his name was called again over the loudspeaker, and shook his fist. "Coming, Mom! Meet you in the cafeteria, William. Wait for me."

"You're taking me home, remember? I'll have to wait for you."

"You might get picked up by a candy-striper. Even you could get lucky." He hitched up the pants of his surgical greens and headed for the door.

What energy Will had went with Jerry, and he took the elevator down to the cafeteria for coffee and something to ease the howl from his gut. He hadn't been able to eat on the plane. The damp food made his head swim. Laura ate his meals as well as her own, then excused herself and went to the restroom. He imagined her, head-down, over the stainless steel toilet. He couldn't manage to talk to her if he thought of her like that—a case study. He'd tried to sleep.

"You're looking glad to be back." Millie checked his coffee, cheese sandwich, vegetable soup on her register.

"I am." When he dug into his pocket he came up with a handful of groschen.

"That ain't money." Her brown arms shone under the neon lights.

"You're telling me." He stuffed the coins back, found a couple of U.S. bills in his wallet, handed them over.

"Save that toy money until you go back there." Millie handed him his ticket. "Wherever you were."

"I'm not going back." He hadn't thought that, but when he heard his words he recognized his conviction. He didn't want to travel anywhere again. He wanted to stay in this ordered, familiar place where he knew his way around with some ease, where the very words reassured him, having nothing to do with emotion, having to do only with things—instruments, injuries, techniques, and the Cubs games. Here he could manage his anxiety. Though it hadn't always been like this, he reminded himself, setting out his plastic dishes, pulling his chair close to the table so he could lean on the scarred Formica top. He ran his palm over the indentations and remembered the desks in med school with their scars: names, numbers, crib notes—the history of their users' hopes and fears.

He'd put his face right down on his nicked desk in that neurology exam. He'd swept his exam sheets to the floor and laid his cheek on the rough surface. The room had grown dark and small around him, closing up over him. He folded his arms around his head. Waves broke over him, in him. He was being sucked under. He would drown. His heart labored as though he'd been running hard and his face was first hot, then cold. He thought he was fainting from lack of sleep, but he didn't faint. He sat there, face pressed against his desk as though it were a raft on the sea, darkness choking him under its weight.

Then two men stood beside his desk. He'd never seen them. They were neither students nor teachers. They were prying his hands off his desk, telling him to stand up, to take a deep breath, to try to walk. He didn't want to let go. He cursed them, wondering at the rage in his voice, wondering that they weren't angry in return. Then one of them gave him a hypo and after a while he could let go of his desk, could walk, could lie down on a bed he found himself beside.

Acute anxiety neurosis—he was a goddamned *classic*. It often happened to med students—the compulsive ones, the overachievers—the psychiatrist told him. He recommended therapy for Will, and a rest.

He told his folks he'd dropped out of school. His father nodded—it was what he'd expected of Will, anyway—he anticipated disappointment in all things. His mother cried. She wanted him to be a doctor. She wanted him to save lives.

Out of school, without a job, he faced paying for his therapy and drugs. He saw the psychiatrist twice a week, and took ten milligrams of Valium four times a day—enough to calm a horse, though he was still tense. He was twenty-two and had no skills to speak of. He had, instead, a list of things he *couldn't* do: sit at a desk, read, write, memorize, be alone in a room. He got work for a landscaper, planting trees and bushes around homes on the North Shore. It was good to be outside, and he was never alone. He worked with a crew of Latinos from South Chicago who asked him no questions, didn't give a damn where he'd been or where he was going as long as he kept up with their trimming, digging, cutting, bagging. They spoke Spanish and ignored him, but he wasn't alone. The pay was lousy. Men supported large families on that pay, but he didn't have enough to pay his psychiatrist. He was afraid to try it without him or without medication. What if the waves broke over him again?

He read the want ads and discovered that welders got the best pay; he studied the trade papers and found they needed welders in the shipyards in Louisiana. He bullied a guy he knew in pharmacology into giving him three refills of his prescription, quit his job and packed up. His mother cried again when he put jeans, some shirts, his work boots in a suitcase and bought a bus ticket for New Orleans. How could he save lives if he was a welder? He told her he was trying to save his own. His father understood: an electrician's son becomes a welder—at last Will made sense to him. Will said he wouldn't stay long, just long enough to get on his feet. He stayed four years.

In New Orleans he got into welding school, found a furnished efficiency on the West Bank, got a job pumping gas at an all-night Shell station. School plus work left him about four or five hours of sleep. It was enough. He discovered he had a gift. He could make his hands do what he wanted them to do. He learned to make V butts that were marbled and satiny. At last, his instructor said softly, "Shit, that's real pretty." The rest of the class turned to look—it was the highest compliment. He'd never been prouder of anything in his life than that "pretty." It proved he could *do* something. When the class was over he quit his gas station job and went to work in the shipyards as a tacker.

The first time the Junkman led him across the deck of the tanker and Will followed him through the hatch into the hold, he thought he'd faint with fear. But his medication kept him steady. With his medication he could do anything. The "hole" smelled of metal, of oil and burning flux from the welding rods. Heat shimmered over the deck and the hatch looked like the mouth of hell. He crouched to look and saw the cavernous vastness of the tanker, shipfitters hooked to the sides like spiders, their safety lines attached to the pieces of metal they'd welded to the sloping, sheer inside of the hull. But he slipped through the hatch behind Junk as though it was the most natural thing in the world.

The truth was he loved it, loved every bit of it, the terrible heat, the sickening humidity, the roughness, even his own fear. Yes, even that—it was *real*. Nothing was in a book. He said it over and over to himself like a Zen koan: This is horrible and I love it.

Of course his drugs made it possible—beautiful Valium!—how could he get along without it? After he used it up, he got along like the others: he drank and did dope.

It had been a hot, formless time surrounded on both sides by the intense, cool order of med school—because he'd come back. In despair. And he'd needed med school as a haven where he could heal himself. He wanted it for the very things he'd been afraid of before: it asked the most of him, and—it was true—he could help people instead of betraying them.

Him, and his good hands. Will spread them on the cafeteria table—short, blunt fingers, backs still pockmarked from welding. But steady.

"Brenner!" Jerry beckoned from across the cafeteria. He was still in his scrub suit, cap and all, his dark beard looking like part of the uniform. He carried a box of saltwater taffy and a wrapped sterile kit.

Will followed him out the emergency entrance and into the doctors' parking lot. His red Mercedes was in the first space. He got here early, another benefit of his insomnia. As Will climbed in his side he pushed out of the way a tennis sock, two hardcover novels, the book review section of *The New York Times,* a box of tapes labeled "Opera," and an empty McDonald's carton. Jerry shoved the box of candy on top of a pile of magazines between them. "You finished early," Will said.

"Sometimes I amaze even myself." Unwrapping a piece of taffy with one hand, he backed up, pulled into the drive. "How was your big trip?"

Will let his head sink back on the headrest. "Good. No, that's a lie. Not so good, especially near the end. You won't believe this, but I missed working. There's nothing to *do* when you're traveling. I was this American tourist, just looking on."

Jerry gunned the Mercedes as they left the lot. "Switzerland, though. I bet you loved Switzerland. I was at that conference two years ago in Zurich. What a classy city. Classy broads. That's the French influence."

Will unwrapped a piece of taffy, put the paper in his pocket. Laura would buy a carful of groceries, cook a big dinner. Maybe he could nap this afternoon. Or would it be better to hang on until evening and try to catch up with a real night's sleep? "I'm a little spaced out. Jet lag, I guess. What's your remedy? You're a world-class traveler."

Jerry turned onto Greenbay Road. This time of day most of the traffic consisted of mothers driving station wagons loaded with very small kids and large dogs. He thought a moment. "I guess I use the same technique stewardesses do. I just pretend I'm on the same time as the country I'm in. Your head can fool your body. Give yourself a lot of positive suggestions. Tell yourself that you aren't tired from traveling, that it's just the end of another exciting morning of medical breakthroughs. It's a form of self-hypnosis. Your body will respond. Try it, you'll like it."

Will was doubtful. He didn't have a very good record of mind over body, but he nodded. Good old Jerry—an answer for everything. What would it be like to have unlimited energy, unlimited confidence that you were right? "What if I'm not a good candidate for hypnosis?" He chewed hard at the taffy.

"Hell, you're an ideal candidate for hypnosis." Jerry smiled, racing the motor as he waited for the light to change. "You're intelligent and you have a good visual memory. I bet I could hypnotize you into believing you were full of zip and ready to break another four-minute mile." Without looking down, Jerry reached for another piece of candy. "You're also basically trusting."

"Not true."

"The hell it's not. It's a fundamental character trait of yours. And a certain crude optimism still clings to you."

Will wondered if that was true. He hoped so. "Then trance me, doctor! Give me that trance!" His falsetto was shaky but Jerry laughed.

"Can't. You've got to have the whole setup—a quiet, secure office, lots of books on the shelves, the subtle white noise of an air conditioner, an hour of time locked in and to be paid for, the permission of your therapist to let you pass out quietly when he gives you the countdown. You can't get tranced between stoplights."

"You seem to know a lot about it."

"I read a lot."

Will closed his eyes, feeling them burn with fatigue. "Push me out when we get to my house."

Jerry carried on without cues. He described the past weeks at the clinic, the schedule for the coming week now that Will was back. Then he detailed his last tennis game, in which he almost took gas in the third set but came back to put away his opponent, a radiologist almost twelve, maybe thirteen years younger. He ran down the names and vital statistics of the women he'd taken out recently—he was divorced and "on the move," as he characterized himself. He reviewed a couple of movies and a novel. He gave a brief weather report: continued hot and fair, Indian summer.

The Mercedes jolted onto Center Road, the familiar potholes under the wheels. The smell of leaf smoke was in the air. The rocking of the car and Jerry's monologue made Will drowsy, and now he smelled Lake Michigan, a salt smell, like an animal nearby. Almost home.

"Must be jelly, jam don't shake like that." Jerry slowed the car.

Will opened his eyes: a green ten-speed bike, tanned legs, white shorts, yellow-striped tank top, dark hair in a ponytail. She waved as Jerry passed her—a flash of white teeth, sunglasses.

"Laura's kid sister! Has *she* changed." Jerry looked back over his shoulder.

"She's starting college. Day student up at Woodcliff."

"Does she run around the house in her underwear the way she used to?"

"I haven't noticed."

"If she did, you'd have noticed, all right. Does she go out with older men?"

"She's got a boyfriend her own age." He glanced back at Jo. Her head was down as she negotiated the gravel and potholes.

What if some guy like Jerry did make a move on her? "She's not your type."

"I've made a discovery, William. They're all my type. I took out a girl so young she'd learned the twist as a folk dance in high school. I admit that was humiliating, but in other ways she was definitely my type."

Jerry turned onto Prospect and pulled up in front of the house.

Out of the corner of his eye Will saw Jo heading around the block to the driveway on the alley at the back. "You old reprobate," he said to Jerry. It sounded harsher than he'd have thought it would—well, that's how he meant it.

Jerry sighed, "I'm all talk, you know that. My fantasies are much grander than my capacities." He leaned forward to peer at the house—white stucco, blue shutters, a row of Japanese pines around the screened porch. "The place looks good. You won't have to cut the grass before Laura will let you in." He slapped Will on the arm. "Listen, I've got a squash court tomorrow night at eight. You want a game?"

"Great!" he said, too loudly. "Thanks for the ride." He pushed his door shut. "I mean it, Jerry, thanks. Good to see you again." Because for a moment he'd wanted to hit him in the mouth. He stood by the curb to watch the red Mercedes cruise down to the park and turn left along Sunrise back toward Center Road. At the corner Jerry waved out of the open sunroof, a disconnected hand.

The front porch was dim and cool, the heavy door to the house open. "Laura?" No answer—she must be out on her errands. He stood for a moment, looking into the long living room, afternoon sun coming in through the Venetian blinds onto the amber-toned Persian rugs. A Peter Max print that he'd liked, insisted on buying, glowed like a lamp over the fireplace. It was an image of a runner, blue curls of air rising like waves at his heels and breaking behind him like surf as he ran through an orange and yellow landscape. It was too modern for the decor, but he'd liked it instantly, wanted it—he wanted to be such a runner, he guessed, his head up, chest out, floating. And he'd insisted on the print partly because he wanted a choice of his own in this room. If he ever left, maybe that print would be the only thing he'd take with him.

The back door slammed and Jo appeared at the far end of the dining room in the doorway. Barefooted, she carried her tennis shoes. He saw her in silhouette, the sun bright behind her in the south windows of the kitchen. "Hi," she called.

"I thought you'd be asleep." He stopped at the foot of the front stairs.

"I did sleep for a while, then I decided I needed exercise. Your friend really crowds, doesn't he?" She leaned against the kitchen door.

"Jerry has an aggressive style, all right. How're you doing, Jo?"

"I don't know." She seemed to recede toward the sun-filled windows behind her. When she reached to the back of her neck and pulled away the rubberband, her hair fell loose on her bare shoulders. "How should I feel?"

"Tired, definitely tired." Her elastic tank top pushed her breasts down and apart. A band of skin, the color of dark honey, showed between the top and the white track shorts. With the light behind her it was hard to see her face. "Jet lag is real."

"Should I feel confused, too?"

He leaned on the curved banister. She was describing his mood. "What are you confused about, Jo?"

"Everything," he thought she said, but her voice was low. She pushed her shoes with her bare foot. "Everything," she repeated, louder.

"Glad to be home?" He wanted to go sit with her in the sunny kitchen.

She held up her hand; at first he thought it was a warning— don't come near—but then he saw she checked her watch. "I don't know where I am, exactly. *Is* this home?"

He wished she'd smile. The shadows made her expression sad, dispirited.

"It's afternoon, but my body's telling me it's midnight. Things are upside-down," she said.

"And backwards." He loosened his tie. Along the living room floor the shadows of vine leaves wavered.

"Does it seem easy to you—coming back?" She didn't leave the doorway where she leaned, one hand above her head.

"Not at first."

"But we were all homesick, weren't we?"

"You could say that. Sometimes, though, I'd like to just keep on going." He wondered at his honesty.

"In *Austria?*"

Her incredulity made him smile. "No." Had he been about to say, Into a different life? "Make new patterns, I meant."

"I want the old, dependable ones." Again he could barely hear her.

He pulled off his tie, stuffed it into his pocket, started unbuttoning his shirt. "Which ones?"

She pushed her hair back, then, and he saw her face, the marks of fatigue under her eyes, her mouth turned down in the characteristic manner of her repose. "I don't know, exactly. Sometimes it all comes back on me, like memories I'm not even sure my mind remembers, maybe just my body. Like Estelle holding me. I woke up thinking about her."

He heard a tremor in her voice. "You still miss her?" Should he go to her? Give her a hug? She was speaking of love.

"Yes, I still miss her. I guess I always will, until someone loves me like she did. After Laura made her leave, she used to call me from phone booths all over Saint Louis. I'd pick up the phone and hear her change dropping in, and she'd be at some filling station, trucks roaring by, calling because she just *had* to hear my voice. She missed me as much as she missed Daniel, she said. She phoned me from coin laundries, and once a library, and drugstores, and the lobbies of movie theaters, from grocery stores. From bars. Everyplace. She never reversed the charges, either. She dropped in her coins, and when the three minutes were up she'd say, 'Love you, toots,' and we'd hang up. When the phone rang I always expected it would be her. You remember, Will, how she called me that last day from the hospital." She crouched down suddenly, as though she were in pain, pushed her folded arms against the bare skin at her waist.

He walked toward her, then. But as he crossed the dining room she stood again, her tennis shoes in her hand, as though that was why she'd doubled over. Maybe it was.

"So. That's not such big news, is it? I miss Estelle, or I miss what I remember of her."

She leaned to pitch her shoes toward the narrow back staircase once intended for a maid. "Will, what *new* patterns were you thinking of?" Her voice was determinedly cheerful. He was stopped at the table.

"I was glad enough to be back at the hospital, but sometimes I'd like to have less responsibility, I suppose. The whole doctor role."

"People needing you?"

"There was a time in my life when I was more carefree." *Was* there?

"Your welder stories?" Her voice held a faint echo of Laura's. She'd broken the thread between them, and there was nothing else for him to say. Time to head upstairs for a shower.

She stepped backward into the kitchen. "I'm exhausted, Will. You're right about jet lag."

"Want to get some more sleep? It's normal to be tired and confused."

"What I wouldn't give to be perfectly normal."

He saw her bare foot last, catching at the tennis shoe which had fallen to the terra-cotta tiles of the kitchen floor. "Sleep tight." He watched her foot disappear before he walked back through the shadows of the living room.

From the stairs he heard her call after him, "You too." As though it were night, as though he were putting her to bed as he had in those first weeks when he came to live here, Laura's husband, trying to make things all right for the ten-year-old girl, who cried herself to sleep because she missed the housekeeper Laura had let go.

The first time he tucked Jo into her bed she hissed at him, "You're not my father, and don't you think so!"

"I don't want to be. Maybe I could be a sort of friend."

She was chewing on the end of her dark braid. "I don't want to talk about it," she said. And they didn't, but after a while, sooner than he imagined, she came to trust him. She needed to trust somebody.

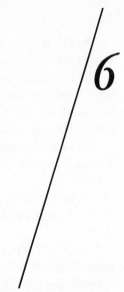

6

Will was stripping off his clothes to shower when he heard Daisy's excited bark and Laura calling "Hello?" from downstairs.

"Up here!"

In a moment she was running up the stairs, and then at the door, her hair swinging, her hands on her slim hips. "Welcome home." Smiling.

He examined her face as though they'd been separated for several days instead of a couple of hours. "Did you get a nap? You look good."

"I didn't have time. Jo was out like a light, of course. I've got groceries and the mail and picked up Daisy. Did you hear her bark? She's glad to be home."

The energy in her voice surprised him. He felt as though he'd been hit on the back of the head, an ache that crept down into his shoulders.

She sat beside him on the bed. "Did they miss you at the hospital?"

That wasn't her kind of question—that was the kind that wives on sitcoms asked their husbands as they handed them dry martinis. Laura usually said sarcastically, "How many lives did you save today?"

"Everyone's expendable."

She followed him into the bathroom and watched as he adjusted the shower. She ran her hands through her hair, seeming pleased with herself, pleased with something. *"I'm* so glad to be home. I realize I've been kind of crazy lately. The trip was more of a strain than we admitted, don't you think? I wish we'd had the nerve to call it quits in Innsbruck and just come home."

He nodded, watching her in the mirror.

"If things were tight between us it was my fault."

Her statement was so straightforward and guileless that he stared. "It was both of us, honey." He was even more grateful than he sounded.

"I mean it," she insisted.

"Me, too."

She hugged him, letting her body sink against his. "We belong here," she said, nuzzling.

He rested his chin on her shoulder, smelling her talc, feeling her taut waist under his palm. "Could you get me a beer?" Anything else he might say would sound sentimental and she might retreat into her sarcasm. With Laura it paid to be careful.

"In a minute." She let go of his neck and hiked herself onto the counter by the sink. "There's something mysterious going on, and I want to talk to you before you speak with Jo." Her brown eyes followed him as he unfolded a towel.

"Yeah? Girls her age are supposed to become mysterious. It's a developmental stage. Increased independence, privacy, separation from authority figures."

She frowned briefly. "You sound like a textbook."

"I mean to. It's right out of chapter three, *Adolescent Behavior.*" The water ran warm on his hand. He wanted to get in, let it soak him, turn his face up into the spray.

"She's not the mysterious one. There was a long distance call for her today from Rome."

That startled him, but he didn't want to admit it. He sat on the edge of the tub.

"That guy from Vienna, the one who intercepted Jo at the airport. I worried about him, remember? He decided to call Jo from Rome. I say that's mysterious."

He remembered well enough Trawick's aggressive pursuit of Jo in the airport. "Listen, Laura, the guy's a prick. Forget about him. Jo can take care of herself."

"You don't believe that."

"I believe he's a prick. She won't be interested." He stood again. He wanted to be alone now.

"You don't believe Jo can take care of herself, do you?"

He tested the water, turned his back to her and stepped into the spray. "I do. As well as any of us, better, maybe."

Through the sound of the spray he heard her. "Well, she can't. She wasn't even ready to move out for college. She's only got one foot in the water and she needs looking after. We need to know what's going on. Thomas didn't strike me as your average guy. He seemed more of a sociopath—"

"Forget that beer."

After a moment he heard her leave the bathroom and bang the door.

He let the spray fill his mouth, spatter on his closed eyes. Then he soaped, starting with his hair and face and working down. He made the shower cooler. God, it felt good. He didn't want to talk about Trawick, didn't want to think about him, didn't want to know of his existence. He didn't like the guy and hoped he wouldn't reappear in their lives, but Jo could certainly make her own choices. That was a matter of principle. People chose for themselves whom they'd love. Or maybe, really, things just happened and later on we concluded that we had some part in making them happen. Perhaps there really was only chance, not choice at all.

He let the tub fill with warm water and slid down in it to soak.

Chance. Chance that Jerry had introduced him to Laura in the first place. Jerry had phoned him, "Come on over to our condo for some tennis. Meet Diane."

Jerry was married then, and put Diane on the phone. "And dinner here, after," she said, "to get acquainted. Jer tells me you're his new wonder boy at Westside Clinic, and I want to meet you!"

After Will accepted, she rambled on—she'd run into the daughter of an old friend and would like to invite her, too. The girl's name was Laura Hale, and her dad had done the insurance work for Jerry's clinic. He'd been killed six months ago, hit by a bus on the Loop. Laura had just graduated from Northwestern. She'd let the housekeeper go and was taking care of the family home and her young sister all by herself—her mother had passed away several years before. It was a lot of work—Laura was very brave. What did Will think about asking Laura to join them for dinner?

Of course he tried to sound pleased. What the hell could he do? He wanted to get off to a good start with his first job. But he pictured the brave Laura Hale like a woman from a Victorian novel: small, shy and yet determined, with glasses.

After tennis with Jerry, Will took a turn in the shower and when he came out, damp in his clean khakis, a slim blonde he guessed must be Laura was setting the table on the deck. She wore a black sundress that showed off her tan, and her hair was loose, thick and in motion as she bent forward to lay knives across the table. Her hair parted, falling along her shoulders, and he could see the raised bones of her spine, each one as discrete as a pearl. She turned to smile at him as if she'd known he was watching.

They had thick steaks and an indifferent salad of iceberg lettuce. Laura brought iced brownies to go with the fresh peaches and at her urging Will ate three, picking up the chocolate crumbs with the tips of his fingers while Diane talked about life in the condos. When Laura described her days—tennis lessons, the gym, real estate classes, sailing—he decided she'd get along just fine running the old family manse or whatever and raising her kid sister. He imagined she knew a lot of people and got out as much as she wanted to—Diane didn't need to do her any favors. But then there was the other thing.

His training had taught him to recognize that she'd been anorexic. He put her illness in the past tense because she was slender, not skinny. But there was a cast to her complexion like a green underpainting beneath her tan, a hollowness above her eyes. Her hands and feet seemed slightly too large for her. He could see her nipples through the sheer sundress but she had no breasts, and her hips were narrower than a boy's. The boyishness of her figure contrasted with the beauty of her face, full lips turned down slightly, straight eyebrows above those brown eyes, narrow nose, thick, tawny hair.

He felt a tenderness for her. It was the tenderness a parent might feel for an injured child, even though the child was not his own. Although she seemed so confident, at one time she had damaged herself and the marks were still on her.

When he thought about it later, he realized that from the very first he was hooked on the certifiably insane idea that he could care for her, somehow nurse and cajole and nourish the woman out of the boyish girl. Had he *chosen* to feel that way? It was an automatic response: he wanted to save her.

While Jerry and Diane were clearing the table and making coffee, Will asked her, "Can I take you home? I've got a car."

"You can take me anywhere," she smiled. "Whoever you are."

"Well, it's *me.*" He smiled down at the brownie crumbs he was chasing, feeling as though he'd said something profound.

But the rest of the evening went differently than he'd expected. He'd hoped to take her to a bar, have a couple of beers, hear her story—maybe tell her his, if she was interested. But she wanted to go home. "Diane told you about my father and my little sister, didn't she?"

She had.

"Jo's home alone. She's been real upset about going to bed since I let the housekeeper go, but she's never had a sitter. I told her I'd be home by bedtime." Then she added, "I'd like to see what it's like to have you at the house, okay?"

He was disappointed, but didn't say so. It was a typical Chicago June night, warm and humid, a faint chemical smell almost like cinnamon in the air from the factories. They rolled the windows all the way down and she put her arm out, as he did— "holding down the roof," they'd called it when he was in high school. He felt almost as though he was in high school again, thrown off his guard by Laura, waiting to see which way she would move.

He pulled up in front of her house, a narrow stucco two-story under oaks so thick they blocked the streetlights from the front walk. Lights were on in the downstairs rooms and a mosquito candle flickered on the porch.

"Let me have a peek at Jo and then let's walk along the bluff.

I want to show you the lake from up here." She directed him to pull around the block and park in her driveway on the lane—the police ticketed cars without town stickers this close to the park.

At the corner a raccoon scurried across the lane, its eyes glinting yellow in his headlights. The trees were heavy-boughed, forming a tunnel in the lane, the air damp and rank, like a rain forest. Night noises came up loud from cicadas and tree frogs dinning away in the wet grass. He parked behind the Chevy that was in the drive and walked back around the corner to the front porch.

Laura was waiting for him on the front steps. "I thought you'd run away." She took his hand and turned toward the park, beyond which he could see the opaque darkness that would be Lake Michigan. "Don't let's talk now. Let's just *be*. This is my favorite place in the world."

So he followed her, enjoying the light, tensed grip of her hand in his. Her bones were narrow, like glass straws. He could easily lift her, carry her on his shoulder the way he'd carried the seventy-pound "come-alongs" the shipfitters used to pull together the seams of the ships. Once he'd been strong enough to climb a ladder with one of those levers slung over each shoulder, their weight dragging him backward. Her weight would be nothing to him. From time to time she turned, smiled, and pointed at an owl circling over the park, visible now and then between the trees, or a cat hunting in the long, pale grass near the edge of the bluff.

Away from the streetlights the night closed in. In the park, trees roofed them over, but at the edge of the bluff where she led him the whole sky appeared suddenly, vast and milky, a sheen of stars seen faintly through the haze. He gasped when she wrapped her free arm around a precariously rooted oak and leaned out to point to the beach below. The sand was lighter than the water. Down the beach two fires burned, tiny figures moving around them. He held her hand more tightly when she swung back to him. She stood still beside him and slowly he became aware of the sound of the lake, sighing like the wind off the plains, and the lake smell, which made him think of rust. Far out from shore, lights of freighters moved south toward the ports of Chicago and Gary.

"Do you want to climb down the bluff with me?" she whispered. "I can do it with my eyes closed."

"Next time." He realized as he answered that he'd made a commitment.

They turned to cross the park back to her house and he slipped his arm around her waist, not pulling her close, but just to feel her there. The distances of the night made him sad. He'd grown used to being alone—but maybe she'd ask him in and they could talk.

At her porch she went ahead of him. "Jo? Me again." A moth beat at the screen, flying out when the door swung wide. In spite of the mosquito candle, he heard a high whine by his ear and slapped. His hand came away from his forehead damp. It was hotter than he'd realized. Her hand had been cool in his.

In the long front room a small girl was sitting in the middle of a Persian rug, a box of crayons spread out around her. She looked up when he followed Laura into the room. Her solemn, round face, sunburned cheekbones and shoulders shone in the soft light. Her dark hair was in braids and she wore a pair of bib overalls cut off short, no shirt under. Behind her a baseball game glimmered on a small TV, the sound turned so low he could barely hear it.

"Jo, this is Will Brenner." Laura paused by the couch, looking down. "Jo got too much sun at the beach today."

"I forgot the zinc oxide," Jo said, as though she and her sister had been over this point several times. "It was in the cupboard with the dog food but I couldn't find it. Anyway, it doesn't hurt much." She touched her shoulder blade with her forefinger, experimentally.

It was his turn to say something. "Do you like the beach?" Discouraged, because the question was such an obvious one.

Jo nodded. "But I despise the pool."

"She takes swimming lessons at the pool," Laura said. "It's important to swim well if you live on the lake."

Jo ignored the lecture. "Are you going to come up with me so I can go to bed?" she asked Laura.

"Jo's afraid of the dark," Laura told him.

Jo made a face. Her bangs were cut off unevenly and a tar mark streaked her chin.

Instead of asking him to wait, Laura led him back to the front door rather formally. "It's a lot less trouble if you walk around the sidewalk to the garage. We've got a puppy in the backyard and she'll wake up and remember we took her away from her mother and howl like she's been doing every night."

Behind him, Jo said, "Her name's Daisy."

He found himself back at the porch door. "I'd like to see you again."

"I'd like that, too. A lot, actually. But not tomorrow. I have to think about you for a while."

Tomorrow? That startled him. He'd thought he might ask her to a movie and for a hamburger after, maybe in a week or so. It was as if she had a plot outline he didn't have, or at least a different set of expectations.

"I'll be in touch." Over Laura's shoulder he saw Jo appear in the lighted doorway, look out at him.

"Was he your date?" Jo asked, although he hadn't left yet.

"Yes and no." Laura smiled as she leaned toward him. It was the most intimate look she'd given him all evening. He wondered what the little girl made of this glamorous young woman who liked to run things.

There was nothing left to do except wave good night and make his way around the corner and back to his car. The sidewalk was tipped by oak roots and pieces had broken away. He watched his step in the dim lights of the old streetlamps. From the ravine he heard a whippoorwill, a falling note that grew fainter and then was gone.

He climbed into his Ford, rummaged for the keys he'd placed under the seat for safekeeping—how had he expected he might lose them from his pocket? Had he imagined he might lie on the beach with her?

While he was fumbling in the dark to find the right key, he sensed more than saw her run to his car from the back gate of her yard. The black of her dress blended with the fence and the hedge, but he caught the pale shape that was her face, a blur that was her bare arm. She darted in front of the car and was at his window, handing him something. Her breath smelled of the fruit they'd eaten. "You *will* call, won't you?" Her lips brushed his cheek and then she drew back. "That's my number." He realized he had a scrap of paper in his hand. "Don't lose it."

"Don't worry." But she was already running back to the gate, had disappeared again. He waited a moment to keep an image of her face before he turned the lights on. When he did turn them on they lit the starkness of the old stucco garage, trash cans inside a rail fence. A metal sign, Beware of the Dog, had been nailed to the gate, waist high, as though the child had been given the task and put it at her own height. A light went on upstairs in the house but no one looked out.

Back at his little apartment he was restless. He got himself a beer, pulled a kitchen chair onto the tiny balcony overlooking Route 41. Below, cars streamed by on their way out of the Sunset Drive-in, couples tucked behind the steering wheels as though both were driving. He propped his feet up on the railing and studied the couples. It would be a warm night to be making it in a drive-in, almost as humid as some nights in New Orleans.

Now that he wasn't with Laura, she seemed more eccentric than when they were together. Earlier, what they'd done was natural. Then she'd both sent him away and run after him—a mixed message. He wanted something more substantial. He was lonelier than he remembered being for a long time. He decided she was making herself more mysterious than she was.

Then his impatience gave way to another, stronger feeling: he wanted a woman. Flesh and blood. He didn't want mystery and intuition and responsibility for the family home and a kid. He wanted a normal woman, one who made it clear what she was about. One with tits. He crumpled his beer can and gripped the iron railing. Oh, yes, he wanted to bury himself like a time bomb in the warm, juicy body of a woman and slowly, so slowly he could feel every pulse beat bringing him closer, explode.

He tried to think instead of the simple pleasure of walking in the park with Laura Hale. She was okay. In a few days he'd call her. He'd see what would happen.

When morning was only a green tint on his curtains, the

phone woke him. The hospital, he thought, but he wasn't on call. An emergency, then. He tried to sound alert. "Dr. Brenner here."

She laughed. "Jerry is really pissed! I woke him up to get your number."

"Laura?"

"Of course. Do lots of women call you at five in the morning?"

He pushed to his elbow. "What's up?"

"I have something to tell you."

"Now?"

"Now is when it's happening. My period."

Was she playing some game? "Your period," he repeated, the doctor reassuring a patient by following a list of symptoms. He was having trouble understanding her—maybe she was on drugs.

"You don't know what that means?"

"You're menstruating." The doctor checking his diagnosis. Why would she call him at five in the morning to tell him she was menstruating? Last night she hadn't even wanted him to stay and talk.

"Yes!" she cried, as though he'd understood something complicated. What should he say now? Before he could decide, she rushed on, "Isn't that amazing?"

He sat up, pushed his pillow behind his back and settled in to try to help her make sense. "Is 'amazing' good or bad?" That was a safe question.

"Mostly it's just amazing. I've never had a period before. This is my first. I've gained a lot of weight these past two years and I kept hoping. My doctor was hopeful, too. Then I met you last night and when I woke up just now I knew. I absolutely knew, and I was right. Don't you see, Will? It's some kind of sign."

He remembered what he'd read about anorexia, the medical reports. A starving woman loses her fertility quickly, the frantic attempt of the organism to save itself—those studies from the concentration camps had provided invaluable data. In a young girl, the most common victim of anorexia, delayed adolescence. What else? "You've never had a period at all?"

"Never. It's all so complicated, Will. The important thing is that I was sick, but now I'm better. I'm well. This proves it. I'm normal, don't you see?"

He thought he did. "So you called me?"

"I had to share this with someone. With you, I guess. It seems connected some way with meeting you, although I know that's got to be coincidence."

"Yes."

"You're angry?"

"I'm glad you shared it with me." Angry instead at himself because he sounded just like the psychiatrist who'd listened patiently to Will's symptoms of anxiety, failure, depression when he went under and dropped out of med school.

She seemed not to hear the professional tone, or his reservations. "Oh, Will."

"Do you want to talk about it some more?" he asked tentatively, wondering if he did.

"Not now. Soon. I'm too excited now."

"Do you want me to call you?" Wondering if he wanted to call.

"Yes. Call me. I knew you'd understand. I trust you absolutely. You'll call me." And she hung up.

He lay staring at the window as the sun came up through the exhaust fumes and mist. His room seemed small and unfamiliar in the faint light, as though he'd gone to sleep in one room and wakened in another. Diane had told him that Laura Hale was twenty-one.

He was very tired, but he couldn't go back to sleep. After a while he got up and fried himself some eggs. She said she trusted him—what was he going to do about that?

He waited two days before he called her. But he had *chosen* to call her, hadn't he? Wasn't that a clear instance of choice? Although he knew that she was waiting; he imagined her watching the phone, trusting it to ring, trusting him to appear again in her life—he'd chosen to call. He had chosen not to betray her trust. But had he chosen *her*?

He called from his new office in Jerry's clinic. He didn't have time to talk, he said, but he'd like to take her out for a bite to eat soon. Tonight? No, he had a conflict. He named a time a few days off; he wanted to stay in control of things.

They went out for hamburgers and beers. This time it was as he'd hoped it would be. They talked long and quietly, sitting in a booth in the Irish Waters, holding hands now and then across the table as they spoke of her life, of his. It was an intimate conversation, the kind he'd been hungry for. She told him of her family tragedies. "Things are going to be better for you," he told her.

"You've been through tough times, too," she said. "I can tell. It's made you sympathetic."

He hoped he was honest, or honest enough, when he described his mixed career as a student, his descent into anxiety, the years in New Orleans. He must have wanted to convince her of his frailties, for he admitted to her, "I was a mess, then. Strung out all the time."

She cupped her chin in her hand. "But you're not like that now."

"I betrayed everything I valued about myself. I'd never thought I was weak or immoral, but I was."

Her hand closed around his wrist. "You're a good man now, Will."

"I *hated* myself."

She said quickly, as though she *knew*, "You'll never feel like that again. Never."

He wanted to believe her.

"No matter what happened then, Will, I trust you. Absolutely."

Then they were in his car, parked out on a deserted lane overlooking the lake. The air was sweet with lilacs, an undertone of onion grass cutting through the perfume. Bob Dylan was singing "Lay Lady Lay" on the radio, and Laura's head was on his shoulder. She took his left hand, kissed the palm, and then slowly and deliberately licked and sucked each of his fingers, starting with the little finger and ending with his thumb. When he kissed her lips, they parted easily, and he felt her tongue there, too. He drew back and looked into her face, the pure oval, creamy skin. Her eyes were open. "I'm glad you told me about yourself, Will. But you can't convince me you're not special."

He didn't want to convince her. She was pulling his damp hand up under her skirt to press against her even damper panties. "Would you like to fuck me?" she asked. As though this was the reward for his honesty.

Yes, he would. Very much.

"Jo's home tonight. She's going to sleep over at a friend's house tomorrow."

How about his place then?

"I want you in *my* bed."

He wanted to be there too.

"So we have to wait until tomorrow. You don't mind?"

He minded. How about here in his car?

"We can do better than that. You understand, don't you?"

He wasn't sure.

"We should go back now. I have to put Jo to bed."

In a daze compounded of his confessions and desire he backed out of the lane, lilacs slapping his face and arms as he leaned out the window to find the tracks. She kissed him once more at her house. "Promise? Tomorrow night?"

He promised.

But when they were alone the next night she was almost formal. She lit candles while he undressed and then she undressed in the bathroom. When they lay down together it was ceremonial, forehead to forehead, hands on each other's shoulders, until he drew her leg up under his waist. When he kissed her he realized she was holding her breath. He'd hoped she'd be wanton.

Later, they had iced tea and talked. Their conversation was more intimate than their caresses. But she clung to him when he left. "I'm so glad!" she whispered.

He *thought* he was.

At three-ten that morning she called him. He sat up in the dark, disbelieving the illuminated digits of his clock, disbelieving that she was doing this again. He tried to make out what she was saying. His name, he got that, but what else? He imagined how her face was crumpled by her sobs, but her words made no sense. Her sobs seemed wrenched up out of her lungs like water from a woman who has almost drowned.

"Laura? For God's sake, are you sick?"

She said something. *Sever? Lever?*

He tried his doctor's voice. "Slow down. Tell me slowly." That worked better, and he made out a few words. "You won't love me! You'll never love me! You'll feel sorry for me but you'll never love me. Never!"

Steadily, as though to a drunk, he said, "Try to calm down. I'm coming back. I'll be there in a few minutes."

He yanked on Levi's, a shirt, and drove the twenty minutes down an almost deserted Route 41, a few trucks passing him in the dark tunnel of night. Had she drunk too much, taken some drug? When he'd left she seemed fine, just fine.

She was waiting for him in the unlighted front doorway. Her face was disfigured, as though she'd been tortured. She fell against him and pulled the door shut behind them.

She let him help her back upstairs, let herself be eased onto the tangled sheets. "I don't know what's the matter! I need you so much!" She turned her face into the pillow and after a moment he took off his clothes and lay down beside her, turning her face to his.

"It's all right."

"It will never be all right! *I* know and *you* don't!"

"It's all right."

"I feel so awful! I don't know what's wrong!" She clung to his shoulders. She wore a sweatshirt and no panties. Her legs were chill when his touched them. He drew up the sheet over the two of them, wondering how this had come about in his life.

"I'm here." He stroked her back.

"You'll never love me! I have no substance!" She faltered on that word and tried again. "Substance. I'm hollow inside." Then she buried her face against his chest. "You'll never love me."

He held her a long time, at first tightly, and then, when her crying eased, more gently. "If I fall asleep, don't leave me," she begged.

He didn't leave her. In the growing light he searched out the shapes in her room that had been lit with the blue candles earlier. Her white skirt lay on the dresser, straw sandals sat on top of a lacquer box, her blouse was crumpled on a chair. There was the open door to the bathroom and a closed door into what must be the closet. The curtains swayed in the wind off the lake. He listened to the lake, its steady breath against the beach—it would be good to swim out into the lake in this pearly light, head toward the Michigan shore.

After a long while she said, "You have to go." She didn't open her eyes and he wasn't sure if she had slept, or just pretended to sleep.

"You're sure?"

"Yes." Then she grasped his hand. "You're so good, Will! You saved me tonight. I don't know what I might have done."

He drew himself out of her arms, and, trying to keep down the edge of panic that pushed him faster, he slipped on his pants and shirt.

"You'll call this afternoon?" The sheet was rumpled, her legs spread slightly, her hands crossed on her chest. The edge of her sweatshirt came just above her triangle of auburn hair. He pulled up the sheet, tucked her in.

He let himself out of the house. He pulled away down the deserted lane and then the empty road, forcing himself to drive slowly. He drove to a donut shop on the outskirts of Fort Sheridan and had two sugar donuts and a cup of black coffee. If he went home, she might call again. He was scared. What the hell was he doing? What would happen now?

When he called her at five that afternoon she laughed about a tennis game she'd won, about Jo's efforts to housebreak Daisy; she was trying a new chicken recipe and was already picking lettuce from her garden. It was as though her weeping hadn't happened.

Except that it had.

"I don't have much appetite when there's just Jo and me, and I'm trying to gain. Couldn't you join us for supper? I made a terrific apple pie."

He hesitated.

"Please?"

She'd hated begging, he knew. Quickly, before his silence reduced her to pleading, he said, "Sure."

The apple pie was great, tart with spices. He had two pieces and then helped Jo do a crossword puzzle while Laura did the dishes. After, he taught them five-card draw and spit-in-the-ocean, betting pennies.

After Jo had been put to bed Laura asked him if they couldn't make love again. This time he handled her more roughly. She was so light, so pliant, he could easily turn her this way, that way. "Do you like this?" he whispered. "This?" But she didn't answer. Her silence had its own seductive power. He did as he pleased.

He must have slept for a while, because he started awake. She was tensed, her breath on his chest shallow and uneven. Against her forehead he asked, "Are you okay?"

"Yes."

"Sure?"

"Yes."

He thought her voice trembled and her wild crying of the night before came back to him. "Listen, Laura?"

"Yes."

"You've got to promise me something. It's important."

"Anything."

"No more crying. It's too hard on you. It's too hard on me. And there's nothing to cry about."

"No, I won't cry. I don't want to. It's too awful. I won't."

Later, when he unlatched the screen door, he reminded her, "You won't cry. What if Jo heard you?"

"Oh, *Jo.*"

"She'd be scared to death."

"Like *you* were." Even in the dark he saw that she was smiling. She was taunting him. She was herself, she was okay.

Except that she wasn't. *She* knew and *he* didn't—she was dead right when she'd told him that, no matter that she'd been hysterical. But in any case even then it was somehow too late. A choice had been made.

He stood nude in the steamy bathroom. He wanted a beer badly and he was suddenly almost ill with fatigue. Clean and thin-blooded, like a patient who has just been allowed up for the first time in many days, he pulled on briefs, a tennis shirt, cut-offs.

The bedroom was cool, the wind off the lake sharp on his

damp skin and wet hair. From the front steps below the open window he heard a whistle. Then it became a song. "Sweet daddy, I need your lovin'."

Looking down from the open casement, he saw Jo seated on the front steps as she rubbed Daisy with one bare foot, a yellow pencil stuck behind her ear and her college catalogue open on her lap. She hadn't gone to bed after all. She was singing a song he'd heard often enough on one of the records Estelle had left with Jo when she was sent back to Missouri, a recording of blues so funky that Laura had tried to get Jo to give the record up—"I know where that record came from, but the mothers around here will kill me if their kids hear it." Of course Jo refused. Estelle had taught her to boogie to those songs. They were ones he'd heard in the strip bars in New Orleans. He rested his forehead against the smooth window frame and listened as Jo's voice lifted to him—high, clear, weightless and true.

> *Sweet daddy, I need your lovin'*
> *But I wasn't true to you*
> *Now you're gonna rock me all night long*
> *I ain't gonna be so blue*
> *Sweet daddy sweet daddy sweet daddy.*

7

The sky was pale lemon, black branches of the butternut like ink marks across it, when Kit pulled up in the old black Pontiac he'd bought with money he made at his after-school jobs. Chilly in her sweatjacket—the wind was off the lake—Jo sat on the front porch. She'd planned to wait until he came to the door, but she ran down to his car as he was getting out.

"Hey," he said.

His face and arms were dark with freckles and there was a line of zinc oxide on his lower lip where he burned the worst, a smear of it on the collar of his blue shirt. He wore Levi's and a pair of rubber thongs. Hadn't he been taller? He could have looked directly into her eyes if he'd look at her; he was looking at her house as though she were still in it.

"I'm back." She patted the dusty hood of his car.

"Great." He repeated it more enthusiastically, "Great!" He studied the butternut at the end of the porch.

"So I called."

"Great."

"Were you expecting me today?"

"Sometime around now." He'd started to say "pretty soon," she thought, then switched when he stumbled on the *p*. He examined the band of his waterproof watch.

"Well, here I am."

He tapped the watch and held it to his ear. *"Great."*

She pushed her hands into the pockets of her gray sweat-jacket and leaned against the fender. What had she expected from shy Kit? He would rush to her, take her in his arms. Background music, the whole bit. "The trip was okay," she said, as though he'd asked her. "But it wore me out. I guess I wrote you that, didn't I? Did you get my letters?"

He looked up then, smiled. White teeth, brown eyes the color of his freckles, a thatch of red hair bleached from chlorine. There was a gold chain around his neck with a small cross—that was new. "Yeah, you wrote that. You write good letters. The kids in my group talked me out of the foreign stamps."

"Maybe I should have written directly to your kids!"

"No way." He reached to her just as she moved aside, their arms bumped and he drew his back.

She tugged at the hem of her jacket. "I wanted to get a good sleep this afternoon, but I couldn't. I'm excited to be home. I don't mean excited like 'great,' but real spacey. Everything is different, do you know what I mean?"

"Sure." He reached again and took her hand in his.

The gesture wasn't much, but it warmed her. She hung on. "Kit, you're really tanned, much darker than you were. That's not exactly what I mean by different, but now you look like a surfer. Do you see?"

"Sure I see. But I'm mostly the same." He ran his free hand down his arm, the fine gold hairs there slicking flat, and she saw that under the tan he was sunburned. "My great Irish heritage. Mom keeps telling me I'll get skin cancer. She knew this dude once with no nose from skin cancer. That's her message for me this summer." He laced his fingers through hers, adjusting his grip. Their hands were exactly the same size—they'd measured once. We could be twins, she'd said.

"You look good," she told him, "for a guy with a nose."

"So do you. You look great."

She pushed at her hair. "I took two showers but I still feel dirty. The air inside the plane had this recycled smell, and I knew everyone was breathing the same air. There was no air of my own."

He swung their hands between them like a gate—open, closed, open.

"Do you want to come in?"

He studied the house again, as though peeling away the walls, looking into each room. "They here?"

"Will's asleep. Laura's upstairs reading or something. We couldn't really crank up the music, but no one would bother us."

"Let's go get some beers instead."

"Is anybody around? I know Betsy and Alyssa have left for school already."

"Everyone's shipped off to college except me and Brian. It's a lonesome town, Jo. Brian and I take turns guarding until the pool shuts down next weekend. Brian's totally wasted all the time. If he had to go in after anyone he'd drown with them."

She took his other hand and moved closer. There was a sheen of sweat on his cheeks and upper lip. "How about you?"

"Like usual. Just now and then."

"Your dad still giving you your grass?"

He released her hand to rub his lower lip, wiped the zinc oxide onto his jeans, rubbed again. After a moment he said, "Yeah. Excellent grass. He only buys the best."

"Terrific!"

"I don't know. I just don't think it's right and I've thought it through a lot lately. I don't think a father ought to give his kid grass. Parents should stay parents, even if they piss you off and ride your ass about stupid stuff like getting sunburned. Dad gives me this 'ole buddy' grin and slips me a sandwich bag of his stuff."

She tried to get a clear focus on his frown in the fading light. "You used to be glad enough."

"I've done some thinking this summer."

"You'd buy it if he didn't give it to you."

He looked down at his feet, at hers in her scuffed docksiders. "But it would be my decision. I'd be responsible. I'm talking values here."

"Oh." She hadn't thought much about values. It hadn't occurred to her that Kit might. While she was on the long trip her mind had seemed to be asleep. She'd absorbed sensory impressions without analyzing them, without thinking.

She wondered what else he'd been thinking about since she saw him last. The night before he left they'd walked down to the beach, where they skipped stones on the calm lake. He'd leaned her against the guardrail there, his hands on her hair, lifting it and smoothing it on her shoulders. He'd kissed her long and deeply, but carefully, she thought, his hands on her bare shoulders but only the faintest weight of his chest against her sundress and breasts. "I really like you," he'd said. She'd leaned against him as hard as she dared. He was almost nineteen and had two older brothers, but he was shy. His oldest brother, who'd gone into the liquor business with their dad, knocked up a girl he hardly knew and had to marry her when he was just Kit's age, Kit told her once—it took him several tries to get the story out, his stuttering growing worse the more he tried. She hadn't asked him any more.

He had his car started by the time she climbed in on her side. "So tell me all about your trip," he said.

She sighed—neither of them was really interested in the trip. "We saw all this stuff Laura has been reading about for her entire life. Will jogged in all the major cities. I ate a lot of chocolate. That's about it."

"Shit. Any parties?"

"How would I go to any parties?"

"I thought you might have met some guys." He turned up Center, gunning the car to scatter gravel.

"Well, I didn't." She had a flash of guilt. Maybe she wouldn't tell Kit about Thomas yet. She hadn't exactly *met* him, anyway. A flush of heat prickled at the base of her throat and she was glad of the dark—funny, how you can lie by saying nothing at all.

She touched his leg, the soft denim. "Did you think about me?"

"How could I forget you? All those letters." He reached for her hand again, and pulled her across the plastic seat toward him. "Of course I thought about you." He had to work hard to get "thought" out, but she waited, as he'd told her to.

She leaned away from his shoulder to watch his profile—-
straight nose, hair over his ears, the glossy line of his lashes. The
clean smell of him made her chest ache. "What did you think
about when you thought of me?"

"I just thought about you."

"How?"

"How guys think about girls, I guess."

"How do guys think about girls?"

He turned right along the railroad tracks toward Highwood
and the nearest spot where they could buy beer. "You're teasing
me." He pinched her leg just above the knee.

The pinch hurt—a warning. He was right, she was teasing.
God, she was such a child. "Tell me what's been going on since
you got back from working at the camp." It was the best she
could do for an apology.

So he told her. He'd registered at Lake County College,
which would be a waste of time, but his grades hadn't been
good enough to get him into the University of Illinois. If he
could get his grades up, he could transfer at the semester. He
and Brian had found a bar up near Kenosha where they had live
music on Saturday nights, bluegrass; he'd take her there. Brian
was leaving soon to live with his brother out in Colorado. He'd
miss old Brian, but he'd met a new guy, Mike Kenny, who was
one of the older counselors at the camp. He and Mike were
going to get an apartment together out in Libertyville where
rents were cheaper. His mom didn't like the idea but he was
sick of living at home with his mom and dad always drinking
and yelling. He had to make the break sometime and this was it.
He could afford it. After the pool job was over he had a job
loading UPS trucks at night. It would be heavy work, but the
money was good. Of course his dad always gave him money, just
threw some bucks down on his dresser. He'd had to open a
savings account because if it was lying around Brian took it, as
though they lived in a welfare state. Anyway, he wanted to make
it on his own without his dad's money. His dad had another new
boat, inboard, twenty-two feet. He was always asking Kit to go
fishing with him and his buddies, but who wanted to fish? That
was about it.

"Who's this Mike guy?"

"He's from Northbrook. He led our retreats and stuff like that. He's got good ideas."

"Like getting an apartment?" She watched the red and blue neon lights of Highwood flash on his face. "You don't know how to cook, do you?"

"What's so hard about that? I figure you go to the store and you get some stuff and cook it. It'll be fine. Just because I don't know how to do something doesn't mean I can't learn."

The lights from Steve's Liquor Store were green, wavering over the gravel parking lot like the shallows of the lake. Steve was Kit's uncle; he sold Kit beer even though Kit was underage. Steve sold anyone beer if there were no cops around. Kit got a six-pack and they headed for the park up by the fort. The cops drove through every hour or so, but this early in the evening they didn't give you grief if you kept your booze out of sight.

Kit popped a beer for her, one for himself, and stashed the others under a towel by his feet. The beer can was cold and she held it between her thighs, feeling the dampness soak her Levi's. She listened to the racket from the cicadas and smelled the sweetly rank scent of goldenrod from the side ditch and oil from Kit's car. His shoulder was tense against hers when she leaned against him. "What else have you been doing?"

"I read some stuff." He wiped his mouth with the back of his hand, pushed around so he leaned against the door and could look at her. Her shoulder chilled where his hand had been—fall was coming on already.

"Read what?"

"We got all these books that came with the new house last spring. A lot aren't real books, just cardboard to fill up the shelves. But there are real ones, too. I read this one by Hemingway, *The Old Man and the Sea*, which is about this old man who goes fishing in the gulf."

"I thought you didn't like fishing." The beer filled her mouth with bitter coolness, traveled down through her chest where it warmed her belly.

"It's different in the book. The fish is a symbol. And I've been reading statistics."

Jo took another long drink and groaned. She was terrible in

math. "Why do you want to *read* it? You'll be in the course soon enough."

"I'm planning ahead. I figure I'll get a start on it. Just once I'd like to get good grades, really good grades. I figure I'm smart enough if I dig in. Mike says you have to think about the future, not just the present. Everything you do now has a bearing on the future. It's all connected."

So it was Mike who had brought "values" into Kit's life. She guessed she'd be hearing more about Mike. "That's a fine plan," she said, thinking it would be good to be excellent at something. Laura had a Phi Beta Kappa key that she kept in with her earrings. She said good grades were a matter of self-control. With Laura, everything was a matter of self-control. But Kit certainly had discipline when he needed it. When he went out for soccer he practiced until he couldn't stand up. In track he never shorted on the training miles; in wrestling he kept his weight down by locking himself in his room at meal-times and chewing gum. She put her hand on his knee. "You'll get good grades if you decide to. You really will."

"You think so?"

"I know it. You'll be the star of Lake County College and I'll be the star of Woodcliff, handing in those little essays right on time, no excuses, footnotes and all. We'll be superstars on the academic scene."

Kit finished his beer and reached down for another. He popped it and rested it against his forehead, then his temples, studying her around the edge of the sweating can. "Do you think this is going to be a horrible year?"

She thought it over. Their friends had left. She was going to a dinky Catholic girls' school and he was going to a county college with burnouts and housewives. She'd be living at home, which was basically the same as high school. He'd have a crummy apartment that leaked when it rained. They'd both be thinking the whole time how to get away and make things better the next year. Still, it wasn't her nature to be pessimistic. Who knows what will happen next? Estelle used to say, "It's a good life if you don't weaken. Live it, baby!"

She leaned to kiss Kit's cheek. "I think it will be okay, really okay. We have to start somewhere."

Kit set his beer on the dash and reached past her to the glove compartment, where he kept his grass. He took out a wooden box with a Boy Scout emblem carved on it, quickly and expertly rolled a joint, lit it, passed it to her.

The smoke came into her lungs as smooth as honey. "This is the new stuff your dad's getting?"

Kit took a hit. "What do you think?"

"Terrific." She took the J back from him.

"Take it easy. It's so good it'll knock you out."

"Wonderful!" The gold honey flowed through her chest, her arms, her legs. In the soft light reflected from the clouds Kit's face had the same amber gloss as the polished wooden box he turned in his hands.

"I made this in woodworking, can you believe that? Sixth grade." He'd showed her how he sorted his grass through the openwork sides of a silver tray his mother kept on the hall table for calling cards. "Use what you have," he'd said. Now he handed her his industrial arts project, the box.

The smell of the dope it contained made her mouth pucker the way a green apple did. She let the box, with its pleasant patina, rest in her lap. She felt herself grinning. "Maybe it'll be a great year." She closed her eyes, leaned her head back against the crisp seatcover. Kit lifted the box from her legs, and she heard the snap of the glove compartment. The music of the night meadow was louder, as if the volume of the tree frogs and locusts had been turned up. A wind stirred in the pines. Kit's breath was on her cheek.

"I did miss you," he whispered. "I didn't want to say. I thought maybe you didn't miss me."

"I missed you," she whispered back without opening her eyes. "A lot. I thought about you. I thought about kissing you."

His breath was on her mouth, then, very softly, his lips touched hers. Neither of them moved. After a moment she parted her lips to breathe and he parted his so that their breath mingled. She timed herself so that she breathed in when he breathed out. She was light-headed and floating. His mouth, or maybe hers, was sweet like mint and tart like the smoke they shared. She held very still, moving neither toward him nor away.

His breath filled her lungs and she swayed, underwater. Then she felt the tip of his tongue. A slow caress, exploratory, first just inside her upper lip where the most delicate membrane was, and then—how much longer?—inside her lower lip. His caress moved through her body with the syrupy smoke. "Let me," she said.

He curled his hands around the back of her neck and she licked his lips slowly, as he had hers, then licked his teeth. After a while he opened his mouth more and she did too, and there was a long time in which, except for their tongues, they didn't move at all. The night hum of the field flowed through the open windows of the car like a current of water; they could breathe under this dark water, it was a friendly element that bore them along gently.

Then abruptly he pushed away from her and dropped his hands to her shoulders. She pressed her face against his throat, tasting salt. Dazed.

"Jo, I've got to take it easy."

"Take it easy?"

"This is a really big test of my values."

"Values?" She shook her head, not understanding, wishing they'd just kiss again. Even the soles of her feet ached with wanting to kiss.

"I've been trying to think things through."

"Yes." She drew out the sound. *Yes* was part of the sounds of the night around them.

"I've got to get some stuff right for a change. Everything in my life is second-rate. Second-rate family, second-rate crummy jobs, a second-rate little college out in the boonies. I've got to figure how to do better. It's the only life I've got."

She kept her eyes tightly closed. Why was his voice so stern? "I'm second-rate for you?"

"No, not you! I mean all the rest of it."

She rubbed her face against his shoulder, the heat from his chest radiant through his soft cotton shirt. "Why are you telling me now?"

"I have to."

"You could tell me later."

"Now. I have to take charge of what I do. Like with sex."

He paused and she snuggled closer, their clasped hands against her breasts. "Sex," she repeated.

"You asked me what guys think about when they think about girls. They think about getting a piece. That's it. That's *all.* I don't want to be like that. Most guys want to get high and get laid, and they don't even care if they know the name of the girl they're screwing."

She nodded against his chest.

"I want to get love right. Not just screwing, but love."

She nodded again, her forehead bumping his chin. She opened her eyes then and saw his face only as a dark shape. She licked his damp throat experimentally, wishing he'd do that to hers. But he pulled away.

"This is awful tough on me," he said, as though confessing to an unusual weakness. "And I found Jesus this summer."

"Jesus?" She pulled back to get a better look at him.

"I've been a Catholic all my life, but I'd never found Jesus."

"Is there a difference?"

"I've taken him for my personal savior and all."

That was something she'd never figured on. "Sin and all that, you mean?"

He settled back against the door again, apparently glad to have a discussion. "Sin sounds so heavy. Negative. Most Catholics are real negative. But some are real positive, those who've found Jesus. My mom always talks about the stuff you shouldn't do. Don't do this, don't do that—and of course Dad does what he wants, no matter what. When you find Jesus you concentrate on the positive. It's like falling in love, I guess, everything is just so clear and simple. There's a lot I don't believe in, but I feel really good about Jesus. He's helped me line up sex with love."

She took a deep breath and tried to clear her head. "That's supposed to be the best way, I guess."

"You don't think I'm crazy, do you? I'm not in a cult or anything. I'm just a believer."

"You're okay, Kit. I mean it. How about your friend Mike? Is he a believer, too?"

"We plan to spend weekends working on retreats for kids,

helping them to understand." He touched her cheek, gently. "You *do* understand, don't you? Is there anything else I could tell you?"

"I'll think about what you've said." She looked back over the seat, pretending to check for cops. She was afraid that she would laugh, though nothing at all that Kit said was really funny.

He pulled her close again, bumping her hip against the steering wheel. "You smell so good, Jo. You smell like those little white flowers that bloom in April and no one's supposed to pick them."

She realized that it had been several minutes since he'd stuttered. He must be at peace with himself, or maybe it was the grass. "Can we have another hit of that excellent J? Then I've got to go home. I've got such a jet lag headache I feel silly." That was in case she did laugh, in spite of her efforts. She pretended to yawn to hide her smile.

They smoked a little more, and then he drove her home, slowly, his arm around her shoulders, smiling at her from time to time.

"Mellow?" she asked.

"I just never thought you'd understand."

She drank her second beer while he drove. She felt sad, now, as though the possibility for loving him had closed up just as it had begun to open. She wanted more kissing like that. She wanted her whole body kissed like that. Instead, it looked like she and Kit were going to be buddies. She sighed.

"Sleepy?" He squeezed her shoulder.

"Very." The truth was that she was lonely.

At her house he walked her to the porch, kissed her quickly on the cheek. "I'll call you, okay?"

When she opened the door Daisy came running, belly low to the floor with pleasure. Under her hands the dog turned in circles, tail slapping Jo's arms and legs. She crouched to press her face into Daisy's soft, musty coat, and kept her arms tightly around her dog, imagining Kit holding her in the dark. "Oh, Kit!" she said against Daisy's soft ear. "You bastard!"

Almost midnight. As she walked into the unlit kitchen the

phone rang, the jangle making her start. She grabbed it on the first ring, then waited a moment to be sure Laura hadn't answered, too. Sometimes Laura listened in.

A woman with a foreign accent said, "Person-to-person for Josephine Hale."

"This is she." Long distance. She rubbed her eyes.

Then his voice came on the line so close he might have been in the same room. "So you *do* exist! I thought maybe I'd just dreamed you up. This is Thomas."

"Thomas? But you're in Rome."

"Right, but I wish I were there in Chicago. I want to talk to you. I tried to write you a letter, but I couldn't."

"I thought you were a writer." She pulled a strand of her hair across her eyes and remembered the intense way he'd looked at her.

"That's the point. I was writing *de la littérature,* not a conversation with you. I thought, call her! Modern technology."

"From Rome? This must be costing you the world."

"You're worth it!" He laughed, although there was so much energy in his voice he seemed to have been laughing at her all the time. "It's morning here, but already the street is loud with—"

"Wait!" Because she'd just heard Laura come down the front stairs. Laura would be pissed Thomas had called. She'd deliver another one of her lectures about playing it cool with men, as though Jo had been leading Thomas on. She put her hand over the receiver and called to Laura as she came through the living room, "It's me. Just a sec."

To Thomas she said, "I've got to go now. Call me when you get back."

"Call! I'm coming to see you!"

She hung up and ran up the back stairs before Laura came into the kitchen. Whatever Laura asked she'd avoid answering. She had a right to her privacy. Thomas was pushy, he made her nervous, but along with her nervousness she had another feeling—a lurid excitement. She'd never known anyone like Thomas and no man had ever chased her before. She wondered how Thomas might kiss a woman. She wondered how he might kiss her.

8

Laura saw Thomas before he saw her. No special skills of hers, there; no accident, really. She'd been on the lookout for him. More than a week had passed since they'd been back from their trip and Thomas had phoned Jo from Rome. Time's up—come out of hiding. She'd known it was only a matter of time.

He was just where she might expect to see him, too, crossing the parking lot to the Evanston commuter station, for all the world like one of the local men going down to the Loop. Except that it was eleven in the morning and the other commuters this time of day were shoppers, kids or household help. Thomas wore faded jeans and a white shirt open at the collar, a tan jacket slung over his shoulder. His hair was so blond it was almost white.

She'd never hunted but she imagined the shiver a hunter must feel when the deer steps out of the shadows—after all that waiting, rehearsing: So there you are. In my sights.

She pulled the station wagon over to the curb and honked. He didn't turn, so she leaned out and called his name. He looked up, shading his eyes. Startled. Then he saw her, and, grinning like a movie star who's been recognized by a fan, he strode across the gravel to her car. She was smiling, too. Now we'll see what happens, she thought.

"What good luck!" Under his reddish mustache his teeth

were lightly stained. When he bent down to her window she smelled citrus cologne.

"Hello!" She wondered what she'd say next, but it didn't matter. It had been inevitable that she'd find him; she'd willed him into existence these past few days. She needed him and his mysteries. She'd even looked up his phone number and address: Sheridan Road near Loyola, not a bad neighborhood—her relief told her she already planned to visit him. "Good luck me spotting you, or good luck because you need a ride somewhere?"

He looked into her car—the back seat was loaded with grocery bags, the very back filled with pots of orange and yellow mums. She looked the typical suburban housewife, but she wasn't. He'd know that.

Glancing at the gold rectangle of his watch, he hurried around and slid into the passenger side next to her, dropped his notebook on the seat between them, left the car door open. "My train will be here soon. I've just got time to be amazed that you remember me. Just time to say hello to the lovely wife of the good doctor."

"That makes me feel like Madame Bovary."

He laughed. Good, she'd got his wavelength: Talk is a game. Don't play for high stakes. She liked that; it made them both free.

Making himself at home, he stretched his arm along the back of the seat. "You come all the way down here from Highland Park to buy groceries?"

"There's a fabric store I like. I had to get something terrific for a robe. What's your destination today?"

"My editor's office. Michigan Avenue." He groomed his short beard.

"Michigan Avenue? I thought you were a writer. I imagined a dingy garret."

"Writers have to eat, Laura. May I call you Laura? I write medical articles for an advertising firm that specializes in drug companies. Surely you read and loved *Behavior Modification for Obese Adults?* Only one of my smash hits." He touched her slim arm. "No, you probably didn't read that one. Maybe you caught *The Use of the Spinhaler,* or *Listen to Your Back Pain.*"

She felt herself redden with pleasure because he'd used her name. She wasn't Mrs. William Brenner or "the wife of the good doctor" any more. "You're in advertising, then."

"No, I'm a *writer*. The crap for Monroe and Barrett, Inc., keeps their accounts with drug firms secure, and my rent paid. A substantial fringe benefit is a lot of lunches on the expense accounts of drug salesmen. But you're looking at a man on the very brink of publishing success. My novel's with an excellent publisher and I've just finished revisions. It's seven hundred and forty-two pages of genius, Laura. My agent says it's only a matter now of time."

"A novel! Published soon?"

"I've only got a contract for the revisions at this point. It hasn't been given the final nod yet, but it's ninety-nine-percent certain."

She swept her hair off her cheek. "Oh, so that's where you've been—doing those revisions. I thought we'd see you before this."

"I was going to look up the Brenner household any day now."

"Look up Jo, you mean."

When he laughed she saw gold crowns on his back teeth. "Jo! Yes, soon. As soon as I can get the courage."

"Courage? She's eighteen." Emphasizing the number—a girl, not a woman.

"I don't want to scare her off. I thought I'd just stop by, if I can find your place."

"Come on, if you can call our place from Rome you can surely figure out a way to get there."

"Jo told you I finally got through to her?" His smile shut down slightly, an almost imperceptible flutter of the muscles around his lips and eyes. "I got the impression that she wouldn't."

"Do you care?"

His smile returned. "Not in the least. Except I also got the impression that you and the good doctor didn't approve of me."

"Not that you wanted approval."

He winked, grinning. "I'd rather have your interest than approval, Laura. But Jo might—"

"Have to sneak around to see you? You wouldn't mind that. Anyway, I'm *not* her mother. I'm only a little older than she is."

"*Did* she tell you I reached her?"

"She didn't have to tell me."

"You guessed?"

"I don't miss much." She meant for him to take that as a warning. She could play these games, too.

"So we're both spies? What else have you picked up about me?"

Close to him, she saw his skin was faintly freckled like a pear, with deep lines around his eyes. He was older than she'd thought, older than she was, certainly. There was something damaged about him—when he wasn't smiling his face went slack. A failure of energy? The power off?

"Oh, I know several things about you." She hadn't intended to sound so coy.

He leaned closer. She'd hooked his vanity. "Such as?"

"I guessed you were a serious artist." That paid off—he smiled. "And that you act on impulse. That you'd show up at our place when the impulse struck you."

"Sheer impulse? Not guile?"

It was her turn to laugh—nerves. She felt she was driving too fast and the brakes were out. "That, too. You've admitted to a bad case of nerves about chasing a teenager."

His smile flared again. He stretched his legs, his grayed tennis shoes shoving the floor mat out of place. "The impulse to come to your place is striking me right now. But I hope you'll quit calling Jo a teenager—at Jo's age Juliet would have been considered elderly. Passion may be a gift exclusive to the very young."

"*We're* too old? Already?" She lifted her hair from the back of her neck with both hands, a gesture she'd often practiced in front of her mirror.

He studied her, rubbing his lower lip with his thumb. "Maybe not. I hope not, anyway." He glanced at his watch again, then at the back seat. "Lots of food. Are you having a party?"

"There's a log-burning at the beach Sunday night. A pot-luck, after."

"Tell me about it." His request was a command.

As she talked he watched her closely; she was glad she'd taken extra time to choose her peach silk shirt, linen shorts that showed off her tan. "Our next-door neighbors, the Millets, have decided that our end of town should clean up the beach and have a log-burning with a sing-along, after. That's their corny style, I'm afraid. It sounds to me like a church picnic, one of the Millets' typical evenings, combining practicality with celebration. They don't plan parties, they plan 'fêtes,' or 'readings' or evenings devoted to a theme. They had a mock-exorcism when they renovated their house. That kind of stuff."

"Old bohos?"

"Maybe not bohemians, exactly, but culture crazies." She felt a tremor of betrayal. Why was she saying these things about old, loyal friends—Cecil and Pat Millet had helped her out at every turn.

Thomas urged her on. "Costumes? Do people still do that?"

"That's why I need a robe. Pat adores robes."

"Wonderful!"

"Not the kind of event *you'd* want to crash."

"On the contrary! A fire? Dancing? Leaping shadows on the waves? In Technicolor?" He winked. "My style."

"It won't be much. A lot of neighbors stumbling around on the sand." Suddenly—too late?—she felt protective of the Millets. Pat had said, "What is authentic never grows old." She'd also said, "We're the last of a dying breed." She continued to work in the Rare Books Room at Seabury even though Cecil had retired from the Museum of Science and Industry. They were genuine; Laura would bet Thomas Trawick wasn't.

"Don't underestimate me," he said, as if guessing her thoughts. "If I come, the party will be a good one."

"Pretty sure of yourself?"

"In some things." He winked again. He'd practiced that wink—it sealed a bargain she didn't know she'd made. "What else do you know about me?"

Now she cautioned herself. Protect Jo. Intercede, draw the lightning.

"What else?" he repeated.

"That you like to shake things up, don't you?"

"Don't *you?*" His answer acknowledged that she was right.

"Not in the way you do."

"Hey, pretty lady! You recognized *me*, called to *me*, remember. A few brief minutes ago?"

"You knew who I was."

"Oh, yes, but I've got a reason to know. Don't forget, I've got a photo of you. Did you ever model professionally? Those cheekbones, those eyes!"

She felt herself blushing. He'd turned the tables so easily. He closed his eyes as if reconstructing the photo he'd taken of her and Jo. His white eyelashes curved on his tan cheeks. He looked tired, his lips dry and a trace of blood at one chapped corner.

Suddenly she was tired, too. She couldn't act in this game any longer; she'd run out of lines. "Thomas," she said abruptly, "why *Jo?*"

Without opening his eyes he asked, "Why not?"

"I mean it. Why Jo?"

"I mean it, too. Why not? She's a pretty girl and I like her lack of calculation. I envy her youth and simplicity. I'd like some of that to rub off on me." His eyelids lifted slightly to reveal a narrow khaki shine.

"You must have known hundreds of pretty, young, simple girls."

"Wrong. Actually, Jo appeared to me in a vision."

"Vision! Like Lourdes?"

Now he wasn't smiling, his lips were tight. "Just reporting the facts, ma'am."

She'd had visions—if you fasted, you *saw* things. Visions were real enough, but they weren't facts, they were an altered state of mind. "What vision did you have?"

"A glimpse of a purer place," he said slowly.

That startled her. "She doesn't live in a purer place. She's a real girl in the real world. Eighteen, remember?" As if the number would explain everything.

"I think she has certain capacities she isn't aware of yet, a certain clarity, maybe."

"You're romanticizing!"

"I hope so! With background music and soft lights. The important thing is that she's right here and so am I. Kismet! And she's so American, you know. You wouldn't notice that quality so much here, but meeting her abroad—she was like a tangerine on a field of snow. Europeans are so complicated—the roles they play. I'm sick and tired of complicated people."

"Like yourself?"

"It takes one to know one." That wink again. What had they agreed to? "Your sister isn't bored yet."

"You're interested in Jo because you're bored?"

He pinned her with his steady gaze. "Aren't *you* a little bored? Or maybe desperate? A sparkling lady like yourself? You look like a woman who's expecting something. You looked like you were expecting me to arrive right here by your side this morning."

She had been. Did she give that much away without even realizing it? "I don't think Jo's your sort."

"No one's my sort," he agreed. "But *you* seem to understand me." He was smiling again. That meant he thought he was in charge. He didn't like it when he wasn't. She'd have to remember that. "And now neither one of us will have to be bored Sunday night. I'll crash the party. The timing's right."

Had she invited him into their midst? But what harm could he do? Nothing she couldn't take care of. And she wanted to see him again. He knew that.

She heard the train in the distance. "Listen," she said quickly, "one promise."

"A code word?" He gathered his jacket off his knees, picked up his notebook.

"I'm serious. I didn't invite you. You just stopped by unexpectedly. Promise?"

He took her hand, cupped it briefly, his thumb pressing her palm. "Our blood is mingled on that point. Tell me how to find your house."

She named streets. There was a metallic taste in her mouth from the lie she'd asked of him. Did everyone around him end up lying? But it was better this way. Will would be furious if he knew she'd asked Thomas to come. "He's a prick," Will had said in his most disgusted voice. But he didn't know everything. He didn't know that there was an unhappy man behind

Thomas's show of bravado. A man seeking a soulmate. She
knew: only someone who's been hurt badly needs so much
camouflage.

The commuter train pulled in with a whine of metal. He ran
for it. "Good-bye, then!" she called after him.

He turned at the train door. "It's hello, Laura! Hello!" Then
he swung up into the car and was out of sight.

She pulled ahead into the parking lot, shut off the engine,
rested her arms on the steering wheel and put her forehead
down on her wrist. Her throat ached as though she'd been running, and she wanted to rest. She'd be okay in a minute. She was
always okay—or almost okay.

Was it his wink? That, and his unexpected "Hello!" that reminded her of her father. And it was here, right here, that she'd
seen her father off that last day. He'd come to have lunch with
her near the campus. He never did that, but that morning he'd
left her a note on the kitchen counter suggesting Kilpatrick's for
lunch. Over hamburgers they'd talked about the Bears, the
weather, her classes. Then she'd walked him to his train. He
stepped onto the train, turned to wave to her, not smiling, his
face gray because he was hungover again, his unfurled umbrella
over his arm and the light January rain falling between them.
Had he waved? No, he was just gone, that's all. When she got
home after classes she found his briefcase on the hall table, a
note with her name taped to the leather; inside, the insurance
papers. That was when she knew what he'd decided, although
the police didn't phone her until after six.

Memories can't really *hurt*. The pain is mental, therefore not
pain at all. It was just that it was so difficult to get her breath.
Will said once of the tragedies of life, "You can rebound, but
you can't recover." In a minute she'd rebound. She kept her
eyes closed tightly.

Thomas's wink. That wink of her father's—she hated it. And
she knew the exact moment she realized she hated it. Her four-
teenth birthday. It was time to start again, a new beginning—
she and Daddy agreed on that. Several weeks before, one of the
doctors at the clinic where he worked pointed out to him that

his daughter was starving to death. The doctor made an appointment for her to see a specialist. So she saw Dr. Bauman, the specialist, for seven visits, and she'd suggested Laura bring her father in with her. To talk, that's all.

"She's always been a perfect daughter," her father told Dr. Bauman. "Never a worry. Never a word of back talk, like some kids. Even after her mother . . ."

He sat with his hands folded in his lap, like a boy called into the principal's office. He wore a new white shirt, the sharp creases still in the cuffs.

"Look, *she's* the one with the problem," he said. "Ask her why she won't eat. Don't ask me."

Dr. Bauman ran her hand through her cropped black hair. She worked the talk around so Laura could ask for what she wanted for her birthday. She wanted to eat dinner in the dining room with her father. Dr. Bauman asked her to promise that if they had a normal meal together, she wouldn't throw up after. Her birthday dinner would be a start to new and healthier habits.

"We need a new start," her father said.

"Agreed?" Dr. Bauman told them to shake hands on it. Daddy's hand was trembling when Laura took it, but his hands always shook.

Estelle was glad to go along; she thought Laura's skinniness reflected on her cooking. Estelle's cooking didn't matter to Laura anymore—she was far, far beyond that, in the grip of something else entirely. She *couldn't* eat; it was out of her control. But maybe Daddy could help her take charge of her life. Oh, please.

Estelle said just tell her the menu, she'd take care of the rest. She'd even put the baby to bed and take the evening off; she needed an evening anyway, she hadn't taken one the week before because Jo had the croup.

Laura typed out the menu on Momma's portable typewriter: barbecued spareribs, mashed potatoes, apple sauce, rolls. She didn't want birthday cake, just ice cream, and pop to drink.

Her job was to set the table. She got out a tablecloth, a pink one Momma had used on Sundays. Then she folded the paper napkins and put them into the glasses like she'd seen in a magazine. She turned the cutting edges of the knives in and polished the bowls of the spoons. Jelly went into one cut-glass bowl, pickles into another. By five o'clock she was ready and Estelle was waiting to serve them and leave.

Daddy came in the back door at a quarter to six. He nodded to Estelle and patted Laura's shoulder. "How's the birthday girl?"

Laura smoothed her white angora sweater over her jeans. "All ready."

He stamped snow off his boots, hung up his coat, put his briefcase onto his desk and went into the sun-room. "Call me when dinner's on."

She poured the pop right away, using wine glasses and lots of ice. She put cream in the silver pitcher for his coffee while Estelle filled the serving dishes. Cinnamon rolls—Estelle's surprise, because there wasn't a cake.

"I like them better than cake!" Everything was perfect.

"I'll bathe Jo, change into my black sweater and be on my way. It's your party, sweetie." Estelle hung her apron on the hook.

"What if she wakes up?"

"She won't, she's a real sleeper. Anyway, you can give her juice."

"When will you be home?"

She adjusted her slip strap. "Whenever." She took the train into Highwood on her nights off and usually a soldier drove her home.

Laura put the serving dishes on the table and lit the candles in the silver candlesticks. She couldn't remember the last time they'd had candles. Then she called, "Daddy!"

He came smiling out of the sun-room, his face soft and blurred. How could he change so quickly? When she was older she realized that always he started drinking before he came home, maybe in that bar in Union Station, maybe even from a bottle kept in his office. He got a head start.

He was silent throughout the meal. Chewing steadily and slowly, reflectively, he kept his gaze on his plate. Once in a while he looked up at her and winked, as though she'd just told him something delightful, a secret, maybe. His eyes were blue and direct. As though he saw her clearly.

For the first few bites she was dizzy with hunger, and Dr. Bauman had said she could enjoy the good food without guilt. Then she lost her appetite—her stomach was out of practice. She should have started with something lighter than the buttery rolls and the spicy ribs. But when she stopped eating Daddy winked again and motioned for her to "eat up" with a gesture of his fork. She held her own fork tightly—she could stick it in his eyes.

After dinner he went back into the sun-room and she heard a football game on the TV. She cleared the table, washed the dishes. She loved the kitchen when Estelle wasn't there—the cosy room, the soapy water. She dipped her fingers in the left-over sauce and ate crumbs of the rolls, although she wasn't really hungry.

After she cleaned up she got her homework and spread her notebooks on the kitchen table. She turned on Estelle's radio for company. It was seven-thirty.

At nine-thirty she turned out the kitchen lights and went up-stairs. Jo slept in her yellow fleece sleeper, her dark head pushed into the corner of her crib, her pacifier in her mouth. When Laura bent close she smelled baby oil and heard the steady snuf-fle of a baby with a cold. But Jo didn't waken.

In her room Laura pulled on flannel pajamas and then a nightgown over them. She was so thin that she was cold all the time; her skin even looked tanned, she was so cold—bluish tan. Nothing could keep her warm. She yanked on knee socks and her rabbit slippers and plugged in her heating pad.

Wind whistled through the cracks around her windows and ice had already formed on the bottoms of the panes. At the edge of the bluff the wind blew the snow like spray curling off the top of a wave. The chill crept under her nightgown so she put on a sweater, too.

Suddenly she held her breath. The house was empty.

She knew Daddy must be in the sun-room. Yellow rectangles of light from those windows spread on the snow in the sideyard. But the house grew more and more silent. The front door stopped rattling, the wind fell back from the windows so that even the loosest panes stopped creaking. She watched her clock—the minutes went by but there was no ticking sound. Her heart was the loudest thing in the house.

Even though the floor was icy, shc crept back to the window. Small clouds raced across the sky—it was a winter night with the weather changing, but inside the house nothing moved. It was as though the air had been sucked out of it, the way Mr. Kelly described a vacuum in science class: a space with nothing at all in it. *Not even me.*

She crept down the stairs. The sun-room door was closed, but a streak of light showed under it. She tapped on the door. "Daddy?" She wanted to tell him that she hadn't thrown up. It was a terrible struggle not to, but she'd won. She'd kept the promise. He didn't answer.

Maybe when they had supper together the next night it would go better. Estelle could have things on the table right when he walked in the door. Before he went into the sun-room.

She knocked again, then she turned the knob. A table lamp with an old green shade gave the room a soft, underwater glow. At first she didn't see him. His recliner chair was empty. Stretched on his back with his arms behind his head, the plaid blanket over his legs, he lay on the daybed at the end of the room. The TV flickered, an old movie with the sound turned off. On the floor beside the daybed was a thick-bottomed glass.

"Daddy?"

He looked at her without turning his head. She was surprised how young he looked in the dim light. His lips were parted and his forehead was smooth. He looked like a boy resting in the grass, watching the trees move overhead, without a care in the world. Dreaming.

There wasn't room for her to sit beside him, so she bent down. "I got scared."

He nodded, or she thought he did. "I wanted to say good night, Daddy."

She steadied herself with her hands on his shoulders and leaned close to kiss his cheek. When her lips touched his cheek he reached up, his arms went tightly around her waist, and he drew her down to him. "Hello!" he whispered. He kissed her on the lips the way lovers kissed in the movies.

She jerked back. "Daddy?"

His gaze didn't follow her. He stared at the ceiling where the green light made circles like ripples on a pond. He didn't recognize her at all. He didn't know who she was.

A horn blared. Laura started, sat up straight in her car, turned the key in the ignition. A taxi honked at her—she blocked the cab lane at the station and the next train was coming in from Chicago. She pulled ahead, trying not to care about the nasty look the cabbie gave her—an obstacle in his path.

She *was* alone. Absolutely alone. "A purer world," Thomas said of his vision. There was no purer world, but there might be one in which some of those who've been hurt—who've hurt themselves—might speak to each other. Thomas was one of them, as she was—she was sure of it. He needed help but she wasn't sure if he knew that. She did. She knew how to pay close attention, decipher his signals, recognize him for who he was. And then maybe he would see who she was, too.

"A code word?" he'd asked her.

Thomas, I can break your code.

9

From the beach the bluff looked like a wall, sheer toward the top, undercut along the rim where storms had washed out the clay and sandstone, the lowest third sloped and covered with weeds, grass, scrub oak and pine. Trees that had fallen from the rim lay at the base, roots exposed, branches tangled with vines and stickweed. Cecil Millet and Will dragged the lighter trees from the slope, pulling them down to the beach where Cecil had his chain saw. Above them, Nate Coleman and his older brother David were gathering brush and dead pine branches. It was Cecil's plan. He was running the show.

They'd begun with the windfalls nearest the beach, then worked farther and farther up the slopes. The other neighbors who'd started with them had left for supper now. When Cecil and Will came to the last whitened oak log that they couldn't budge, Cecil sent Will to drag out the few logs from the opening where the creek ran into the lake. Cecil went to his chain saw. It whined and then howled as he pressed it into rotten wood.

Near the creek the air was cooler and smelled of leaf mold and sour mud. The fallen logs were damp underneath, slugs clinging to the rotting bark, fans of fungus like orange flowers blooming from the splits. Will dragged those down to the beach until the creek opening was clean.

Cecil came to help with the last log. Boots digging into the squeaky sand, Will strained on his side of the sapling.

"That's feldspar that makes it squeal," Cecil huffed between steps. His specialty was metallurgy. Every summer he still went for several weeks to mine gold in western Canada, using a method he refused to describe, but involving long pipes and drill bits that he assembled in his basement and then completed in his backyard. He wouldn't reveal how much gold he'd found, but Pat confided once, "Just enough to pay his expenses. But he keeps hoping."

"Thought my bones were complaining," Will said.

"Or mine, more likely." Cecil was tall, stooped in one shoulder, white-haired; a red ski hat was pulled right down to his white eyebrows. The tendons stood out on his throat as he strained with the log.

The boys came down off the bluff and stacked the wood as Cecil directed. "Small, dry stuff under, big logs over. Right out of the Boy Scout manual." He worked slowly, as though he'd just as soon the job would go on for several days. As he finished the last logs, the boys and Will piled the others up until the stack was about seven feet high and maybe six feet long.

"Now that's what we're aiming for." Cecil's hiking boots were thick with mud and sand and he knocked at them with a stick.

Will sat down on one of the logs, found his handkerchief, wiped his face and throat, feeling sand sift into his cotton shirt. The beach was deep in shadow. As the sun dropped lower the sky paled to a thin blue. It had been a long time since he'd got tired working. The good ache in his shoulders and thighs brought back the earlier, better moments at the shipyards—the way they'd helped each other carry their tools, the awful, obscene, continuous, horrible jokes that went on nonstop. When he left he swore he'd never miss it. Right now he did. He felt like soldiers when they reminisced about combat, smiling, saying, "Shit, it was living hell," but remembering, too, their own intensity, youth, purpose. Back in New Orleans, sweat streaming into his eyes, aching for a drink, crawling up a ladder that threatened to break apart, he'd never have believed he'd be capable of remembering anything good from that time. Maybe what he missed was being young, with everything ahead.

"Will this stuff burn?" Nate Coleman asked.

Cecil didn't look up from gouging mud off his boots. "I have my secrets. Gasoline."

"That's not in the Boy Scout manual." A fifteen-year-old who'd suddenly grown lanky, Nate swiped at his nose with the back of his wrist.

"There are a few things worth knowing that aren't in books. If you want to get wet wood going, you've got to give it some help."

David Coleman checked his watch. "Mom'll kill us. Are we going to start this fire when we come back?"

"Will and I'll get it started now, let it burn down. What we're after is low flame and glowing coals, not bits of brush flying off and singeing hair."

David slapped Nate's skinny rear and they started back behind the boathouse to the steep, dirt path the kids used. "See you later."

"Don't forget your guitar," Cecil called to David. Then he checked the pile one more time, unscrewed the cap from the gasoline can and dashed some on. The odor was pleasantly heady, like anesthetic fumes. Cecil rolled cones of newspapers and lit them, handing them to Will to stuff into the pile. The small sticks caught in a rush that sounded like wind coming up in the oaks before a storm, and in moments the pile was burning, its dark smoke lifting toward the bluff where the Coleman boys scrambled through the scrub pine.

"You've done this before," Will told Cecil.

"Few times," he grinned. His white mustache yellowed in the firelight and around the edge of his cap his hair reflected the orange flames.

The fire warmed Will's face and he yawned in the cool air, glad to be here. "I haven't had much chance to talk to you since we got home. How did the mining go this summer?"

Cecil seemed to be memorizing details of the fire. "I know where it is but I can't get deep enough to get it."

"Gold?"

"Of course, gold. Got just enough to tease me. I used to get angry, so close but not into the lode. This year it was different. I was just so damned glad to be there, damned glad to be able to work hard at my age. Sixty-six and still mining a little. Gold or no gold, it was good, hard work and it was my own."

Will turned to look out over the lake. Its surface was the color of iron. Cecil's words hurt: "Good, hard work and my own." It had been a long time since Will'd felt that. Now he wanted something hard to do, he wanted an act of sheer physical discipline that might clear his mind. All week he'd examined his life, questioned it. He liked his work well enough; Laura was in unexpected good spirits. But something was missing. Something enormous was missing.

The lake darkened, charcoal gray now under the surface. He looked back down the beach toward the boathouse. He could take his Sunfish out. It would be cold as hell in the water; it would be a hard thing to do—dumb-ass, really. But he could do it. A test?

"See you later, Cecil. I'm going out for a final sail."

"She's not put up yet?"

"Didn't get around to it." Putting up the boat was on his list of things to do, but he'd cleaned out the garage first. Now he was glad.

At the boathouse he pushed at the door, setting his shoulder to it to force it in. The door gave slowly, as though someone were pushing back. Then the refuse of stones and sticks washed up by the last storm gave way, and the door creaked open. The smell of alewives and mold and dead fish met him.

Two starlings flapped out of the open place between the screen wire and the roof. Around him in tiers were the berths for Sunfish, only two boats left—the red one, his. When he touched the hull, a raccoon started from beneath, scurried out the back of the boathouse through the torn screen. He listened a moment. No sounds except the lake, and from far away, the faint laughter of the Coleman boys at the top of the bluff.

He tried the combination of his lock, missed the third digit, turned it again, getting it right that time. The mind remembers random numbers—he'd forgotten the date of his father's death, but remembered his lock combination. The lock fell open and he pulled the chain free, sand and bits of dirt scattering onto his wrists as he tugged it from the boat.

Then he went to the back of the boathouse where rhododendron leaves pressed in against the torn screening, and yanked the rusted boat trolley out of the corner. It creaked forward on the gravel, reluctant on its skewed wheels. Once on the board runners it came along more easily.

He dragged his Sunfish carefully onto the trolley. As though lit from within, the red hull gleamed in the dim light. Hand over hand he pulled out the mast that was laid in beside it, the wrapped mainsail rumpling as the mast slid forward—Jo was the last one to furl it and she didn't have the patience to get it smooth and tight. Laid onto the gravel, the mainsail unrolled a single turn as his foot hit it, revealing two feet of yellow-striped sail. A gaudy outfit he'd chosen himself.

At the put-in, an underwater barrier of corrugated iron blocked waves and debris from the north, and on the south slabs of concrete salvaged from torn-out pavement formed a wall. Between those two breakwaters was a launching chute about thirty feet wide and sixty feet long into which waves traveled at an angle. The churning water there was grayish green; flecks of orange, like confetti, flashed on the surface from the sun setting behind the oaks on the bluff. The wind was from the southeast and tasted of tar and salt. He pushed the boat into the edge of the water.

Slipping on the wet stones, he went back for the mainsail. As he unrolled it pebbles scattered out onto his boots—he'd have to teach Jo to do a better job; he should teach her about elegance, the scientific kind, getting the best results with the least effort. She was quick but careless. She'd tangled a line and he had to kneel on the chill stones to unknot it, then make a second trip for the centerboard and the paddle—she could have stowed those in the cockpit, but she overlooked that, too. That time he closed and latched the boathouse doors, as though he were leaving a barn with animals nosing behind, eager to escape. Compulsive—was he like that before he went into medicine? He guessed he must have been.

He took off his boots, stuffed his socks inside, set them on the trolley, rolled his khakis up to his knees. He dropped the centerboard and the paddle into the cockpit and, working half-in, half-out of the water, began to rig the mainsail. Almost at once his feet were blue and numb and the ache began to travel up his calves. What he was doing was crazy. He kept at it.

He laced the halyard through the eye at the top of the mast, pulled hard to draw the sail up, cursing as the sediment from Jo's sloppy job spattered down into his upturned face. Then he tied the halyard off to the cleat and ran the mainsheet halyard through the eyes along the bottom of the boom—the way Estelle threaded a needle, Jo told him when he was teaching her how. With the rudder up and the centerboard within reach, he tested the water a last time. He couldn't believe it was that cold. He could still stop if he wanted to. But he didn't.

The wind was coming in harder. It would be tough to do, but he'd try to get past the breakwater without tacking. He glanced down the beach toward the fire. Cecil stood there, hands in his hip pockets, but no one else was in sight. Will decided to take off his pants and leave them behind with his shoes—he'd want them dry when he came back and if anyone saw him in the Sunfish they'd think he was wearing swim trunks.

When he pushed off the water numbed him to the knees at the first step and with the second there was a furious arc of cold to his groin. But he ran another step, jumped into the cockpit and crouched, hauling at the sail. He traveled a few feet on the momentum of his running push, then he dropped the centerboard and let the sheet out. He waved once to Cecil, who wasn't watching, and then turned his attention to the open lake.

The water was rimmed with white, slate gray in the furrows. It left a slick of oil on his hands. He'd learned to love Lake Michigan as a boy, taking the bus down to the harbor to watch the sailboats come and go; he came back gratefully from New Orleans to this northern, demanding chill. Self-discipline was easier in a cold climate—that was one of the ways he'd explained to himself how from the very first day in the shipyards he'd failed to do what was right. What was humane. He went along because it was much too hot to take the harder route. The rationalizations of a very young man.

In New Orleans the waters of the Mississippi had been a flat, opaque brown surfaced with iridescent yellow rings of oil. The current moved with a slow steady surge past the shipyards, oil refineries, grain elevators, out into the gulf, miles away. On the surface it was hard to see movement at all, but underneath the pull was immensely strong.

"Don't get your feet wet," the man who'd hired Will warned, and sent him to Wet Dock Three to wait for the foreman to call crews. He took his lunch bag and welding shield and went to the edge of a group of twenty or thirty men who already lounged on the wharf beside the looming steel hull of a tanker, their hard hats pulled down against the glare of the late-afternoon July sun that glanced off the iron hull like a solid wall of heat. Some of them talked despondently, some called to friends coming off the day shift. Inches from the hull an enormous black man with a handlebar mustache slept with his head propped on the bumper, the others stepping over him carefully.

At four-thirty sharp the foreman appeared on his motorcycle, his clipboard under his arm. He parked next to the sleeping black man and hefted himself off, his Pelicans T-shirt stained with sweat and rust. He called off names until the men were divided into twos, a shipfitter and a tacker to help him. Then he sent off each pair either to the outside scaffolding or into the hold. Will was the last one.

"You get with the Junkman and I get with you later," the foreman told Will.

"The Junkman?"

"That's his CB handle." He winked, probably because Will's clothes were so impossibly clean, his faded Levi's unstained, his work boots dark with neat's-foot oil. "His tacker broke his leg yesterday. Fell off a ladder. Junk was pissed."

The sleeping man rolled to his side, got onto all fours, pushed to his feet. Six feet five, maybe, possibly 260 pounds. His skin was so black it was purple in the reflected light. His heaviness made Will think more of an animal than of a man, more of a particularly well-muscled bull or an enormous horse. White mingled with gray in his mustache. "Folla me," he said, and then he said something Will had to work to understand—he hadn't caught on to the way the blacks talked yet. As he hurried behind, he decided it was, "We got the motherfucking hole."

The Junkman led him across the ramp and down the deck of the tanker, dust and smoke issuing from the hatches. "I show you where to set up for us, and when you set up you wake me."

Wake him? Will glanced into the hatch through which the Junkman was disappearing. The heat was 120 degrees easily, maybe more. Inside the hold the noise reverberated through his body like electrical shocks. All around him the ship trembled. The Junkman signaled for him to keep up. It was impossible now to talk and be heard.

The ladder swayed under the Junkman's weight. Had his tacker broken his leg here? It occurred to Will that he could die here. It occurred to him that he didn't care—that must be the Valium. He followed the Junkman down into the howling tanker.

That first time it took him two hours to set up their tools and get them connected to the welding machine. The Junkman slept beside the welding machine, his head pillowed by one arm, his other hand tucked between his knees like a comforted child. The noise was so loud that Will had to tug on his shoulder to wake him.

His wide, mild eyes opened. His eyelashes were crisp and thick, curled to expose whites round and unblemished. He crawled to his feet, motioned to Will to bend close, and shouted, "Don' try to keep up. You cain't keep up. Jus get it right." He attached his whip to the lead, jammed in a welding rod, and was quickly at work on a seam.

After a minute or two it was clear to Will that he could neither keep up nor get it right, and after five minutes the Junkman had doubled back to help him, like a mother encouraging a clumsy, stupid child who is, after all, her own. The welds he made were beautiful; Will had never seen any like them, not even his instructor's. The Junkman nodded to himself as he worked, his welding rods dissolving into pure light evenly and steadily, the stub tossed into the rod can, another one thrust in from Will's anxious grip and another beautiful, undulating seam begun under the Junkman's calm, damp gaze.

At nine o'clock the Junkman signaled to the tacker next to

him, and motioned for Will to follow the black boy who nodded
to him without smiling. They climbed back up the ladder into
the heavy heat of the night. "Eats," the thin-faced boy said.

He led Will to a '66 Thunderbird with blue flames painted on
the sides. Two men sat in front, two in back—all white. "Junk
say take him." The boy flowed back onto the ship, clicking his
fingers.

The two men in the back seat crowded to make room. The
man in the center reached out a blackened and pockmarked
hand. "George LaFleur, and this here's Po'kchop."

"Will Brenner."

"No handle?"

"Nope." Wishing he had one.

"We're getting some grub at the Seven-Eleven. You're coming with."

Bald, his lumpy skull shining, Porkchop leaned on LaFleur's
shoulder. "Meet LaFleur here, Yankee. LaFleur is your basic
happy married man. Ask him about the wife. She's his queen.
Ask about the kids. He's got pictures. Everybody else has an evil
woman except LaFleur, who has his goddamned queen. *He*
says."

"You're drunk, Chop," LaFleur said.

"Course I'm drunk. Show Yankee the photos."

LaFleur scratched his dark hair where it was matted to his
head from his hard hat. He wasn't so ugly when he smiled.
"Want to see the family?"

"Sure." Will settled back as the driver threw the car into
second and it jerked forward.

LaFleur reached out his billfold and extracted a crumpled
black-and-white photo. Three dark-headed little girls in swim
suits leaned against the knees of a heavy young woman in a
shiny bikini. She'd struck a thirties pin-up pose, her hand on her
hip, one hand behind her head. Her thick, curly hair covered
her shoulders. Through the nylon of the bra Will could see her
raised nipples. Two of the little girls had their arms around each
other's waists; the smaller looped her arm around her mother's
thigh. None of them smiled.

"Helen and the girls," LaFleur said.

"Nice family."

"Damn right." LaFleur smiled.

Helen LaFleur. The whole time Will was in that swamp New Orleans he was hot for her. At first Will saw Helen only when LaFleur took him home for meals, "looking after the Yankee kid." They ate spicy Creole jambalayas. Helen claimed she was part Cajun. Will believed her, believed her dark eyes and the purplish nipples that showed through her gauze blouses. The little girls looked like her—dark-haired and amber-skinned. Their panties stuck in the cracks of their behinds. They leaned against Will, their eyes small lakes. Helen flirted with him, though LaFleur didn't seem to care. She laughed and brushed against Will, asked him to reach up for platters from her kitchen shelves—"I jus cain't jump that high!"

Then she started coming to his dank efficiency apartment. The first time she appeared it was nine-thirty in the morning, the girls off to school and LaFleur temporarily on the day shift. Will was only two or three hours into a drunken sleep after the night shift. "You want me, don't ya," she said. It wasn't a question.

He did. Foul-mouthed and hungover he drew her inside. "Why'd you come?"

"Because I figured you wanted me. And I'm pregnant, so it don't matter."

He pulled her on top so he could feel her weight, bits of her hair brushing his face, her breasts crushed between them. "Sugarpie," she called him. "Suck on me, sugarpie!"

After that she came to his place whenever she wanted to. They never made any plans. When he opened the door to her tapping she jumped into his arms. He'd slide his hand up under her skirt or down her blouse almost as he caught her.

"I don't exactly love you," she said, older than he and careful about her categories, especially after the baby was born. "But I have a sorta love *for* you. And George is the best friend you got, you know that?" Ashamed, he rubbed his face against her shoulder. Did he ever say anything to her about love? He *wanted* her, wanted her kneeling for him on his bed, her head down on her hands, looking up sideways through her tangled hair as he lifted her skirt and threw it forward.

Her morning visits to him were like dreams—he slept again

after she left. When LaFleur invited him home, they played poker as always. Maybe nothing has happened between her and me at all, Will would think then, watching Helen washing the little girls' faces, putting them to bed, bending over the side of the playpen where the new baby girl slept. She treated him no differently than she always had—half maternal, half playful. But the line of her panties showed through her wrap-around skirt— she wanted him to see that, didn't she? And even the next morning she'd visit him again. When he was sober he'd think of cheating on LaFleur and feel as sick as he'd felt looking down into the hold for the first time, except that now the cavernous darkness was in himself. And after all he did nothing to stop Helen's visits.

Memories of a sad lust—well, he didn't have that one any more. He had other problems now, and for the most important ones there were no solutions. Laura had taught him that; life had taught him that.

The wind had died down a little, but his sail was full and steady. For a moment it seemed to him that his Sunfish stood still on the water and the shore moved, receding to the west. If he stayed right where he was the Michigan shore would catch him by morning. The thought made him smile—a half-naked man drifting toward Michigan in a Sunfish, his teeth chattering with cold and the memory of old shame.

He came about and began to tack down the shore. It was going to be hard to get back into the water to pull the boat out, and what had he proved to himself except that he could still force himself to endure discomfort?

When he reached the breakwater he looked up at the bluff and saw a figure in a yellow windbreaker, waving. "Hello!" Jo's voice reached him on the water.

"Hello!" His legs cramped with the cold—had he been out only half an hour?

Then to his alarm she started straight down the bluff, right from where she stood by the roots of the oak. There was no path there. She simply leapt, arms flung out, onto a sandy ledge about eight feet long, tumbled into a somersault, ran a step or two, leapt again. She skidded along the next ledge to a slope, slid, jumped, and then, running through scrub pine, hurtled down through the copse and onto the beach. He saw her sureness: it was a journey she must have made many times when no one was watching.

When he yanked up the centerboard, she was waiting on the beach. She'd taken off her tennis shoes, rolled up her jeans. As he jumped out she waded in to help him, grabbed the prow, hauled with him so they easily pulled the boat onto shore.

"You're probably crazy," she said.

"So are you. I saw you come down that bluff." His lips were numb with cold.

"I wanted you to see."

"Showing off?"

"Are *you?* What's this sailing bit?"

"Take down the lines, Jo. I need my dry stuff." He grabbed his pants and stepped inside the boathouse, whistling through his teeth as the stones hurt his feet. Behind him he heard her, "You need all the help you can get, mister."

He swiped at his feet with his sweater sleeve before pulling on his socks. Then he stuffed his wet briefs into his hip pocket, slid his feet into his boots, and, without pausing to lace them, went out to join her.

She was already lowering the mast. When he reached past her, her hand brushed his and he felt her warmth. "What's up?" he said.

"I couldn't wait for you to come home. I've got something to show you, but it's in my backpack, up in the park." She took the stern and with him at the prow they carried the boat into the boathouse. "Anyway, Laura wants you. Supper's ready."

"I thought we were eating after the bonfire."

"Both times. You know her."

"What have you got to show me?"

She hopped, unrolling her jeans, brushing sand off her feet. "Aren't you freezing, Will?"

"Yes."

"I guess you wanted to do that, right?"

"Right."

"You looked so lonely out there by yourself with the lake getting dark and the fog coming in."

He'd been very lonely. "It was a test of manhood."

"You passed, huh?"

"I survived."

"And now you're a man?" She tied her tennis shoes, looking up at him through strands of hair.

He handed her the centerboard and paddle. "You should stow these. I made three trips because you didn't."

"Sorry, mister. So now you're a man?"

"Now I'm a mouse. Come on, let's finish this. And don't get crap in the sail when you furl it. Lift it and tighten it."

"Sorry!"

"What have you got to show me?"

"I forget."

He slid the stick into the boathouse latch and followed her to the short path up the bluff. Once, when he first knew Laura, she'd had him follow her up, climbing hand over hand, holding onto vines and roots. That had been a test of some kind, too, though not of his making. He hated that climb, dirt in his mouth, her heels kicking down stones on him. But he kept following. Why, he wasn't sure, except that it was important to finish what you started. Now he followed Jo's quick steps up the split log stairs. She'd come after him to share something; she stayed to help. He'd been gruff. He caught up with her and tried to follow what she was saying.

She was talking about her ceramics class that had started last Monday, about photographs of the pots, about her teacher who made the pots, about a light meter for the camera she used, an old Minolta of his. He couldn't get it all. Below, the crack and roar of the bonfire trailed them through the woods, which were filling with smoke and fog.

She'd left her bike by the bench at the top of the stairs, her backpack on the ground. By the time he caught up to her she had the pack open and was pulling out a brown envelope.

"I took lots, but these are the best."

"Lots of what?"

"I've been telling you. Photos, of course. It's been my test of manhood."

She was still angry. He guessed he deserved it. "Sorry."

"I know. It's okay." She sat down on the bench and made room for him beside her.

"Wouldn't the light be better at the house?" His fingers were clumsy with cold and he wanted a hot shower. And a drink.

"There's plenty of light. Anyway, I can't wait."

He took the photos as she handed them to him, five of them, five-by-sevens, black-and-white, although the evening light gave them a sepia cast, uncentered on her printing paper.

In the first she'd used a framing technique, shooting a portrait of the potter through a shelf of bowls and plates so that they surrounded the figure of a dark-headed man bent over his wheel. She'd caught the man from the front, the intensity of his heavy-browed face the focus of the picture. Will studied her technique. The potter with his hooded eyes was small, but in focus; his bowls were large, but blurred. The depth of field was adjusted to render his figure precisely: spots of clay on his forearms, a silver chain at his neck, the lines around his mouth, the furrow between his lower lip and his chin.

"That's Mr. Coutris, the teacher. I told him what I wanted to do and he said he'd just forget all about me. He's making plates for a set that was commissioned, that's why he has those calipers. They have to be the same rim size. I didn't ask him any other questions. He said he'd throw me out if I did, but he didn't mean it. I just wanted to *see,* anyway." She took the photo back from him. "What do you think?"

"You know it's good." Why was he so irritated? He held out his hand for the next one.

The second photo was of the bowls themselves, or at least parts of them. She'd moved in close, caught the smooth, rounded surfaces with the potter's finger marks on them. In the upper right-hand corner the rim of one of the bowls was visible, giving the shapes definition. The bowls were monumental, vast as mountains.

The last three photos were a series. She'd taken them from directly behind the potter, his hands and wrists entering the photos from the bottom corners, his work in the lower center. "He's centering the clay," she said, her forehead at the level of his chin as they bent over the pictures.

The muscular hands of the man were cupped around a breast of clay, the wheel was obviously turning swiftly, for water ran from under his hands out onto the rim of the wheel. The potter's thumbs met where the nipple would be.

"Then you press in and clay moves up like this." She lay the next photo on top. She'd moved in even closer. His wrists were cut out, his hands cupped around the base of what seemed a wet and shimmering phallus of clay.

In the final photo she'd moved back again, the clay had been pressed back down into the breast shape, and, while the left hand still cupped it, the right hand was turned, rested at an angle, the thumb thrust straight down into the clay. Water spun away from the hands, which were slick and coated. "He's opening the clay here. I can do this, too. This far, anyway. I can't make a pot yet, but it's only the first week. Mr. Coutris says I'm a natural. I go into the studio between classes and practice. But this day," she rested her hands on her photos, "I just spent the afternoon watching." She leaned back. "What do you think, Will?"

"I think you're a natural." Why was his voice unsteady?

"The pictures are good?"

"Great."

"I mean *really?*"

"I don't lie to you." He studied the photos again. Each was a statement about work, commitment, form, and, finally, the erotic nature of creation. Did she know the meaning in what she'd seen and photographed? But they were *her* pictures. Even if she didn't have words for the experience, she knew. The pictures were the proof.

He looked down at her, then. She didn't look any older, her face naked of makeup, small gold hoops in her ears, dark eyes watching him from under those long lashes.

"What were you saying about a light meter?" He slipped the photos back into the folder.

"I want to borrow yours, if that's okay."

He handed her the folder. "Of course it's okay. But I've got another idea. You could use better equipment than my cast-offs. Let's get you one of your own."

"Really?"

"Sure. How did you learn about depth of field, Jo?"

"I figured it out. It's so logical."

So she was inventing photography all by herself.

"Better idea. Let's get you a camera with a light meter built in. It looks like you're taking this seriously."

"Will!" As she did as a little girl, she leaned against his shoulder and slipped her hand into his. Hers was small, warm and firm in his chilled palm. He gave her a quick squeeze and stood. "Let's get inside."

The streetlights were on, and under the oaks in the park it was almost night. He helped her wheel her bike over the roots of the old trees. There was an ache of longing in his chest, although he wasn't sure what he could be longing for. Sailing, and his sad, old memories had done nothing to clear his head. "How old is your teacher, anyway?" He wondered why he cared.

"Pretty old. About forty, I think."

The sweet, rotting smell of chinaberry leaves came from the ravine and behind them the lake soughed softly, more fog rising. The idea of the log-burning exhausted him now, as much as he'd liked piling them up earlier. The best part was over. The best part of everything was over. Maybe he wouldn't go down at all, although Cecil would be disappointed. Maybe he'd stay home and look through some camera magazines, decide which kind would be best for Jo.

The bike wobbled and bumped his leg, and he grabbed at it, saying "Hey!" But Jo didn't hear. She'd stopped at the porch steps, her mouth open in surprise.

"Do you know who's in the house?"

He straightened the bike. "Who's here?"

"That guy I met in Vienna. Thomas!" She stepped back as though she might run.

"Laura will get rid of him. She doesn't—"

"Laura! Laura's *smiling* at him!"

10

The way the fog had come up. That spooked Jo. A thick, dense presence moved across the park like a low cloud. But then the whole situation spooked her. She'd guessed that sooner or later this guy would appear. Thomas liked to startle and surprise, that was part of his gig. But she couldn't figure Laura. She'd thought Laura might have slammed the door in his face. But there she was, standing on the lowest step of the staircase, pulling on her blue caftan over a black shirt and white Levi's, and there was Thomas arranging the folds. They looked like actors dressing for a play.

Laura's face was flushed, her hands busy at the throat of her caftan. "Look who's here! And look what he's brought." On the end of the newel post perched a small, beaded Indian headdress, feathers dangling—the size for a costume, not massive, like the real ones.

Thomas turned then, elegant in tan cords and a leather jacket. His cool dude outfit, Jo thought.

"I hear this is the evening the whole town goes up in flames." He spread his arms. "And here's Jo!" A wink for her, white lashes fanning down. Then he reached past her to Will. "And the good doctor."

"Hi." Something's crazy here, she warned herself.

"Call him Will," Laura said. "He's not wild about this 'the good doctor' stuff."

"I'm frozen. Excuse me." Will ducked Thomas's handshake, headed past them to the kitchen, where Jo heard him getting ice, probably the whiskey, and clumping up the back stairs.

She made a quick assessment: Will was pissed, Laura was excited, and Jo wasn't sure what she felt, except off-balance because she hadn't expected this. Which was probably what Thomas would want. He looked terribly pleased with himself.

"How long have you been here?" Laura and Thomas seemed to have been interrupted in the middle of a joke.

"Days!"

"About fifteen minutes," Laura said.

"I don't believe this." Jo looked up at Laura. "I didn't know you two were seeing each other." Good—she'd made Laura blush, a hard trick.

But to Jo's surprise Laura laughed instead of giving her a dirty look. "This park isn't exactly hard to find." She hadn't denied anything, Jo noticed.

A piece of the puzzle was missing—why was Laura so *pleased?* But Jo couldn't think what question might clear that up. "You just stopped by?" she asked Thomas. She slipped off her backpack, wondering if she could get upstairs to clean up. She had clay on her Levi's and the last time she'd looked there was clay in her eyebrows, too. Upstairs, Will's shower went on—she'd love a shower. That would give her a chance to pull herself together.

Thomas launched into some story about a friend of his telling him there was a log-burning right *here,* where he wanted to be anyway, and what great timing that was for him, a story she didn't pay any attention to because she was mentally checking the wet hems of her jeans and the Disneyland sweatshirt she wore under her windbreaker. She was a mess.

"Our good luck!" Laura said. Thomas had tamed her somehow.

Jo edged toward the dining room and the escape route up the back staircase. "Will you be around long?"

"I asked him to stay for supper. And the log-burning, as long as he's here," Laura said.

"My luck's going right."

"It'll be a super-dull evening." Jo made it to the kitchen. "Anyway, I'm cleaning up."

When she closed the door of her small bathroom she realized she was shaking. Cold. And scared? He could have called and told her that he was coming by, that wouldn't have been too hard. That bastard! She might even have said, Don't. Though she doubted that. But she'd certainly have asked him to meet her at school, or somewhere on neutral ground. And damn, Kit was coming by after he finished loading the UPS trucks tonight, joining her for what was left of the party. Of course she hadn't said anything about Thomas to Kit. Not that she *had* to. She bit her lip.

When she yanked off her sweatshirt and glanced in the mirror she found dabs of clay on her chin as well as her forehead, her hair wild around her head, as though sparks might fly from it. Then she thought, What the hell. This is how I am, let him take it or leave it. What did he *want?*

After a minute the water pressure came on hard—Will must be finished with his shower—and she soaped herself, held her hands up, palms open, water drumming down under the rims of her fingernails. She even washed her hair. There was no special hurry, and she wasn't anxious to go back downstairs. When she tried to get her breath her chest ached. They could all get lost.

When Jo came down, her damp hair pulled back by a head-band, Laura was piling chicken sandwiches onto a platter and Thomas was grinding pepper onto the salad. They were talking to each other in a way that made no sense at all, jumping from subject to subject, laughing a lot. It was a language game that Jo didn't know how to play, and apparently one that Will refused to. He was wrapping a sandwich in waxed paper, stuffing it into the pocket of his sweater.

"Hey," she said to him. "Where are you going?"

"I promised Cecil I'd watch the fire while he had supper." He'd pulled on a gray Irish sweater with holes in the elbows, and his dad's old Navy watch cap. The hook in his nose was red from scrubbing and there was a faint stubble on his chin—if he and Laura went out in the evening he usually shaved again.

Jo followed him out onto the back stoop, pulled the door

behind her. She hugged herself against the chill that came in through her plaid shirt. "When shall we come down?"

"Any time. Now. Never."

"Will, *I* didn't invite him. He called me, sure, but I didn't even suggest he could come here."

He stopped by the gate, Daisy circling at his legs, sniffing his boots. "Listen, I'm in a foul mood and it doesn't have anything to do with your friend."

"He's not exactly *my* friend!"

"Whose is he?"

"I don't know! Anyway, no fair!"

He turned up the shawl collar of his sweater. Underneath it, she saw one of his old blue cotton work shirts, holes burned in the collar. He couldn't have looked raggier if he'd tried. Maybe he *had* tried.

"No fair!" she repeated. She didn't bother to whisper. She'd scream if she had to—if Will wasn't on her side, who was?

"Okay. I'm no fair. Okay?"

"Okay." Although it wasn't. Nothing was okay.

"Come down whenever there's a pause in the dialogue. Cecil has some plan. It doesn't matter. It's just a fire." He pulled off the cap, ran his hand through his wet hair, pulled the cap on lower, the rim straight across his forehead. Then he turned and was gone through the gate, shoving Daisy back with his foot.

All the neighbors seemed to have left their houses and started for the beach at the same time. Jo spotted the Coleman boys running across the park through a thin patch of fog, David with his guitar slung over his shoulder, Nate followed by his retriever. The dog leaped at Nate's feet, jumped to bite his wrists, to catch at his flapping windbreaker, her loud, high bark pitched even higher with excitement. Mrs. Simon limped along the walk with her cane, Mrs. Mikelson there beside her, the other seven Mikelsons right behind. Mr. and Mrs. Rodenberg were waiting at the top of the path with a young couple who were visiting them, the woman with a baby in a sling across her chest, the man scratching his throat and looking surprised at the sudden gathering, which grew larger as the Hudsons and their three grandchildren, the whole Polk family, and Miss Goldbaum materialized on Center Road. "Martinis anyone?" Mr. Rodenberg called, holding up a shaker, and the smallest of the Hudsons' grandchildren cried, "It's dark!"

"It's supposed to be dark, it's night," some kid yelled. Everyone laughed, and the child cried harder. "Carry me!"

Pat Millet wore her red autumnal robe over a white turtleneck, her gray hair loose on her shoulders, bronze bracelets clinking as she hugged everyone. It occurred to Jo that maybe the little girl who was crying thought Pat Millet was a witch.

Mrs. Coleman had a flashlight, and so did one of the Mikelson boys, and so did Laura. They led the way down the split log steps, Laura calling back, "Everyone, this handsome stranger is Thomas Trawick!"

Thomas was right behind Jo. "How many names do I have to learn?" he whispered.

"None. It's up to you."

"It's perfect!"

Was he making fun of them? While eating their sandwiches he and Laura had seemed to be making fun of something all the time. "I'll fill you in on names, but it's hard to see. Let's wait until we get down to the beach."

"I don't want to spoil this by knowing who anyone is." Feathers from the Indian headdress he carried brushed her hand.

The tart smell of woodsmoke mingled with the sweet damp of pine needles. Dew fell on Jo's face as they passed under the trees—wet already. That must be from the fog. Thomas's smell was of limes, too strong, as though he'd spilled some on his shirt. When she glanced up at him she saw dew glitter in his beard. He was leaning over her.

"Do you do this every year?"

"This is a first. The Millets organize something every year, though. The vernal equinox, the Fourth of July, maybe carol singing at Christmas. We go along."

"You must like these events, then."

"I guess." Actually, the parties the Millets came up with reminded her of the ones they'd had in Campfire Girls—themes carried out with crepe paper and place cards and music chosen for the occasion. In other words, corny. She liked the parties her friends had at whichever house happened to be available each weekend—"available" meaning parents away. Someone's parents were gone every weekend, if you asked around. Everyone took grass and beer, or maybe jug wine, and their favorite records. You just sat around and laughed at those parties, danced a little, got wrecked. Usually they ordered pizza and tried to get the guy who delivered it to stay and dance. That was part of the fun, jumping on the delivery guys and hauling them in the door. "This log- burning business could be a total waste of time," she warned Thomas, wondering if he'd say, Come on back to the house, then. Or, Let's get a drink. Why was he *here?*

"We'll see what happens," he whispered. He liked to whisper.

Then they were out of the trees and onto the asphalt drive. The bonfire was on the widest stretch of beach, a fire taller and wider than Jo had imagined it could be. The Hudsons' two older granddaughters were turning cartwheels around it on the sand, Cecil Millet waving at them to stay back.

Jo didn't see Will. Maybe he was on the other side of the fire. Mrs. Simon had been settled in an aluminum folding chair and the Mikelsons and Rodenbergs had spread their blankets beside her. The younger kids were chasing Nate Coleman around the fire, weaving in and out of the light, wild with the strangeness of the flame and the misty night, wild with being down on the beach at this forbidden hour. They dashed back and forth. No one stopped them. The beach was an illuminated path between the bluffs and the lake and they all knew it by heart. Then Nate threw a stick into the water for his dog to retrieve, and her sleek, polished head snaked up out of the dark water. When she shook dry the kids all screamed and ran. Jo thought that not so long ago she'd have been running with them, splashing into the shallow water now and then.

Mr. Rodenberg called "Drinks!" Miss Goldbaum produced a corkscrew from her raincoat pocket for Cecil's Moselle and the adults passed each other plastic cups. Mrs. Coleman called out, "Cider over here!" but the kids didn't pay any attention. Cecil had started in with his mandolin, a song that was thin and painful and quick and made the kids run faster. Pat Millet shook her tambourine. "What shall we sing?" she cried above the noise. "'On Top of Old Smokey'?"

"This isn't your *Beach Blanket Bingo* scene," Jo said when Thomas joined her at the edge of the lake, a bottle of Moselle tucked under his arm. He had his own opener in a folding knife. The wine was cool and not too sweet and she drank hers down quickly.

Thomas snugged the bottle back under his arm. "Let's sing 'On Top of Old Smokey'!" he yelled, and Jo saw Pat Millet focus on him, smile, raise her tambourine. He'd volunteered to be her assistant.

"This is absolutely crazy," Jo said, but he was already singing.

The next song Cecil started in on was slower, "Early One Morning." How many times had Jo heard Pat singing it, her voice soft and reedy? Thomas joined right in, lower and huskier than Jo had expected. Pat hurried over to stand by him, adjusting her tones to fit, smiling and tossing back her gray hair.

> Early one morning, just as the sun was rising,
> I heard a maiden singing in the valley below.
> O don't deceive me, O never leave me,
> How could you treat your poor Mary so?

A stupid song. A girl walking in the valley, lamenting lost love—how half-assed stupid. But suddenly Jo was filled with a heartbreaking sadness, as though she had lost *her* love forever. Tears stung at her eyes. Stupid tears. But they welled up and over. As though all love had been lost forever. And she'd never even been in love.

She poured herself another cup of wine. It went down like pop, cooled the fiery part of her throat, though she still felt like bawling—big *boo hoo hoo*s that would float above her head like they did in comic strips. When she tilted her head back to drain her cup she caught Thomas's gaze.

She sat down cross-legged. Then he was beside her, crouching. He touched her shoulder.

"I don't get why you're here," she said. "You put on a good act, but this isn't your kind of place."

"I wanted to see you."

"Now you've seen me."

"I've seen you *and* I've seen you."

"You're spooky."

He smiled.

"You *want* to be spooky."

"About some things, yes. But not about you." He had his hand on her shoulder. She didn't look at him.

"Thomas? What do you lie about?" She closed her eyes a moment, steadied herself with her palm on the chilly sand. "Practically everything, like everyone else does. But not about seeing you."

"Then you're a tease."

"You're right, there." He laughed, and to her surprise Jo found herself laughing, too, a shrill sound that didn't seem to be her own.

"What do you mean, 'I've seen you *and* seen you'?" She kept her eyes closed.

"I'll tell you."

"Now."

"Later. I promised your neighbor I'd lead a circle dance."

Jo groaned. Pat Millet and her pageants, her carnivals. Tomorrow she'd say to Jo, "Wasn't it magical last night?" That was what she always said, as though the parties took place more in her imagination than in the real world. Whatever the real world was.

"Let's get it over with." She opened her eyes, leaned on Thomas's knee to stand.

Pat had already pulled the adults and some of the kids forward, had them take hands in a ring around the fire. She made a place for Thomas between herself and Laura, and Jo found herself between Mr. Rodenberg, who smelled of gin, and Nate, who smelled of sweat. "Two steps right, one step back. Follow me!" Thomas called, and Cecil struck up the tune of a Greek circle dance. It was easy, and everyone caught on right away, keeping step with Thomas. The circle moved faster when Cecil's song sprinted ahead. Jo caught a glimpse of Laura's face, her blond hair bannering as she moved. Thomas changed the steps, and when he introduced the first variation Jo got it, although Mr. Rodenberg slipped and giggled. Then suddenly Nate began to run, and in a moment the circle wasn't dancing any more, it was turning faster and faster, spinning out, all arms stretching.

Jo let her head fall back, let Nate pull her along. Now and then
the amber moon flashed through the mist. She heard Thomas
yell, "Don't let go!" and the music became faster yet.
Then someone let loose, the ring broke, Nate was tearing off
into the dark. The Mikelsons had formed their own ring. Mrs.
Coleman was spinning the Hudsons' little granddaughter, and
Jo thought she saw Mr. Rodenberg kissing the young mother,
whose baby was wedged in between them. Thomas was twirling
Laura, who had her hands clasped behind his neck, her caftan
flying out behind them.

Then Jo saw Will near the boathouse. She ran to him, her feet
unsteady in the loose sand. "Will, you've got to spin me! You've
got to!"

She linked her hands around his neck and pulled him to her,
stumbling backward. His hands were on her hips then and they
began to turn, much more slowly than the giddy music, but fast
enough that the moon streaked a circle overhead. She closed her
eyes, leaned back, feeling the warmth of Will's neck, his thick
hair against her wrists. He wouldn't let her fall, he would never
let her fall. And she wanted to dance.

Then suddenly he stopped, straightened her up.

"Don't stop! It feels so good!"

"That's enough for me." He kept his hands on her hips until
she got her balance.

When she opened her eyes he wasn't smiling. Her face was
hot from running and she had a stitch in her side.

"You okay?" he asked her.

She shook her head—yes or no, she wasn't sure how she felt.

"Dance with me?"

"It's not my thing."

"But it's easy. I could teach you the steps."

"I suppose you could." Frowning, he pulled his watch cap
lower.

A hand on her shoulder. Thomas, of course. Right behind
her. "My turn."

He took her hand and led her to the gritty asphalt drive
where the Mikelsons were circle-dancing. Cecil was playing
"The Tennessee Waltz," Pat's thin voice lifting, "I was dancing
with my darling." Jo glanced toward the log steps—would Kit

be coming? But it was still early, and he didn't get off until ten. So she could dance with Thomas without chancing Kit's anger—Kit acted possessive, though nothing much was going on between them.

To her surprise, Thomas wasn't teasing any more. He took her hand the proper way, settled her against his side. "This is a waltz," he said, although of course she knew that. Then they began to dance. She hadn't expected it would be so smooth, so calm to waltz with Thomas. Their feet slid easily and she turned the ways he moved her, not dizzy any more.

"I like this," she said.

"Of course you like this. This is one of the great inventions of the Western world, ranking close behind ripe Brie."

He seemed to know where to move on the drive without faltering. His beard brushed her forehead, a good feeling. "You *talk* a lot, Thomas. You know that?"

"You're right. Why talk when you're dancing with a beautiful girl?"

Was she beautiful? "Do you ever have the feeling that you're sad but you don't know why?"

He held her closer. "That one's easy. Of course I do. That's called the human condition. This is the hard question—Do you ever have the feeling that you're happy and you don't know why? How about that one?"

"Yes."

"What's it like?"

"Just a lighthearted feeling."

"When would you get such a feeling?"

"Well, coming home on my bike today. I'd done some work I liked, and little yellow leaves were coming down around me."

"And how do you feel right now?"

"Pretty good." Better than she'd expected to feel.

He didn't say anything else, maybe because she'd told him he talked too much, and after a while she added, "Except about Will."

"Ah, good old Will."

"He's in a rotten mood, you know."

"I know."

"He's usually not like that."

"I suspect he is more than you might guess. He certainly will be if I'm around you."

"Why do you say that?" Cecil had stopped playing, although now Jo wished he would go on and on. Instead of answering her, Thomas led her over to the blanket where Pat Millet, Laura, and now Will were sitting. Laura wore the headdress.

Then Pat was on her feet, shaking her robe out around her ankles, beaming up at Thomas. "You're a welcome addition! We need a shaman now and then, though I haven't seen you in that headdress yet."

"Seeing the headdress on Laura, I've decided it was meant for a tall, blond woman with brown eyes," Thomas said.

Laura smiled, then looked down, as though she was afraid Will would see how pleased she was. She did look exotic in the headdress—her big eyes tipped up at the corners—the beads and feathers brushing her throat.

"What's a shaman?" Jo asked.

"A medicine man," Pat Millet said. "A magic man."

Jo tried a joke. "Will's a medicine man." But he didn't look up from filling his pipe, as though this familiar job required his full attention.

"Will and Thomas come from different tribes." Pat Millet settled back down quickly so that her robe belled around her. "Thomas probably has a leather pouch around his neck crammed full of eagles' claws and garlic."

Jo sat down on the sand, cross-legged, and Thomas squatted beside her. "I am definitely in touch with the secrets of the gods," Thomas said. "And I have visions, certifiable visions." Both Laura and Pat Millet were smiling at him—of course Pat would love that bit about the gods. She and Cecil were into myths.

"Do you predict the future, too?" Pat asked.

"Absolutely. My predictions about the future are invariably accurate. It's the one area of my life where I've managed complete precision and control. Do you want to have your future predicted?"

He was watching Jo—he meant the question for her. She wasn't sure, but then she thought, it's just a game. "I know you'll do what you want, no matter what anyone says," she said.

Thomas raked the sand with his fingers until he found a small driftwood stick, one end forked, the other end charred from an old fire. "Here's my diviner. I've had better, but in a pinch one uses what's at hand." He smoothed the sand and then drew spirals, one on top of the other, like a skater practicing school figures.

Laura leaned foward and Pat Millet seemed to be hypnotized by the motion.

"There's your future, Jo," Thomas said at last.

She peered down at the circles he'd drawn in the sand. "Doesn't look like much to me."

He traced the circle with his forefinger, as if perfecting it, polishing it—presented it to her again. "Here. The gods say love is your future. Love."

To her surprise her pulse sped up. "They'd say that to any girl." As if there were gods.

"It's hot news." Thomas smiled. "You have to believe the gods."

Laura touched his knee. "How about my future?"

He placed the tip of the diviner on her hand, keeping her palm on his knee. "Concentrate."

Laura frowned with concentration. The feathers of the head-dress swung forward across her temples, feathers like leaves, red and orange. Thomas let the stick rest on her hand a long time, as though he was taking her pulse. Cecil had started playing again, soft, tired chords that floated up in the smoke. After a while Thomas said, "The feeling I have the most strongly is 'new.'"

Laura seemed doubtful. "New?"

"It's a powerful message," Thomas said. "Don't ignore it."

Laura leaned back and propped herself on her elbows, smiling to herself. "Do Will's now. I like this game."

"It's no game," Thomas said at the same time Will said, "No!"

"Why not?" Laura settled the headdress on her brow.

Will shook his head. "I know the future. It's just like the present."

"That's either terribly cynical or terribly optimistic," Pat Millet said, "depending on how you feel about the present."

Thomas pushed the stick down into the sand as if he were probing for water. "Let the gods speak."

Will stood up. "Don't."

"It's too late now. When the power's running through me I can't stop." His voice had the sing-song cadence of a preacher delivering the "good news." "Here comes the message, the news for our brother. Brother, are you ready?" He didn't wait for Will to answer. "Hold on, brother, there is more! That's the message. Hold on, there is more!"

"What the hell does *that* mean?" Will had his hands on his hips, the pipe clenched between his teeth as if he might bite through it. His shoulders hunched forward as if he were defending himself against a blow.

"That's a *real* Indian tale," Pat Millet cried, excited, her clasped hands raised to her chin. "When a young man goes out into the wilderness to communicate with the spirits who will guide his life, he has to fast and wait for the gods to speak to him. In one story the young brave was near exhaustion, in a trance of hunger and pain, and his special spirit spoke to him in those words. 'Hold on, there is more.' So he held on until he understood the meaning of his life." She rocked back and forth as she spoke, her bronze earrings swinging along her cheeks.

Laura clapped as though the game were still fun. "Terrific! That's a much better prediction than 'new.' Will got the best one."

"Go to hell," Will said.

Jo shivered. Will's anger frightened her. Thomas should cut it out.

Head cocked, smiling, Thomas looked up at him.

Will turned and walked away from the fire. He was almost instantly invisible, swallowed up into the fog. Jo heard his first step onto the wooden stairs as he left them all behind.

"I offended him," Thomas said after a moment.

"You meant to." Laura didn't seem angry, but she got to her feet, brushed sand from her caftan, started after Will. "See you at the Millets' later."

"Time to go back," Pat Millet said. "We have to recognize

when the mood shifts," she informed Jo, as though Jo might not have noticed. Pat began making the rounds of the other groups, inviting the neighbors back to her house. The Mikelsons first, and then the others shook out their blankets, began the climb up from the beach, disappearing one by one into the mists that lifted and then settled back as the wind changed.

The logs had fallen into the center of the fire and a heap of coals shimmered red and blue—it was the kind of fire she'd loved to watch when she was a little kid. Shapes like animals or ghosts came and went in the branches as they crumbled into ash. Cecil Millet had kicked sand around the edges, doused the largest logs with buckets of sand. The center would burn all night, he'd said—no danger. And left her and Thomas alone on the beach.

She couldn't see the moon any more. She tilted her wrist so she could read the time by the red glow: almost ten. But Kit wouldn't get here for a while. Thomas was quiet for a change, rolling a joint.

He handed her the J and leaned against a log he'd dragged over for a backrest. The dope was sweet and rich, melted into her lungs. She should really stop smoking so often, but it was hard when such good stuff was offered to her. She handed the J back. "Thanks."

He stretched his arm behind her along the log. After he took a hit, he asked, "Did I make a fool of myself?"

"Do you care?"

"If you do."

She shrugged. "You like to break things, don't you?"

"Some things need to be broken."

"You shake people up."

"I guess I do. Is that wrong?"

"Don't know. It's just that what happens after might not be so good for some people."

"Good old Will?"

"Don't call him that, okay?"

"It's not my fascinating presence that's eating good old Will. I don't have that kind of power."

"What did that bit mean, 'Hold on, there's more'?"

"There's always more. Unless you pull the plug. People who
pull the plug have decided they don't want any more. That's all
suicide is, a simple 'No thanks.' If you're still alive that means
you want more. Good old Will wants something he hasn't gotten yet, just like the rest of us."

"How about Laura? 'New'?"

"Your sister is a foxy lady. She's looking for excitement, I
think." After a moment he added, "A wise man bribes the
chaperone."

"Except she's not my chaperone."

"I know that. But I know who your chaperone is, Jo."

"Who?"

"You. No one could do a thing with you if you didn't allow it.
You're in charge."

"That's the same for everyone."

"You'd think so, wouldn't you? But it doesn't work out that
way. Cause and effect isn't so simple once you get out of science
class."

"Most people do what they want."

"Most people do what they *can*."

Accepting the J back, she looked at him sideways. He
watched her, his hair flattened over his forehead by the damp.
"Is that why you're here? You can do a few dances and shake
up Laura and Will? And me?"

He settled back against the log, his leg against hers. His hand
grazed her shoulder and stayed. "I'm here to report on my vision, and its meaning. Don't you want to know what I saw?"

"Why do you keep on with this bit about visions? Why don't
you just talk about who you are?"

"You sound impatient. My visions *are* who I am."

"Like, for instance, what do you do? What kind of writing?"

"For money, I write articles which explain the uses for vari-
ous drugs. It's ad-agency work, and it's incredibly boring, but
the pay is good. In my real life I'm a novelist. Believe me, I'd
choose to write my novels full-time, if I could. That's the difference between *want* and *can* right there."

She sighed. "Why don't you do that, if that's what you
want?"

"It's strictly a question of money. Sometimes I think this is exactly the job Princeton prepared me for—a lifetime of term papers, carefully documented and footnoted, all adding up to zero. God, my alma mater, the fount of culture! It sprung me right off my dad's farm and into the laps of the Great Minds. Full scholarship. Ivy growing everywhere. Einstein's old think tank right down the road, folks in there *thinking,* whatever that means, day and night. I thought that was wonderful, 'sweet tit,' as my old man says. His greatest superlative, 'What a sweet-tit tractor.'"

"Princeton?"

"I fooled you? Ah, but we Princeton men aren't all Poppin' Fresh doughboys. Even a million years ago, when I was there, there were some bona fide weirdos like myself. Except that I wasn't a weirdo then. No, I was straight as a die, the Greenwich Mean Time of straightness, the Paris platinum meter bar of straightness. Hippies all around me, and I've got a haircut— that straight. I got a degree in English, along with those first brilliant beauties they let into our all-male haven. I repudiated the old man's narrow Republican prejudices, marched for black rights, marched with the welfare mothers. Then I woke up one morning after a friend of mine was killed in a car accident and realized I was wading around in a lot of cosmic bullshit. Nothing *means* a damn. There is no meaning in life."

"That's your vision?"

He picked up the wine bottle, motioned for her to hold out her cup, but she covered the top with her palm. "I have to go back in a minute. A guy's coming by for me."

"A guy? You would have a guy. I hadn't thought of that."

For the first time since she'd met him he seemed unsure. She pressed the advantage. "My boyfriend." And stood up.

He got to his feet, put his hand on her shoulder. "I'll let you rush to his side in a minute. Don't you want to hear about my vision of you first? You must be a little curious." His narrowed eyes reflected the dying fire. "You won't admit you'd like to know?"

"Is it important that I have to *ask* you to tell me?"

"You don't want that responsibility?"

Her mouth was dry. But what difference could his "vision" possibly make? "Just tell me! You try to make everything so dramatic." She started away from the fire but he drew her back, his hand closing lightly around her wrist.

"Stay a minute. Sit down."

She didn't pull her hand away, but she didn't sit down, either.

"What, then?"

He took a deep breath. "Remember Vienna? But of course you remember Vienna. Halcyon days, the great city gilded with sun. I turned and there you were."

She did pull her wrist away then. "I don't want to hear this romantic crap. You're putting me on."

"Listen!" He took her wrist again, not so loosely. "This is important to me."

He shifted so that he blocked her way to the path. "When I said I'd look you up back here in the States I meant that. People always say they're going to do that, but they never do. I knew I'd see you again. I liked your freshness. No, your eagerness, your simplicity. After you left the Spanish Riding School I decided, why wait? I could see you right there in Vienna. I decided to ask you out for a late supper. I think I saw us in one of those dark little restaurants with the polished mahogany and silver trays with piles of iced cakes. So I wrote a note inviting you to join me. I was going to leave it at your hotel, asking you to ring me up at mine if you could join me. Very, very proper, English-major prose, a straight-arrow proposal in my best cursive. I even wrote another note to 'Dr. and Mrs. Brenner,' requesting permission! Nineteenth century! I was in an altered state, I suppose. You're young. I thought for once I'd get things right. Maybe I even saw myself arriving with a small bouquet of flowers in my hand, a musical-comedy number, singing and tap-dancing like Gene Kelly. No, don't look at me like that—I'm making fun of myself, not of you. It was the straight old me following the rules.

"I walked to your hotel, my notes signed and tucked into my pocket. It was a lovely evening, leaves swishing underfoot, the smell of a storm in the air. I felt about twenty, the young suitor—a feeling I don't remember ever having. I was proud of myself, you see. I was participating in the arena of tradition, and it had been a long time . . .

"God, when I think of it! I can hardly believe I was on that errand. I should have saved the notes to teach myself humility. I'm capable of any folly. But, I thought maybe formality was necessary. Not for you. When you slipped me that piece of paper with the name of your hotel, I knew you'd take a chance. But it seemed to me that your brother-in-law was running interference for you, and your sister. I was wrong about her. She wants out of whatever straitjacket she's in. And nothing will help with the good doctor. *Anyway.* I advanced upon your hotel, the letters in my pocket, plumped up, like one of those Viennese pigeons, with good intentions. Are you listening?"

"Why didn't you leave the notes, then?"

"Because I had a vision. A real one. I found your hotel, I rushed inside, no one was at the desk, so I took the stairs to search for your room. I don't know what I thought I was going to do—knock on your door, slip the note underneath. Something romantic, I guess, as you accuse me of being. Then, across the airshaft, I saw you. You were opening the casements of the *Badezimmer.* You were so lovely, Jo, in your pink blouse, the blue-and-white tiled wall behind you. I wanted to call to you, but the window wouldn't open. So I watched. Then, like the answer to my prayers, you took off your clothes and bathed."

"Damn you!"

"No, don't run! Listen!"

"Damn you, Thomas!" She remembered too well how she'd stripped to bathe. How she'd stood in front of that long mirror, after, how she admired herself, posed, played, teased her nipples. Touched herself until she came. And he'd been watching. She took a step to pass him but he blocked her with his arm.

"You don't understand yet. Look, don't be shocked. I had a vision and you're not going to stop me until I've told you all of it. I *have* to go on. You have to stay." He took her by her elbows and shook her lightly.

But she wouldn't look at him. He couldn't make her do that. She fixed her gaze on her sand-crusted docksiders. "You spied on me!"

"I'm no voyeur. Just let me explain. It's important to me and it might be to you. I'd never seen a girl alone with herself. I had the most intense sensations—oh, yes, sexual ones—but mostly I felt tenderness for you. I thought I could actually *see* your inno-

cence, your spirit, as if those qualities were something for the
eye, like your hair or your skin. I imagined I looked at *you*.
When we're alone we reveal so much—I mean, when we're
without roles, without costumes."

A buzzing in her ears covered his words. "That's cheap and
dirty, Thomas, you know that? Spying!"

He shook her again, and this time her head snapped back and
she looked up at him. His lips were drawn back on his teeth as
though he were in pain.

"You aren't paying attention. I saw your naked *being*, or at
least I imagined that I did. I looked right through your lovely
body. I kept repeating to myself, 'That's who she is!' The way
you were washing and whatever, I guessed that was what you
were saying, too: This is who I am. Affirming yourself. I said
your name over and over. I didn't want a damn thing from you.
And I didn't make this effort to find you just to tell you I'd seen
your tits! Do you begin to understand me?"

She clenched her teeth. "Fucker!"

"But I'm not talking about fucking! Christ, don't you get it? I
had a conversion experience! Listen, there I was with those
notes in my pocket, remember? I was playing the old game,
buying right into the play. Act I, Scene I—the whole stilted
ritual of courtship, or whatever we play when we do these bullshit social acts. I thought about those notes, and I realized that
if I left them, if you phoned me and we met like that, we'd be
locked right into the social fictions of the Western world, the
fine civilization that gave us the waltz, and World War II,
Korea, Nam. The great stage set, all of us entering on cue, either
with the music or with our bayonets set, depending on who was
directing the scene. But none of us under our own volition. So I
took a big risk, Jo. I wanted to keep my vision, so I took a risk. I
wanted to know the girl in the lighted window *as she is,* or
I didn't want to know her at all. I wanted the honesty of that
silent encounter that was given to me. I wanted nothing but
that."

"You're crazy!"

"No, I'm not crazy. I'm completely sane, the sanest man
you'll ever meet. What have I just told you?" He slowed, as
though he spoke to someone who might not speak the language

well. "I've told you that I saw through the fiction of our lives, that's all. You helped me to do that."

Because he'd slowed down it was easier for her to hear him, but the burn that had begun in her face had spread down through her chest and stomach. "Whatever you call it, you stole my privacy!" His hands hurt her, and hers were going numb from the pressure of his thumbs just above her elbows. "I don't want a guy who doesn't love me to be looking at me naked. That's total shit, no matter what you say."

"I told you my intentions. I don't want to hurt you."

"Well, you are. You make me ashamed."

"Jo!" His head went back in exasperation. "You're not ashamed! I don't believe that. You say that because you think that's how you should feel. That's just what I'm talking about, feeling what we really *do* feel, not what we think we should feel."

She considered that. He didn't loosen his grip, but he didn't move any closer. "It's true that I feel violated."

"God, you're stubborn!"

"You said what I really feel is important. I feel violated."

"But I didn't violate you. It was your purity I saw. I don't mean goody, goody, is she a virgin or not. I don't give a damn. I mean that I saw a young woman who belongs to herself. I don't want to violate that. There are a million things I hate about myself, but that will never be one of them." Suddenly he dropped her arms, pushed his hands into his trouser pockets. "I couldn't change that, anyway. You're too strong."

Strong? The blood rushed back into her hands, making them ache. She rubbed her forehead, tucked her hair behind her ears. What was this heat in her chest? "Look, I don't think I understand you." She kept her voice steady. "But I don't want to understand you, especially. You pushed in here. You pushed us all around, primarily me. You said a lot of fancy stuff, some of which sounds okay. But you're a bastard, you know that?"

He wiped his lips on the back of his hand, shoved his hair out of his eyes. "Please, listen. I think this is the only chance I'll ever have for something *simple* with a woman."

"But it's too late. Already it's not simple. You're not simple!"

"I'm only telling you one thing: I am going to love you."

Love—he'd whispered the word, and she heard it more clearly for the whispering. "It doesn't feel like love to me."

"Think about what I've said. You'll begin to understand."

"No!"

"You'll see things my way."

"I don't want to see things your way."

Gently, he stroked her cheek with the back of his hand, then tilted up her chin. "But you want me to kiss you, don't you? You want that, I can tell. Maybe that's enough to understand for now."

Her curiosity was even stronger than her anger and distrust. She let him pull her against him. He brushed her lips with his, then their hard pressure on hers seemed part of his persuasion. He held her around the waist, tightly, as though they were waltzing again, but now she felt how urgently aroused he was. No matter what he said about her "spirit" he was after sex, that was all. For a moment his determination excited her, but when his hand went to her breast she wrenched back. "No!"

"Yes, Jo. Oh, yes."

"I want you to stop."

For answer, he kissed her again, even harder, trapping her head with both his hands. "I do love you. You can't stop me," he said against her temple.

She ducked, grabbed his hand, and sank her teeth into it above the thumb, feeling the skin break, tasting salt, then blood, hearing him gasp with pain. He flung himself away from her.

Then she was running. She took the path up through the trees, stumbling, pines slapping her face, her heart racing, too. Not that she thought he'd chase her, he couldn't find the way. But she needed to run. She could have bitten his hand off! Torn it right off with her teeth if he hadn't grabbed it away.

At the top of the bluff she stopped, dizzy, and huddled down by the big oak. Her temples ached from the pulse that slammed there. Even though she'd run off some of her anger, that intense heat still radiated through her body.

Then she caught sight of Thomas at the far end of the park, walking down Sunrise to Center Road. Heading for the train station. He didn't look toward her house, nor was he glancing around as though he hoped to catch sight of her. Now he'd leave her alone, that bastard! Still, she stayed hidden, balanced on her heels.

Tires splattered gravel as Kit's junker pulled up in front of her house and parked. Neighbors were going in and out of the Millets', and she didn't want to be seen, so she ran across the end of the park and waved to him from the middle of Sunrise. After a moment his car lights came on again and he drove slowly to her.

She yanked open the car door almost before he'd pulled to a stop.

"Hey!" He helped her pull the door shut when she slid in next to him.

He smelled of clean sweat. She put her face against his shoulder. "Let's just drive, okay?"

"What's wrong, Jo?" He brushed her hair from her face.

"I'm drunk, I guess." For the first time she realized how she must look, her face smeared with tears and dirt, leaves and pine needles in her hair. "Would you please just kiss me first?"

His lips were light, soft, molded to hers. When she parted hers, so did he. His breath tasted of chocolate and coffee.

"I mean *really* kiss me." She wanted to be saved, from whom she wasn't sure. "I can't explain right now, but I want you to hold me for a while."

He held her, rocking her slowly and gently—like Estelle, she thought. Oh, Estelle, you didn't tell me enough about men. You didn't tell me about Thomas.

"You're so sweet," Kit said against the top of her head. "I think about you all the time. I think about how sweet you are."

She wanted him to lie down on her, smother her, cut off both imagination and memory, fill her with something so deep and intense that it would blot out the queer desire she'd felt for Thomas. Why had she ever been attracted to that bastard? Why had she given him the name of her hotel? This whole mess was her fault, but she didn't know what she'd done to bring it on. She buried her face against Kit's chest, heard the steady beat of his heart, tried to slow her own.

"You're really upset," he said.

"I guess."

"Something happened."

"A guy made a move on me. I didn't want him to."

"Did you tell him off?"

She nodded. "Could we drive now, Kit? Let's go out on the highway. Let's open all the windows and turn the tunes up loud and drive real fast."

"Excellent!" One arm around her shoulders, he turned onto Center. The trees were a gaudy orange and yellow, like crepe-paper decorations, the streetlights lemon and lime. She longed for the sanctuary of darkness and speed. In a few blocks they passed Thomas, who walked fast, his head down, his left hand—the one she'd bitten—tucked under his armpit. His yellow hair looked like a helmet.

She closed her eyes as they passed him. That's over, that's all over. He's gone, gone, gone. And when she looked again Kit was driving over the train tracks and entering the bright stream of cars leaving the outdoor concert at Ravinia and heading west.

11

Will woke before his alarm went off. His gut was tight and churning, his breath coming fast. Something was wrong; something awful had happened. He lay still and listened. Pheasants clucked in the ravine, but the house was quiet. His clock made its insectlike tick: five-forty-one. A soft light sifted in through the yellow curtains. In her bed Laura slept on her stomach, hugging her pillow, her breath shallow and even as the sigh of the lake.

His head ached and he rubbed the tight knot between his eyes, wondering if he was hungover. He'd had only a couple of whiskeys, maybe three, none of the sweet wine Cecil had brought. The night loomed back with its confusion of images: mists and the bonfire, figures appearing and disappearing on the beach, Laura in her robe and Trawick leering at her, at Jo. *Jo.* Her head flung back, lips parted, eyes closed, arms around his neck.

And he remembered what was wrong: holding her like that, he'd realized he was in love with her. Oh, God.

He got up quickly. He needed to get a hold on himself.

Showered, shaved, dressed for his day at the hospital, he was down in the kitchen by six-fifteen. He glanced at the back staircase, but Jo would never come down this early. Her classes had been in session for several days and she'd continued her high school habit of rushing off without breakfast, Laura had said. Usually he was gone before Jo wakened. Why would this morning be any different? And Laura still slept. Under the circumstances, it was much better to be alone until he got his feelings figured out.

He put on the kettle for instant coffee, poured himself a bowl of cereal. His hand shook as he lifted the milk carton. He noticed, too, as though for the first time, the pattern of shadows on the white counter top, the copper pans glinting on their hooks. Both light and shadow hurt, so he closed his eyes for a moment. In fact, all his senses felt stripped and raw, as though he'd been very ill, in a cave of fever, and had just come to consciousness.

Jo's windbreaker lay on the tile, the hem caught in the back door. In spite of his fight with Laura, in spite of their closed door, he'd heard Jo come in last night. He'd thought he heard her crying, but he didn't go to her, though he always had when she was younger. When a bad dream wakened her, when she imagined a bogeyman coming after her, during those weeks when her nose was broken and she couldn't sleep easily, he pulled on his pajama pants and padded down the hall to her. But not last night. What could he offer her now? He unlocked the door to free her jacket, then folded it, laid it on the counter.

When he finished his coffee and cereal he put on his sunglasses against the light from the east windows and rinsed his dishes, slipped them into the washer. Then he pulled on his suit jacket, checked for billfold, handkerchief, comb, car keys; he reminded himself to go slowly, to take it easy. Giving Daisy the pat she'd been waiting for, he let her out into the yard, and she followed him to the gate.

Before he opened the gate he looked back up at Jo's window. A slice of pale blue sky as evenly tinted as house paint showed between the roof and the overhanging oaks. Her window was shut, the curtains drawn. Even if he called, she wouldn't waken. And what would he say—"Are you okay?" She was probably fine. He was the one in trouble.

As he drove to Saint Mary's he marveled at how much of his life he'd reduced to the security of habit. He followed his route without really noticing where he was; his feet worked in harmony on the clutch, brake, gas pedals; he remembered to fill the gas tank, check the oil. He was doing all right, but anything could happen. He didn't know what to expect. Once, long ago, his father forgot how to knot his tie. One Sunday morning he came yelling down into the kitchen, "I don't know how!" As though it was Mother's fault, he thrust the tie at her, his expression angry, baffled, scared. Standing on a stool behind him, she tied it for him, showing him how again. Had some new fear entered his father's life that morning? Will guessed things had gone on as they always had—he didn't think his father had forgotten again. And maybe it would be the same for him: he'd simply do exactly what he'd always done, and no one, especially not Laura, would notice any change.

The morning was sunny and chill, all traces of last night's fog were gone. Sun cut through the protection of his sunglasses and his eyes teared. At seven-fifteen he pushed his card into the gate of the doctors' parking lot. His sight was better now that the hospital building blocked the sun, but his hands still worried him—when he spread them each finger jumped as though triggered by an electrical impulse.

He told himself to walk slowly—no hurry. In the elevator he watched the lighted numbers to make sure he didn't get off too soon. On the fourth floor, the staff was assembling. As he walked through Radiology, he called "How was your weekend?" to Heintz and Comber, who glanced up from an X-ray they were examining.

"Hunky-dory," Heintz said.

"Have a good day," Comber said. Jerry claimed that Comber sounded like a TV preacher—his greetings kept pace with the current media—and Heintz had frozen his at pre–World War II.

"Same to you," Will said. Then on impulse he ducked into Recovery for a glass of ice water. At home he'd slipped two Valium into his pants pocket as a safety measure, and now he was glad he'd thought of them. He was breathing too fast. And his *hands.*

In Recovery the beds were already made up, everything ready for the patients who'd be brought in as the morning progressed. A nurse and an aide were seated on folding chairs near the ice machine. "Headache?" the nurse asked.

He filled a plastic cup, tipped his head back to swallow.
"Allergies, I bet," she added. "It's that time of year."

"Right." If you don't have an answer, someone usually sup-
plies one for you—he'd have to remember that.

In the doctors' lounge, Stuber and Walsh, the two anesthe-
tists, were drinking coffee. "How was your weekend?" he asked
them—the usual question.

"Nothing special," Stuber said, his head bent over the *Trib*.

Walsh didn't bother to look up from pulling paper covers
over his shoes. Will hoped to God he wouldn't have to work
with Walsh for the day's surgery.

He loosened his tie as he entered the dressing room, hung his
clothes in his locker with his watch and wedding ring tucked
into the jacket pocket. Then he pulled on his scrub suit and
stepped into his white conductive shoes. He adjusted his paper
surgical hat and tied a mask around his neck; both mask and hat
were a clear, pale blue, exactly the color of the sky over the
house when he'd looked up to Jo's window. He could tell her
that. But of course he wouldn't.

At the control desk he said, "Good morning, ladies," to the
chief surgical supervisor and the receptionist. As they smiled
and chatted, he checked the list of patients he'd be working on
that morning. He remembered each one—that was a good sign.
And his anesthetist would be Stuber. He smiled back at the
ladies. Then to his surprise he said, "Have a good day."

He drank a cup of coffee in the doctors' lounge and listened
to the residents comparing golf scores, planning their ski trips.
Stuber read World Series statistics aloud. Walsh was chain-
smoking. Will looked out the window at the deepening blue sky
over the pink maples. After fifteen minutes, he could feel the
Valium kick in, though he knew that had to be only his imagination. Or hope. He began a second cup of coffee when his name
and Stuber's came over the wall mike, "Room seven."

Stuber slapped his paper closed, stretched. Will set his cup
down, his mouth dry. He thought his hands were steady, but
was afraid to check. "Let's go get 'em," Stuber said, and Will
followed him, feeling as he had that first day in the shipyards
when he'd crawled into the hatch behind the Junkman. Let it be
okay. Let me be okay.

The automatic doors parted with a whisper, and he inhaled the stale benzoin gases, a good smell that reminded him of balsam: the safety of the familiar. And there was Mr. Fowler, his first patient, lying on the table and looking up sideways from under white eyebrows. Septoplasty: remove his nasal obstructions and straighten the cartilage. Easy enough, if his hands steadied.

"Good morning, Mr. Fowler." The man's hand was wet and limp in Will's. He was scared, too.

"I don't like this business of no breakfast." Mr. Fowler hung onto Will's hand.

"Take it easy," Will told him. Trying to take it easy.

"We don't want you tossing your cookies," one of the nurses said.

"How was your vacation?" a nurse asked, turning to Will. "Haven't seen you since you got back."

Vacation? For a moment he couldn't think, then he remembered. "Austria? Just fine."

He watched Stuber start the I.V. on Mr. Fowler. "A good vein. Things look good," Stuber said.

"That's because *you* had breakfast." Mr. Fowler stretched to watch the nurse attach electrocardiograph pads to his chest and wire him to the cardioscope. "Everything okay?" he asked Will.

"You're in good hands," the nurse said before Will could answer.

A pattern appeared on the scanner. Will wondered how his own pulse would read if he were wired to the cardioscope. "I'm going to wash up and we'll get started," he told Mr. Fowler.

At the sink he brushed and soaped his hands even longer than the required ten minutes. Then he checked: his hands seemed steady now. His breathing was almost normal. Beautiful Valium. Get on with it, then.

Shoving the door with his hip, he crossed the operating room to the scrub nurse. She handed him a towel, held his gown for him, opened his gloves. "Okay, Stuber." He hiked himself onto a stool to watch as the patient was injected.

"Tell me when you see double," Stuber said to Mr. Fowler.

After a moment the man blinked, squinted. "I see two lights."

"Good!" As though Mr. Fowler had performed a difficult task well. Stuber gave him the drugs.

Will crossed his wrists against his chest as he waited. *Shadows on her throat. Her hair brushing my mouth.*

"Ready," Stuber said.

Will pushed off his stool, helped to drape Mr. Fowler. Don't think about her, he warned himself. And then to his relief his good hands took over. Behind him he heard the nurse who'd asked about his vacation whisper, "He hasn't lost his touch." It was the most reassuring thing he'd ever heard.

When he'd finished, he packed Mr. Fowler's nose and the nurse put on the dressing. "What could be simpler? You should turn pro," Stuber said as he and Will wheeled the patient to Recovery.

"Done so soon?" the nurse asked. "We've got two in here already. It's a fast track this morning."

"See you in a minute," Will told Stuber, who snapped him a salute and headed back to the lounge. Will had to make out his surgical report, and an edge of panic pressed back into his chest now that his fears about whether or not he could work had been set aside. He wanted to be alone.

At the control desk he asked the supervisor if he could use the phone in her office. She nodded, not seeming particularly surprised at the request.

He closed her office door and chose the least used line. It was eight-forty; Jo would be heading out the door right now. He might catch her. He dialed the number, then hung up as soon as he'd dialed. He couldn't *do* that. He had to stay under control, he had to think things through.

He sat down, leaned forward, put his head in his hands. Oh, God. The worst thing that he could imagine had happened to him, and he was going to have to act with absolute caution or they'd all be damaged beyond repair. He *loved* her.

Of course he'd loved her for years, but now, for reasons he couldn't figure out yet, he was *in* love with her. He said her name over to himself several times, the way a man rubs a wound that aches, rubs because it hurts so badly he can't leave the pain alone.

Maybe he'd been in love with her for a long time and hadn't realized it, but he'd made the discovery with unmistakable ferocity last night. When Trawick danced with Laura, Will felt nothing at all. But when Trawick seized Jo's hand to lead her back to the fire and Cecil's waltz, Will imagined bashing in that blond head with a log, kicking him in the face and groin and dragging his bloodied body into the lake. That *prick* with his arm around Jo. That stupid prick.

Watching Trawick holding Jo, Will's heart had actually ached. A green pain spread through his chest. It was a feeling he'd never had before, but he recognized it instantly. There it was.

What the hell would happen now? In the supervisor's quiet office, he heard himself groan. He had to think it through. He had to *think*.

There was a tap on the door. "Dr. Brenner? Did you hear your name on the mike? Room seven."

"Okay," he called back.

At least he could work. But he clenched his fists, wishing he could smash something—a pane of glass, say, that would burst with a decisive crash and splintering of shards. Wishing he could smash in Trawick's face.

Wishing he could hold Jo in his own arms. Except that was impossible.

Carrying a sandwich encased in plastic wrap and a sundae in a cardboard cup, Jerry threaded his way toward Will between the tables in the cafeteria. He sat down at the table across from Will, who was hunched over his bowl of soup and glass of milk. "You've got that Mona Lisa smile, William. What were you thinking about just now to make you all dewy-eyed, my friend?"

Will took another spoonful of the thick soup. He'd been thinking of buying Jo a camera. It was an innocent fantasy and he was grateful that it had come to him in the midst of so many anxious thoughts. But he knew this game with Jerry. "The stock market."

"Turns you on, does it? Bulls and bears?" Jerry unwrapped his sandwich and lifted the decorative slice of olive between his thumb and forefinger. "Transparent. The person who slices these should do skin grafts. We must search out this naturally gifted surgeon."

"Busy morning?" He was glad of Jerry's distracting banter.

"Yes, busy. I started off this 'first day of the rest of my life,' as Comber insists on calling it, at three a.m. A drunk kid wrapped himself and his motorcycle around a tree. Have you ever noticed how anger wakes you up faster than anything? I kept thinking, you shithead kid, why'd you *do* this to yourself! He isn't even seventeen yet. Goddamned kid, stinking drunk and his head split open. His parents . . ."

"Wire him back together?"

"Not much to wire to." He took a bite of the sandwich and looked at the label on the wrapper. "Tunafish, says so right here. Can't tell the players without a program."

"How was your weekend?" That question had been useful today — what could he ask people tomorrow?

Jerry pulled his chair closer, lowered his voice. "Last night was terrific! I was sauntering down Michigan Avenue about six-thirty, heading for one of those sandwich-and-jazz spots, when this woman I dated a couple of years ago walks by going the other way. Gorgeous. But I couldn't remember if I liked her or not. If I'd liked her, why hadn't I seen her again? She passed me without nodding and I thought, that's not Kelly after all. Then she stopped to look in the window of Marshall Field's, and I stopped, too, and she gave me this 'come here' gesture with her shoulder." Jerry demonstrated. It looked like a shrug to Will, but he nodded.

"I winked. She grinned like a little kid. Cute! I eased on back to her and said, 'I would really like to buy you a drink, Kelly.' So we had drinks, and, later, sandwiches. Then we went to her place and I got back to mine just in time to pick up the phone and come here to wire up the kid who'd hit the tree."

"Six hours in her apartment?"

"Of course we weren't screwing all that time. First we danced, and later I found the right covers for all her records and repaired the light switch in her bathroom. But the rest of the time . . ." Jerry put down his sandwich crust and started in on his ice cream. He liked to say he'd never let a woman down.

"The life of a bachelor." Will tried for a casual tone. More than anything else he didn't want to think about what Jerry called "screwing." He'd got through the morning by letting only the smallest edge of his feelings for Jo surface. He didn't think any graphic details of Jerry's lovemaking — if he chose to offer any — would help him. He tried for a variation on the theme. "Tell me, Jer, as a guy who plays the field, why do men go for some women and not others?" He wanted to say "love" but he was afraid to try the word out loud.

"Get us some coffee, and I'll give you a brief but thorough analysis."

Will took his dishes to the kitchen window and got two cups of coffee, black for himself, cream in Jerry's. His hands weren't shaking at all now, and he quickly calculated how long it would be before the Valium wore off. He should save it for operating until he was sure of himself, but he might need something to help him through the dinner hour. Would Jo be home for supper? Sometimes she ate at the college or at a friend's. It would be a good idea to try to carry on a normal conversation with Laura before he saw Jo, especially since they'd fought last night. He'd have to think it all through. He felt like a man who's been blind in one eye, but getting along pretty well until all of a sudden he's smashed in the good eye.

He set the coffee cups on the table and slumped back down across from Jerry, who was licking chocolate from his plastic spoon. In the border of his white chest hair a heavy, square-linked gold chain showed above his scrub shirt.

"My friend," Jerry said gently, "you have a nervous tic in your right eye. Stress? What's on your mind? Trouble right here in River City?"

"Just talk to me for a while, Jer. Give me the lowdown on the male and female of the species."

"And you'll talk to me if you want to?"

"Sure thing." Knowing he never would.

"You ought to have more fun, William. *Do* you have fun? Carefree moments?" Jerry's tone was halfway between buddy and father.

"Sure." Wondering what his carefree moments might be. If Jerry pushed, he'd say running.

"The steady joys of married life?"

"Whatever."

"You look like a man with a pain in his ass."

"The great diagnostician."

"Get off it, Will. You have a fight with Laura?"

He nodded — that was an easy way out. "How'd you guess?"

"I remember the pain in *my* ass. Diane and I used to tear up the condo on weekends, with regularity, especially toward the end. Too much to drink, tired, trapped, I guess. My life's been a lot more pain-free since the divorce. Not that I recommend such action." He tasted his coffee, grimaced. "You two doing okay?"

"Except for a fight now and then. That's normal. We're doing okay." He wanted to smile for emphasis, but that was impossible. He took a drink of his coffee instead. "You aren't giving me the analysis." He couldn't talk about himself and Laura, and it would only take Jerry a couple more questions to find that out.

Jerry cleared his throat. "Okay, take notes. And remember there are lots of individual variations in sexual attraction, and we mustn't forget to include those. That's the very basis of the scientific method. But I'll give you an overview."

Will wanted to fold his arms and put his head down. "Go on."

Jerry leaned back, hefted his feet onto an empty chair. "Men love women because women are beautiful. Women love men because men have power. This is axiomatic and amply demonstrated by, say, the alliance of Jackie and Ari."

Will took another sip of coffee and congratulated himself: Jerry had said "love" twice and he hadn't flinched. But of course Jerry wasn't talking about *love*.

"Let's start with beauty. Men are drawn to physical beauty because this is the proper quality for primary attraction — that's Aristotelian. Of course what's considered beautiful changes with trends, and also with how much booze has been consumed. There's also the compelling attraction of opposites. Wasp men with pale body hair find women with black hair and dark eyes beautiful. Swarthy, greasy Mediterranean types like myself get it on for blondes. You're an aberration, Will. You're basically a

Scotch-Irish-English type, but you married a blonde. Maybe you married the wrong woman, have you thought of that?"

He looked down into his cup. "How about the power thing?"

"Women love men with power because women have so little power themselves. If this situation ever reverses itself, then power won't count for so much. But even with women's lib I'd give power another few thousand years, minimum, on men's side."

"Pretty standard stuff. Somehow I hoped for something more insightful after six hours in Kerry's arms."

"*Kelly*. You're right, William. I'm your mentor, am I not? Haven't I been assigned the task of guiding you safely through the Highland Park vale of tears?" His feet came down and his chair legs slammed the floor. "What I'm saying is true, but it doesn't mean shit. And the bit with Kelly wasn't all that great, either. Maybe that brutally honest confession on my part will help your nervous tic." He looked up at Will from under his heavy black brows. "And of course I know that both beauty and power are in the eye of the beholder. The actual size of her tits or his bankroll don't have much to do with it, if that's how you were going to attack my theory. It's all in the mind. *And* you know all this!" He threw up his hands.

Good old Jerry. Yes, he knew all that, and he was only half-listening anyway because he wanted a few minutes alone to think about Jo. Not the problem of loving her, just the girl herself. The *girl*. Remember that. But to keep the ball in play, Will said, "I liked your dramatic monologue."

"I also perform at bar mitzvahs." He reached to grab Will's forearm, one of Jerry's versions of a hug. "Walk me home, honey?" The signal for Let's get out of here.

On the way to the elevator Jerry talked about bike racing. Will didn't bother to respond and Jerry clearly didn't expect him to. When Jerry punched four, Will asked, "See you at the office later?"

"The usual." Then as Jerry stepped through the elevator doors he swung around, made a clown face—corners of his mouth turned down, eyebrows lifted. "Hey, I forgot to tell you that Kelly couldn't remember my name. She called me Gary.

How are the mighty fallen." The chrome doors closed and he was gone.

H*er hands laced around my neck. The pressure of her breasts against me when I steady her.* As Will headed across town to his appointments at the clinic he said her name out loud—it sent warmth down into his chest. Jerry's banter about sexual attraction prompted him to wonder whether he would desire her if he didn't love her. Would he be attracted to her? Certainly he'd registered her as a woman—the vision of her, nude, in Vienna sealed that. But now it was impossible to separate any response to her physical being from his response to her as a person, and there was just the one feeling: love.

He imagined her again as she was yesterday—just yesterday—on the bench beside him in the smoky evening. In spite of the smears of clay on her hands and face, his primary sensation of her was of her cleanness: clean Levi's, though spattered; under her sweatshirt a clean blue shirt. Clean cotton bra.

He visualized her hands, fingernails clipped to the quick, her left index finger circled with a silver ring set with a carnelian chip. She wore a Timex, having refused the gift of a Swiss watch because if it was a good one she'd have to worry about it. She didn't like worrying about *things,* she said; it was all right to worry about people.

Her knees were crisscrossed with roller-skating scars. A hairline scar traced the curve of her lower lip, just below the rim. When she was first learning to ride her bike, at the age of seven, she told him, she'd plunged through the Millets' hedge. Estelle didn't think the cut looked deep enough for stitches.

Because of her widow's peak her hair wouldn't part in the center. It was her nervous habit to push her bangs to the side as she talked.

What else? Last summer she wore a yellow bikini with a wooden ring fastening the two triangles of the bra. The skimpy bikini bottom gave him a close look at her minutely skewed lower spine. Its tipped curvature thrust her stomach out very slightly, and very slightly emphasized and raised her buttocks. Just above the upper edge of the bikini panties, in the depression between the roundness of her cheeks, he spotted the two out-of-line vertebrae. But why was it that until this moment, driving down Greenbay Road, he hadn't allowed himself to admit how very, very badly he wanted to kiss that secret place where her spine dipped?

He wanted to make love to her because he loved *her,* not just her body. In fact, he could no longer imagine making love to a woman for whom he didn't have some love. He'd gone past those other days. Just last week, picking up a copy of a magazine at a newsstand, he saw a photo of some celebrity with his arms around attractive twins whose long hair had been artfully arranged to cover their breasts—the guy was dresssed, the girls were nude. Apparently the guy made it with twins—somebody's fantasy, but not Will's. Jerry would call him prehistoric, a moral dinosaur, but love and sex were bound together for him now. That's how it was; that was his character, though *character* was an outmoded term. If you try to go against your character you go crazy—though no psychologist he knew would put it that way.

Another fear—if he loved Jo, *could* he go on making love to Laura?

And how the hell could he ever make love to Jo? Ever in his *lifetime?*

Sex and love hadn't always been joined for him, of course. He remembered that after Helen LaFleur there were several nurses, a dental technician, an eighth-grade teacher who'd recently been divorced. And then Laura. Even with Laura there had been a time when he'd easily imagined screwing other women. Those fantasies began shortly after they were married—that they came so early in their marriage was the most troubling part—but he'd never acted on those impulses. Laura was in her most frantic period of wanting to conceive a child then. For two, maybe three years, each time they made love he imagined her focusing on his semen as though it was the very essence of their marriage. Legs wrapped around his waist, arms gripping his shoulders, breathless with effort, she seemed to be willing her womb to open and his sperm to enter. Afterward, she'd lie for half an hour with her hips elevated on a pillow; her doctor had suggested this.

During that time Will looked at other women and imagined fucking them mindlessly, with no thought of names and certainly not of outcomes, handing them rubbers to unroll over his cock. His throat grew thick, wanting that. He remembered watching a young woman cross in front of his car as he drove home one day—a woman not so different from Laura. Tanned arms, tanned legs, beads of sweat showing between her breasts in her white V-neck shirt, her sandals slapping as she ran. But a woman he didn't know, would never see again. "Split her and screw her," he whispered to himself. And he was ashamed.

Of course he never spoke of this to Laura. After a while, when she gave up trying to conceive, and their loving became less earnest, he was content. What he had was enough. Often now he didn't particularly want to make love at all, but they were in a couple-of-times-a-week pattern that would require explanation to change. He'd have to try to stay in that pattern, now. He had to keep things as they were. Oh, God. *Jo.*

When he got home for supper her bike wasn't there. He was more disappointed than relieved, but he guessed it was probably a lucky break. He had to straighten things out with Laura. He owed her that.

But Laura—instead of the sullen and withdrawn frowns she often had after a fight—smiled him a hello. She wore a blue sweater he'd never seen before. The kitchen smelled of yeast and onions.

"Hi, honey," she said. "Brisket tonight." His favorite.

Will sank down on the kitchen bench. He'd decided to apologize as quickly as possible, but she'd beaten him to it. He pushed on anyway. "I'm sorry about last night." It was a line he'd rehearsed, and it surprised him that it sounded so sincere. But then why shouldn't it? He *was* sorry, desperately sorry. "I don't know what was wrong with me." Of course that part was a lie.

She turned from the stove and gave him a nod of understanding. "You were jealous."

He looked down at his clasped hands. "I guess."

"I don't blame you. After I thought about the way I behaved, practically fawning on Thomas, all that schoolgirl giggling, I understood your reaction. I guess I made a fool of myself." She came to stand in front of him, hands on her hips, looking not at all like a woman who thinks she's made a fool of herself.

Why was she making it so easy for him? "You looked good last night. And why wouldn't you be pleased to have all that attention? He even gave you that headdress. But he better keep his hands off you." He added that to support her version of his jealousy. "And I don't think he's good for Jo." He couldn't *help* adding that.

"He's terrible for Jo," she agreed quickly. "He's much too old and there's something sneaky about him." She pushed her hair behind her shoulders. "He's not all that attractive, either."

He leaned back, feeling very, very tired. "We're okay, then?" He wanted to fix himself a drink, a lot of Seagram's and very little seltzer; he wanted a shower.

"We're fine." She bent to peer into the oven at the brisket. Her jeans were new, too, with someone's name on the back pocket. "Boiled potatoes, or mashed? We can defy tradition if you'd like mashed."

"Yes, the hell with tradition. Mashed would be great." He stood wearily, reached the whiskey down from the cupboard over the refrigerator. So far, so good. As though he'd just thought of her, he asked, "When's Jo getting home?"

"Not for days," Laura said over the *whirr* of the electric mixer she'd already thrust into the pan of potatoes.

His chest tightened. "Days?"

"All the townies at Woodcliff are spending the week in the dorms to get to know the residential students. They're supposed to be integrated into the community and all that. They even have to go to mass each morning. Jo will hate that. But she said she'd have more time to work in the ceramics studio. That and her photographs are big for her right now. She'll be back on Friday in time for supper."

He wouldn't see her for four nights, then. A furrow of pain stretched under his ribs. "How was she doing this morning?"

"Hungover."

"Does she want us to call?"

"She says she doesn't want *anyone* to call. Especially Thomas. After we left they had a fight or something—she wouldn't say." She eyed the drink he was pouring. "So much?"

"It was a tough day." Then, without thinking, he took a chance he hadn't planned. "How about a quickie before supper, then? Since we're alone."

It was his good faith gesture because she'd helped him make up with her when he needed her to, and he hoped it would go all right. He also hoped she might refuse—she hated having her dinner plans changed. Anyway, he'd offered.

To his surprise she wrapped her arms around his neck. "Hey, there!" Her voice was as determinedly friendly as his. Efficiently, she unzipped her jeans and slipped down her nylon panties. "Downstairs? We haven't done that for ages, and we don't have to worry about Jo walking in on us."

He was afraid to try it without a drink first. "Let me get a quick shower. I stink."

"I like your sweat." She stepped out of both jeans and panties.

Why was she so cooperative? "Just be in my bed when I get out of the shower." He patted her slim ass as she passed him up the back stairs. He'd do his best; he wanted to make things right. He even detected a stirring of sexual anticipation that he wouldn't have guessed was possible. And the smallest streak of joy, connected somehow with that new power. Along with love and guilt and fear, the feeling of power, wholly irrational, was there: that he had it *in* him to fall in love.

12

Laura memorized both of the letters Thomas had written to Jo, and the poem he'd marked in the Sappho. She memorized them so that they'd be hers. She even called them *her* letters, meaning letters he'd written to her. They certainly weren't *Jo's* letters— they had nothing to do with Jo at all. Really, they were letters which Thomas had written to himself, talking to himself—and Laura had happened to overhear. And to understand, oh, yes, understand what he said as though she'd spoken the words herself. Now she wanted to talk to him about what he'd written. Meaning, she wanted to talk to him about who he was.

Meaning, she wanted to talk to him about who *she* was, because he would understand her. There wasn't a single thing she could tell him that he wouldn't understand, because he was as crazy as she, or she was as crazy as he. Or, neither of them was crazy at all. He'd say, Every fucking one of us is crazy as a loon and the only hope for sanity is to recognize that.

It was sheer luck that she found the first letter. An accident, Will would say, in his pragmatic way. She'd say, fate. She was fated to find that letter. Sooner or later she had to meet up with a message that would make some sense to her, and Thomas's letter made sense. It was like news from the homeland, a sheet of paper crumpled and greasy, carried thousands of miles wrapped in a handkerchief, unfolded finally and bearing words in a language she'd always imagined existed somewhere. But not here. Sooner or later she was fated to find real words, not the everything-will-be-all-right tape that Will played or the let's-pretend tapes that most people played.

It didn't seem like a time when fate might help her out. She'd come downstairs on the morning after the log-burning with her senses still thick and deadened from the stuff she'd taken to get to sleep. At bedtime she and Will had fought horribly about Thomas. Will accused her of inviting him, then encouraging him; of course she'd denied it. Then they'd gone on fighting because they were both so angry about everything—*every-thing*—things that couldn't be named, so she accused him of ignoring her and he accused her of suffocating him. The usual. From their window, as Will was berating her, she saw Thomas heading up the street in the smoky night, hands under his arms, shoulders bent, collar turned up. Later, she heard Jo come in, bumping into things, drunk, maybe; maybe stoned. Unhappy. There was no way to make anything better, so Laura took her sleeping pill and buried her face in her pillow. The Dalmane did its potent work of tying her down into sleep and letting her forget everything she ever knew. Especially her dreams. It kept her asleep until after Will left in the morning.

Holding the wall so she'd walk straight, she came down the back staircase into the clean, quiet kitchen. She set the alarm on the oven to ring at quarter to eight so she'd be sure to wake Jo, who would have to have a ride up to her college—with all the gear she needed to stay there for a few days. Laura put water on for coffee and picked up Jo's windbreaker from the counter. Jo left her things everywhere; Laura piled them on the stairs for her and everyone tripped on them. She shook the twigs and sand from the jacket into the wastebasket and an envelope fell out of the pocket.

Crumpled slightly. Airmail weight, but no stamp. No address. Sealed. Of course it would be from Thomas.

Sealed. That meant Jo hadn't wanted to read it, or that he'd slipped it into her pocket and she hadn't found it yet. Sneaking it into her life was certainly his style, but Laura guessed that if Jo knew it were there she'd either have read it from curiosity or

torn it to bits from anger. Or read it and *then* torn it to bits.
Laura held the envelope over the steaming kettle. It was just
like those English spy movies. The flap curled up like a flower
petal. She decided to read it, then to glue the flap again, put it
back into the jacket pocket and things would move right along,
the only difference being that she'd know a little more than she
had before. The other funny thing—besides that spy technique
of opening it—was that she imagined he'd written Jo a proposi-
tion, Meet me at such-and-such and don't let anyone know.
Playing the bad boy.

But his letter was in dead earnest.

Two pages typed with a manual typewriter on airmail stationery. She spread the sheets out on the counter and leaned down
to read, her chin in her hands. She didn't want to handle the
tissue too much—she was still playing the spy game.

Dear Jo,

A long time ago there was a guy who loved me. I didn't
know he loved me and he didn't know either, though later we
both knew. Before we knew, he asked me to come home with
him to his family's house in Atlanta. It was spring break at
Princeton; he wanted to go white-water canoeing, wanted to
take me with him. He was an expert, he said. He didn't say
that to brag, or even with any special pride. He just said how
things were—good or bad—about himself as easily as about
another. He said about himself once, My trouble is that I lay
everything on the line when I should hold back. That was
before he knew he loved me, but he was right about himself.
He said about me, Your trouble is that you'll always be afraid
of the wrong things. Now I'm afraid of *you,* Jo. Believe me?

I was afraid of the white-water canoeing. In Atlanta we got
up before dawn and drove fifty miles upstream to a put-in on
the Nantahala. The rapids start right away, he said. He was
excited, a big, redheaded guy with freckles. He laughed a lot
and told me jokes about accidents he'd been in. The closer we
got to the put-in the more frightened I was.

The morning was warm, but where the river bursts through
the dam it comes out like ice—forty degrees, fifty, maybe. I

gasped when I put my hand in. He talked about hypothermia as we climbed into our wet suits, paddling vests, helmets, knee pads. We're monsters, I said. I am, he said; you're just a skinny guy in a wet suit.

Even though I hadn't been able to eat breakfast, I threw up. He did, too, but he said he was glad we were scared. That was part of it. He wanted us to have it all, he said.

The first rapids seemed like tidal waves to me. Paddle! he yelled. He yelled other things and I tried—Draw toward the shore! Pry back! The river wrapped itself around us, water over and under. We hurtled down. The last rapids were the worst. Our canoe slammed sideways against some boulders and we came down that way because I wasn't strong enough to push us around. Water flooded the canoe, our noses, our mouths. I felt my pulse stutter from the cold. But he didn't let us turn over. I was right to trust him. I'd have been right to go on trusting him.

Why am I telling you this? Because I'm going to see you in a day or two and I'm frightened. Something dangerous is about to happen and I want you to trust me. I want to trust myself. I've gone too far to make it without the risk of trying to know you. To let myself be known. I am so fucking lonely.

That guy? His name was Lucian, a family name, but he was called Luke. Luke Monroe. He's dead now. But you and I are alive.

Thomas

Laura whispered his name as she folded the pages, put them into her robe pocket, made the coffee. Then she unfolded the letter and read it again. How many times? She stopped counting at four. She felt as though he were calling to her from across a canyon. She could barely see him on the other side, but his words came to her on an updraft, as clearly as if he were beside her. He wasn't calling Jo. Jo wouldn't understand him, couldn't understand him. That stricken way he'd walked off last night told Laura that much. He'd blown it with her.

Whether he knew it or not, Thomas was calling out to *her*. Because she could understand. She knew the white-water fear and the desperate need to *do* it. She knew the loneliness. She imagined talking to Thomas, just the way he spoke in his letter; "A long time ago a woman loved me," she'd begin. "She was my mother and—" Then the alarm went off and she went to waken Jo.

She didn't give Jo the letter. If Jo did know it had been in her pocket she'd think she lost it in the park. If she didn't know Thomas had put it there, she wouldn't miss it. Laura wanted it, the thing itself—his distress signal, Mayday.

Fate. Would he mind that word? She used words like that to herself: destiny, existence, truth, karma, fate. She'd never used those words with Will. He was the original Rational Man. If he couldn't see it, hold it, turn it over in his hands, he didn't believe a thing existed. He didn't believe, for example, in love. He believed in care. Care was a matter of evidence; love, a mystery. Will didn't like mysteries. Thomas had guessed that about him. That was why his message for Will was so accurate: Hold on, there is more. There is so *much* more that Will would never allow himself to discover. But she didn't want to think about Will and his heavy ways.

She found herself thinking of a cave she'd visited once with her mother and father—a cold stream ran through it, icy, like the one Thomas had described. She must have been ten or eleven. They'd been on vacation. She remembered an elevator down into the cave, rickety steel creaking down a poured concrete shaft. At the bottom a single trail led off into the dark, and their group followed a guide who held a lantern aloft. Yellow light glittered on the secret stream beside the trail. Their shadows wavered and fled from them across the water. All around quartz sparkled in the cracks and fissures of the limestone rooms.

Then Momma became hysterical. She cried that there was no way out. She was so frightened that she fell to her knees. Is she scared of the dark? the guide asked Daddy. They got her to the elevator. Let me out! she cried. When they reached the surface Daddy made her lie down on the front seat of the Ford and later he held an Orange Crush to her lips. I couldn't breathe down there, she said. I knew I'd never get out alive. I'd never get back!

Momma was right. There is no way back, and everything

waits in the dark. Thomas knows that. He knows how the dark swallows everything light and hopeful, like a huge mouth that eats up consciousness and plunges you into a black cave. Which is why she didn't want to dream, ever. In her dreams it was she who was devoured.

That night, when Will came home, she had brisket and Parker House rolls for him. She smiled at him and ignored him and his clumsy, predictable loving—she concentrated on Thomas's intimate confession, "I am so fucking lonely."

"Fucking"—the ultimate modifier. Your fucking letter is mine, Thomas.

Two days later his second letter arrived, and the little book. The letter was delivered first, sailing through the mail-slot onto the floor beside the usual catalogues and bills. Airmail stationery again, addressed this time in an elegant cursive. Blue ink. With Jo gone for the week, Laura didn't bother to steam open the envelope; instead, she slit it with the paring knife. The letter belonged to her; she could do anything she wished with it. She'd make Thomas understand when they talked.

Typed again, a new ribbon.

Dear Jo,

I think it was you I dreamed about last night. Shall I tell you my dream? I was in a desert, sleeping on my side, wrapped in a blanket. It was that kind of bright blue night that Metro-Goldwyn-Mayer creates with a blue filter over the camera lens. I could see clearly.

As I slept a naked angel came to me, the way an angel came to wrestle with Jacob. She was small and muscular, like a Russian gymnast, her long, black hair braided. She strode to me and put her bare foot on the edge of my blanket. I knew we must fight. I wasn't afraid, in fact, I welcomed the wrestling match. I threw off my blanket so I was as naked as she. I put my arm over her back, seized her wrists. Already I tasted victory.

But like a snake she uncoiled from under my arm, and spun me over onto the stones. My head hit, my back, her knees pinned my arms. She'd won, of course she'd won. Angels don't lose matches with mortals—the Bible's got all the scores.

But Jo, dear Jo, between us there can be no contest because no one can win. There's only the chance to experience our own lives. That's all. There can be no more games, no trials, no exhibitions, no tournaments, no more costumes or masks. I am speaking of my sanity. I am speaking of my life. Please understand me.

Somehow I got it wrong with you. You didn't hear me. You aren't hearing me now. You ran from me because you were afraid. I understand that. I've done the same. But you don't need to be afraid. And I need you. You are the only way out from under this blanket of despair that covers me. Beauty and the Beast—I'm the poor beast. Read your fairy tales, *ma petite,* before it's too late.

Do I dare to write love,

Thomas

When the doorbell rang and Daisy set up her commotion, Laura started from her chair, confused. As she read the letter over she'd forgotten for a few moments where she was. The UPS man was at the door with a delivery. Laura signed for the box, and took it into the kitchen.

She eased the tape off the end; she might need to seal it again. She wasn't sure. She wasn't sure of anything except that she wanted whatever Thomas would bring into her life.

"My life." The echo of her words in the kitchen made her smile. As if her life had some sort of coherence, a straight line leading toward some fixed point on the horizon. Actually, her life had been more like being trapped inside a pinball machine—bounced around, flippers knocking her back and forth, signals going off, a bell, then through the gate at the bottom and silence. And nothing to add up on the board, no big numbers, no free games.

She was a good pinball player—she'd tell that to Thomas and he'd smile with her at the irony. The guy she went with before she went with Will was an obsessive player, and he'd taught her. They used to cut their classes sometimes to play pinball at the

Union. They'd spent whole evenings at the Game Shack, drinking beer and playing pinball. And balling—his word—later, at his place. Actually, it was the same thing—erratic, random flashes of green and blue electricity, red neon traveling down to the base of her spine and curving up inside. Sometimes a shock of white at the back of her throat, and swallowing fast.

She and Will never talked about that guy. Will said he didn't care about anyone in her "past," as he referred to her college life. He meant he didn't want to go into detail about the women he'd known, and there had been a lot of women. Will's position on the past was reasonable, logical, sound, mature. What had gone before was over for them both. Except, as Thomas knew, nothing was ever over, ever completely over. The past hung in lunar balance like a tide that could sweep back in across the sand and carry them all with it.

When she opened the package she found a delicate gold bracelet wrapped in tissue, and an old paperback of Sappho's poems.

She put the bracelet on. The snaky links caressed her wrist as she looked over the book, playing spy again. *Sappho, A New Translation,* by Mary Barnard, 1965. The book looked even older than that—yellowed, cover loose, the edge bashed in as though it had been jammed into a box. Why would he send Jo a used book? A penciled name had been erased from inside the front cover. None of the pages was turned down, nor was there a bit of paper to mark a place. But in the index, a penciled check-mark at page 39.

> *He is more than a hero*
>
> *He is a god in my eyes—*
> *the man who is allowed*
> *to sit beside you—he*
>
> *who listens intimately*
> *to the sweet murmur of*
> *your voice, the enticing*
>
> *laughter that makes my own*
> *heart beat fast. If I meet*
> *you suddenly, I can't*

speak—my tongue is broken;
a thin flame runs under
my skin; seeing nothing,

hearing only my own ears
drumming, I drip with sweat;
trembling shakes my body

and I turn paler than
dry grass. At such times
death isn't far from me

Reading the poem, she heard it as if in Thomas's voice. She shivered. She'd never felt intense sexual passion, but she imagined this was how it would be—"a thin flame runs under my skin . . . trembling shakes my body."

Upstairs, she slipped the bracelet into her jewelry box, closed the box with the letters tucked inside the book, and hid it in her safest place, the old hatbox on the back of the closet shelf where she kept some of her mother's things. Right beside the Indian headdress.

After she got dinner started she walked out onto the screened porch. The weather had changed; the day was autumnal, chill and overcast. Wasps droned under the porch eaves, leaves flicked against the screen. She heard each sound separately, just as she smelled, singly, the yellowed ferns, the boxwoods, the juniper bushes. Her senses were as alert as if she were being tortured. Or loved. She sat in the hammock and watched the cirrus clouds move over the pale sun like a veil.

She would get in touch with Thomas, of course. Talk to him. He was in desperate trouble and he didn't know it. He was writing about death. Both letters spoke of it, and the poem as well. Not love, not naked knowing, not sharing. Only death.

She knew this because she'd discovered that same heightened world he described when she realized she could let herself die. Not kill herself, nothing violent and bloody. Just choose to unclench her hands and let her life slip through. She was only fourteen when she realized that possibility.

When she was fourteen not a soul in the world would even have cared. Momma was gone. Daddy wouldn't have noticed for more than a day. As long as Estelle had Jo, she didn't want anyone else. Laura was dying, then, and she knew she *could*. How easy it would have been. It didn't seem right to her that a fourteen-year-old should know how to die, wanted that knowledge, and that no one would care.

Apparently *she* cared, though. Here she was. Apparently she'd chosen not to die. As Will often said, Examine the facts. She knew how but she didn't do it. Why not? She'd come up out of the cave, that was all. She could imagine herself so clearly as bones strewn around a cave floor, but her bones had tightened and straightened. She rose and walked.

Why had she gone to all that trouble to live? She supposed she must have hoped that something might happen. She might grow up and fall in love. She might find someone who would make her life worth living.

How humorous that she'd once thought Will would make her life worth living. She'd thought she couldn't live without him. After all, she and Will were strangers to each other. They'd always been strangers. There was no way to draw closer to him, and now she didn't want to. He wanted to "fix" her, that was it. That was all.

No, the only reason for staying around is for your own self— no man, no child makes life worth living. Sometimes she hated herself, but she was all she had. She knew a better way to live than she was able to live, that was the thing. Her helplessness in the grip of her compulsions disgusted her. Again and again she let herself down. No one but herself.

As Thomas had become his own enemy. But why was he confessing that to Jo? She would be no help to him at all. The more she understood what he was saying the more she'd abhor him. Of course she'd be frightened. Of course she'd feel burdened by his outpourings. She didn't *know*. Thomas had made a terrible choice of confidante, but Laura could help there, as well. If she intercepted these messages she could both protect Jo and give Thomas the real emotional intimacy he was looking for.

She knew a few things that might lend comfort to his life, and her own. And if she couldn't stand her life any more she knew how to call it quits.

The thing about Thomas was that he made her want to stick around. Not that she'd been thinking of calling it quits lately, because she hadn't. No more than usual, anyway. But if she could make contact with Thomas she'd have an anchor, a reality. He'd understand her. Although no one else needed her, Thomas did. She could love him for that.

13

Kit sat on the kitchen counter behind Jo, who was doing the dishes. With the edge of the longest blade of his pocket knife he lifted and smoothed the bleached hairs on his wrist. He'd arrived, unexpectedly, just as she and Laura and Will were sitting down to Laura's stir-fried chicken—Jo's welcome-home dinner after her get-acquainted week at Woodcliff. Of course Laura had insisted that Kit eat with them—she loved feeding everyone but herself. She jumped up and got him a plate, a glass for milk, and a wine glass for some Vouvray—all very classy. During dinner she'd kept asking him questions about his college, his new apartment, about his job loading packages for UPS, her gaze fixed on him as though Kit were the most interesting man in the world. He loved her attention, of course. Will ate quickly and nervously, his brow furrowed as though he had a headache. Jo was too tired to be very hungry. She hadn't slept well this week. The dorm was noisy and it was drafty on the floor in her sleeping bag. Tonight she wanted more than anything to be alone. But when Laura and Will went off to the theater, Kit hung around. He thought he had rights.

"How was the retreat?" he asked.

"It wasn't a retreat, I told you that. It was get-acquainted time for the day students." She wiped out the wok with paper towels.

"You said you had silent meditation. That sounds like a retreat to me."

"It wasn't meditation like prayer. We were supposed to think about our college goals. I don't have any, I discovered." The truth was that the guitar music a nun had played during Vespers each evening had made Jo's throat ache, as though she were about to cry, but she didn't feel like telling Kit that. He was acting as though the whole damn religion was *his*. She nudged his dangling leg so he'd move out of the way of the wastebasket beneath the counter, and tossed in the greasy towels. "Look, you could help. Put the silverware in the washer, okay?"

He slid off the counter and stood beside her. He smelled good, that clean soap smell of his. His leg brushed hers, their shoulders rubbed. After all, she was glad he was here.

"They sure had you locked up," he said. "You told me not to call."

"Not calling in was one of the rules." That was a lie; she hadn't wanted to talk to him. Last Sunday, after she'd run to him across the park, they'd driven around, fast, as she'd wanted to do. Then he'd brought her right home, although she'd suggested they stop at Albrect Park for a while. He was pissed because she'd said a guy had made a move on her, as though she'd wanted that. Had she? Maybe. Certainly she'd been curious. All week she'd tried to decide if she'd led Thomas on. There wasn't an easy answer to that, but no matter how she thought things through, Thomas came out as a bastard. A voyeur, for God's sake, a pervert. Anyway, he was out of her life now. And here was dependable Kit. She sighed, and tucked a strand of hair behind her ears.

"I thought about you. I worried about you," Kit said, stuffing a handful of forks into the washer.

"Worried?"

"Sure. No law against that, is there?"

She leaned against the counter and took a good look at him. His eyelids were reddened, his lips dry and pale. He looked as if he wasn't getting enough sleep—his UPS job and school and his activities with his roommate, Mike, added up to a lot of hours. Well, she knew how Kit felt. Her legs were rubbery with fatigue. At Woodcliff she'd never been alone for a moment, but she'd been lonely, though she didn't know for whom. Not for Kit, anyway, but she was glad he was looking at her like this, tenderly. A soft autumn rain streaked down the windowpanes behind his head.

"Is it okay there? At Woodcliff?" he said.

"I don't know yet." If she criticized the school, Kit might think she was criticizing Catholics. Actually, she'd decided she'd made a terrible mistake, but it was too late to do anything about it now. A girls' school—she must have been crazy. And the sisters had an earnest cheerfulness that made her uneasy. They were interested in her as a person, they assured her. She believed them. It made her tired. It was only in the ceramics studio that she was comfortable, or in the darkroom. When she was working with her hands she didn't think. Not thinking was becoming important.

She rinsed her hands, wiped them, and put her arms around Kit's neck. After a moment she felt his hand on her nape, stroking rhythmically, the way you stroke a puppy. He slid his other hand inside the waist of her jeans at the small of her back as she pressed against him. This was much better—she didn't want to talk. Words just dried things up. She wanted to be loved, instead.

It was good to kiss him, his soft lips and his swirly tongue. If he didn't have this thing about not making love, they could try it. She'd try anything with Kit—he wasn't the kind to have his own way. She could lead him along, tease him; she could be in charge. Already he was excited.

He pushed back against the counter to make a space between them. "Have you got some beers? Let's have one and play some tunes."

She took a deep breath. She didn't love him, but he had this queer way of making her want to cry. Maybe she was premenstrual or something.

She opened the refrigerator door. The bottles were beaded with moisture. Kit popped the caps and held one to her cheek like a gift—a cool, fresh touch. She bumped the door shut again with her shoulder.

"Mom's got this new piece of modern technology in our refrigerator now," he said. "It's this big cardboard carton with a plastic bag inside and a little spout like gallon milk dispensers have. But it holds wine. She can just open the door and refill her glass. Doesn't even have to tip a bottle." He took a swallow of beer as he put the last dish in the washer. "I wish I had a normal family like you do."

"Normal?"

"Like you guys eating supper tonight. That was normal. Everyone sitting down together."

"Kit, my folks are dead, I was raised by a hillbilly, I live with a sister who's probably certifiably insane, my brother-in-law goes to my PTA meetings and helps me with my homework. That's a normal family?"

"It feels normal around here."

"How does it feel at your place?"

"Weird. Mom doesn't talk sense once she starts on the sauce, and this lady who cooks for us leaves everything in the oven and we just wander in and eat whenever we're hungry. Janie eats standing up at the sink. She doesn't even make herself a plate and take it into the TV room like the rest of us. And she's only nine, for crying out loud. Lots of times Dad doesn't eat at all, he just zonks out in his study. Living with Mike is a lot better."

"You want *The Little House on the Prairie?*"

"I guess I do."

Sometimes she did, too. She reached for his hand, damp from the bottle, and he squeezed back.

"Like what do they bring you for a present when they've been away?" he asked.

She thought. Will and Laura practically never traveled together. Laura depended on her own routines, and Will didn't like to leave his practice for longer than a few days at a time. They'd planned a whole year ahead to go to Europe. But Laura and Will had been to Saint Louis for a long weekend last spring, when Dr. Perrone rented a riverboat for a party. "They brought me that orange nylon bag for my racquetball gear."

"That's what I mean! A normal gift, right? Well, I drove to O'Hare this afternoon to pick up my old man from a business trip, and when he got into the car he handed me this." He reached into his shirt pocket and held out what looked like a square of toffee wrapped in foil. "This is my homecoming present from the old man." He slapped the square down on the counter between them.

She touched it with her forefinger. "So?"

"It's not grass this time. It's hash."

"Hash?"

"Right. Now he's giving me hash. I'm wondering when he'll start laying crack on me."

The idea of turning on made her smile. God, it would be so good to get mellow after this awful week.

" 'It's great stuff,' the old man said. 'The top of the line. Have a good time, kiddo,' he said. 'You only go around once.' Like he'd just given me a Christmas stocking full of candy."

She picked up the square and sniffed.

"The top of the line," Kit repeated, shaking his head. "As though he was talking about stereos or cars."

She unwrapped the square. It looked like a piece of clay. "Let's try it. Do you know how?"

He looked at her, his tan fading and his freckles dark across his cheekbones and forehead. "My old man taught me how to ride my bike and to water-ski. Do you think he'd overlook an important life skill like doing hash?"

"We'll be alone here for at least three hours. Or, we could go to your apartment."

"Mike's studying tonight. He's not into drugs."

"Always Mike! We could just forget it," she said abruptly.

He took his pocket knife out again. "What the hell. Get a sewing needle, will you?"

When she came back to the kitchen with a needle from Laura's sewing basket, Kit had cut the Vouvray cork in half and positioned a piece on a saucer. He stuck the needle in the piece of cork, flicked off a tiny chip of the hash with the point of his knife, and stuck the chip on the point of the needle. The chip flared briefly when he held a match to it, then burned steadily. He turned a coffee cup over the burning chip and leaned back. "When I have kids of my own I'm going to be completely different from my old man."

"Pretend I bought this."

"You couldn't begin to afford it." He raised the cup a half inch and sniffed the smoke that curled under the rim.

"Good?"

"Try it." This time he tipped the cup over quickly, catching the smoke that had filled it, and held the cup to her.

The smoke eased into her lungs. She closed her eyes. For a moment she imagined sun glancing up off the lake on a spring day. The warmth melted her arms, her legs. "Excellent."

Kit took his turn from the cup.

"What do you think?" she asked.

"I think we'd better be careful. I've never had any this good. It'll knock us on our asses." He breathed in again, and smiled. "Here's to the old man. Excellent taste in the finer things in life." His smile went crooked.

But she saluted. Pleasantly dizzy, she smiled at her reflection in the darkened window over the sink.

She and Kit were lying side-by-side on the living room floor on a spot he'd judged to be in the exact center between the two stereo speakers. He'd made his calculations by stepping off the distance, then Jo had spread the blanket Laura kept on the couch. Lying on her back, holding Kit's hand, and listening to music felt good. The songs were all of love, hot and restless love, but this kind of closeness was good enough for now. She was high, and the floor under her drummed like a heartbeat, as though the house had a life of its own.

Kit had been quiet for a long time. Once he'd said, "Clapton was born to play that guitar. It kind of circulates inside your bones," and another time he'd said, "I should make a tape of this cut." Then she thought maybe he'd gone to sleep, because he didn't even squeeze back when she pressed his hand. Maybe she'd slept for a while, too.

But suddenly he was sitting up and looking down at her, his face so close his breath warmed her forehead. In the dim light from the kitchen she saw her own eyes reflected in his. "I forgot to ask," he said. "Who sent you the box?"

She tried to bring his face into focus, but he was too close. "What box?"

"The one that was delivered here on Wednesday."

"I wasn't here on Wednesday."

"I know that. But a package must have come for you. There I

was, loading junk onto the UPS truck Tuesday night, thinking about you, and there's your name on a package! It blew me away. Who was it from?"

"Nobody sends me packages. The only person who sends me stuff is Aunt Hattie. Last Christmas she sent me a little plastic reviewing stand with a place to put a tiny doll of each president of the United States. Each president was individually wrapped."

He shook her shoulder, lightly. "You didn't get the package?"

She closed her eyes. "No, no package." Then she opened them again. "How big was it?"

Kit's hands described a square. She'd thought for a moment it might be a big box, the kind that would hold clothes. Though who would send her clothes, or anything else for that matter? "If it came, I didn't get it."

"UPS doesn't lose packages."

"Maybe Laura forgot." Laura had picked her up from the dorm at four-thirty, they'd stopped at the Chocolate Shop to buy ice cream for dinner, then Jo had showered while Laura cut up veggies. Will had come home, and it was time for dinner. Laura had forgotten—she forgot about everything else when she concentrated on food.

Jo crawled to her knees, then to her feet, marveling at her good coordination and balance.

"Where are you going?"

"I'm going to write Laura a note, since you're so sure something came for me."

"You could just ask."

"I'll forget."

In the kitchen she printed *package?* in big block letters on the blackboard by the phone. After the word she drew a little smiling face, so Laura would know she wasn't mad. Then she wrote, *Kit loaded it,* as though an explanation were necessary.

Maybe Laura had put the package in Jo's room—though thinking in a straight line about the problem was difficult right now. She went up the back stairs, checked her room, and the spare room next to hers. Then she looked in the linen closet where Laura kept Christmas gifts, and on the chest of drawers in the room that had been Estelle's. Nothing. That left Laura

and Will's room. No packages. Jo peered into Laura's half of
the divided closet that she and Will shared. Nothing new except
the orange-and-red feathered Indian headdress Thomas had
brought to the bonfire. The headdress was on the highest shelf
with out-of-season shoes.

She'd wanted to try on that costume. She took the desk chair
into the closet, climbed up, and, stretching, just managed to
snag the headdress. She tugged it on and checked herself in the
mirror as she passed Will's dresser. The beaded headband set
off her dark eyes, her straight eyebrows. Even her short nose
looked exotic.

She ran down the front stairs, the headdress firmly in place.
Kit still lay on the floor, his eyes shut. In repose he looked older,
his face thin—a man. She stood at his feet.

"Kit?"

He opened his eyes and peered at her in the headdress.
"Wow! That's it, right?"

"I didn't find any package."

"Where did that Indian thing come from, then?"

"The guy gave it to Laura." She nudged Kit's ribs with her
bare toes. "Don't I look sexy?"

"What guy?" He folded his arms behind his head.

"The one who made a move on me last Sunday night."

Now Kit sat up, fast. "Him! Take the thing off."

"I like it."

"And you liked him, too, didn't you? Who is he?"

She kicked his thigh. "Nobody."

He caught her ankle. His grip hurt.

"He's just a creep."

"He messed with you, right?"

"No way. Not really."

"What did he do, anyway? What the hell did he do, that's
what I want to know. You came running out of the park like a
rapist was after you."

His grip on her ankle twisted skin and her balance faltered.
She took off the headdress, but the weight of the leather stayed
around her forehead like a band—her head ached. "He did
what guys do. *You* told me all about it." She shouldn't have
mentioned Thomas. That was dumb. She hated the man. He

was certainly no rival to Kit, but she didn't like Kit pushing her around as though she belonged to him.

She kicked him again and caught his shoulder. It felt good to kick him. Why was she so angry?

He got to his knees. "You let him—"

"He kissed me. He put his hand on my breast. I bit him, if you want to know!"

She slipped on the blanket and sat down hard, her back against the couch. He swatted her leg, sharply, to hurt, so she tried kicking him with both feet, but missed. He grasped her ankles again. Then he was crawling up over her, his hands on her knees, waist, breasts, shoulders. He was shaking her and kissing her at the same time. Her head hit the couch, his teeth cut against her cheekbone. He sat across her hips, his hands gripping her hair.

"If there's another guy, you've got to tell me!"

Before she could answer he shook her again, his mouth on hers, as though jealousy and anger and sex and dope had overloaded his circuits, too many messages registering. He wanted to hurt her and to love her at the same time.

She pried her head back. "Kit, it's okay!"

"I have feelings!"

Her teeth rattled when he shook her, but she put her arms around his waist and hung on. "Kit, it's okay. He's no one to me. No one. I'd tell you."

He pushed his face against her throat and after a moment crawled off and sat beside her, clutching her hands, stroking her hair, gentle again. "Oh, Jo, I'm so fucking sorry! What's the matter with me?"

"We're stoned, that's all. It's okay."

"It's not okay."

By staring steadily at the lighted kitchen doorway she managed to get the room to stop moving. She was so dizzy. Waylon Jennings was singing cowboy blues, and she held Kit's head against her shoulder. After a long time he said, "I'm so fucking stupid, that's what kills me. Just because he gave it to me I didn't have to get us wasted. I just wanted to be with you, that's all."

"I know. It's my fault." Though she didn't think it was her fault, really. Somehow Thomas was to blame. He was poison.

"No, *mine,*" he insisted, as though responsibility were something he owned. "I know better."

She closed her eyes, feeling sick at her stomach.

Then he was on his feet and pulling her up. "Jo, you should go to bed. You go to bed and I'll go home. Let's forget this scene, all right? Tomorrow we'll talk over everything."

In the kitchen he scrubbed out the cup and wrapped up the hash, put it in his pocket. "I could put this stuff down the disposal, but I think I'll give it back to Dad. It's a gesture."

The headdress in her lap, she sat on the windowseat, watching him clean up, put soap in the washer, turn it on. He took a handful of Oreos, gave her a couple, and she walked with him to the front door. A gust of rain blew across the porch, bringing the smell of wet leaves and fallen plums.

"Are you okay, Jo? Did I hurt you?"

"Mostly I'm tired."

"Are you angry with me?"

"It's natural to have feelings." She felt only a numb fatigue now, and wanted to crash on her bed. "We're tired, that's the main thing."

He kissed her hard, possessively, as if roughing her up had made her more precious to him. As if he hadn't known how much he felt for her until now. "I'll call in the morning, right?"

"Right."

He let go of her and the heat from his face went away. When she opened her eyes he was running across the front lawn in the rain, waving, as though he were leaving on a long journey.

Bed, now. But she still had a few things to do. She turned off the radio, straightened the couch pillows, folded the blanket, picked up the headdress again. Watching herself, she admired her poise; she was fine, just fine.

In Laura's closet she pushed the chair into the row of clothes that hung beneath the shelves. The headdress had been between an old hatbox and a pair of espadrilles. When she pushed it into place she knocked the shoes to the floor. Damn! She crawled down from the chair, groped behind the pants and skirts that held Laura's Ombre Rose, found the espadrilles. Back up on the chair she reached high to get the shoes in place, and this time knocked down the headdress. Lunging for it, she tipped the shelf, and the hatbox bounced off. It spilled a litter of photos, valentines, baby shoes, beads, gloves, dried corsages onto the closet floor. When she crouched to scoop up these old mementoes of Laura's, Jo found among them a box addressed to Ms. Jo Hale.

"Christ," she whispered. A red UPS stamp blurred in the right-hand corner, Tuesday's date on it. It was the package Kit spoke of, but what was it doing here? Why had Laura opened it and done this clumsy resealing job? Why had she hidden it? Bitch!

She cautiously layered everything back into the hatbox. Laura could invade any place in the house, but she'd be burned if she knew Jo had been in her private things. This time the shoes easily went back on the shelf, the headdress. She left room for the hatbox, and sat on the floor to open the package.

A box from Marshall Field's, and inside, a watermarked paperback of poetry. Slipped inside the cover of the book were two letters. Both were written to Jo, and they'd been opened, too. Damn her.

As she read them a buzz began in her head. The noise, like a hive of bees, almost drowned out her racing pulse. Letters from Thomas, horrible letters, really—whining, complaining, ominous, threatening. She leaned against the closet wall to get her breath. Oh, God, what did he want from her? What was he after?

He'd sent black messages. The world was more dangerous than she'd imagined: a man could attack a woman for no reason at all. In his smooth way, Thomas was a madman. It was as if he'd taken a photo of what he'd like a woman to be, untacked it from his wall, and pinned it right onto her forehead. Now she was his target. But he was writing to someone who didn't exist.

And Laura, what could she have been thinking of to take these things, to hide them? If she'd wanted to protect Jo, she would have thrown them away. Why would she want them? Sick, Laura was sick, too.

She and Will would be home from the theater soon. Any time

now. Jo closed the package carefully, like someone handling a bomb. She put the package into the hatbox, the hatbox onto the shelf. Done.

She scrubbed at her eyes with the back of her hands, drew her fingers through her hair. Her face felt thickened, numbed, as though she'd been given Novocain. She touched her lips but could scarcely feel the pressure.

Thomas was after her. What could she do?

In her own room she crawled beneath her quilt and blanket without undressing, pulled the pillow over her head. The sleep that pushed her under almost at once carried her down and down through a passage so narrow she could neither lift her head nor cry out.

14

The steady rain had plastered yellow maple leaves to the windshield, and before Will got in he scooped off a double handful. Their nutmeg scent stayed on his hands as he drove home from the clinic—he'd managed to finish his Saturday appointments before lunchtime. He'd told Jo he'd be back around noon so they could shop for her camera. Now he was early enough to be able to take her for a sandwich first. He hoped that was a good idea. Last night would have been a test of how he'd act with her, but Kit had come by. Laura did most of the talking, and maybe that was just as well. His throat had been tight. Trying to relax, he'd drunk too much wine. And how to get control over this ache in his chest?

Traffic was slow on Greenbay Road. At each intersection the curbs disappeared under lakes of rain where leaves blocked the drains. It had rained all night. He slept fitfully and wakened often to the beat of it on the porch roof. He got up once to check the windowsill; his hand came away damp, but he left the window open anyway. If Jo wakened, she'd hear the rain. Down the hall. Down the hall she slept under her orange and white quilt. After the play, he'd come upstairs before Laura, glanced into Jo's room. Only the crown of her head was visible above the quilt. He left her door ajar. She might call to him. Though that was wishful thinking.

Laura stayed up late. She was hyped from the play, she said.

She stayed downstairs to read. He was glad enough to have their room to himself. It was better to be alone. Much better.

Driving down Greenbay with Jo this afternoon, this dense, heavy rain would shut them in together.

When Laura went to her tennis doubles Thursday evening, he'd gone upstairs to sit in Jo's room. It was a reward to himself for not driving up to Woodcliff to look for her—an impulse he'd found very, very hard to resist. Soft evening light drained the colors from the oval braided rug by her bed, dimmed the orange squares in her quilt. He leaned in her doorway for a moment before he entered. He'd always liked her room—the sloped ceiling, low casement windows against which butternut branches scratched, the sliver of lake visible beyond the trees.

After a minute he sat down at her desk. A chipped Quimper bowl, one of its blue handles missing, was filled with safety pins, paperclips, pennies. On top of the coins rested a chestnut pip, its star markings black incisions in the brown surface. Once she'd told him the pip smelled like a cat; he sniffed, but the pip was too old to have kept a scent. A stack of colored folders held old high school assignments. On a few he recognized his own penciled corrections and math computations. Placed on top of a paperback Spanish dictionary was a red ceramic heart she'd made in sixth grade. She'd offered it to him once, making friends with him after he and Laura married and he'd moved in.

On the wall behind her desk Jo had hung a cork bulletin board. Snapshots of her friends overlapped into a confusion of colored squares. His heart sped up when he saw she'd tacked three new photos of herself there—black-and-white self-portraits. He unpinned them, snapped on the desk lamp and bent over the photos.

In the first she held the camera up to her eye. Behind her were reflected what looked like the stall doors in a bathroom. He guessed she'd gone to the first mirror she could find when she'd got the idea to photograph herself. Her exposed eye was closed; she was seeing only through the lens.

She must have thought about that closed eye, for in the next one she'd opened it. Her eyebrow was raised with the effort and her face still halved by the line of her camera.

But the third picture. He leaned closer. She'd shifted her camera to rest it against her cheek, and the whole of her face was visible. In the soft, even light her face was without shadow. From the bandanna tied around her head, a tendril of dark hair escaped and followed the line of her narrow chin. Her mouth was set in concentration, but her upper lip curved slightly, as though she were amused by her efforts. Her eyes looked directly into his. She'd focused so precisely that when he touched the photo he imagined he could feel the texture of her skin.

He looked at the photo for a long time. He even considered taking it. God, he wished she were here. Right now. Just that. That was all he wanted.

At least he'd been trying to convince himself that was all he wanted. All over the world men rushed to meet their lovers, and here he was, filled with guilt because he loved a girl to whom he would never even speak of his love. It wasn't fair, but that's how he was. He'd dropped out of med school when his anxiety became too much for him, but he couldn't just "drop out" of his marriage. He was married to a woman who depended on him for her very survival. Jo was only eighteen—remember that— and Laura's sister. Nothing could be done. There was no future to hope for. There was only the present, and in the present it was his job to watch out for them all. Among other things, that meant that he mustn't do anything for which he'd feel guilty.

Not even take the photo of her. He pinned it back up on her bulletin board, and went downstairs to try to read until Laura got back from tennis.

At eleven-forty-five he pulled up behind their garage. A silver line of rain streamed off the roof and onto the stepping-stones to the back gate. He turned up his raincoat collar and ran to the house.

At the back door he saw Jo sitting at the breakfast table. She wore a red sweater, her hair pulled up in a twist at the back of her head. When he came into the hall, she stood up. He stamped water from his shoes, shrugged out of his raincoat and dropped it onto a hook.

"Hello!" Too loud.

"Hey, Will." He could hardly hear her.

"It's raining." He pointed to the puddle forming beneath his raincoat as if that were the only proof.

"Yes." She hugged herself and sat down.

"Are you cold? We could turn the heat on." He loosened his tie, pulled off his suitcoat.

"Tired, I guess. You know how you get chilled when you're tired?"

He wiped his wet face on his shirtsleeve. "You got a few hours in the sack. You were sound asleep when we got home around eleven."

She turned the silver ring on her index finger. "I passed out."

"Passed out?"

"Kit brought some dope. It was a bad trip."

So she wasn't going to lie about doing dope any more. Her trust pleased him. "Smoking the weed?"

"Something like that."

He stopped by the table. "How're you feeling now, Jo?" Wanting to kneel beside her.

"Wobbly." A reddened edge showed along the lower rim of her eyes.

He remembered the feeling. "Dry mouth? Did you have some juice?"

"Yes, and coffee." She bent her head, rubbed her eyes. Her hair was looped at the back of her neck with a bamboo ornament. Fine, dark strands escaped along her exposed nape. He kept his hands in his pockets.

"Got enough energy to go looking for that camera?"

"Yes."

"And a sandwich first? How about Ella's Deli?" His plan sounded artificial to him now. He should think of what would be best for her. He should probably fix her some soup, but Laura would be back from her Saturday errands soon and more than anything he wanted to be alone with Jo. "Let's go, then. I saved the afternoon."

She slipped her red-stockinged feet into her clogs. "Thanks, Will." Then, as if she spoke his thoughts, she blurted, "Let's get out of here!"

"I'll change and we'll do just that."

As he headed upstairs he took a deep breath—his nervousness was gone.

Ella's was crowded, but they got a table without too long a wait. He suggested cocoa if she was still chilled, but she wanted coffee, and a plain hamburger instead of corned beef. He ordered whatever she did. Service was slow, but he didn't care. He was where he wanted to be.

He asked about her photography. One of the nuns in the art department had loaned her a Pentex, and she was experimenting, she said. This week she was seeing the effect of using different f-stops on the same subject. Along with bracketing, she was experimenting with what would happen if she photographed black objects against a black background. It seemed black came out gray. She wasn't sure why.

"Doesn't Woodcliff have a course in photography?" he asked.

"Not this semester. I'd rather teach myself." She smiled. "The nun who loaned me the camera helps me. She's really good."

"It takes a long time to reinvent photography."

"I'm not in any hurry. I'm not in a hurry for anything, Will. I feel like I'm in some holding pattern like those planes they keep out over the lake while the runways clear at O'Hare. I'm not sure I want to land."

She slid down in her seat, pushed her hands into the pockets of her jeans.

"What would happen if you landed?"

"I don't know. That's what I don't like. Not knowing what's going to happen."

"Something going wrong at school?" He'd forgotten how hard it was to adjust to college.

"Nothing *can* happen at Woodcliff. I figure my best bet is to learn to make pots, try to get good grades, and get out of there. A girl I like pretty well might want to transfer to Illinois State with me, or maybe the U at Urbana."

His heart constricted at the thought of her leaving, and he was proud of how casually he asked, "When would you transfer?"

"Next semester, I guess. If I can." She looked down at her untouched hamburger.

"I'll be sorry."

She glanced up then, her brown eyes regarding him as though she read his mind. He looked away first.

"I don't know what I'm talking about, actually. That's what I mean about being in a holding pattern, Will. I'm in a sort of limbo. I haven't made very good choices, but I don't seem to know what to do. All my friends are away except Kit, and we don't really have much in common. I can't stay at home forever. I have to make some plans. Will you help me?"

Briefly he imagined sitting with her at the dining room table where he'd helped her with her homework, going through a pile of college catalogues, the printout of the Strong-Campbell Interest Inventory, discussing undergrad credits and strategies for apartment living near the campus of her choice. The scene filled him with grief. But she was right—of course she needed to take charge of her life. That was the task of her life now. But not just yet.

"You've just got started at Woodcliff." He hated the false optimism in his voice, but selfishly kept on. "There's a period of adjustment, Jo. Things will look up."

She slid lower. "I'm not really talking about college. I'm talking about everything."

He knew that. It was just that he didn't want to lose her. Although of course he didn't have her. "You need your lunch, Jo." The damned paternal—it was all he could think of.

She took a bite of her hamburger, and he asked about ceramics. What was she inventing there? Keep things light, that was best. He was framing a question about the composition of clays when he realized she'd dropped her sandwich back onto her plate and started to cry. Tears rolled down beside her nose and she rubbed at them with her red napkin.

"Jo!" he whispered. "What is it? Are you sick?"

She shook her head, trying to swallow the bite that was in her mouth. She got it down with difficulty, then her lips turned down and she hid behind her napkin.

"It's okay to cry."

"Not here!"

"We'll get out of here." He grabbed their check, helped her out of her chair and led her to the door, handing her his handkerchief to replace the napkin.

"You didn't get your lunch," she managed through her tears.

"Who cares?"

"God, I'm so sorry!"

"*Jo.*" He bundled her into her jacket, tried to zip it for her, but gave up and paid the bill instead. She ran ahead of him across the street to the parking lot.

Pulling on his raincoat, he thought, Did I say something? Remembering all that he hadn't said, he splashed across the asphalt toward his car where Jo was already huddled.

When he climbed in beside her she was crying hard, her face splotched and wet, his handkerchief bunched in her fist. So it was all right for him to put his arm around her, to pull her to him, settle her against his shoulder. He heard himself repeating her name over and over, as though that might heal her. The softness of her hair was against his mouth—even that was permitted because he was comforting her. "Jo? What's wrong? Just tell me. There's nothing you can't tell me, nothing at all."

After a long while she did tell him. At first he couldn't fit together the jumble about the beach, Trawick seeing her nude in the hotel in Vienna (that prick! He'd kill him!), Kit and the package and the hash, the headdress, the letters and package. He had her go back over it all more slowly. This time she was less headlong.

Most of what she told him he understood all too easily. Of course Trawick was struck by her nakedness—so had Will been. Of course Kit was jealous—so was Will, all of us, the same, the same. He could even imagine Laura hiding the package and the letters to protect Jo—Laura's kind of manipulative logic—though why she'd opened Jo's mail he couldn't guess. But surely Jo was too hysterical about Trawick. She insisted he hated her, that his letters were filled with hate, though when Will pressed her for details she spoke of a canoe trip he described, of Jacob wrestling with an angel. Sick! she said. But if Trawick were genuinely threatening, wouldn't Laura have spoken to him of the danger? Maybe Jo had been even more stoned than she'd realized; maybe other fears had tangled with whatever Trawick had written.

"What should I do?" she said.

He imagined smashing Trawick's face, running him down with his car—the bastard. His rage tasted of salt—a clean, righteous rage. He'd take care of her. That much was allotted to him.

He said they'd talk it over with Laura, call the cops if the letters were threats to Jo's life.

She slapped the dash with both hands. "Why would he want to hurt me? Saying all that love stuff but really hating me?"

His knees bumping the gear shift, he cradled her. Rain flooded across the glass sunroof. In fact, floods and famine were everywhere out there in the world. There were real problems, significant ones, as the news commentators called them. Whole populations starved because of an unending drought, ancient cultures were being systematically obliterated. Everywhere human misery was of dimensions so immense that he couldn't comprehend the suffering. Yet here he sat, joyful, because he held a crying girl whom he loved. Forgive me, he said silently, as though the suffering world could forgive him. The moment was banal, but he was so goddamned happy. Oh, forgive me.

"Let's go home now," she said finally. "I'll ask Laura for the letters. You'll understand when you see them."

With enormous reluctance he took his arm from around her shoulders, helped her to sit up. She pressed the collar of her green ski jacket up over her chin.

"My face is puffy. It always is when I cry."

He looked down into her face. Her eyes were swollen, her nose red, her skin blotchy. "You're beautiful."

"Oh, Will. You told me that even when I had braces."

"How're you doing now?"

"Better, I guess." But she shuddered. "Estelle used to say that someone was walking on your grave if you jumped like that."

He didn't want to start for home yet. "Do you cry often, Jo?"

She reached behind her neck to unpin the bamboo ornament from her hair, brush it through with her fingers, twist it in both hands and pin it up again. Why hadn't he noticed before how lovely such a gesture could be?

"Do you cry often?" he repeated, sliding the key into the ignition.

She sighed. "When I feel really lonely. When I think I'm never going to love someone who'll love me back." She blew her nose in the corner of his handkerchief. "Let's go home."

Laura sat curled up in a corner of the couch, a cup of tea balanced on her lap. "You look like you've caught a cold," she said to Jo as they came into the living room. The fire Laura had laid crackled on the hearth—the first of the season. He went to stand by it, holding his hands out to the heat.

Jo sank down on the footstool by the coffee table.

"Are you getting a cold?" Laura set her cup on the end table.

"No." Jo looked up at him as if asking for directions.

As if she'd guessed the unspoken question, Laura said, "Your little package is over there on the desk."

"You saw my note?"

"Sure."

Jo quickly retrieved the package, sat down and laid it on her knees to open it.

"You look jittery," Laura said to Will. "Things go all right this morning at work?"

"Too much coffee today."

"Caffeine will do it to you," she agreed.

He was studying the package in Jo's lap as she ripped off the tape. Inside was a paperback with a bright blue cover. He read the title upside down: *The Norton Anthology of Modern Poetry*.

She glanced up at him in dismay.

Laura tapped the rim of her cup with her fingernail. "What is it?"

"A book."

"Who sent it?"

"I don't know."

"Maybe there's an inscription or a card. Or a bill."

Jo opened the book. A single sheet of notepaper lay inside the front cover. She read the message to herself, her brow furrowed, lips moving slightly.

"Who's it from?" Laura asked again.

"Thomas."

"Ah. What's he have to say? Some Indian proverb?"

She read, "Dear Jo, I hope this helps you with your brilliant career as a student. Just wanted to wish you luck and thank you and yours for letting me join the Great Marshmallow Roast. Upsetting you in any way wasn't part of my plan. Not to worry. Best, Thomas." She looked up at Will again, eyes too bright.

"I guess that's his idea of an apology," Laura said. "What *did* he do to upset you?"

Jo examined her hands. "I don't want to talk about it."

He closed his eyes. For a moment Laura's form had wavered as he looked at her. Was she lying? She lied all the time about her compulsions; she could lie about other things as well.

As he opened his eyes, Jo dropped the book under the coffee table and handed him the note.

He glanced at the lines—a typed signature—and handed it back. She crumpled the paper and flung it into the fire. It burst into flame and quickly folded into a sheet of black ash. Had she fantasized those letters she'd described to him?

As if she'd intuited that brief failure of his trust, Jo turned and hurried from the room, her clogs clattering on the back stairs. Upstairs, her door slammed. He jabbed at the fire with the poker and the ashes of the letter dissolved.

"It looks like Thomas is persona non grata," Laura said mildly. "He can't seem to get his act right."

He wanted to shout What the hell is going on here! Instead, he asked, "What note did Jo leave for you?" Wanting to smash the Japanese vases on the mantel. Behind the vases, the Peter Max runner sped along, heading for the mat yellow horizon, leaving behind him all unasked questions. The artist drew a world in which clarity of purpose triumphed.

"A scribble on the blackboard. It seems Kit noticed she'd got a package when he was loading at the UPS station."

"And?"

"And nothing. I forgot to put it on her bed with her mail."

"When did it come?"

She raised her eyebrows as though curious that he would care. "Wednesday."

"You didn't mention it." The dogged detective. The fool. Either Jo had hallucinated the letters, or Laura was lying. Did it matter? Of course not.

"Why would I mention it?"

"You were going to protect Jo, the last I heard in this melodrama. It was from Trawick."

"How would I know that?"

She was right, and he was disgusted with himself. "Forget it."

"I already have."

With her foot she pushed the book farther under the coffee table, then came to his side at the fireplace. "I don't remember that we talked much about anything Wednesday night. We were busy."

She stood with her hands held out to the fire, head bent so that her hair fell forward across her cheeks like curtains. He couldn't see her eyes. Wednesday night? He remembered his squash game with Jerry, remembered pretending to read *The Wall Street Journal* later, while he daydreamed about Jo. It was Wednesday night that Laura had knelt before him as he read the paper, pushed the pages aside, and unzipped his pants. She hadn't even looked up at him before her cool hand was searching for his cock. Twisting like a snake she skinned off her jeans and pressed her face into his crotch. He'd watched his body respond as though he watched another man, curious that the mechanics of sex worked so predictably when his feelings were numb. Where had that chill sexual directness of Laura's come from? What fantasies did she have—his wife?

"Laura?"

She didn't look away from the fire.

He wanted to ask, Who are you? Instead, he said, "Jo was wondering if she got any letters. She misses her friends."

"Just the couple I put on her bed, and a few catalogues. 'Frederick's of Hollywood.' How she got on that mailing list I'll never know."

He heard nothing in her voice except calm reason. If she was lying, she was a master at it.

He couldn't go question Jo; he certainly couldn't search Laura's closet. He wanted a drink but knew the futility of that.

He imagined himself running along Center Road, the rain

pelting his shoulders. Cold rain. That would be good. Running
on the beach would be good, too—the hard-packed sand, the
drone of droplets on the lake. He could go until his chest ached,
until his legs were spent.

"I guess I'll go out for a while, okay?"

Laura was settling another log onto the fire and didn't
answer.

A curved strip of sand soaked to a dark gray, the beach was
deserted. Running close to the water's edge where the sand was
the hardest, he kept his head up into the rain. He'd pulled on
his waterproof poncho and tied the hood tightly. His sweat
pants were soaked, but he was warm enough. He'd been running for a long time, first through town and now up and down
the beach, guessing how he might look to someone watching
from the bluff: a running man, shrunken by distance, splashing
through the darkening afternoon.

Finally he stopped at the boathouse to smoke his pipe. He
was whipped now, but he didn't want to go home. When he
opened the boathouse door two raccoons scuttled from the
rafters and scurried out through a gap in the screen. His boat
was the only one left. He'd haul it home in a minute, drag it up
the road on the boat trolley. He'd get tired and his back would
ache. The work and discomfort might distract him.

He set his pipe on the hull, opened the lock. It started to rain
harder. Waves of rain howled on the tin roof overhead. He tied
his poncho hood closer against the rain that blew in the open
sides of the boathouse.

He didn't hear Jo when she came in. Suddenly she was just
there in front of him, her hair slicked against her bare head,
drops of rain in her lashes, her hands deep in the pockets of her
yellow slicker. "I had to find you!"

"I'm glad." He was more than glad—he was elated.

She planted her feet as though ready for a fight. "You think I
was dreaming about those letters, don't you?"

He sat on the Sunfish, fingering his pipe, and looked up at
her. Her anger had brought the blood up in her face. "You told
me your truth, I'm sure of it."

"The truth," she insisted. "Nothing but the truth." One hand placed on an imaginary Bible, one hand in the air.

She whirled around and began to pace back and forth in front of him, kicking gravel at her turns. "Laura is lying. I don't know why, and I don't care why. She's my sister and your wife and all, but she's crazy! I don't know where I am with her, I never have!"

Her lips trembled with anger, or perhaps she'd cry again. If she cried, he could hold her.

She crouched to pick up one of the larger stones and hurled it overhand at the wooden door left ajar behind her. It whacked and caromed onto the planks near his feet.

"All afternoon I've been trying to figure out Laura and Thomas. I can't get it straight about Laura. All I know is that she wants to run everything, be in charge of everything, and of course she can't be. And her blaming me the whole time for Mother, as if that was my fault! Thomas is easier to figure out in some ways. He's on a power trip, too, and he's after sex. But since he could get that anywhere, why did he pick me? Why is he after me when I have nothing at all for him? That's sick, don't you see?"

"I'm listening."

"Laura's got something she wants from him, though. She took those letters he sent me and she's lying about it. I don't care, but I can't stand feeling like this! Angry! Scared!"

The door slammed shut in a sudden gust of wind and she turned, startled, then shook her fist at it.

"Hey."

"Don't slow me down, Will. I mean it! I wanted to tell you that most of all I'm sick of crying. No more crying! Do you hear me? I'm going to do something about my life."

He nodded. "I hear you. What are you going to do?" His careful question. But what could he say?

She took a deep breath, let her shoulders drop when she blew it out. "To begin with, I'm going to get out of the house. I'm sure I could move into the dorm. There's tons of room. Even the Catholics don't want to go to Catholic schools any more. I can get along there until I can transfer somewhere I'd like better."

He gripped the edge of the hull, felt his hand tingle before it went numb with pressure.

She picked up another stone, larger than the first, but instead of throwing it she seemed to weigh it in her hand. "I've been thinking about everything this afternoon. Like how things got a lot better for me when you came, Will. Dad, well, he was a drunk, a sneaky drunk. And Laura killing herself because she wanted his attention, or something, but of course he didn't notice her. Estelle loved me, I had that, but she was paid to mother me. And then she died, too. You remember, she called up and said, 'They cut off my boobs, but it's spread everywhere.' She actually *said* that." She stopped, tears coming, though she sniffed them back.

Then she did hurl the stone. It cracked against the tin roof and crashed back near her feet. He flinched, but she didn't. "I'm sick of feeling sorry for myself, too. 'Poor little Jo, no momma, no daddy,'" she singsonged. "No more of that! I'm really okay, don't you think? I'm really a normal person when I'm with people who don't make me crazy, right?"

"You're a wonderful person." He couldn't keep the emotion from his voice, but she didn't seem to notice.

"I owe you a lot, Will. When I'm with you I'm a normal person. When I'm with you I feel like myself."

She was quieter now. He wanted to grab her, embrace her. The elation he'd felt when he held her in the parking lot had faded. He wished now she could hold *him,* comfort *him.*

She stopped in front of him and spread her hands, fingers parted, as though offering him the rain that had spattered onto her palms. "Will, would you help me get out of here?"

She opened her arms to him.

When he stood his pipe dropped somewhere behind him onto the stones. Her arms went around his neck and he rested his cheek on the top of her head. Her teeth chattered and her shivering entered him as though it were his own.

Then she lifted her wet face and kissed him on the mouth, hard at first, then pulling back so that their lips parted gently. As though they'd kissed like lovers a thousand times.

Heat radiated through him in a clean stroke. He would have expected that, if he'd imagined this at all. What he didn't expect was that he would no longer think of her as a girl; she hurtled ahead into womanhood as she pressed herself into his embrace.

Suddenly he was seeing the two of them as though from a great height. *There they are down there.* The woman, soaked from rain, her arms lifted, her face lifted, the line of her drenched hair as slick at her temples as a scarf. The man, hands hard at her waist, raising her to him, leaning over her and trying not to move, trying neither to break the kiss nor to force it further, letting it happen—not willing it—that important point he will need for his conscience later.

Then Jo abruptly pulled away.

He grabbed for her shoulder to stop her, but she ran from the boathouse, brushing through the weeds and rhododendron, heading for the path up the bluff. He kept himself from running after her. Her yellow slicker flashed as she ran through the pines, then he caught a last glimpse of yellow near the top of the bluff. She'd vanished. The boathouse door swung in the wind.

He picked up his fallen pipe, knocked it out and put it in his pocket, sat back down on the Sunfish. Down the beach a dog barked. Rain streamed from the tin roof and a green mist rose from the battered lake. The taste of her—he wanted to set that in memory along with the feel of her in his arms. He closed his eyes and saw again the surprise on her face just before she kissed him. She hadn't known what she felt, hadn't known what she would do, but when it came to her she seized it simply and without question. Without an instant of hesitation she changed all the rules.

Listening to the rain, he touched his lips tentatively, as though probing a bruise. There was nothing girlish or coy in her kiss. She meant business. And he'd accepted it all, even pulled her hips against him so she'd feel his wanting her. Things were different now—it didn't do any good to pretend they weren't.

He went to the boathouse door, leaned against the rough wood, and thought again of kissing her. Though home was where Jo must be now, it was a long time before he made himself go back. At home, things must go on exactly as they always had.

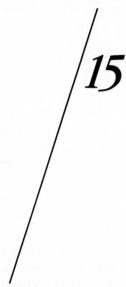

15

Jo slammed her bedroom door behind her and leaned against it. Pines had whipped her face as she ran up the bluff, and she tasted pitch on her lips. Her eyes smarted and she closed them, tight. When she opened them again her room was in motion; the walls and floor seemed to sway in the smudgy, late-afternoon light. Reflections of the rain on her windows swam on the floor, lifted her desk and chair. Her bed seemed tipped. She remembered a Chagall print she'd seen, a picture of a whole village that had become unmoored. Flowers, donkeys, chickens, a man and a woman floated over the rooftops in a green sky. As if Daisy might drift in now through her window. As if Will might swim to her through the tops of the oaks.

But she didn't want to think about him yet.

She grabbed her blue bathrobe from her closet, hugged it around her soaked shoulders. The ceiling lowered itself onto her—why wouldn't things stay in place? Such a small room, she thought, trying to squint it steady. How could she have lived all her life in such a small room?

Don't think about him.

The leftovers of her careless childhood were everywhere: nail-holes in the faded wallpaper with its rose-and-trellis pattern, stains on the curtain hems where rain had soaked them, the ascending line of pencil marks on the closet door where Estelle had measured Jo's growth. There hadn't been a new mark for a long time. The little room closed around her like cupped hands cutting off light and air. Why was she still living in this tiny space? She had to leave.

Would he be coming across the park?

She pushed the curtains aside so that she could look out over the park to the edge of the bluff. The lake was leaden gray, pounded flat by the rain. The park was empty.

The horrible curtains were practically rags; chips of cream-colored paint lay on the sill. Everything needed painting, papering. She should crumple the room, throw it away. Or burn it down. There was nothing here that she wanted. What did she have that was worth saving? Will's camera, a few scrapbooks, some silver jewelry with chips of turquoise and coral, a red cashmere sweatshirt—one of Laura's extravagant Christmas gifts. Nothing else was worth anything. She could leave it all behind in a moment, leave the whole house behind her the way a sand crab leaves one shell and moves into another.

The Colemans' dog streaked russet across the park and disappeared into the ravine, but no one was in sight. Will hadn't followed her.

Nothing in this room was really hers, when she thought about it; everything was a cast-off. The maple bed had once been Laura's, the sewing rocker Aunt Hattie's, the oval mirror with its chipped "gold" frame Estelle's. The desk had been Jo's mother's—but that didn't mean anything. It meant only that some little girl Jo had never known had once carved tic-tac-toe games in the birch top, spilled ink in the top drawer, scratched a boy's name by the inkwell—"Dean," not even Jo's father's name. The desk had been stored in the attic for years, but when Laura took over the house she dragged it down. "You should have something of your mother's," she'd said. As if Jo had had a mother. It was a useless desk, too tiny, drawers too small for notebooks, rickety legs. Yet she'd used it all this time. She'd never even questioned that it was here.

This pathetic little room with its cracked plaster and gashed woodwork—her *sanctuary?* How glad she'd be to leave. The place was a trap. Like Alice in Wonderland, her size had changed. Now her head might bump the ceiling, her hands might flip over the chairs, her knees knock the casements. She would have to crouch down in order to live in this room.

She sat down on her bed and leaned back against the wall. She wasn't breathing so fast now. Gradually the room settled into a kind of order. If it wasn't as she remembered it, at least it wasn't tumbling around her. But the world was upside-down, that was the truth. It was also true that she'd already left this old room of hers. She'd left it behind when she kissed Will.

She remembered an old trick that Will had taught her to use when she was frightened: "Ask yourself, What's the worst that can happen?" That had always been easy enough. If she was frightened of an exam the worst that could happen was that she'd fail (but she could take a makeup exam, no course grade was based all on one exam). If she was scared before a track meet the worst would be that she'd fall (but runners fell all the time and got up again). If you asked yourself that question, you could bring things into perspective, he said. Rehearse the situation, he coached her, cut it down to size. Once she'd asked him, "What's the very worst thing that *can* happen, Will?" She thought he'd answer her, "To die." But he said, "To lose hope, I think. Christians are right about that. Without hope, there's really nothing at all."

She grabbed her pillow and doubled it into a ball to hug. *What's the worst that can happen, Will? I mean now.* Now.

She tried to keep her mind from going in circles. tried to make a list of fears, each one coming dependably along behind another, like the stations on the Northwestern commuter line. She tested possible disasters, trying to find a name for what was lodged at the base of her throat.

Laura could find out. Will wouldn't tell her, of course, but she'd know, in that uncanny way of hers. Jo punched her pillow in dismay—worrying about Laura made her feel like a baby, a guilty child. But it was undeniable that a sick rage surfaced from the flood of feelings in her chest.

She threw herself out lengthwise on her bed, pushed her fist against her mouth. A taste of revenge came like old blood after a nosebleed, or bile after having thrown up on an empty stomach. *I have something with Will, Laura! He wants it, too. And he won't tell you about it. You're not in charge anymore, Laura.*

She rolled onto her back, hugging her pillow hard against her stomach because the cramps of anger were real. They doubled her over. She imagined pounding her fists against the wall, knocking her head against the headboard, hurting herself because it was true, she did want to hurt Laura.

Damn you! I hate living with you, Laura. I hate your lies and I hate your sickness or whatever it is. I hate your trying to feed me too much so you can be in charge. I hate your stupid intrigue about shit like Thomas's letters. I hate it that you'd want them, save them, hide them. I hate you because we could have been okay as sisters, you know that? I didn't have so much, Laura. What if you'd *been* my sister? What if just once you'd talked to me? What if just once you'd said something true and real? My friends talk to me, you know. Women talk to each other, magazines are full of that stuff. Estelle talked to me. But not you. Not my *sister*. What if just once you'd told me what you were feeling? What if just once you'd asked me what I felt?

As though that would have made any difference. I don't care anymore, Laura.

Jo had clenched her teeth so tightly that her jaw ached, but no more crying. And the time in which she and Laura might have been friends had never existed, never, never. Magical thinking.

She let out a long breath, and some of the tightness went out of her chest. She hugged her knees and rocked back and forth. No comfort came, but gradually the anger eased. "It's over and I'm glad," she said out loud against her pillow. But she wasn't glad, not really.

She got to her feet, went to the oval mirror that hung by the closet door. Estelle had given it to her "to remember me by, cutie." She'd hung it up for Jo before she left. Later, Jo moved it higher. The mirror needed raising again, but she hadn't bothered. Some silver had worn away from the backing so parts of her cheek and chin were barely visible. She rubbed her face with her rough, chilled hands. Had her mother looked like this—transparent, dark under her eyes? She'd died when she was thirty-eight. A year older than Will.

This is how I'll look when I'm middle-aged. "And then, I'll be old." She'd never said that aloud, and the words startled her. Time would go by like the wind, just like Estelle had said, "It's a dream, cutie. Life."

But if you loved the right man, it would be all right to grow old, wouldn't it? *I could love the wrong man. Is that the worst?* Estelle had told her all about that. Love was Estelle's favorite topic. According to her, love was an accident that left you maimed with no way in the world to mend. Estelle talked about her own love all the time, the way a patient relives over and over the operation that has injured her. Every time she came to visit Jo she talked about love. There Estelle was at the kitchen table in her black peasant blouse and silver hoop earrings, wiping a rim of lipstick from her coffee cup with her little finger.

"The first man you love, he's the *one*. That's the way love is. If he leaves you, you go around looking for him the rest of your life. Like me. Still looking for John Holden! Why, he's right there in town, going gray, face getting puffy. But me, I'm still looking for him the way he was. Slim and dark, that way he had of setting his hands on his hips with his thumbs in his pockets. That way he had of looking at me with his eyes almost closed, just a dark shine and lashes two inches long, I bet. I'm not even looking for a man who *looks* like him—no one could. That's not it. Sometimes I get a quick glance at a fella, a sailor, maybe. A fella kind of restless and lazy at the same time. Just like John, I tell myself. But if I strike up a conversation, in a moment or two that idea's gone. Something reminded me of John Holden, but something in *me,* not in the sailor. Me—I'm still dreaming of the way John kissed me the very first time, his face coming close, the beginning of it all in me. You see what I mean? That's what happens when you fall in love—you get that man printed on you, the same way they print a president's face on money. You go everywhere looking for a match to that man stamped on your heart. And of course there ain't one! Do you know why? Because maybe that first man you loved didn't even exist! That's why. Like maybe I didn't know John Holden at all, maybe I just loved something I made up about him, loved something I made up about me. And all I've got printed on me is a ghost. Here I am trying to find a match-up for a ghost. You can spend your whole life looking for someone who never even *was,* and that's how it is, toots."

Estelle, winking at her, "That's woman-talk, honey."

Jo hunched down on her bed again, crushed her pillow to the

hollow in her chest. She wished she could talk to Estelle. She wished she could say, It's the other way around. Will isn't any ghost. He's real.

She could tell Estelle about that photograph her psychology teacher had shown the class to illustrate field-and-figure perception in Gestalt theory. The photo was blown up large, maybe two feet square, pasted on cardboard. It looked like a maze of random black and white forms, like abstract art. The teacher explained that the photographer had simply pointed his camera at a plowed field of black earth on which snow was melting. At least that was the photo he thought he'd taken. When he'd developed the photo he'd seen in the pattern of black earth and white snow the face of Christ.

The class studied the photo. How long would it take them to see the face emerge from the shapes? One by one the students laughed with recognition. It took Jo a long time, but suddenly what had been a black half-oval metamorphosed into an eye, and with complete clarity she saw a man's face, bearded and tenderly severe, looking right at her. Once she saw the face in the pattern she couldn't make it disappear again. Your perceptions are altered, said the teacher; the specific emerges from the general.

It was just like that with Will. He'd been there all the time, but now, suddenly, he had appeared and she'd kissed him. And he'd kissed her back. He'd held so very still that she'd felt only her own chest move when they breathed, but he'd kissed her, all right. His lips were a warm pressure that didn't move away, his cheekbone a hot pressure that hurt her. He'd held onto her as tightly as she'd held him. Hold on for dear life, Estelle used to say.

For dear life. Because he'd seen her for the first time, too, recognized *her*. Somehow, in that kiss, she had appeared for him to see and know.

She would never be able to make him disappear again, she was sure of that. And it would be the same for him, wouldn't it? He would never be able to make her disappear. Trembling, she traced the shape of her lips. You make me exist, Will.

How he'd hate it if she said that to him. "Be your own girl!" he'd insisted, giving her courage against unfair teachers, teasing friends, a stern employer. And what a burden, to make someone exist!

Is that the worst that could happen, Will? That I'd need you in order to exist?

She leaned across her bed to open her window a crack. A scatter of rain stirred the curtains. The air smelled of wet earth and of the pork roast crisping in the kitchen below. As the clouds shifted, the oaks along the bluff were lit by a thin light. From the Millets' came the faint, lonely sound of a flute—one of Pat Millet's favorite recordings of those old Irish songs. Jo tried to follow the melody, but it curled and twisted in its plaintive way, like a live thing. Those few notes made her ache with longing to be held. To hold.

"Will." As she spoke his name she caught sight of the top of his head at the back gate. He must have come up by the road; she hadn't seen him cross the park, and she'd been watching.

In a moment the gate opened. The mast, wrapped in the red sail, appeared first, then came Will, his pipe clenched in his teeth, smoke trailing up beside his chin through the fine mist of rain. He'd pulled back the hood of his poncho, pulled his watch cap low. Was he frowning? He rested the mast against the fence, latched the gate, opened the door into the storage section of the garage. Then he picked up the mast and disappeared with it into the gloom.

What he did was familiar enough, but the world was different now. In one of the talks during orientation, a priest had spoken about the difference between essence and appearance. He'd been talking about transubstantiation, of course. She didn't believe the bread and wine changed, but she believed the principle that something could appear to be one thing and yet really be something else entirely different. She and Will might seem the same, but everything was changed. You couldn't love someone and have the world stay the same. Something would have to happen now.

She rehearsed: In a moment he would come out of the garage and she'd be at her window. He'd look up at her, and she would know that what he felt was real, too. She opened the window a little wider so that she could call down to him when he came to the back door. She'd only say his name. That would be enough.

After what seemed a long time, he appeared in the doorway again, Daisy at his side. He closed the garage door, yanked off his cap and ran his hand through his hair. Didn't he sense that she was watching him? She moved even closer to the open window so that her face would be clearly visible, and drew the curtain aside. He strode up the back walk, leaning to ruffle Daisy's fur as the dog leaped beside him.

He was right beneath her window, opening the back door. "Will?" Only a whisper. Maybe he didn't hear. She tapped the pane. He held the door open to let Daisy in and then passed from Jo's sight into the back porch below.

Why hadn't he looked up? Had Laura been right there by the door? Jo stared down at the floor by the bed as though X-ray vision would allow her to see Will as he took off his shoes and toweled Daisy dry.

Then she heard his voice from the kitchen. He must be standing by the back stairs, because his words were clear. He'd bring the Sunfish up tomorrow, he told Laura, the rain was too heavy today. He thought he'd strained a tendon, running. He wanted a hot shower. Were they out of seltzer? Never mind, he'd drink it neat, it would warm him faster.

Then, at a distance, she heard him climbing the front stairs, heard his bedroom door closing behind him. He'd gone up that way instead of passing her room.

At her closet she stepped out of her wet Levi's, rubbed her damp hair with her bathrobe. She was alternately chilled and flushed as though she had a fever, as though love were a disease that attacked the central nervous system. She looked into her mirror again, brushed back her hair, and saw the face of a girl who has done too much dope and slept too little. Not much to see. Everything was just the same. Except the world was tipped upside-down.

Dinnertime. Jo didn't know where to look, what to say. What she'd always done naturally she now felt as the movements of a mannequin. Laura had assembled one of her usual huge spreads which she'd urge on others and only pick at herself: pork roast, sweet potatoes, apple and nut salad, biscuits. She was busy putting all the dishes on the table. Jo stood in the kitchen door, in Laura's way, she supposed, but she couldn't seem to move.

Will came to the kitchen, his shirt collar damp from his wet hair. He made another drink, the whiskey honey-colored in his glass. When Laura turned to the oven he glanced at Jo as if assessing her, but she read no message in his narrowed blue eyes. A drop of water ran down his temple. "Let's eat," he said to no one in particular.

The scents made Jo's mouth water, but after the first few bites she couldn't eat any more.

"You're not hungry?" Of course Laura would notice.

"I think I might have flu."

"Do you have a fever?"

"No, a headache."

Will pushed his food around for a while as though he didn't care if he ever ate again, then determinedly settled to his meal as though it were work he'd just remembered he must complete.

Laura looked from Will to Jo, then back again. "This is a lively group."

Now that Jo's anger at her had flowed away, she looked at Laura more clearly: a thin, nervous, pretty young woman with no friends to speak of, no kids of her own, and not much family. Tonight Laura was especially agitated, too busy with the jam dish, the butter plate, the biscuit napkin—the hostess whose party won't take off.

Jo thought briefly of saying, Let's forget about Thomas's letters. I don't want them. I wish I'd never seen them. Maybe you were protecting me; anyway, you don't have to lie. Instead she pleated her napkin in her lap and remained silent. If only Will would look at her, give her some signal.

Laura talked with brittle animation about the tennis lesson she'd taken that morning from the new pro at the club. Jamaican. Named Esau, of all things. Terrific power on his backhand, and that sweet-but-smarmy way island blacks had learned to please the white folks. She liked him when he let up on the "milady" bit. She'd worked at blocking at the net. He hit them hard and it was good practice. Esau called everyone "mon," too. You had to get used to that. If she hit one wrong, he said,

"No problem, mon." That was his answer to everything, "No problem, mon."

Then she seemed to run out of energy. Her shoulders slumped and she fingered the collar of her white shirt. "How's the roast?" she asked Will.

He nodded, and took another long drink of his whiskey and water.

"I wish I had a drink," Laura said. "I think I'm going to start drinking. I wouldn't mind being mellowed out on a rainy Saturday night."

Jo tried her milk, but it coated the inside of her mouth. Maybe she could startle Will into responding to her. "I want a drink, too." She went to the kitchen for Will's whiskey bottle and poured an inch into each of two juice glasses, brought them back to the table. She set one glass by Laura's place, one by her own.

"At least put ice in it," he said.

"Who cares?" Laura peered down into the amber liquid as though it were medicine. "I used to like gin and tonics." She sipped and made a face.

Jo tasted her drink. The whiskey burned her tongue but it cut through the milk, traced a hot path down through her chest. All this acting was too difficult. What she really wanted was a joint. Except she'd vowed to lay off dope for a while. She glanced at Will again, but he appeared to be absorbed in buttering a biscuit.

"You've got that rash of yours," Laura said to her.

Jo touched her throat. "The whiskey?"

"We're crazy to drink stuff like this," Laura said, but she finished hers in tiny sips, as though there were no way out. Jo knew she was calculating the calories in each sip. "How was your morning at the clinic?" she asked Will.

He said they were considering the possibility of taking a new doctor into the group. It was time they expanded, Jerry thought, shared some of the overload. They were all working too hard.

"Find a young one for Jo," Laura said, her face worked into a smile.

He said they were considering several, none especially young.

"Did you and Jo find a camera when you went shopping?"

Not yet.

He'd lifted her against him. Her feet had barely touched the ground. She'd broken the kiss before he had.

Laura passed Jo the bowl of sweet potatoes, although Jo hadn't touched what was on her plate. "Are you seeing Kit tonight?"

She'd forgotten Kit. "He might come by after his job, but he doesn't get off until late." She would make sure she was asleep before he came—she didn't want to see him. They'd talk about everything, he'd said. She didn't want to talk to Kit about anything at all.

"He comes and goes as he pleases," Laura said. She folded her arms across her chest, caved in, her shoulders bent as though she were sheltering herself against a draft. "I guess you don't mind or you'd tell him to call first."

"I don't much care what he does." She wanted to leave the table if Will wasn't going to acknowledge her, but where would she go? His presence held her here. She studied his hands, his blunt fingers with fine, brown hairs above the knuckles. He hadn't buttoned the cuffs of his blue shirt and they lay open on his wrists. Look at me, she commanded him silently. Make me real.

"Laura, I've been thinking about moving into the dorm. I'd be more a part of the school that way, and it'd be a lot more convenient. Could we afford that?"

Laura looked up, eyebrows raised. "That's your decision. You've got that trust fund from Daddy for your education. Is the dorm what you want?"

"It's what I want."

Will trimmed the fat from a slice of pork, pushed the trimmed edge to the side, cut the pink slice into sections. Without eating any, he took another long swallow of his drink.

Then there was a silence. Rain spattered on the windows in a sudden gust of wind. The grandfather clock in the living room clicked forward. But it seemed to Jo that time had stopped, as though the three of them were underwater, each in their own diving mask, isolated. She imagined yanking the cloth from the table, flinging the water pitcher at the window to break the spell.

"There's a new movie down at Eden's," Laura said after a while, stuttering slightly, as though they were in a play and she'd suddenly remembered the next line was hers. "One of those murder-on-a-train things. It's supposed to be campy."

"Okay," Will said.

"Jo, why don't you come along?" Laura suggested.

That was new. Laura didn't usually try to include her. Maybe she was as much at a loss as Jo was, with Will so withdrawn. Maybe she was feeling guilty that she'd taken the package and the letters.

"The movie sounds dumb," Jo said.

Then Will did look at her. His gaze slid across hers quickly, flashed like a lighthouse signal distinguishing safe water from the reef. "Why the hell not come?"

She caught her breath. He was giving her a message of some kind. "I don't like mysteries."

"Come on." This time he looked at her steadily, as though he'd got his balance and made a decision. "Something up with you, Jo?"

"I'm just tired."

Then he held his fist out, thumb up, purposefully, Jo saw— his old signal for her to take it easy. He had calculated the paternal gesture. She understood the conscious effort. He'd thought it over, chosen a path. He was telling her things must go on as they always had.

She looked down at his hand that he held out across the table.

"Hey," he said quietly. "Come on."

To her surprise she thought of slapping his hand away. Let Laura think what she would. That's not it at all, Will!

But what was there to do? She held out her own hand, pressed her thumb to his in agreement, feeling his heat, imagining a spark leaping between them at the moment of contact. She put her hand back into her lap.

His fingers had dug into her waist, drawing her close.

But she'd agreed to do it his way. At least for now.

Will drove and Laura sat beside him. As usual, Jo had the back seat to herself. She huddled, her knees pushed against the back of Laura's seat. At every intersection sheets of water splashed onto the windows. Laura fiddled with the radio for a moment, then turned it off. Will's profile was lit by the pale light of the dash—the ridge of his nose, deep-set eyes, pipe in his teeth.

A burst of rain slowed their progress to a crawl. "My God," Will said, "has it been raining forever?"

Laura slipped her arm along the back of his seat behind his shoulders. "No problem, mon."

"In the shipyard the blacks didn't try to please *anybody*. Junk would have died first." He stopped, then after a moment went on. "The others would sooner knife you than please you." He sounded his horn at a pickup truck that swerved into the lane ahead of them. "Of course the whites were the same way."

"Hey, mon, take it easy," Laura whispered.

The pickup honked back, and the beer truck beside them honked, too, like dogs snapping at each other. "Bastards!" Will said.

Jo watched him in the rearview mirror. The rectangle reflected his right temple, his glasses, his right eye. He watched Route 41 ahead as though there were some answer there.

After a while she rested her head against the window now muddied where the beer truck had flung up water. Her mouth tasted sour and metallic from the whiskey, and she was more frightened now than she'd been this afternoon.

This is the way it is, she told herself. Remember the realities. This is the only way it can be. I can love him until my heart breaks and it won't make any difference. There they are and here I am. It's like a dream, but it's the truth: Will is driving and Laura is beside him. I am here behind them in the dark. After a while I'll get out of their car and they'll drive on as before. Nothing will be different except that I love him. Nothing will be different. And that's the way it is, cutie.

Is that the worst that can happen, Will? That nothing at all will happen?

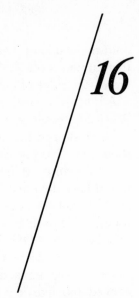

16

On Monday morning, as soon as Will and Jo were out of the house, Laura phoned Thomas. When he answered on the fifth ring he sounded groggy. "Did I wake you?" she said before she said her name.

"Christ, what time is it?"

"Almost eight. This is Laura."

"Ah. Lovely Laura. I should be on my feet and running toward the Loop right now. Thanks for the wake-up call."

"I'd like to talk with you."

"Not now, honey. In half an hour I've got a meeting with the folks who pay my outrageous rent. Two doctors are coming down from Mayo, the pharmacists, my editor and I are 'conceptualizing,' as they say, this morning."

"For lunch, then?"

A pause. She waited, wishing he'd been the one to ask.

"Good idea, but I won't be through in time today. Maybe next week?"

"I'd really like to see you today. It's about Jo," she added, her strong card. "Look, I know where you live. Why don't I meet you there after your conference?"

He laughed, then coughed, his morning cough, she guessed, a dry hack. "Laura, you always surprise me. I've never met a woman I could say that about. Sure, here at my digs, why not?

About three, then? I'll tell the manager to let you in if I'm not back. You'll wait, right?"

"Yes," she said. "Yes. I'll be there. I'll wait."

So here she was, in Thomas's apartment, waiting.

She stood just inside the door, listening to the manager's footsteps slap down the stairs, and looked around. She was in a long, underfurnished room with books everywhere—a wall full of them on shelves of boards and bricks, books stacked under the table he used as a desk, books in piles by the leather reading chair and beside the bed that would probably serve as a sofa if it were made up. Magazines and newspapers littered the tops of filing cabinets. Through the open doorway into the kitchen she saw a round table, the single plate lying on top of an open book.

Aside from the books, there was hardly a personal item of any kind. The off-white walls were bare except for a bulletin board beside the table-desk, at the two tall windows a bamboo shade served as both blind and curtain, the lights were goosenecked tensors for reading, the carpet was regulation tan. No photographs, no posters, no bibelots on the tables or shelves. No mirror.

She slipped her jacket off and dropped it on what she supposed was the chair for guests, black canvas on a curved metal frame, the kind for decks or porches. Well, what had she expected? Something quietly elegant, or an artist's garret. Something romantic. She smiled at herself. Oh, this was much better than her fantasies; it was the home of a man who lived inside his own head, who had no sentiment and no apparent ties to anyone. A man who needed her more deeply than she'd guessed—needed her love, not her decorating skills, though she thought her first gift might be a couple of really good prints, a few ferns to hang in the bare windows against that bleak light, and he could use a TV larger than that tiny one on the coffee table.

Before she went to the windows to watch for him, she ducked into the bathroom to check her looks in the mirror. The bathroom was white, too, spartan, although it smelled of sandalwood soap. The lights over the sink came on with a neon buzz. She looked good against all this white, looked even more blond, more tanned. She was the only color here. The splash of her gold earrings and the pale peach of her silk shirt had never looked richer. Without knowing her, he'd created a setting to show her off. She smiled at herself in the mirror though she was trembling with eagerness to talk to him. Hello, Thomas, hurry home.

But he didn't hurry home. For a while she stood at the windows looking down into the flow of traffic on Sheridan Road three floors below, at the signs in the next block for pizza and Chicago Hots, at the mix of elderly men and women and students in jeans and denim jackets on the sidewalk. Where the street turned west she saw the white stone buildings of Loyola, and in the distance, the taller steel-and-glass structures of Northwestern. Maybe he'd lived here as a grad student and just stayed on. Maybe he'd just moved in recently and hadn't finished unpacking. Either conclusion seemed possible. The light from the overcast sky was flat and harsh and made her head ache.

After a while she turned to sit at his desk instead. His writing chair was the heavy oak kind she remembered from the university library. It faced away from the windows. On the table was an Apple IIc computer setup and an elderly manual typewriter, office model. Among the stacks of folders on the table rested a couple of coffee cups, maybe a half dozen chewed-on yellow pencils, a box of saltines and another of cookies. Pinned to the bulletin board were sheets of legal paper covered with his script, each sheet with a heading naming chapter and character. A novelist, he'd said. She read some of the sheets: a description of a young girl masturbating in front of a mirror in a hotel in Paris; a cycling scene from *Le Tour de France;* a love scene in which a woman named Catherine "—kissed him passionately, as though her kiss had the power to raise the dead."

So this was where he lived—in his writing—and in his imagination women and men kissed passionately. Oh yes, she and Thomas would kiss passionately, but first there would be talk, real talk, talk powerful and intimate enough "to raise the dead." She turned the chair to the window and leaned her elbow on the sill so she could watch in the direction of the commuter station. Once she'd hated waiting, but she'd changed, she'd learned how. It was an art.

She'd learned it the one time she was pregnant. That was several months before she and Will married. She remembered waking one morning to the scuttle of squirrels on the porch roof and knowing even before she opened her eyes that something was different. She touched her face, breasts, belly. She slid her fingers between her thighs where she was still moist—Will had been with her the night before. He'd gone to his place, later, and she'd slept deeply; now when she woke in the early mist she *knew:* she was pregnant. No, not from the night before, nothing crazy like that. She was pregnant from one of the many times they'd made love in the last six months.

They were still in that first stage of courtship, that heightened, hopeful time when it seemed possible they both might become the new people they wanted to be. That never really happens, of course, that kind of elemental change. People in love act differently for a little while and then go back to the way they were before. But she and Will were in that drama of first discoveries, and that morning she sensed something newer yet—the child in her womb, yes, it had to be that—and she was glad.

"A child," she said out loud, to test the possibility. "Oh, a child!" She hadn't realized how much she wanted to be a mother. She had been so busy lately being in love. There was a desperation in her feelings for Will that jerked her around. All of her emotions were extreme, and that frightened her. She phoned him at his office even when she ordered herself not to, she begged him to come to her house and when he did she threw herself into his arms as though he'd been gone for months. Often, after they made love, she cried violently, as though pleasure unclenched old sorrows, too. She bawled against his chest and he held her. *Don't leave me.* He stayed.

She wasn't sure why he stayed, because she knew he didn't love her. There are many possible bonds between lovers, and only one of them is love. They were bound together by her love for him. Meaning they weren't equals. She drew equations in her journal: I need him more than he loves me / I love him more than he needs me. They didn't add up, but she was helpless. She would die without him. Poor Will. Romantic love—the twining of one neurotic temperament around its natural mate.

But when she was pregnant the first clear thought she had about Will was, I don't need him anymore. Now she had what she needed most, and she could dispense with this man who caused her such complicated and humiliating anguish. She could get on with her real business.

Oh, she had a love for him, but how wonderful it would be to dump him, push him away, forget about him. How glad she'd be not to worry if he'd call, if he was coming, if he'd stay, if he would ever really love her. Anger was on the other side of needing him. She hated herself because she wanted him so badly. It all tangled together—love and need and rage.

That very first morning when she suspected she was pregnant she made two decisions: First, when the baby was born she'd put the bassinet right by the bed where she could reach out and touch it, and, second, she wasn't going to tell Will that she was pregnant. At least for a long time, as long as she could conceal it.

Now she had something he didn't have. He didn't even know he'd given it to her. She'd stolen it. After all, she'd been lying to him about using contraception. She must have wanted his baby, and wanted the baby even more than she wanted Will.

Before they made love the very first time he asked her what she was using. She was lighting candles, and his question startled her—she'd only had one period. "Using?"

"So you don't get pregnant."

"Oh. A diaphragm." It was the first thing she could think of. He said he didn't mind using something himself, but a diaphragm was more reliable—he approved, the medical man as lover. So she had to go into the bathroom before they made love and stay long enough so that he'd think she'd put it in. Her *thing,* he called it, as if it existed. He said it was a fine invention, much better than rubbers. She didn't want to know so much about his past, about women kneeling to sheathe his cock. But she let that go. She was pleased with her lie.

Her lie—that was it, all right. A lie was lodged right in the middle of their loving. The lie was the real diaphragm, the real barrier. His semen traveled where it would, but she'd blocked off their real intimacy.

No matter. In the weeks that followed her discovery that she was pregnant, she knew her lie was worth it. She forgave herself because she was saved. Everything she'd ever done was washed clean, especially the guilt of not letting herself grow up, not letting herself become a woman. She was in the lifestream, moving with the great human tide toward the normal human destinies. She wasn't crazy any more, she wasn't self-destructive, as the doctors liked to say. She wasn't alone; her child was with her. Her existence was justified.

She bought one of those books, *You and Your Baby*. She studied the drawings, the tiny curled spines, finger forms, enormous eyes. She imagined the face of her child, eyes shut, a sleeper closed on its dream.

Her daze of fulfillment showed. She knew this because strangers would smile at her as though she were a friend they'd almost forgotten, someone from home encountered here in the impersonal city. And after a few weeks Will asked her, with calculated casualness, if she'd met some other guy. He was curious, he said. Did she realize they weren't seeing as much of each other?

"What guy? I like to be alone now and then," she said, smiling.

The fact was that she'd stopped calling him, except occasionally. She didn't ask him for supper unless he suggested it first. When he stopped by the house she was often out in the garden or walking in the ravine. She liked discovering little things, tiny shells and fossils, acorns; she liked watching the squirrels storing up nuts and the birds eating the last of the berries. She was preoccupied. He liked that.

He began to feel safe with her. They fought, once, about something insignificant and he angrily stomped out of her house. She didn't call him to say she was sorry, as she would have done in the past. Instead, he phoned her. He woke her at eleven that night and said he'd got carried away, he was sorry.

"What did we fight about?" She was honestly baffled.

He laughed. "You're doing better!" He was hearty, as if he were welcoming her into the club of normally insensitive men and women, as if he were welcoming her into the company of the cured. As if he'd cured her.

When she was pregnant, she was healed—it was so simple,

after all. What none of the doctors or psychologists could do, the baby did. It was as if the child were her own self-esteem fattening inside her.

"I shouldn't have stormed out," Will went on. "That was dumb. We should have a better way to resolve arguments."

"Yes." She wanted to go back to sleep. She wanted to sleep all the time, now.

"Shall I come back?" That meant he wanted her to forgive him. He couldn't bear to hurt her, he'd said. That also meant he wanted to get laid.

She'd made other discoveries since she'd been pregnant. Not attached to a man, she could study the behavior of men more clearly. What men really wanted most was their work. Love didn't have much to do with anything real; work was real. That discovery didn't make her bitter. She felt the same way. She wanted to have certain comforts and then to be left alone with the baby. She and Will were in perfect balance.

"Sure, come on back," she told him. She knew she'd sleep until he arrived, and sleep again immediately after they made love. Her arm over his side, her legs tucked behind his, her forehead against his shoulder—that was a good way to sleep.

"You've got a key. Let yourself in," she said.

"You're a sweetie," he told her.

The next morning he asked her to marry him. It was a Wednesday, his day off. She'd got up and packed Jo her lunch and come back to bed where he dozed on his back, the sheet pushed down to his waist. She was thinking she liked that curly hair on his chest but that it was too bad his beard was so rough in the morning. She was wondering if she'd left the carton of milk out on the counter.

He lifted the covers to welcome her back to bed. "I think we should get married."

She smiled, knowing she couldn't tell him why she felt like laughing. "Wait a minute, let me get hold of this concept. You're asking me to marry you?" A few weeks ago she'd have been kissing him with gratitude, weeping on his chest with appreciation.

"Hey." He grinned, his breath sour from his pipe. "Don't you think we should?"

"Should?" Did he know?

"It feels right." He kissed her, still grinning, and their teeth bumped.

"Should!" No, he hadn't guessed the baby, but she wondered if she wanted to get married.

"I'll make an honest woman of you, you'll make an honest man of me. How about it?" He kissed her shoulder, then her throat, his beard scratching.

She remembered that *You and Your Baby* included a chapter, "The Role of the Father." She hadn't read it. She did laugh, then, she couldn't stop herself. He began to laugh, too, belly laughs, like hers. He was so relieved, that was it. He wanted so badly for her to take things lightly. Even marrying him.

"Yes or no?" he asked through their laughter.

They rolled on the bed, laughing, laughing. It didn't matter to her, that was what was so funny. It didn't matter if he married her or not. Which was why he *wanted* to marry her, but he didn't know that. It was all so ironic and she couldn't explain. She slipped a hand to her belly. Soon he'd realize she was getting fat. That made her laugh harder—his imminent surprise. "Give me a few days to think it over," she said, hugging her knees.

He pushed at her knees so he could move closer. "Listen, kid, marry me." His Humphrey Bogart imitation, and he kissed harder. "Have you got your thing in?"

"Yes, from last night. Yes."

He scooped her to him, his hands under her ass. "You'll come around."

After they made love and he slept again, she studied him closely. Not a handsome man, but she liked the way he looked—sturdy, intense, muscular. He smelled good to her. Of the men she'd known, she liked him the best. But only a short time ago she'd worshipped Will, thought she couldn't survive without him. She touched his forehead. What do we feel that we can ever trust to last?

But a child needs a father. She wondered if Will would be the kind of father who'd want to be in the delivery room. There was nothing for a man to do there, really; no work. She'd have to tell Will she didn't want him with her when she delivered the baby.

But there wasn't a baby. Two days later when she was doing breakfast dishes she felt a warm flood between her legs. Quickly, quickly she jammed a towel there and drove herself to Highland Park General—not Saint Mary's, no, no, Will mustn't find out. He must never know. Never. By the time she got to Emergency the towel was soaked and it was all over. They cleaned her up, examined her, gave her a shot to help her rest. They said, You will have other babies, don't worry; your womb wasn't ready yet, next time it will be. She was home in time to fix supper for Jo.

Will phoned while she heated chicken noodle soup—did she want to go out for dinner?

Jo sat at the breakfast table, chewing her braid as she read the comics in the paper. "I'll stay here with the kid," Laura said. "To tell you the truth, I think I've got the flu. Maybe in a few days?"

"Too bad! Get a good night's sleep. Dream of me," he added, his tone softer, romantic. He was wooing her—if you reject a man, his instinct is to chase you. It's in their hormones.

She made her voice light and crisp, then. "Listen, darling? Just to make sure you get it on your calendar, we're getting married, right?" As though they were making a date for tennis.

There was a pause, then he laughed. "Right! I knew you'd see it my way."

She closed her eyes. "Pretty sure of yourself?" she made herself say.

"Sure of *us*." It was a line he might have been quoting from any of the movies they'd seen lately.

She made a kissing noise and he smacked back. "Have a good night, sweetie. I'll phone you tomorrow morning."

That night, in her feverish sleep, she dreamt of a toad or frog, its body flattened like a dried leaf and pressed onto a steaming highway somewhere in the West. Heat waves shimmered over the frog print as she gazed down at it, noticing how it resembled a little human, those muscular leg shapes, reaching arms. Then she saw that the small, squashed body had no hands, only stubs where the hands must have been before they were torn away.

The mangled thing in the dream was not her baby. The damaged creature was she, herself. She awoke crying and could not stop. Gone, both of them, mother and child, gone.

In the morning the florist delivered a large bouquet of white daisies. She'd got just the right tone with Will, then—chin up and cute, feisty, sure of herself—the young Kate Hepburn.

She said nothing to Will about the pregnancy. What could she say? And she tried to hold herself back from him, not to hang on, but she needed to cling again. It was all that it had been before. He was a matter of life or death to her, but this time she couldn't let him know.

More babies, the nurses had told her in Emergency. But there were no more pregnancies. Nothing worked. Will suggested adoption, that was how little he knew of her needs. And what had she learned in all that time? How to wait and wait and wait.

Steps outside the door, a key—Thomas was back. She stood up quickly, moved away from his desk. The door swung in as she ran her hands through her hair and he was framed in the doorway, dust motes in the panel of light that reflected off the white wall beside him. His face was flushed, his eyes too bright. She knew before he spoke that he'd been drinking, maybe a lot—living with her father had taught her all the signs.

"Sweetheart," he said, shutting the door and tossing the jacket he carried onto the unmade bed. He wore a blue shirt and tie, gray trousers; even writers dress up for doctors. "You waited! They started with vodka martinis at lunch and now they're sobering up on margaritas. I excused myself. I claimed an emergency. That's you."

Her hands trembled, so she pushed them into her pants pockets. "I like it here."

"How can you like it here? What's there to like? Even I don't like it here and sometimes I don't leave it for days." He shoved his hair back, and paced by her to the window, where he turned, the five-o'clock sun directly behind him.

"It's quiet."

"Oh, quiet! Christ, is it quiet."

She shaded her eyes to look at him. She hadn't remembered that he was so thin, and how did he get that tan if he locked himself in here all day to write? Sun shimmered around his dark form. Maybe she'd waited for him too long. She should have left, made him come after her. "Actually, I was just going."

That pushed him from the window and toward her. He took her elbow to turn her away from the door. "No, not yet. I ran all the way from the train station. I was sure you'd given up on me. But here you are! We'll have a beer, okay? You said you wanted to talk."

She let him lead her to the kitchen. He grabbed two beers from a six-pack in the refrigerator and popped them, poured hers into a glass and handed it to her. He circled her and came to rest against one of the counters. She leaned against the sink.

"Your day was—"

He held up his hand. "Hold it. I'm not the good doctor. I don't want to talk about 'my day,' Laura. My days are all the same, white on white. Right now you are the gold warp through the gray woof in this fabric. For God's sake, let's not be polite."

She smiled. Good, they could leap into it. She'd been wrong to doubt he'd want that headlong rush, too.

"What's on your mind?" he said.

"How would Jo fit in?" She hadn't intended to ask that, but she should trust her instincts. She repeated, "How?"

He narrowed his eyes. "Fit in?"

"Here."

He spread his arms, moons of sweat, under. "In this place?"

"In your life."

He laughed, then took a long drink of beer. "You're a trapeze artist, do you know that? You execute these sudden leaps and twists. Jo has already pried me out of 'my life,' as you delicately put it, your eyebrows lifted. I don't want anyone to *fit into* this muck. I've been trying to worm my way out of it with very little success."

Now she was confused. "You could move."

"It's not the place, Laura. It's all in here." He tapped his temple. "Depression is serious business. It's like that black hole the scientists have discovered in the universe, a dark appetite that eats up the surrounding stars. Jo is the faint light at the end of that tunnel."

"She's not strong enough."

"Oh, she'd be strong enough if I could convince her to let herself be. I'll admit that my first foray into her domain didn't go so well. She didn't understand . . ."

"But I do." She let the silence following her words stay. It grew around them both.

After a minute he breathed, "Ah. You didn't come about Jo."

"I wanted to tell you she's moving into a dorm this week. She wants out of the house. It's time."

"You didn't wait two hours to tell me she's moving into a dorm."

"I want to help you get clear about her. You expect too much. You'll be disappointed."

"I'm already disappointed. There is practically nothing in life that doesn't disappoint me. I think that Jo's spirit—"

"Spirit!'

He rubbed his lower lip with his thumb. "She has one."

"Thomas, what you feel for her is sex. That's all." She leaned back, her hand on the cool porcelain.

He came to stand by her, turned on the faucet and let water run over his hands, then splashed his face, wiped it with a paper towel. His shoulder against hers, he looked out into the parking lot where shadows carved the brick buildings in half.

"Sex," he said "Sex with a capital S, of course. Yes, that's there. Maybe it's the basis for everything between men and women. What do you think?"

She shivered. "I think there's understanding."

"Do you? What do you *understand?*"

The heat from his shoulder passed into hers. She turned to face him and saw he watched her warily. Go slow, she told herself. Play the game. Change the pace. "I understand that right now you're drunk, right?"

He laughed, his chin tipped up. "Oh, God, yes, I'm drunk. Never try to keep up with the doctors. They will drink you right under the table and while you're lying there at their feet they'll plan, coherently, new tax shelters."

"So I'm not sure I believe anything you say."

His hand slid down her arm to her elbow. "Hold on. You can believe me, Laura. There's no reason to lie, and I don't have enough excitement in my life to pass up an electrical storm like

you. Yes, it's true, sex draws me to your sister. It draws me to
you, too. That's only the beginning."

"*Then* there's understanding, that's what I'm saying. Jo can't
understand you."

"But you've got it backwards. I can understand her, you see. I
really don't want a woman 'understanding' me, Laura. No, not
even you. Actually, I have something else in mind."

Without kissing her, he stroked her breast with the back of
his hand until her nipple rose stiff as a thumb to meet his.

She held her breath. She wanted to fling her arms around
him, but he kept her at this distance. He liked to be in control,
she remembered. She would tell him all that she understood
about him, and he would be glad of it, but this wasn't the time.
That time would come later, after they'd made love, in the safer
intimacy that follows.

"There's an erotic promise, isn't there?" he said softly.
"Sometimes the promise is so much sweeter than anything that
comes after. Do you keep your promises, Laura?"

She nodded.

He drew a cross over her heart, and waited for her to answer
that question.

She nodded again.

"Because I'm drunk right now, you said you have to head
back up the shore, and what I have in mind will take a long,
long time. You'll come back? Promise you'll come back."

She leaned to kiss him, tasting salt on his lips. His kiss was
gentle, then suddenly fierce, his teeth cutting. When she didn't
flinch, he took her face in both hands. "So, it will be violent,
won't it?"

She parted her lips to invite another kiss, but he said, "I think
I'm going to be sick in a moment and I'd rather face that alone.
I'll phone you when I sober up."

Before he could say anything else, she swung away from him,
crossed the kitchen and grabbed her shoulder bag from the
black canvas chair. He was right behind her, his hand on her
waist as he opened the door. "I shouldn't have had the booze. I
sabotage things sometimes," he said. "I sabotage what I want
the most. That's the way I am."

She stood a moment in the hallway outside his closed door,

heard him fling himself onto his bed. *Sabotage*—a word for war games, for broken machines and botched assembly lines. He was afraid, that was it. She put her hand to the burn at her breast where he'd touched her. But now they knew each other better. Now there was, as he'd said, an erotic promise. If the doorway was sex, the rooms beyond the door were the hopes and disappointments of their lives. She would teach him that there was nothing they couldn't share. She would wait for him, there was nothing else to do. *New,* he'd said, foretelling her future. He was that new person who made life okay a little while longer. Without Thomas to wait for, what would she ever, ever do?

17

As Jo worked the clay it warmed her hands. That comforted her—a little, anyway. Although rain drizzled steadily onto the windows, the heat from the kiln behind her pressed against her shoulders like July sun. Except for her instructor, Mr. Coutris, who was mixing clay, she was the only one in the studio. He hadn't even seemed to notice that she'd been here all this long Sunday afternoon, ruining the pots she tried to make. Maybe Mr. Coutris wanted to be alone, too. Maybe he didn't want to think.

If you worked with your hands you didn't have to think. It must be that way for Will, too. After that day, over two weeks ago now, the day they kissed, he'd begun to schedule more surgery, more appointments. "It's an expanded schedule," he'd said to Laura, although Laura hadn't asked. Jo wanted to say, "I know, I understand," but she hadn't been alone with him to talk. He'd seen to that. Every evening he'd gone to meetings, or planned games of squash or tennis. It seemed to her that Will had moved out of the house before she did. And when she went back home for a meal, as she had today, he was cool and distant. He didn't know what to do, either.

The days would have been impossible if she hadn't been able to do this work with her hands. It was difficult to concentrate on words—if you were in love. She didn't have any control over her thoughts. One moment she'd be reading her assignment and the next moment she'd be staring blindly into space, seeing only his face. "Will." When she spoke his name a shimmer of longing traveled over her skin like the heat from the kiln. Even her bones grew fiery and molten.

Sometimes she observed this pattern of heat as though she watched dye spread outward from her heart through her body. She traced its journey through all her nerve endings, even into the tips of her fingers. But no matter how scientifically she observed herself, the force of those feelings didn't lessen. Her thoughts about Will went around and around, like the potter's wheel under her hands, always returning to his expression of pain and desire just before they kissed. He loved her. And he regretted it. What could come of that love except pain?

Now and then she paused, her wet hands holding a ball of clay, and watched Mr. Coutris, bare-chested under his work apron, a bandanna tied over his mouth against the dust, as he slit open the bags of clay compounds and dumped them into the mixing tub. Clay dust matted his white chest hair and collected in the creases in his forehead and under his eyes. The jagged furrow between his eyes made her think of Will. Maybe Mr. Coutris, too, had once been in love with the wrong person.

She had no power to make anything happen, that was the worst of what she'd learned. Will had always urged her, "Choose for yourself, be your own person." But what choices could she make now? Estelle had said once, calling from a grocery store somewhere in Missouri, "You can choose and choose until you're all choosed out. Life just throws it back in your face! What *you* want doesn't matter none. What's gonna happen will happen. That's just how it is." Estelle said that even before she knew she was dying.

The side of the pot Jo was working on wobbled and then collapsed. She'd let her fingers go slack, let them follow the clay. A beginner's clumsy mistake. Another pot ruined. She hadn't made even one worth saving all day. Who cared? She pushed the clay to the center of the wheel and forced it into a ball.

"How long are you going to keep this guy waiting?"

Startled, she looked up to find Mr. Coutris standing a few feet away, wiping his hands on his apron.

She stood, knocking her shins against the wheel. Was Will here? "What guy?"

Mr. Coutris rubbed his eyes with a corner of his apron. "A guy in an old Pontiac. He's been looking in the window for five minutes. He's not watching me, so I figure he's yours." He gestured with his chin to the windows behind her.

Kit, in his windbreaker, hands in his jeans pockets. He waved. They'd seen each other twice since that night they'd smoked the hash. He'd apologized too much. She'd told him that a friend of Laura's had sent the package, a text for English. She and Kit had found it difficult to talk—what was there to talk about? "He's not *mine*," she told Mr. Coutris.

"Talk to him about that." He gestured again to the window where Kit stood, head bent in the rain.

"He's just a friend."

"A wet friend. I've got to lock up here in a minute," Mr. Coutris said, not unkindly, looking at her over the red and white bandanna—a bandit.

So that was that. There wasn't any choice. "Couldn't you just brick me up and let me stay here?" she asked Mr. Coutris.

In spite of his bandanna mask she saw that he smiled at her. "At my age you hide out. You're too young to be talking that way."

When she'd cleaned up and got outside, Kit was back in his car, the heater going, a Dire Straits tape on the player. She slid in, zipping up her jacket against the chill. Her hands ached from the caustic clay and cold water, so she wedged them under her thighs to warm them.

"Hey, Jo."

"Hey." She took a quick look at him. His tan was fading, his nose peeling. His face was thinner than she remembered, his cheekbones showed, the way they had when he'd starved himself for wrestling. A nice guy, but how could she have imagined that she'd grow to love him? "How're you doing, Kit?"

"Okay. No, not so good. It's hard to find you now that you're living here. How's dorm life treating you?"

She looked up at the brick wall of the dorm. Lights were on already in some of the rooms, here and there a plant or pop bottle showed on a windowsill. In the dorm there was no place to be alone, none at all. Darlene Mohs, Jo's roommate, got up at six-thirty every morning to wash and air-dry her permed hair. She was a pre-drama major; she wore an enormous sweatshirt over skin-tight Levi's and Popsicle-red sneakers—what theater people in New York wore, Darlene said. Sometimes she said "You Nork" instead of New York, to be funny. Oh, God, it was awful.

"I think it'll be okay," she said; she didn't want Kit to try to save her.

"You want to show me your room?"

"Actually, I'm going back down to the house now. Laura made a big deal out of inviting me to spend part of the day with her. She said she remembered how rotten dorm food is on Sundays. You could take me to the train station."

"I'll drive you home."

She didn't want to spend that much time with Kit, but there was no choice here, either. As they traveled down the long drive willows brushed the roof. She crossed her legs and looked out of her window at the stark college buildings sitting on the crest of the hill. Maybe if she just kept quiet she could ease Kit out of her life without a confrontation.

"I've wanted to see you all week, but I've been afraid, too." He pulled out of the gravel drive onto Sheridan Road too quickly, the tail of his car skidding.

"Why afraid?" She didn't really want to know, but she was stuck. She watched the road, the dripping willows giving way to the open fields of Fort Sheridan where a ground fog hung over the brown grass.

"Something's wrong between us."

"Nothing's wrong." She wanted to say, There's nothing between us, really. But that sounded too harsh.

"I want to know what's wrong, Jo. I care for you, you know."

Her heart sank because he was going to play detective. It didn't matter—if he pushed her she'd tell him she didn't want to go out with him any more. The only thing she had to protect were her feelings for Will. She knew exactly how the world would judge her: You don't fall in love with your brother-in-law; you don't fall in love with a married man almost twice your age. Will couldn't guard his reputation if he were seen with her in intimate circumstances. But there was no way that Kit could find out. "I know you care for me. Nothing's wrong, really."

The stoplight turned red at the fort. Kit slowed too quickly and his brakes grabbed. She caught the dash with her forearm, saw him bump the steering wheel.

"Sorry!" he said.

He was proud of his driving, so he must be upset, she knew. It wouldn't hurt her to help him out a little. He'd have her home in a few minutes and she could figure out a way to explain that she didn't want to see him again. "Just tell me what's going on, okay?"

He bit his lip. "I saw Nate Coleman last week."

"Nate Coleman?" She huffed out her exasperation.

"I ran into him at Walgreen's. He said he'd seen you."

She sighed impatiently. "I see Nate all the time. He delivers the paper. He speeds up on his bike making noises like it's a motorcycle."

"He's got a crush on you."

She knew—Nate was exactly at that age when boys start sneaking looks at a girl's boobs. "It's not me. It's his hormones. What's the big deal about Nate seeing me?"

Kit slowed behind a white-headed lady in a Lincoln, and followed, too close. It wasn't like him to push like this. He sped up suddenly and passed. "Nate's dog is in heat. He says she got out a couple of Saturdays ago and he had to run her down. He followed her to the beach. He said that when he passed the boathouse he saw you kissing some guy. What I want to know is who's the guy."

It took a moment for Kit's story to register, and then blood rushed to her face and she heard a roar that she knew was her pulse. So Nate had seen her kissing Will. She remembered this feeling of violation—so Thomas wasn't the only spy in her life. She looked away, tried to catch her breath. Through the tumult of guilty panic, she heard Kit repeat, "Who's the guy?"

A scene from a storybook flashed before her: Peter Rabbit running from Farmer MacGregor. She'd hated that book. "Nate didn't say?"

Kit looked at her sideways. "He says it was that guy who came to the bonfire. The one you said made a move on you. The one you said you couldn't stand."

She unclenched her fists. Some of her adrenaline began to flow back into the space under her ribs. Nate thought she'd been with Thomas in the boathouse. Then Thomas it would be. Anyone besides Will. Anyone at all. She made her voice contrite. "Nate's right, that little rat." But she was afraid to look at Kit, because he might read the whole of it in her glance.

"I thought you despised the guy."

He was jealous, of course. But she was on safer ground, because she didn't need a clear head to talk about Thomas. "Kit, listen, it's nothing. I didn't know how to tell you, it's complicated and I thought you'd be upset. It's true that he's after me, but he's nothing to me, really."

"He's *something*. He comes up here to the party, Nate says you spent the evening with him. When I come by you're crying and drunk. The next time he comes by you make out with him in the boathouse."

For a moment she considered jumping out of the car, but he was going too fast. "I didn't make out with him! He kissed me. I couldn't stop him."

"Nate says you didn't even hear him when he ran by the boathouse. He says neither of you moved."

"Nate's a punk kid! The truth is that I hate Thomas! I wish he were dead and I've never said that about anyone!" She was convincing, here.

Kit touched her knee. "Okay, okay, just tell me about him."

"Don't be jealous!"

"I am. I can't help it. Just tell me."

So she did. She reminded Kit she'd been upset enough about Thomas's advances to bite his hand. About the scene in the boathouse she was vague—he'd come to apologize, grabbed her. He was horrible, really, a psychopath. She gained strength with the telling.

She watched Kit as she hurried with her story, her words stumbling. A flush appeared and faded on his face and a single vein stood out blue under the thin skin at his temple. He believed her. She had more power than she'd realized; she could mold reality the way she'd worked the clay.

"Are you angry with me?" she said finally.

He turned onto Center Road, driving slowly now. "No. I just wish I'd known. You should've trusted me. You could have, you know."

Easily, gratefully, she accused herself. "I know there wasn't any reason to hide anything from you." They would be at her house soon, and she was exhausted.

Then, as they approached her corner, she saw Thomas. He stood on her front porch, right at the door, as though delivered on schedule to verify her story to Kit.

She slid down in her seat and grabbed Kit's arm. "Turn into the lane and stop!"

He pulled over. "What's up?"

"There he is on my porch." She sank lower, but for once she was glad to see Thomas. Now any doubts Kit had would be resolved. Laura opened the door to Thomas—to sick Thomas with his sick talk—what did Laura want with all that? Never mind, just wear the disguise—it fit.

Kit leaned forward. "He looks sleazy."

"He is."

Thomas stayed in the doorway. Jo couldn't see Laura, but he must be talking to her. Then he stepped into the house and the door closed behind him. "Damn!" she said.

"What happens now?"

"Let's just wait a minute. He'll leave."

Dusk had brought more rain, the steady kind that brimmed the potholes and would leave the ground mushy. Kit switched tapes to a new Bob Dylan. They waited. Dylan's voice whined, and something about the music made her throat tight. Oh, Will, please, please—wanting to be with him, anywhere at all, wanting to be done with everything else.

"They haven't turned on the lights," Kit said.

"Laura wouldn't mess around."

"You never know."

But even as he spoke the light over the back door came on like a yellow star. Kit started his car and inched down the street to the Jacobsons' drive, where he backed in. "Let's see what happens."

When the back door opened, it was Laura who came out first, her blond hair glistening under the yellow light as she paused to pull on her raincoat. She held the door for Thomas. With his hand on her waist, they ran through the rain to the garage.

"Now what?" Kit said.

"Now she gives him a ride to the train station, I guess. They're going to drive right by here and spot us."

"Let's see."

Though they couldn't see, really, because the garage blocked their view of the station wagon. Headlights flared a halo over the garage roof. Then the station wagon appeared at the corner. Thomas drove, and as the car turned left, away from town, he kissed Laura, she leaned on his shoulder, then slid lower. She must have her head in his lap. Jo bit her thumb. Not *Laura*.

"They're getting it on," Kit said. "He's not after you. He's after her."

"Maybe." She had a sick feeling in her stomach. She wanted to be alone now, to gather herself. And Kit didn't know Laura. Laura didn't really like men. Oh, she flirted, and liked attention, and she probably loved the intrigue Thomas offered, but deep down she distrusted men. That was because their father was such a mess. And Laura needed Will too much to take any risks.

But Kit eased out of the drive and followed the station wagon, a block behind.

"Let's turn back," she told Kit.

"In a minute."

She didn't say anything else. Kit's attention wasn't on her now, and that was enough.

Thomas turned into the drive of the old Macalester estate. The mansion and the outbuildings had been torn down, all the trees marked for razing. Apartments were going in there. In the meantime, kids went onto the grounds to party. By the time Kit pulled up at the entrance, Thomas had driven almost out of sight down the winding, tree-lined drive.

"They're going to stay a while," Kit said.

"Laura's life is her own business." But what if Laura were

under Thomas's thumb? What if it was more than pretend? Scary, but not beyond imagination. And if she were, Will would feel differently about her.

"They're gone," Kit said, though she could see that for herself. The drive was empty, puddles shimmering.

"He might hurt her," Kit said.

"He's crazy, but he's not evil."

Kit slid his arm behind her. "Sometimes it's the same thing. At least you're safe."

Safe? Her life looked so simple, so enclosed, but inside she was walking a tightrope. Oh, Will, catch me if I fall. "Will you take me home, Kit?"

He smiled. "Your dinner's going to be late, but I don't think you have to worry about this guy any more. Let's have a beer and take it easy."

As Kit drove to his uncle's liquor store, Jo pushed her hands inside her jacket sleeves. Her chapped fingers scraped against the rough wool. She thought of the lane where Laura and Thomas were parked. Surely they were too old to make out in a car, but why else come to this place? Oh, Laura—she'd been right all along: Beware of strange men. She should have followed her own warnings. But now things would change between Laura and Will. Jo pulled the collar of her jacket up over her chin—hope could make her blush in the same way guilt did.

They each had a beer and Kit drove her home the long way. He didn't want to talk and neither did she, so they cranked the music loud. By the time they got back the station wagon was in its spot behind the garage again. He parked beside it. To her surprise he grabbed her shoulders and kissed her, his lips parted, his breath pressing into her. Her head bumped the door as he leaned against her. It was the kind of kiss she'd wanted from him once, but now it was too late. All she wanted was Will.

"I don't want to lose you," Kit whispered when she broke the kiss.

"Call if you want," she said quickly, so she could get away.

He opened her door for her. "I will." He waved as he backed out of the drive.

She closed the back gate behind herself and looked up at the house, seeing it as though she'd been gone a long, long time. All the lights were still out, and the house was shrouded by the green evening rain. The place seemed to hang suspended from a taut line, as slack and as temporary as a canvas backdrop. She was glad she'd left, although Will still lived here. Maybe he'd leave someday, too. Anything could happen, Laura had proved that.

The kitchen light went on, sending streaks of light across the grass. Laura appeared in the window by the breakfast table. Because the room was so bright, and it was dark outside, she'd be looking into her own reflection in the window.

My sister. The same mother, the same father.

Laura leaned close to the windowpane, raised both hands, as though searching for support. The tips of her fingers came to rest on the glass, ten small circles on the faintly clouded surface. She seemed to test her weight against the pane, against the dark beyond the window. She thought she was alone in her bright cell, her kitchen. Her lips parted, as though she might be having trouble breathing, and she leaned forward until her forehead touched the window, too. Then she closed her eyes and flattened her palms onto the glass.

The ache started in again under Jo's ribs. It came from loving Will, and her own loneliness, but now it tangled queerly with regret for Laura. How unfair life is. How stupid and blundering the ways we choose to live it, and no second chance to make things better.

Jo slammed the garage door, so Laura would hear her coming and not be caught with that stricken look, and trudged down the walk to the house.

18

Laura had vacuumed the whole house, been to the Sunset for groceries, stopped at Walgreen's for a Sunday *Times* and a bottle of hand lotion, had coffee at the Inn, taken an armload of books to the library drop-off, washed the kitchen windows, done an hour and a half of exercises to her tapes, and still it was only three-thirty. Not time yet to start dinner. No place left to go, nothing left to do, nothing even to be invented. As if for the rest of her life it would always be three-thirty on a rainy Sunday afternoon, with hours and hours left ahead of her before she could even pretend to sleep, and nothing to distract her from what she did not have or whom she could not be. Not one thing to look forward to except Thomas. Almost two weeks had passed since she'd gone to his apartment, and he hadn't called her yet. Although she'd left two messages on his answering machine, he hadn't responded. When she was with him he'd promised; she'd promised. Where was he?

After her exercises and shower she put on a cream-colored blouse and a tan wool skirt she liked for its pleats and deep pockets. Dressing for Thomas—he liked silk, didn't he?—she magicked him right into her bedroom. And why not? He wanted her as much as she wanted him; he'd said so. Synchronicity, that word he'd used with Jo in the airport in Vienna—a meeting of equals in space hollowed out by mutual need. That wasn't magic; in fact, maybe it was simple common sense to believe that within the limitless variety of human encounters such a meeting was not only possible but probable. Except he had not come.

She'd invited Jo for brunch today, but at table Jo was sullen and Will was preoccupied and silent. Since Jo had moved out of the house and into the dorm, she and Will had lost the ease with each other they'd always had. They weren't talking to each other much these days, though now and then they exchanged their old "hi pal" glances. Neither of them noticed Laura's blue mood. Not that she needed Will to understand her now; Thomas would love her instead.

Love—after all, what did the word mean? She "loved" Jo because she'd been responsible for the girl, and because they'd spent so much time together. And often she'd liked Jo for her animal energy, her scruffy good humor, liked it that there was someone else in the house. Now that Jo lived at Woodcliff Laura was alone more and more. Will had started working through dinnertime, fixing himself a bologna sandwich which he ate as he stood at the kitchen counter. Did she *love* Will now? They walked side by side, not touching, toward some juncture where their paths would branch. If she stepped away from him he wouldn't come after her. She must follow him. Neither of them had ever said that, but it was understood between them. She listened for the sound of his steps at the back door during these interminable afternoons or evenings when she was alone in the house. Without him, she would have no one. Is that love?

Probably she didn't really "love" Thomas, either. She desired him. Yes, that was a better word: desire. Hungered for him and his complicated inner world so like her own. She'd been thinking of Thomas at brunch when Will asked her to pass the syrup and she handed him the whipped cream instead. "Are you feeling all right?" he asked her. "Sure." And he went on shoveling down his waffles and fresh strawberries. She thought he was relieved that she didn't say any more. Silently, she cut her waffle into small pieces, poised a sliver of strawberry on each morsel, waited until Will and Jo carried their dishes to the kitchen and went into the living room, then washed her meal down the disposal. She'd started starving herself again, as though this would make something happen, make Thomas call her. Love her.

She was stacking up sections of the *Times* which Will had left strewn across the sofa when there was a quick footstep on the front porch. Thomas was at the door. Although he must have seen her at the same time she caught sight of him through the frosted-glass window, he rang the bell anyway, announcing his arrival. Rang again, even as she dropped the newspapers into the kindling box and hurried to let him in. She'd thought she was ready, but she wasn't. He was here too soon, too suddenly.

As she released the latch, he turned the knob himself and pushed in the door. In a hurry.

"Thomas!"

His lips were tight, his hair plastered to his head with rain, droplets in his beard. He looked over her head, around her, so intent on his purpose he might simply have pushed her aside. Then his gaze snapped back to her as if he'd just remembered old lessons in manners. "Hello, Laura. Is Jo here? I went to her dorm but she wasn't there. I've got something to tell her."

She shook her head. That she was alone was fortunate. Neither Will nor Jo would be home until five-thirty or six at the earliest. "She's working at the ceramics studio, but she'll be here for an early supper before she checks back into her dorm. Come on in."

He looked up the staircase as if willing Jo to appear there, as if he couldn't believe she wasn't where he wanted her to be.

"*I'm* here." She touched his arm. His skin was darkened around his eyes, his jaw tight. Waiting had been hard on him, too. "Come have a glass of wine with me. I've wanted to see you."

"And good old Will? No, you wouldn't be asking me in if he were here, right?"

"He's playing squash."

"The boy athlete."

"We're the only two actors on this empty stage."

He refused her his smile.

What could she say now? He had business to finish with Jo,

that was the thing. He'd rehearsed a speech for her and wanted to deliver it. Laura touched his arm again. His trenchcoat was soaked and dripping, a pool forming around his feet in the doorway. "Hey, there," she said softly. "I want to know more about you, you know. While you're waiting for Jo we can talk."

"You want to know more about me?" But he didn't step inside.

"Yes. You fascinate me. I have some theories about you I'd like to try out." She kept her voice light, teasing. Except he'd know she wasn't teasing.

"I fascinate you?" Then he did smile. A secret joke? Maybe women said that to him all the time.

"Does that surprise you?"

"Nothing surprises me." Looking over her shoulder again, as though Jo might be coming in the back door.

"Come *in,* Thomas."

"What would you like to know?" He leaned against the door-frame, impatient.

Start with something safe, anything would do. "Tell me about your novel, for one thing. I read some of your notes—"

"My novel! It's been rejected. Finally, irrevocably trashed. It sat on Hindon's desk for a year, I did all the revisions he requested, and yesterday it came back to me with his cryptic note about 'his editor's final decision.' Four years of work down the drain. My entire career!"

"Thomas, I'm sorry!'

"I don't want to talk about it." He pulled an envelope from his coat pocket. "Listen, Laura, give this to Jo when she gets home, will you? I'd hoped to read it to her myself, but I'm too pressed for time to wait around for her to show." He tossed an envelope onto the table inside the door. "There. That's done."

She caught his outstretched arm. "I've been waiting for you!"

Now she registered the shift of his attention, which he made as precisely as though he'd exchanged lenses in his camera. Unburdened of his message for Jo, he gazed down at Laura as though he brought her face into focus, studied it, refined the image.

"I've been waiting for you to call, you know that." A flush spread across her throat, prickling.

"Have you, now?" He smiled again, friendlier, taking her hand.

"You said you'd get in touch with me when you sobered up."

"Christ, I thought maybe I'd hallucinated that scene with you. Drunk as a skunk. What did I say? Anything compromising?" He squeezed her hand, hard.

"You remember. You said there was a promise between us. I left messages on your answering machine and—"

"Ah! It all comes back to me now." He pressed her hand to his dry lips. "Lovely Laura, I remember your visit vividly, a flash of color in my drab life. I didn't want to call you until I could say something definite about seeing you."

He brushed past her into the hall and she pulled the door shut behind him. Images spun through her mind too quickly. She wanted to slow herself down. She'd get them some wine, they'd sit in the sun-room to talk, she'd gather his attention to herself and keep it. His fantasy about Jo would soon be over, if it wasn't already. Now it was her turn. She snapped the lock on the door, bumped his side when she turned. He'd stayed close, waiting.

"Well!" Her laugh was too high, not her own.

He didn't seem to notice. "Let me get it straight about Jo. She won't come to the phone when I call her dorm. Would you say she's telling me something?"

"She has a boyfriend her own age. Anyway, you're too much for her. You know that."

He caught his lower lip between his teeth. "She hides when I come close, like a rabbit under the shadow of a hawk."

"It saves her from being snatched up. She's probably wise. She's not your match." She knew her lines, and she wasn't nervous, now, but she hoped she wouldn't laugh like that again.

"I wrote her some letters, revealing ones. She's refused to answer them. Everything I write gets rejected these days."

She knew she'd been right to keep those letters from Jo. Even if Jo had read them, what could she have said to him except what he'd learned: Jo didn't want any part of him. And if an unmasking were to take place, Laura must begin now. "I read them."

He raised his eyebrows—she could startle him; she liked that. "She gave you those letters?"

"I found them. By accident, of course. I wanted to tell you that your letters are wonderful! You mustn't care that Jo didn't respond. She simply doesn't know what—"

"You read them!" He laughed, but the laugh didn't reach his eyes. "So what do you think of me as the heartsick lover?"

She leaned against the hall table. This is crucial, get it right, she told herself. Don't frighten him now. "I respected you in your letters."

"Respected?"

"Respected your intelligence, your aloneness, your search."

He cocked his head. "It's always a revelation to discover how one appears to another."

"You need someone."

"That's your appraisal of me, is it? A needy—"

"You're a man who speaks a language only a few can understand." She was hurrying, but it was too late to worry about that. "You and I speak the same language, I'm sure of it." She took his hand again so he wouldn't move away from her.

He raised their clasped hands. "What would you say is the word for this in *our* language?" A thin, pink scar curved over his thumb. "Look. Jo told me that I'd invaded her privacy. She bit me to make sure I'd heard her."

No, that was too violent for Jo—he could have got that scar anywhere, Laura thought. It was one of his metaphors. She touched it, as though it still needed healing. "You and I have more of these inside, don't we? Scars."

"Scars?" With his damp thumb, he touched her chin, traced a line down her throat to the neckline of her blouse. "You and the good doctor aren't doing so well, are you?"

"Is it obvious?"

"I've caught that high-pitched sound a bat makes guiding itself from a cave. You've got a certain attractive desperation, Laura. *Laura.* A beautiful name. Did you know it was the name of Petrarch's mistress?"

"Tell me more about this signal I give off."

"It's more in your tone than in your words. You want . . ."

She waited. Would he say "love"? He caressed her throat with his open hand, his face came nearer. She didn't close her eyes until he kissed them.

"Laura," he whispered against her temple, "I remember your visit to my apartment very clearly. I remember that I wanted to devour you. Let's get out of here, beautiful Laura. Let's take your car and get the hell out of the good doctor's house. He doesn't deserve you."

She felt it, too—they must leave. They must go quickly while they were still alone. She grabbed her London Fog, her shoulder bag and car keys, and led him to the back door. All along she'd trusted it would happen like this. Now they would unwind their lives to each other like films shown in slow motion, all the complications revealed.

They ran together through the rain to the back gate, then to her station wagon. When she unlocked it he climbed behind the wheel, held out his hand for the keys. "Where would you like to go?"

"Somewhere we can be alone. Where we can talk. Your place."

"Yes, but there are these damned constraints of time. Here, come close."

She slid against him as he put the car into reverse, backed around, headed out of the lane. As he pulled to the corner, he kissed her cheek. "Put your head in my lap. I want to feel you there."

She lay down on the seat, her head on his thigh. When he raised his foot from the brake she felt the pull of muscle. He settled her closer, stroked the back of her head, smoothing her hair, cradling her when they jolted over potholes. She closed her eyes tightly. Borne along through the dark, the man-smelling cloth against her cheek, she thought of her oldest memory, of the time her father carried her in his arms to the edge of the bluff to see her first fireworks.

"Where are we?"

"Heading south down Sheridan."

Then he brushed her lips with his thumb and she didn't ask any more questions. At his place he'd undress her, make love to her, and then in that quiet intimacy, naked, they'd talk nakedly to each other. Although there was only a little time, it was enough for a beginning.

The car swung left; her feet slipped from the seat as they wove slowly down a rough stretch of pavement. When they came to a stop, he helped her to sit up.

He'd parked at the end of a narrow drive lined with dripping black spruce. Beyond the trees, the pewter gleam of the lake. Beside them, an immense basement foundation was exposed where a mansion must recently have been torn down—piles of dirt, an uprooted pine, bricks strewn where the foundation toppled outward. Beyond the cellar rooms and corridors of the foundation, a white gazebo tilted on its side, vines trailing from its roof.

"Where are we?"

"A family I know lived here. They made a fortune they don't need when they sold this property to a developer."

Directly in front of the car, the small swimming pool offered its cracked blue rectangle. On the slope of the overgrown lawn around the pool lay broken plaster urns. "We aren't going to your place?"

"It's too far." He unbuttoned his coat and pulled it off, slung it into the back seat. Underneath, he wore a gray shirt tucked into his jeans. "If it weren't raining we could walk in the ruins. It's like a secret city uncovered by archaeologists, isn't it."

"Let's not stay."

"Why not?" His tongue traced the curve of her ear. "I like it here with the spirits of the dead."

"We could go somewhere else. I don't have to be back for a while. I can make excuses."

His hand slid under her coat to her breast. "You're a dangerous woman, do you know that, Laura?"

A No Trespassing sign hung crookedly from a tree. Under the overgrown lilacs a scattering of beer cans glittered dully. "Kids come here, the police—"

"We're alone, don't worry." He pressed her hand into his crotch. "Didn't we agree to be a little wild? Here, kneel on the seat."

As though in a trance, she did what he told her to do. Roughly, he pulled open her raincoat, pulled up her skirt.

"No," she said, but she didn't stop him. Maybe he didn't hear her. He turned her away from him, pushed her skirt to her shoulders.

"We wanted to fuck, didn't we? Wasn't that the promise?"

"Not like—"

He put his hand across her mouth and knelt behind her, dragging down her panties. She tried to brace her arms on the back of the seat, but his weight against her forced her chest onto it instead. She felt him unzipping his jeans, his hand went between her legs, and then, with an abrupt and painful thrust, he entered her, battering into her, slamming her against the seat until she couldn't get her breath. She tried to turn but he had her around her waist. No way out. No words, just his breath raking her ear and her own gasps against his palm. "No!" she said, "no!" But he kept on. What he wanted was to hurt, to punish, and with her skirt over her head like this she could be anyone he imagined her to be. She could be Jo. Or no one at all. She had ceased to exist.

When he finished he slumped back down in the driver's seat and started the car as soon as he'd fastened his pants. She wouldn't look at him. While he drove she straightened her clothes. No, she wouldn't cry. She wouldn't question or accuse him—a complaint might make him smile. He'd tell her she'd gotten what she asked for. She pressed her hand to her lips. Hold on, hold on, in a minute he'll be gone.

He didn't speak until he'd parked by the commuter station in Winnetka. "Make sure Jo reads my letter, will you? Before you do. It's my final statement." Without waiting for her to answer, he grabbed his raincoat from the back seat and jumped out to run broken-field between the honking cars crowding the street.

Daisy circled against Laura's legs as she let herself in the back door; she pushed the dog away with her knee. She ran upstairs, stripped off her underwear and shoved it deeply into the clothes hamper, turned on the shower. Waiting for the water to come up warm, she looked at herself in the mirror. She must wash her hair, too, get his touch out of it. It was difficult to think, but some decision must be made, though she couldn't remember just now what that could be. In her hands, although she didn't remember picking it up, the letter he'd left on the hall table for Jo.

You slammed all the doors on me, Thomas. No exit. *Huit clos.* Where do I go from here?

Ah, Jo baby,

Nothing from you but silence? That's like wielding a .38, leveling it at me and shooting me full of those bullets which explode upon entry, leaving shards of metal in my brain, my chest, my groin. Ya got me. I thought I should tell you because you didn't get to see the body fall. Silence is a special form of brutality. You may be in training to be a killer, honeychile. Except that I suspect your silence is casual. It's easier for you not to respond, therefore you don't bother. I was kidding myself about your simplicity. You're not simple; you're narcissistic. Which is another word for young. Of course, *young.* And cruel, too. Maybe that's a surprise to you—your cruelty.

I'm surprised that *I'm* surprised. I understand now that I was drawn to you because you reminded me of myself. Yes, I saw myself in you—not as I am now, but as I was. I was once almost simple, almost hopeful. I was also very frightened, and cruel because of that fright. I have to consider that your silence might mean that you are frightened—no, no, not of me. I mean frightened of your feelings for me. Maybe your feelings are too powerful to handle. Maybe you felt yourself going out of control and so you hid. For me, the outcome's the same. I've got the internal bleeding to prove it.

You don't believe I know how damaging silence can be? *Silence kills.* Here's one last act of self-disclosure, and then I'll bow out of your life. The truth about one's self is often so hideously humiliating, but now I don't care. The dead don't give a shit, you'll find that out some day.

I know about the weapon of silence because I used it on my friend Luke. Beautiful Luke—my roommate, my friend, my river guide. That was his book of Sappho that I sent you, thinking you'd read the disarming candor of longing there. Luke marked a poem for me. That was his way of telling me that he loved me. He was shy and fearful. I mean, that can't have been such good news to him—discovering that he was homosexual. And in love with a coward.

He left the Sappho opened to the poem on my desk one night. I pretended not to see it. I pushed it aside casually, as though it were simply out of place. He was watching me. When we turned out our lights I felt him still watching me. The next morning he confessed that he loved me. He cried when he told me. He was twenty, a big red-bearded guy crying. And me? I was scared shitless. I left our room, went to the library and stayed there all day and most of the night. I slept in another dorm room that night and went back to our place in the morning when I was sure Luke had left. I bundled up my things and moved out. Proud of me? Brave man, afraid even to *talk* to his best friend. And why was I so fucking scared? Because it had come to me that I just might love him, too, and that was unthinkable.

Although I do love him. Do you believe that it's possible to love a man who's dead? I mean really dead, not just dead in spirit, like most of us. Luke put the book of poems in my mailbox and drove his car into a bridge abutment. The cops estimated he was doing eighty and no skid marks.

Not to worry, honeychile. That was love. That's not what I'm about, here. Your silence is really more of an inconvenience for me than a rejection, and I'm used to being judged. I thought we could talk plainly to each other, but you don't know how, and I doubt if you ever will. How easy it is to remember you as I first saw you, nude, in that steamy *Badezimmer* in Vienna. Artemis to my Actaeon. That night, anything seemed possible, even the simpler life I've wished for.

My experiment with transparency comes to an end. I suppose I wanted you to forgive me for my whole wasted life. But you are not the one to save me, nor, in fact, is anyone. Being pulled back from the brink is right out of *The Perils of Pauline*. Now, the sun sets behind the potted palms, soft music swells—aloha, paradise.

Thomas

Fantasy, yes. *One for you, one for me, Thomas.*

She folded the letter, slipped it back into the envelope. She'd put it with the others to burn later. She'd burn them all—no more illusions. A single match would destroy the evidence. As Thomas said, the truth about yourself is so horribly humiliating. But that didn't matter anymore. She wasn't even sad. She felt nothing. Nothing at all.

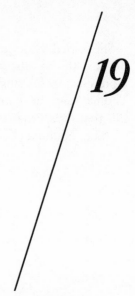

19

Will woke from his dream with a gasp. He scrubbed his eyes, relieved to be out of danger, though he couldn't remember what in the dream had frightened him. He turned on his side. In her bed Laura was curled up like a child, knees to her chin. In the faint light he made out the back of her head, her exposed nape. Maybe he hadn't cried out in his dream as loudly as he'd thought—she hadn't wakened. Sometimes she woke if he so much as coughed. Or maybe she *was* awake, staring into the dark. He couldn't tell.

He smelled the raspberry scent of her soap. She'd pulled up an extra quilt—she was always cold—but if he reached out he could touch her shoulder through the many layers of cloth. If he spoke her name she'd turn to him in an instant. She was right there, except that she'd left: absent, AWOL, missing in action. She was starving herself again, had been for at least three or four weeks, maybe longer.

He reached to touch her hip, but then drew back. What would he say? Would she even want him to touch her? He didn't know what she wanted. He knew she'd needed him. Their marriage was founded on Laura as the needy one and him as her savior. But he hadn't saved her. And after all, what had he given her that any other man in the role of "husband" couldn't have given her just as well, or better? Her continuing sickness wasn't her failure, it was his.

It was an irredeemable failure because their relationship was one of commitment, not of passion. No one expects passion to last. But he'd seen his commitment for what it was; he wasn't deluded by being in love. He'd given himself to a life task and he'd failed at it. He'd heard hundreds of songs and stories about the end of love, but what had been written of the bewilderment and sorrow of the helper who cannot help?

Even though she refused help, refused even to talk with him about her starvation, all of it would come out soon enough because she'd have to be hospitalized. This time the guilt for her sickness was his alone. He loved Jo. Somehow Laura had guessed, and she was destroying herself because of it. It was the only reason he could think of. But what had he done? What terrible thing had he *done?* There he was innocent, unless the Christians were right, and your intentions, your desires, were as real as any acts.

He turned away from her and hugged his pillow, wishing for sleep to come again, no matter how bad the dreams. What he was going to do about his own loneliness he couldn't begin to guess.

"You look like hell," Jerry said with good-humored bluntness. "But then so do I. What are we doing here at this ridiculous hour?"

It was six-thirty in the morning and, except for the one they'd just entered, the squash courts were deserted.

Jerry slammed the heavy door shut. Will pulled his sweat-band down to his eyebrows and swung his arms tentatively. His body ached, his head ached, and he hadn't been able to eat any breakfast. After his bad dream, he hadn't gone back to sleep. "I had a hard time sleeping last night. What's your excuse, Jer? Booze or a gal?"

"*Gal* is an outmoded term. I've been instructed to say 'woman.'"

"Ah, a woman, then." Actually, Jerry looked good; his face was ruddy, his dark eyes shining with no circles underneath. "Whoever she is, she seems to agree with you."

Jerry stretched first one leg, then the other. "She agrees with me that I'm terrific."

He wasn't ready for Jerry's banter. He'd prefer silence, but Jerry usually set the tone when they were together. "You left the warm bed of your woman to come to this dismal squash court?"

"She went back to the warm bed of her husband several hours ago."

He kneaded the cold squash ball as he watched Jerry stretch. "I thought you didn't date married women. 'A matter of principle,' you said. 'Singles should stick to other singles.' Am I quoting you correctly?"

Jerry bent over to pull his arms up behind. He'd dislocated his shoulder last year in a beach-party volleyball game; now he tried to be careful. "Not really a date. Betsy's an old friend of mine who comes to me with her troubles."

"An altruistic lay. That's a new category for you."

"I don't need an excuse."

"Help out an old friend. Screw her and fix up her shaky marriage."

"Hey, she knows where I'm coming from. Why the hell do *you* care, William?"

"Her husband knows where you're coming from, too?" He caromed a forehand shot just above the tin. It rebounded toward Jerry's side of the court.

Jerry let the ricocheting ball pass and continued his methodical warm-up. "Her husband's a nice guy. Sells real estate."

Will hit himself a few hard ones, an easy one thrown in now and then. "One big happy family. Everyone understands."

"It works out." Jerry stretched, arms over his head. "Damn shoulder's stiff. Advanced age."

"You're doing fine. Just fine, Jer. Want to get started?" He was light-headed, but didn't want to say so. He should have had some juice, at least. His mouth was dry and the pressing headband numbed his forehead.

"Slow down," Jerry said. "Take it easy." But he himself hit the ball hard, grimacing, when Will tossed it to him.

Will smashed it so that it came back hugging the wall, and when Jerry missed it he felt an intense satisfaction. What the hell did he have against Jerry? No one was straighter with him than Jerry—he never lied. "You should be locked up for wife-molesting." Will tried to convince himself he'd just made a joke.

Jerry rubbed his shoulder. "Old shrapnel wound."

"Let's play."

"In a minute." Hands on his hips, Jerry did slow side-twists, his gold chains chinking softly. "After I get some points off you maybe your outraged moral fiber will have shrunk to normal."

Will spun his racket to determine first service. "What's *normal,* Jer?"

Jerry crouched to pick up the racket; it was his serve. "Consenting adults understand the term *normal.*"

"You wouldn't recognize an adult if you met one."

Jerry raised his eyebrows, then stepped to the side to take a few practice serves. The ball fell back deep into the corner behind Will. Nice stuff. The old fox—he always had it his own way. Jerry dropped another serve back—he was on.

"Let's *play.*"

"First you warm me up, William. Nice and easy. I'm tired of pain."

They hit for a while, changing sides. The toc of the ball grew gradually louder. Will broke a sweat almost at once—maybe he was really sick, not just sick at heart. He'd be done in before Jerry was ready to start.

"Serve it up," he insisted finally.

He was running almost before Jerry's first serve drifted aloft and died on the back wall. "Perfect. Let's go!" He wanted a good solid connection, a clean blow.

Jerry served again and it came back down the right wall. Will bashed his shoulder when he overran it.

"You wanted a game," Jerry grinned.

"Just play!"

"This isn't the championship of the cosmos. Take it easy."

The squash court closed in around Will. He wanted to kick the court wider, push the ceiling higher, put his fist through the hardwood walls and let in fresh air. Was he going under? He was winded, his chest leaden.

Jerry won the first game easily. "Today's my day," he laughed. He was into it now, sweat glistening on his tanned forehead. He hit his next serve casually, too sure of himself, and

Will saw it coming toward him—a sitting duck, two feet away from the wall and knee high. It was the one he'd been waiting for. He moved quickly into it and smashed it with his backhand. Ferociously. The ball smacked the side wall, ricocheting, at the same moment that Jerry screamed.

Will whirled around. Behind him, Jerry knelt, holding his face in both hands. Blood gushed from between his fingers.

"Jer!"

"You goddamned son of a bitch!"

"Oh, God, Jer!"

"I had the fucking T!" Beneath Jerry's bloody fingers a slash split the skin over his right cheekbone. It looked deep.

He knelt beside Jerry. "I'm so sorry!"

"You know how to play this game! You knew I was right behind you!"

He touched Jerry's wrist but Jerry shoved his hand away.

"You're a goddamned *weapon* on the court, you son of a bitch!" Blood ran down his forearm, dripped onto the floor.

Will ran to grab the towel he'd stashed just outside the door, then thrust it at Jerry. "Pressure."

"I know!"

"Push hard."

"Bastard! I've never seen you hit a roundhouse backhand in your life! Are you crazy?"

Will held the towel to Jerry's head. He'd caught Jerry full in the face. It was inexcusable.

"Stay away from me!"

"It's not your eye. It's nowhere near your eye." Unaccountably, the blood made Will dizzy. He sat on the floor beside Jerry. "Pressure."

"It's my goddamned life I'm worried about, not just my eye. You could have killed me!"

"Don't get up."

"I *can't* get up." He took a deep breath and moved the towel so that Will could see the edge of the slash. "How's it look?"

"It's deep. Clean."

"A lot of stitches, huh?"

He nodded. He could have wept.

"Then get twenty fucking cents and call Tim Ryan and have

him meet us in Emergency. After he stitches me up I'll detail for you why I've decided you're a madman. Lucky, lucky you, William."

Jerry was propped up on his brown sofa with two bed pillows. A neat gauze bandage crossed the right side of his face from his eye down to his chin. He held an ice pack to his eye. With his good one he followed Will's efforts to make coffee.

"Want milk in this?" He wished Jerry wouldn't watch. He was slow and clumsy, as though he was the one smashed in the head with the racket.

"If you made it strong enough, yes. Lots of milk."

"How far wrong can you go with instant coffee?" He was unwilling to be wrong about everything. He didn't want to stay here at Jerry's condo, but he didn't want to go home, either. Every place he turned he found reason to judge himself. He laced both cups with milk and took them to the living room a few steps away.

Jerry patted the seat of the rocking chair next to the sofa. "Sit right here in this Scandinavian-style chair. You'll notice that nothing in my place is genuine. It's all *style*. Danish-style. Oriental-style. Outside is a tiny Olympic-style swimming pool. This Scandinavian-style rocker was made in Taiwan. Things used to be marked Made in Occupied Japan, you remember? Jesus, the good old days."

The Novocain had made Jerry woozy. He looked drained and pale under the blue blanket that Will had yanked from the unmade bed. The morning had turned a flat white. A gentle battering of sleet and rain coated the windows. It was eight-thirty.

"Thanks for this coffee-style beverage," Jerry said.

Will eased into the rocker. "How are you doing now?"

"My skull aches, my cheek is still numb but will hurt like hell shortly, and I find it difficult to focus my eye." He sipped his coffee and made a face. "I'd rather have a medicinal beer. There's some in the refrigerator."

Will got two cans and popped them. He wasn't on call today, and what difference did it make if they drank beer at breakfast time? Who cared? He should eat something, but the idea of food sickened him.

Jerry took a long swallow, his throat working. Then he closed his eye.

Will gulped his. He was dehydrated, and his own head felt skewered by a sharp throbbing above his left eye. A sympathetic pain? The lamp beside him cast a soft, yellow glow through its parchment shade. He leaned toward it as though it might warm him. If he had a blanket he could sleep in the rocker, sleep better right here than in his bed at home. Maybe he should ask Jerry for a blanket.

"I think I'm in shock," Jerry said reflectively. "God must have invented shock to keep people from running around revenging themselves. Shock is like a crib: inside, you nap."

"You want to sleep now?" He'd ask Jerry for a pillow, they'd both sleep.

"No, my friend, I don't want to sleep. I was drawing an analogy. I was comparing the body's shutdown mechanisms to a loving mother's command to her kid to lie down for a while."

"I did a lot of damage." He tried not to sound apologetic. He'd already apologized too much. Jerry had yelled from where he lay on the operating table, "No more mea culpas!"

"You did a moderate amount of damage, but you might do more." Jerry angled himself up into a sitting position. "Why the hell have you been so angry lately?"

"Anger is not my *style*. This morning I was dumb and careless."

"Anger may not be your style, but it's how you've been acting lately."

"What's that mean?"

"Just what I said. I pay attention to you. You're my friend, or at least you were before you attacked me on the court this morning."

"Pay attention to what?"

"To what you've been doing lately. A catalogue of behaviors. I have a list."

Nudging aside several paperbacks and a box of crackers with his ankle, Will propped his feet up on the coffee table. Jerry's unbandaged eye didn't seem to be having any trouble keeping Will in focus. He didn't want to hear what Jerry had to tell him, but there was no way out. "Let's have it."

Jerry finished his beer, pitched the can into the teak-veneered wastebasket at the end of the sofa. He folded his arms, the prosecuting attorney. "Let's start with a week ago and move forward. Last Monday, I'm told, you threw a sterile surgical pack at the wall in the operating room. Actually, you threw it at Crandell, the world's slowest OR, but because your aim was poor you missed her and hit the wall."

"How do you know about that?" He sat up, wide awake, now.

"My spies are everywhere."

"There was a reason for that! She didn't have suction. She was going to let me start an operation without suction. What if my patient had vomited and aspirated it? I'd have been repairing the sinus passages of a corpse. Crandell said she'd called someone to fix it but no one came, so she thought we'd get started anyway!" It all came back. Heat swelled like a balloon in his chest.

"Unpardonable. I agree. She might just as well have written 'operational pneumonia' under 'Cause of Death' before you even started the operation. Still, that's happened before and you haven't thrown a surgical pack at the nurse."

"I didn't hit her."

"You tried. She said you threw overhand, 'like a baseball pitcher.' Those were her words."

Will looked down at his can of beer. Crandell was stupid and negligent and had endangered a life. He'd wanted to hurt her but lost his nerve. Luckily. "Go on."

"You accused a resident of malpractice because she'd neglected to get a child's records down from Peds. She was scared to death. Excessive?"

"Yeah."

"On Wednesday, I think it was, you backed your Honda into Belzer's Porsche and shook your fist at him when he complained that the doctors' parking lot wasn't intended for bumper cars."

"You know what an ass Belzer is. I gave him my insurance agent's card."

"Belzer is *head* of surgery."

"What else?" He heard the dourness in his voice.

"At lunch yesterday I saw you try to hit the wastebasket with an empty milk carton. When you missed you kicked over the wastebasket."

"I picked up all that crap later."

"Are you listening?"

"Yes, damn you."

"Now we come to the most telling incident of all. I can understand your trying to bash Crandell. I can relate, as they say, to your flattening Belzer's Porsche. But on your way home yesterday you snagged a handicapped parking spot in front of Walgreen's. I know this because I was behind you. Directly ahead of you was a van with 'Disabled' license plates. You slipped by the van to get the handicapped spot, stalked into the drugstore, bought a paper, I guess, and stalked out again. The van and I were circling the block when you backed out into the oncoming traffic and pulled away amid the honking of many horns, one of them my own."

"*That's* an act of anger?"

"William, you are a man who tries to help. It's part of your character. You don't have any control over that trait and it doesn't have anything to do with the Hippocratic oath or your profession. You try to help folks who don't even *need* help. You would never, never ace out a handicapped driver from a parking spot unless you were so distracted—or angry—that your judgment was impaired. It was a small occurrence, but a crucial one. Something is wrong. Very wrong."

The damned rocker made Will's back ache. He stood and walked to the window. Sleet and slush piled up in the gutter. "So?"

"You tell me. So?"

He drained his beer, tossed the can in with Jerry's. He wanted another and went into the pullman kitchen.

Jerry said, "If *I'm* not your friend, who is?"

He brought them each another beer. "I've had some ups and downs lately."

"Tell me about the downs."

"I'm not depressed. At least, I don't think so. I mean clinically depressed."

"I doubt if you are."

What could he say now? If you're on the end of a diving board it's better to leap. "Laura's in trouble," he said quickly. He didn't want to give himself a chance to change his mind. In a day or two he'd be spilling it all to Jerry, anyway; her bones were beginning to emerge like the spines of those phosphorescent fish whose bodies disappeared when viewed with infrared light.

"That means you're in trouble, too."

"I guess."

"Tell me about Laura."

"You know her." He knew he sounded sullen, but he couldn't help himself.

"Of course I know her. Most of the time I think she's an okay lady. Then sometimes I wish my ex-wife had fixed you up with someone right down the center lane of sanity."

"Someone like Diane herself, you mean?" He couldn't resist that dig—he guessed he was angry. A little.

"Ouch!" Jerry pretended to grab his head again. "Actually, Diane is undeniably without neurosis. The guy she's married to now is a dealer's rep for outboard motors. He's home for lunch every day and takes her and their three kids fishing every weekend. They snowmobile in the winter. She likes baking casseroles with potato-chip toppings and taking disposable diapers on camping trips. Anyway, we broke up because of me, not her. Not only was I gone all the time, not only was I opposed to having children, but I wasn't monogamous. I was a lousy husband. You, on the other hand, are probably going to retire with some kind of goddamned husband *trophy.*"

"I'm a lousy husband." Even that much admission eased his chest.

"And why is that?"

"Don't know." That was the mystery: Given who he was, how could anything be different? Given who Laura was, how could he change? "Laura's starving again. This time's the worst. She's getting weaker and weaker, but she won't admit it or talk about it."

Jerry's eyebrows shot up. "So *that's* what you're so angry about!"

Everything was so simple to Jerry: black or white. "It's not like that. I'm not angry with her, Jer. She's sick. Anger is a useless emotion with someone who's sick."

"Okay, she's *sick*." Jerry leaned forward, pushed one of his pillows into an armrest. His face flushed briefly as though he'd been exercising. "Forget *why* she isn't eating for a moment. I'm talking about what it does to you. You know how parents react when a kid stops eating? You know why hunger strikes work in a prison? Because everyone around the person who's starving goes crazy with anger. Passive resistance isn't really passive. It's a different brand of hostility, but no less hostile than shooting a gun. Look at Gandhi. Such a quiet little guy. He was a goddamned warrior! He knew what he was doing. He had the most powerful weapon there is. The other side can't get in any punches at someone who's starving. His enemies turned on themselves in their rage and frustration." Jerry sank back again, tried to put his ice pack onto the coffee table, but couldn't reach it.

Will took the pack from him, and sat down on the end of the couch by his feet. The beer had chilled him. He ached with cold. "All that's okay as classroom psychology, but what battle is there for *Laura* to win?"

Jerry scratched his beard next to the taped bandage. "What does she want from you? I know that's too simple, but has she got something on you?"

What she had on him was that he didn't love her. There was no remedy for that. "I don't give her what she needs, I guess."

"Maybe no one could."

"Maybe not." But another man might have loved her. The way he loved Jo.

"Can you change what you give her?"

He'd thought once that affection would grow into love. It hadn't worked that way. "No."

"Can she change what she needs?"

"We don't talk about it."

Jerry lay back down as though he'd just remembered that he'd been hurt. Maybe the Novocain was wearing off. "If you two won't confront anything with each other, I guess you're going to go around blowing up shopping centers—and then when your anger's great enough you'll blow up yourself as well. Terrific."

"It's not like that." The beer had made him groggy as well as cold. He slumped back against the arm of the sofa.

"Shit, Diane knew lots of young women besides Laura." Jerry closed his eye.

"Huh?"

"Marriage at a young age is a random act. At least it was for me. It's like taking notes for a marriage that will come along later. Laura was ready and so were you. Proximity was enough. That, and your neurosis."

So even Jerry thought of their marriage as an accident of time and place and interlocked "conditions." Perhaps all his life things had just happened to him, Will thought. He'd imagined he made decisions, but he was only taking the path of least resistance, like a single-celled creature under a microscope, an organism capable of nothing more than moving away from heat or toward light.

"I guess I don't want to talk about it anymore."

"I still want to talk about it. What are you going to do, my friend? About Laura."

"Get her some help. Whether she wants it or not."

Jerry opened his good eye. A dark, glittering slit. "Then you could leave the scene and try to save yourself for a change."

Although he'd said that to himself, it shocked him to hear Jerry say it out loud. "You can't leave someone who'll die without you."

"Or who'll die *with* you. Who'll live or die as she damned well pleases."

"She wants to live!"

"Look at behaviors, my friend, not just the words."

But if he left Laura, under any circumstances, how could he see Jo? It was unthinkable. There was no solution. "If I stay, it's because I choose to."

Jerry pulled the blanket up under his chin. "Oh, William! And knowing you, you just might prefer being miserable to being guilty. Just don't smash up too many of us who care about you, okay?"

His head spun. Talking had made him ill, or maybe it was the beer on his empty stomach. He wanted Jerry to be quiet now; he wanted to sleep. "Could I borrow a blanket and lie down? I don't feel so good, Jer."

Jerry gestured toward his bedroom without opening his eye. "Join me in the enlisted men's ward."

He pulled himself to his feet. He wouldn't crash on Jerry's bed. He wanted to lie on the firm floor, on neutral ground. "Which ward?"

"The enlisted men's. They did a study in World War II. The same guys who would try to curl up and die in the quiet, private isolation of the officers' ward would heal and live if they were put in with the footsoldiers, who were slugging it out day and night, fighting over bedpans and bashing each other when someone's groan of pain interrupted their sleep. Dog eat dog. They got well fast. Think about it. Get into the fray instead of wasting yourself away."

Will got a pillow and the plaid bedspread and dragged them back into the living room. He chose a spot beside the rocking chair, pushed his pillow against the end of the couch, and rolled himself up in the spread. God, it felt good to lie down. He wanted to thank Jerry for letting him, but Jerry was already snoring softly.

Then, maybe as punishment, Will dreamt about the day the Junkman fell into the Mississippi. It was a day he tried hard never to think of, for his fears and his guilt were still fresh after all these years.

A freighter christened *North Star* had been given an extra *r* when her name was welded on: *North Starr*. A visiting senator had pointed out this costly error, and the boss was mad. Grinding that extra letter off was exacting work, and the boss was in a hurry. To correct the dumb-ass spelling error of the sign welder, the boss sent up the Junkman. He was lifted up with his tools in the iron basket suspended from the boom of a barge crane beside the huge ship.

It was nearly quitting time. LaFleur was the first on the deck of the tanker berthed next to the *North Starr*. "Holy shit!" LaFleur yelled. "Get up here!" In a minute the rest of the crew was on the deck, watching across the sixty or so feet of brown river that separated the ships.

The crane operator had let out too much cable as Junk was lowered to the ship's side. The basket jumped and bobbed like a fish on a line. Tossed about in it, Junk shook his big fist at the operator. Everyone watching laughed. It was the violent, nervous, explosive laughter that comes with fear, for the operator was hauling in the extra cable too fast as he tried to get it taut again. If the ball and tackle hit the boom, the basket would pop off like a ripe berry.

Junk saw that. He dropped his tools and fell to his knees in the jiggling basket. "Sweet Jesus, save me!"

They all laughed harder to hear Junk praying. They believed the crane operator could save Junk without Jesus having to lift a finger. All he had to do was slow down his reeling.

But, maybe because of all the laughter and hooting above him, the operator panicked. The slack cable spun upward, the ball hit the boom, and the cable snapped like a shotgun going off in an empty room. The report echoed between the ships.

The basket hung for a moment on a shred of wire, and then hurtled the hundred yards down into the oily water, Junk still on his knees, his hands clasped and raised high. "Jesus! Save me, Jesus!"

And all of them laughed until he hit and went under because it was impossible, horrible, monstrous that the Junkman should be falling into the river.

Then it was quiet. The foreman yelled for divers. Two professionals went in right away. Will thought he should go, but he was afraid. Not a single man who'd ever fallen into that river had lived. A man on the pier uncoiled some dragging lines and a few others went down to help.

Will waited on the deck of the tanker in the thick, early-morning heat. Running lights on the barges drew near and then faded as the ships pushed on toward the gulf. He pulled off his welding mask and his hard hat and stood unprotected as they dragged.

LaFleur stopped by his side. "You shouldn't wait around here, Yank."

"I'm okay."

"Sure, you're okay. Come on home with me. We'll have us some beers."

"Thanks, LaFleur."

"I mean it."

"I know you mean it. Just leave me alone."

"Why? Why the hell leave you alone?" He jammed his hands into his pockets.

"I'm so tired is why."

"We're all fucking tired. What the hell does that have to do with anything?"

"I'm gonna wait."

LaFleur shrugged. "Wait, then." Rubbing his chin with his fist, he turned back just before he stepped onto the gangplank.

"See ya," Will said.

"Yank? I ain't mad about you and my old lady, if that's what you're thinking. That's just how she is. She can't help it. It don't have nothing to do with you."

Before there was time for shame to register on Will's face, LaFleur clumped down the gangplank and was gone.

In less than an hour they pulled out Junk's body. Will went down for a last look. Junk's mouth was slack, his legs sprawled on the dock as though he were sleeping. His huge hands were still rigidly clasped in prayer.

Junk had plenty of time to *know,* that was the worst part. Too late to choose and no way to hang on. He was going down and he'd known every bit of the way that the deep river lay beneath him and that there was no way back. No way at all.

When he woke his head was under the rocker, his legs tangled in the spread. The dream was still with him. He had packed up that morning and headed home from New Orleans. He drove straight through, keeping himself hyped on coffee and Cokes. As he passed Gary, Indiana—his eyes dry and aching from fatigue and the long effort not to cry—he squinted at the crisp skyline of Chicago. The pale distant towers glinted in the early sun, a mirage, an illusion of order and clarity above the bruise-brown tide of factory smoke.

He'd thought that if he couldn't save the Junkman, he could

at least save himself. But he couldn't do that, either. And now it was Laura who might never find a way back and he had no way to help her.

He crawled stiffly to his knees, to his feet. Jerry still slept, his mouth open, hands crossed on his chest. It was almost eleven. Will rinsed his face at the sink, and, resisting the impulse to write "Sorry" yet again, scrawled "Thanks" instead on a scrap of paper and placed it by the coffee pot. He left Jerry's place as quietly as a thief making good his escape.

20

But Will didn't go home. Light-headed and dizzy, as though he'd just given blood, he pulled into a closed gas station across from the commuter platform. There was a phone booth on the corner. Eyeing it, he stacked dimes for the phone on his dashboard. He stared at the coins. Should he call Jo? Should he allow himself to see her? It was dangerous for him. If she put her arms around him, wouldn't he kiss her? And what would follow? It frightened him that he didn't know what he'd do. No matter what, he had to stay in control.

But, turning up his jacket collar, he climbed out into the freezing sleet, stepped into the phone booth, shoved the door shut. A passing truck sprayed a wave of slush against the glass. The light was dirty gray, the smells of motor oil and urine. He chinked in his dimes.

The girl who answered told him Jo was in the shower; he said he'd hold. She shouted "Hale!" A stereo blared, and high laughter joined the voices. Sleet rattled against the plexiglass booth. An upright coffin.

"Hello?"

"It's me."

"Will?"

"Yeah."

"How *are* you?"

"Not so hot. How are you, Jo?"

"Wet. Darlene got me out of the shower. She thought you were the guy who followed me around at this party last night. I wasn't going to answer."

"But you did."

"I did!"

"You sound good." Delicious was how she sounded, her voice sweet and energetic. He leaned on the metal counter under the phone, rubbed his forehead. "You sound clean."

She laughed. "What are you doing today?"

"I played squash with Jerry. I smashed him with my racket. He had to have stitches."

"Will!"

"Only one of my stupid mistakes. I've made a lot lately, Jerry tells me."

"Don't put yourself down. Is he okay?"

"Angry as hell."

She sighed. "How about you?"

"Sorry."

"You can't bear to hurt anyone."

Only his wife. "Tell me some cheerful news."

"Like what?"

"Something to lift my spirits. That party last night." Biting his lower lip to make it hurt all the more.

"Just a sec, Will, this place is wild." He heard her yell, "Cut that music!" Then, "Look, why don't you come have some coffee with me? It's a madhouse here by the phone."

His breath had fogged the metal of his phone. "Let's just talk."

"Maybe I can find another booth where it's quieter. Can I call you back?"

"I'm at a gas station."

"You're not home?"

"On my way back from Jerry's."

"Where's Laura?"

"At the gym, I think."

"Hey, come here! You've never seen my room."

"I just wanted to say hello."

"Please."

How could he? Now, this day, when he felt too sad, too

lonely for her. How could he help but cling? The hell with everything! "I'll be right there."

He ran to his car. Watching for cops, he broke the speed limit on Greenbay, rolled through a red light, passed a van on the right. Then on impulse he skidded into the no-parking zone in front of Ella's Deli. Leaving the motor running, he ran inside. He grabbed a carton of orange juice, cookies, a package of cream cheese, onion bagels, slices of corned beef, and a chocolate bar with cherries. While the clerk wrapped his purchases Will swigged from the juice carton. His gut howled and he munched a cookie to quiet it as he wove through the Sunday traffic up the shore to Woodcliff.

The brick buildings were a pink blur through the sleet. The steeple on the chapel and the smokestack reflected silver.

Jo waited for him under the arched gate to the circular drive. She wore gray sweatpants and her parka, a red ski hat on the back of her head.

Smiling, she slapped the hood as she rounded the car to jump in beside him. "You were fast!" She touched his knee. "You look rotten, Will."

He grinned. "I am rotten. To the core."

"Are you growing a beard?"

"I haven't shaved."

"I meant you look strung out. I guess that accident with Jerry?"

He reached his bag from the back seat and handed it to her. "I brought lunch. Or is it breakfast? Are you hungry?"

"Yes! I thought I smelled something terrific."

"Is there somewhere we can eat?"

She kicked her tennis shoes together to dislodge the snow. "My room. When Darlene goes to lunch in a few minutes we can have some privacy. She never misses a meal. She says she paid for it and she wants her money's worth."

She pointed to visitors' parking in front of a building with an oversized portico. Somehow, he pulled into an empty space.

"Will, I'm so glad to see you!" The strands of damp hair outlined her face, a dark, glossy hood. As it had that day in the boathouse. He was saving his vision of her that day for his deathbed—her astonished, loving face.

"You look great," he said.

"You mean you miss me?"

He couldn't help his smile. Then, because he loved her, he seized her hand. How simple the gesture was, how *good*. She squeezed back, her grip strong through the thick wool of her mitten and his leather glove.

"I miss you like fire!" she whispered quickly, as though if he'd guessed what she was going to say he'd have found some way to stop her.

He wanted to gather her against him, just that, hold her for a long, long time. Instead, he said, "Let's go."

She took his arm and led him around the building with columns. At the entrance of a smaller, more modern brick building to the rear, she held the door for him. "This is Whitby. Faculty offices on this floor. I'm on the third."

She went ahead of him up the metal stairs. There was a rust stain on the right hip of her sweat pants, and the hem of a navy sweatshirt showed under her parka. When she pulled off her cap and lifted her damp hair with both hands, he stopped himself from taking her around the waist.

The stairwell smelled of sour milk and wet wool. At the first landing music boomed through the fire door; "Believe it or not, Jesus loves you!" in blue Magic Marker on the concrete block wall.

"High-class graffiti," she said. "You should see the bathrooms. All these conversations on the backs of the doors. Do guys ask each other questions when they write in the john?"

"Guys aren't so nice, Jo."

She stopped on the landing, one step above him, their eyes on a level. He saw his own face in her wide iris. If she kissed him now, as she had in the boathouse, he was done for. "So, you like it here?" he asked quickly.

"I hate it. You must know that. I wanted to stay in the house with you, but it was too difficult."

He looked away first. She pulled open a door labeled 3, then waited for him a few yards down the corridor. "Home sweet home."

Room 304. A narrow length of green-carpeted-floor separated two built-in closets, two built-in beds, two built-in shelves which were desks. On the left a washbasin and mirror were crowded in; windows stretched across the end of the room, the deep sill covered with red plastic milk crates for books and a cage holding a gerbil. Darlene, presumably, fed it seeds.

"Come on in," Jo said.

He followed her.

"This is Will, Darlene."

"Right! Your brother-in-law. Hi!"

"Will, meet Darlene Mohs."

Darlene brushed sunflower seeds into the cage and offered Will her hand. She wore a loose black cottony dress, white anklets, and open-toed pumps like those his mother had once favored.

"Darlene's in theater." Jo pulled off her parka and held out her hand for his jacket.

"An actress?"

"She's in this musical, *Joseph and the Amazing Technicolor Dreamcoat*. Darlene's Potiphar's wife."

"A good part?" he asked politely.

"Just one line." Darlene's ears were double-pierced and she wore four different silver earrings.

"But a good one," Jo said.

"Let's hear it," he said.

Darlene lowered her kohl-darkened lids. "Come and lie with me, love."

"See what I mean?" Jo said. "Sit down, Will."

He sat. Darlene took the gerbil from its cage and held it out. The bright dark eyes were unblinking. "His name is Turtledove. I think it's important to humanize a place like this, don't you?"

Jo crawled onto her bed and crossed her legs. Her knee brushed his. "He's supposed to be diurnal, but he runs on his wheel all night."

"Sometimes we turn the wheel on its side to stop the racket, but then he digs." Darlene popped the gerbil back into the cage, where he leaped onto the exercise wheel and began to circle.

Will settled heavily into the unyielding desk chair. If you paid attention, metaphors for life were everywhere.

"Jo tells me you're a doctor." Darlene, the hostess. "That must be exciting."

"He's a surgeon."

"Do you think they portray doctors accurately on TV? I mean, like on *All My Children?*"

"Are you going to lunch?" Jo said.

"Will could come with us as our guest." At the mirror Darlene ran a brush through her short brown hair.

"He brought us lunch from Ella's."

"Thanks, anyway," he said, watching Darlene draw on more dark lipstick. Maybe Jo tried on roles, too; maybe he was a stage in her life. At eighteen, he had imagined himself in love with his English instructor's wife, who served her husband's class spaghetti and jug wine one winter night. She wore a floor-length, quilted skirt and played opera recordings while the students sat on the floor and tried to talk about literature. He'd fallen for her bare feet under the long skirt.

At the door with her hand on her hip, Darlene said, "Catch you later."

In the sudden quiet he heard Jo sigh. "Hard work here?" he said.

"Basically, she's not bad. She has this big act she puts on, but almost every night she cries in her sleep."

"Like all the rest of us," he said, pretending to read the titles of Jo's collection of books on the shelf over her desk. On the wall over her bed she'd tacked up a calendar with a pseudo-oriental drawing of peonies and a poster of a Chagall painting. It was one of the village series, a bride and groom floating over the housetops along with a donkey, chickens, a fiddler, white flowers exploding like constellations across the green sky.

"Do you like it?" she said.

"Yes, very much." He was earthbound, six feet under.

"I got it at the art museum. I'll get you a copy, if you like."

The black-bearded groom clasped his slender bride.

"I'm starved," she said, when he didn't answer.

He opened the sack, laid the deli packages and bagels on her desk.

"Let me borrow a coffee pot. I'll be right back." She climbed from her bed, her hair swinging, and was quickly out the door, bumping it closed again with her hip.

The thin winter light played over the yellow wall, over the orange and white quilt on her bed. He laid his hand on it, imagining it still warm from her where it sloped to the center. A smear of mascara on the flower-sprigged pillow case. He wanted to press his face into the scent of her. Her sweet, wet mouth. He curled beside her. Her thighs opened, sweet, wet, and she clung to him, all, open at last.

Clatter at the door. He started, jumped to his feet, yanked open the door. She carried plastic cups, plates, a roll of paper towels and an electric coffee pot. "Did you miss me?"

He took the coffee pot from her. As she set her tableware on the desk he propped the door half open with the rubber wedge. Protecting himself.

She gave no sign. She sawed at the bagels with a plastic knife, laid them on plates. "Would you fill the pot with water, Will?"

He washed his hands at the basin, then filled the pot, plugged it into the socket under the windowsill. On his wheel the gerbil dashed along.

Watching her spread cheese on the bagels, he leaned back in the plastic chair.

"You didn't want to come to my dorm, did you?" she said.

"No, I wanted to come."

"But thought you shouldn't."

"In my day men couldn't go into girls' dorms."

"I thought you should know where I'm living. All in all, I guess I made the best choice I had." She handed him half a bagel.

"You've got to be on your own."

"If you can call this being on my own. At least I don't have to battle Laura at meals." She poured juice into two pink cups, then, balancing her plate, crawled back onto her bed.

"You have to start somewhere." Marveling that he could sip the juice, chew, when he ached so for her.

"That's what I tell myself." She leaned against the wall, her legs stretched out, and slipped out of her shoes. They dropped by his feet.

"I brought corned beef, too." He unwrapped the package, peeled loose one of the iridescent slices, but the scent made his head ache and he put the meat back, gulped juice instead.

She watched him take a bite of his bagel, devour it. "You're hungry, too."

"I should be, but I don't know if I am or not."

"You never told me where you went to college, did you?"

"Sure I have. I lived at home when I was in undergrad at the U. I've told you all my old war stories." The bread was dry and tasteless in his mouth.

"You could tell me all the stories again. Maybe now I'd understand them. You could tell me how you feel about everything you've done. I want us to talk about *real* things."

"It's all real."

"You know what I mean." She gobbled her sandwich. He laid his on the plate, but he really should get something solid in his gut, something to steady him. He tried another cookie.

"Are you sick, Will? You look funny."

"Hungover, I guess. I had some beers with Jerry this morning." He held out his cup for more juice.

She leaned to pour it, a black enameled heart he'd never seen her wear dangling on a silver chain in the V-neck of her sweatshirt.

"Is that new? The heart?"

"Kit gave it to me."

"Does he come up here?"

"Once. We've kind of broken it off."

"Was he at that party last night?"

"Will, I think you should probably eat something. Beer on an empty stomach can knock you out."

"How about the party? Some guy followed you around, you said."

"He was a jerk."

"His party?"

She got up to check the coffee pot, then leaned against the windowsill. Behind her, around her, the light was so white it hurt his eyes.

"A guy who's the assistant in ceramics asked some of us to his place. It was an older crowd. They were doing coke. They asked me if I wanted to buy some."

With difficulty he swallowed a mouthful of the cookie. "And?"

"I didn't have any money. So I got drunk, instead. Then this totally stoned guy decided I was the answer to his prayers."

"Jo."

"I agree, it was dumb." She wiped her lower lip with her thumb, looking hard at him.

"But something could have happened to you. The drugged-up guys, the icy streets later—"

"Sometimes I feel so low I just want out."

As she poured the coffee, he had the sensation that the room was stifling. He wished for fresh air, wished to be out in the country with her, walking through a pine copse, or maybe in the mountains. He could take her to some island, a Greek one—he could breathe there, and she'd be safe. Except that he couldn't take her anywhere. And any guy who chose to could follow her around, hold her, kiss her.

She sipped from her cup. "The trouble is that I don't fit in, Will. I'm just too old. I don't mean age. I mean something else. Around here I'm just acting all the time."

He nodded.

"I feel like I've got this third eye in the middle of my fore-head. It's like I can see through all of it, see on all sides of everything, the way you can be both inside and outside a house at the same time in a dream. Life here is a big game. That's because of you, how I—"

"Don't."

"Will! Please talk to me."

He drank his coffee, steam clouding his glasses as the room seemed to tilt.

After a moment, she looked away from him. "I think I'll have to find a place of my own when I transfer to the university."

He gave up on the cookie. "You're better off here. I doubt if Trawick likes a girls' dorm." That surprised him—he hadn't realized he'd had that bastard on his mind all this time.

"Thomas?" She set her cup down carefully.

He wiped his glasses on his sleeve. "Is he still after you?"

She turned to look out the window. Her face tightened, or maybe that was the light etching her profile. "I won't hear any more from him."

"You will. You're too fascinating for him to pass up. He could be persuasive—"

"He's already passed me up. He's found someone much more interested in him."

Something in her tone pulled at the back of his neck. It came to him that Trawick had invaded this room already. "You've seen him, then?"

The silence went on too long. She was seeing him, after all. Anger can so easily turn into attraction. Maybe he'd been at that party she'd described, one of the older crowd. A man like Trawick could get a girl drunk and high, have her like that if no other way.

He stood, holding onto the desk to steady himself. "There's something you're not saying, Jo."

"There's a lot *we're* not saying, but I'm not seeing Thomas." She frowned, her face strained. "Thomas has something going now with Laura," she said abruptly, and turned away.

The dangers that love lays out—a minefield. "That's hard to believe," he heard himself say.

"I'm not a liar."

He wanted both to slap her and to kiss her as he tasted the rise of jealousy into his mouth—Laura, now, as well as Jo.

"We saw them."

"Who's *we?*"

"Kit and I. We saw them drive off in our station wagon. Thomas was driving." She shook her head as though tossing off a last constraint. "She put her head down in his lap, and he drove her to a place where kids make out."

He went to the basin, emptied his coffee into it. Trawick's *lap*. It was the kind of detail Jo would never have invented, the kind that could stay with you a lifetime.

"She's wanted Thomas all along," Jo said softly.

"I know Laura." His gut churned.

"So do I, Will!"

He set his empty cup on her desk, reached for her hand, but she pushed the chair between them. "Don't stop me, Will. I'm telling you the truth. I wasn't going to, but—"

"It doesn't matter."

"It matters! It's not fair, Will!" The thin scar under her lower lip whitened.

"Anyway, it's not true." But as he said it he knew it was.

"It's true, all right. You're crazy if you don't think so!"

When she ran from him out of the room he was pinned against her desk by a dark wave breaking over him. It was like that time in med school, not his stomach, after all, but a landslide of anxiety rushing down on him.

He found two Valium in his sweatpants pocket, downed them with a mouthful of juice. Trying to get his breath, he heard her footsteps in the corridor and a distant door slam. On a piece of notebook paper he scribbled, "I'll call you. It's okay." Then he yanked his jacket from her closet and headed from her room, which now smelled thickly of corned beef and coffee and his own acrid sweat.

Once he was outside in the raw wet air he felt better. Warning himself not to look back—she might be watching, she might call to him, and he couldn't take that now—he crossed the ice-coated grass to his car. He drove slowly down Sheridan Road. Get it together, fella, he coached himself. Get it together.

In town, he parked by the closed post office and walked the streets. In every store window he saw himself, head bent against the wind, his eyes wary under the edge of his watch cap, his shoulders hunched. A guy on the lam. But he couldn't outdistance the certainty—Laura and Trawick. Well, why not, why the hell not? Why not that *too*—he hadn't cornered the market on love or need. Where do we go now, wife?

After a long time he turned back toward where he'd left his car. He'd go home and take a shower. When the Valium had kicked in solidly, he'd eat some soup, then shovel the walk, fix the weather stripping on the back door, split some more logs, take Daisy for a run in the park—do what could be done in grief and desire.

21

The cold snap of early November didn't break; already crusts of ice washed up on the beach. Though there had been no more snow the landscape was whitened, the oaks, maples, even the rust-colored willow branches bleached by the cold. When Will ran now his chest ached with each breath unless he held his mittened hand over his mouth to warm the air. He liked the ache. There was absolution in pain, wasn't there? He couldn't forgive himself but he could make himself suffer. If the meaningless small discomforts of a healthy man could be called suffering. Even his anguish seemed no more significant than the most banal distress. He was in trouble.

Hating himself for it, he drove by Woodcliff every day. Once he thought he saw Jo, but when he looked more closely it was another girl in a green parka. He called her often, allowing himself to ask only the few questions he carefully wrote down before he dialed—what was her Social Security number, did she know where Daisy's leash could be, had she taken the garage key by mistake? When she answered the phone his pulse sped; when he hung up his hand was wet and trembling. Neither of them mentioned his visit to her room.

With Laura he'd become cautiously thoughtful, as though they both suffered some debilitating illness like influenza. He persuaded her to see her doctor again. She went three times a week but would say nothing more about her visits than "It's my

problem, it's intrapsychic. I have to work it through myself."
He wanted to believe that, though he suspected his wanting to
was another form of betrayal. Once she came to where he sat
reading, crawled into his lap like a child, and wept. "I'm going
to feel this way forever!" He cradled her. "You'll beat it," he
told her, wondering if he believed that. He stroked her cheek.
Maybe she was still seeing Trawick, too. There was so much
which it was important not to ask.

He was on his evening run down Center, sidestepping potholes, his face burning from cold and his knees aching with it,
when desolation slammed his chest so hard he stopped right in
the middle of the road. He grabbed his ribs—they felt cracked.
Couldn't get his breath. It had hit him that there was no hope.
Theirs was an unfortunate marriage; it could only get worse.
When he'd imagined *marriage* he'd had no idea how deep it
was, how it would stretch out behind him and before, how long
it would go on. Nor had he known that there are bonds much
stronger than love.

Yet he couldn't leave it. He'd pledged his life to Laura.
Though he'd never thought of himself as a religious man, his
vow had been profound. He'd given his word. If his word had
no meaning, what was left of him? Obligation, commitment—
to his dismay, he believed in them. What another man could do
in good conscience, he could not. He was trapped by his own
character as much as by Laura's needs. There was no way out of
that one.

He stood bent over for a long time, his hands clamped under
his arms. He stared at the ice webbed through the cracked asphalt, the grass bristled with frost, at his own labored breath
blossoming white. At his side, Daisy shivered and whined, her
tail wrapped around her paws. He couldn't stay out here forever, and there was no place to go except back home. He'd have
to try to talk honestly with Laura. What he'd say he didn't
know, but the attempt was the one choice left to him. In their
loneliness they might reach out to each other, make some comforting human touch.

He let himself into an empty house. He still expected to hear
Jo's radio, to see her sucking her lower lip in concentration as
she punched away at the old portable typewriter at the kitchen

table. She'd been gone five weeks now, years, it seemed, since they'd kissed in the boathouse—oh, God—the pressure of her hips and breasts, her hands on his neck, the taste of her. Like honey. To be able to *love* her. He wouldn't allow himself to think about that again.

Though his teeth still ached with cold, in the kitchen he broke into a sweat. Instead of a shower he made himself a double Scotch and settled down to wait for Laura, who was at one of her tennis games. He was anxious, but taut nerves were better than the despair he'd smashed into like a wall. Or maybe that was the whiskey easing his chest. He turned on the back light for her and sat in the darkened living room with his glass.

By the time he heard her light footsteps he'd begun a second drink.

"Will?"

"In here."

She stopped in the dining room doorway, the kitchen light behind her. With her heavy hair pulled away from her face by a sweatband, the hollows gathered around her eyes, the lines pulled at the corners of her mouth. Her vulnerable throat. Her shadow reached to where he sat on the sofa.

"No lights?"

"I was thinking."

"Smells like you've been drinking."

"That, too. How was your game?"

"Boring. Women's tennis is boring and I can't get you to play mixed doubles any more."

"I'm sick of tennis. People talk too much when they play."

"And you don't like people?"

"Not very well."

"Is that what you've been thinking about while you sat here in the dark tying one on?" She pulled off her sheepskin jacket, disappeared into the closet. From inside she said, "You don't like people. You just like curing them."

Maybe she'd summed him up right. He should go back to welding—it was cleaner work, after all. "Laura?"

Unzipping the ankles of her blue warm-up suit, she stepped into the living room again. "I'm going to take a shower."

"Could you wait?"

"I'm a smelly mess."

"I want to talk. I *need* to."

Looking down at him as if she'd been accosted by a stranger—that alarmed—she stood at the end of the sofa. "Well?"

"Could you sit down?"

"I think I'll see if I like the conversation first. Your voice sounds funny."

"How *funny?*"

"Grim. Are you sick?"

He shook his head. In spite of himself he'd shown his anxiety; now that he had her attention, he'd forgotten where he wanted to start. He drew an ice cube into his mouth and sucked, trying for a casual tone. "Just some ideas to talk over."

"What, then?" She drew in a breath and held it.

"I was thinking about when we got married."

She breathed out slowly. "That's eight years ago, almost nine."

"I know. I was just thinking about us, I mean, who we were then."

"The same as now, I guess. Younger." He saw the effort in her smile.

"Come on, sit down."

"I'm not crazy about melancholy reminiscence."

"I was trying to think through what we wanted."

"Why?"

"To understand myself better, I guess. You could help me."

She sat on the arm of the sofa, swung her racket in its plastic cover against her tennis shoe. "So?"

"When we married what did you want?'

"Will!"

"I know it sounds dumb. But what did you want?"

"To love you, you know that."

"But what else?"

"Is this a cross-examination?"

"Not at all. I was thinking about our expectations. As you said, we were young."

"A family. Look, you know all this. I don't want to go through the whole baby thing again just because you're plastered."

"I'm not plastered, and I don't want to put you through anything."

"I'm dying for a shower."

"I guess love and a family is what every couple wants. I was wondering, well, what did I seem like to you then?"

She snapped on the table lamp, the linen shade dented where Jo had kicked it once doing a back walkover. With the light her face leaped closer—the fine down on her upper lip, the mole by her eye. "Is this some kind of self-analysis you're putting yourself through?"

"I guess."

"I think it's morbid."

He swirled the ice in his glass. "What qualities did you think I had? I mean, back then."

"I always thought you were a good man."

"I'm not looking for compliments."

"What do you want, then?"

"I don't know. You have good insights into people. What kind of a man was I, Laura?"

Her face softened. "You look so blue."

"I am. Depressed, actually."

She touched his shoulder. "You were my hero, I guess."

"Hero?"

She rubbed her forehead with her thumb. "We're both tired. Let's not go on about the past."

"Seriously—hero? That's too much."

She looked at him steadily, her lips pressed together, as though she calculated the risks of going further. "I've thought about this, you know."

"Tell me."

The clock ticked forward, the ice-maker in the refrigerator discharged a shower of cubes.

"You were more than you were, Will."

"Now you're telling me something new. Go on."

"Will!" She pushed against the end table as though he had hurt her.

He reached for her, slopped some of his drink onto his sweat pants, set the glass down. Then took her cool hand in his. "Let's just talk like old war buddies."

Warily, she leaned back. "Why are you asking this stuff?"

"I'm trying to understand myself better."

"Ask your friend Jerry, he's with you all day. Women don't understand men so well."

Using his doctor voice—the even intonations, the reassuring calm—he urged her, "Tell me how I was bigger than I was."

She pulled off her sweatjacket. Her upper arms were no thicker than his wrists. "I mean more important. You stood for a lot of things that didn't have anything to do with just you. My needs, and yours, I guess, made you bigger than life. That's as close as I can come to it."

"But that's good. That's what I want you to help me with."

Quickly she said, "It wasn't you who built yourself up. *Just* you, anyway. I was part of that. When you'd try to pare yourself down to size, puncture my illusions, I'd just discount that. I wanted you to be my hero and to come save me. That childish dream!" She pushed her head back against the sofa, pressed her fingers to her cheeks. "Anyway, we were conspirators in that. You didn't mind so much being worshiped, did you?"

Maybe he'd wanted that—he couldn't remember. His eyes ached from the light behind her head. "I guess we were in it together."

"That's what I think, anyway. I mean, you can't maintain a heavy fantasy like that all by yourself. Both people have to play, don't you think?"

"Is this something you've talked over with your doctor?"

She pulled her hand away. "It's not some shrinky insight. I'm just answering your question."

"Don't leave now." He caught her elbow.

"It's so long ago."

Meaning, he thought, You're not my hero anymore. He hoped that was what she meant. "But I want to know. What else?"

She sucked in her cheeks. "I don't know much more to tell you. I know I wanted you to be one certain way, and not to change. And I wanted to be a certain way. I know that sounds crazy, because we can't just freeze."

"What way? How did you want to be?"

"Even though I believed that you'd saved me, I wanted to

stay free of you. It was as though my outline blurred sometimes. You did that to me, I think." She looked up from under her thick lashes, checking to see if she'd gone too far.

He squeezed her arm, her muscle moving under his fingers. This was what he'd been after, wasn't it? Somehow he'd persuaded her to share a piece of her truth. "How did I do that, Laura?"

"You had them, too."

"Had what?"

"Illusions. If I tried to be just myself you drew me back into your illusions. It wasn't just my giving in. Anyway, it's all so mixed up and I don't like talking like this."

"What were my illusions?"

"Oh, you know!"

"Tell me."

"I was the cool blond beauty."

"You were, you are." Though she wasn't any more—Oh, Laura.

"I was this blond female, all the things you imagined you wanted in a woman. It didn't have anything to do with who I really was. To you I was the—"

"I can't hear you."

She sat up straighter, but still she whispered. "I was the princess and you'd come to save me. There's this fairy tale I used to read to Jo, and every time I read it I thought it was about you and me. There was this miller who cut off his daughter's hands because she wouldn't do what he wanted. I thought I was the miller's daughter. My father had cut off my hands and you were the prince who'd married me and given me silver ones."

"Silver, that doesn't sound so bad."

"You don't get it, Will. It's a *terrible* story. The hands the prince gave her were beautiful, but they were artificial. Just things. They weren't her own."

"Maybe we should just talk about us."

"This *is* about us. I'm really trying to tell you." Her knuckles were white.

He nodded.

"In that fairy tale the princess goes into the forest alone and grows her own hands back. But I can't make mine grow. I've tried and I can't. I don't have any power, don't you see?"

"I want to."

"I'm telling you I don't have any power except the one. That's why it's so important!"

"Eating?"

"And I think sometimes you want it that way! There's some weird payoff for you when I'm helpless. You want me rigged up in *your* gift of silver hands!" Then she was on her feet, standing in front of him, eyes wide, as though she didn't know how she'd got there. "You wanted to know!"

He looked down into his glass—the chips of ice, the oily surface—and took a gulp. He'd thought he would deserve anything she might accuse him of. Maybe he'd wanted to be punished. But this seemed too much.

"Did you hear me?" The confession he'd twisted from her had made her fearless.

"Yes."

"What do you think of that?"

"I don't know yet. I have to—"

"I think you're sloshed, Will."

"I'm sobering up."

Hands on her waist, she was the one who looked drunk, he thought—she rocked back and forth, yanked the headband from her hair and shook it free.

"*You* wanted to talk."

"Laura, sit down. I meant talk quietly."

"It doesn't always work the way *you* want it. Now it's your turn. I'll ask you questions. Okay?"

He nodded. She had her own agenda, it seemed—how long she'd had it he didn't know.

"What did you want? When we married what did it mean to you?"

He wished she wouldn't lean over him. And, though she only repeated the question he'd asked her, he had a hard time thinking. He'd thought he knew exactly what he wanted to say, but he had to push each word out. "I wanted to get it right with you. My life, I mean. I thought with you I could get it right."

"Our marriage was your self-help project?"

"Don't make it sound like that. I was grateful to you. You gave my life meaning."

"And what did you think was going to happen to me while I was busy giving your life meaning?"

"Don't yell. I thought we were good for each other. I thought you'd get well." He was clear about that, yes, he'd wanted that. "What you said about some payoff for me in your illness, that's not fair."

She brushed that aside with a toss of her head. "You would help me get well—"

"Because I loved you."

"Loved *saving* me!"

"Wanted to help. Loved you." He heard the awful finality in his words—*loved,* not *love*—but she chased her own grievance, her face shining with sweat.

"Wanted to be the great gift-giver of the silver hands. Wanted me to be grateful!"

If he had had too much whiskey, the growing fury in her voice cleared his head. "No, not that. You'd just get well. I believed that."

"And then what?"

"We'd be like everyone else. We'd *be* married."

"As opposed to getting married?"

"I guess I thought that we'd be friends." He hadn't realized until he said it that he'd wanted that. *Had* he? Did he? God, where was the truth? How could you ever, ever know?

"But, poor Will, I didn't get well, did I?" Singsong.

Her tone scared him—what had he started? She was on fire now with emotion but his own feelings were leaden, stuporous. Doggedly, he repeated, "Be friends."

"Lies!"

"Laura, I mean it."

"Tonight, drunk, you may mean it. But never, never have you been my friend. I'm your wife. That's it. You haven't wanted to know me. Admit that! Even right now, while you're pretending to want all this deep disclosure, you're only sinking deeper into the role. You're the reasonable healer and I'm the sick bitch. That's how you want this scene to play, right?"

He stood. At the window he drew his finger across the fogged glass. It was like that time on the lake when the storm had come up, wind lashing his small sail, the boat swinging wildly. Too late, too late—and he'd come about wrong, overturned. Black water over his head, the cold.

She turned to the mantelpiece, rested her head on her arms. "God."

"Laura—"

She looked at him sideways. "This was all your idea, Will, Why? Why did you start all this?"

"I wanted to know—"

"You wanted me to know that I was the one in trouble, not you." She rubbed her teeth on her fist.

He tried to think how to calm her. "You've been honest, you—"

"What is it you *want?* You make me wild and you won't tell me what you're really after!" Her lips drew back—in pain? Or ready to bite?

He felt as though a blood vessel burst in his temple. He couldn't help himself, or didn't want to. "I thought maybe you'd tell me about you and Trawick."

"What?"

He hadn't realized he wanted to hurt her. The good man, the *healer.* Hopelessly, he said, "Trawick."

"What's he got to do with this?'

"I don't know. He gives you something you—"

"The man has given me nothing! No, I take that back. He gave me a phony Indian headdress. Jo despises him and she's right to, he—"

"He made love to you."

He held his breath. Tell me the truth, he'd asked her; the truth was that he was her enemy.

But if a bullet had struck her, she didn't show it. If anything, the accusation calmed her; her trembling stopped. "You're out of your mind."

"I know he has."

"You can't know what's not true."

"I think it is true."

Carefully, she said, "What's true is that he paid attention to me and Jo. You're jealous. That's understandable."

He tried to breathe around the fist in his chest. "But it's true, isn't it."

She swung toward him as though she drove a car and had just caught him in her headlights—the one she wanted to run down. "I just realized how you'd love to have an unfaithful wife. Then you could forgive me. You could walk anywhere with your head high. He saved her, folks, and whatever she does, he chalks it up to her weakness. You'd be happy if I'd had a lover."

He watched her.

"I'd still be the handless maiden, you'd still be the—"

"Screw it!"

"You're into a fairy tale of your own."

"I just want you to tell me." There was no way to escape it: he didn't wish her well. She had slept with Trawick, and if she admitted it, *she'd* be the guilty one. He'd be innocent. God! Was there nothing more to his compassion than a frenzy to save his own life?

Her face went white. "I don't think you know what you're saying. You were sitting here in the dark, trying to think of a way to trap me into admitting something that isn't true."

He circled, looking for a way out. "I was mourning. Mourning my own life, and yours. I was so sorry for both of us, how we've missed it somehow."

She swung at him. Her fist glanced off his shoulder. He grabbed her but the crown of her head smashed his jaw, her nails scraped his cheek. He pinned her arms.

"Don't—"

"Will, you're hurting me! Let go!"

He did. But she looked so bereft that he took her in his arms. He tried to kiss her cheek but she buried her face against his chest. "I'm sorry."

Against his shoulder, she whispered, "You said that thing about Trawick to hurt me."

"It's nothing. Nothing. Jo said she'd seen you with him, that's all."

She quivered. *"Where?"*

He pressed her against him. He didn't want to see her face. "Driving through town." Because now he didn't want to know any more. Jo was right. Laura's fear of discovery told him all of it, and her humiliation was his own. "It doesn't matter."

Her damp hair was coarse on his lips. Under his fingers her pulse pummeled in her throat.

Her hand stroked at his waist. "I gave Thomas a ride to the train station one day when he stopped here to look for Jo. He was late so I offered, more to get rid of him than anything else."

"So there it is."

"Jealous for nothing. All this confusion! We were all doing fine until Thomas came along. But I'm glad we talked, you and me. Now we know each other better."

"Yes." Lie upon lie, heaped on each other like the ice floes on the beach, a trash of lies.

He walked her to the front steps, his arm around her waist. Cold wind blew in the crack of the front door. A stripe of streetlamp light slashed her cheek. He kissed her forehead. "You need your shower, and I'd better close up down here. Those drinks really hit me."

"In the morning it'll seem like a dream, just a bad dream. We shouldn't fight like this." She made a kissing noise, and climbed the steps, dragging her sweatjacket behind her like a shadow. "Don't forget to let Daisy out one last time or she'll wake us up."

"I'll take care of everything."

In the sun-room Daisy slept by the radiator. At his touch, she swarmed awake, licking and nuzzling. Heavily, she jounced ahead of him to the back door. Nine years old, as old as his marriage—a lifetime. He leaned against the door to watch the dog sniff the hay piled over the roses, then squat. "Good old pup," he said when she huffed back to him. He poured fresh water into her red bowl. Already she slept again, her rump against the lowest step of the back stairs. Sometimes Jo had lain on that step to pet the dog. He sat, ran his fingers up into the dog's matted coat, felt her heart throb. He sat like that for a long time, then he locked the back door, pushed the rug against the sill to stop the draft, and, one by one, turned off all the lights behind himself as he made his way upstairs.

22

Once Jo could rely on Will for everything, but nothing that he did now could be counted on. When she'd asked to come home to pick up some things he told her that Laura had the flu, Jo had better wait. When she invited him to have lunch with her, he said he'd try to work it out, but wouldn't name a time. She rehearsed telling him right out loud what they both knew—he was avoiding her—but she didn't say it. "Be straight with me," he'd always told her. Now he wanted anything but that.

One night, reaching him at home on the phone, she began, "That day in my room, Will, I—"

"We can't talk about it."

"Can't?"

"Please."

She knew he meant, I don't want to talk about it. When he chose for himself, he chose for her, too. There was no way around that. Although she wanted both to protect him and to confront him, most of all she wanted to please him. That was nothing new. The only new thing was that now the way to please him was for her to remain apart, silent, closed, polite. Polite! It came down to *manners* when he phoned her at the regular intervals which he chose.

"How's it going for you, Jo?"

"Just fine." What she didn't say was that she was terribly lonely.

"How's it going with Darlene?"

"Smooth enough." Everything Darlene did set Jo's teeth on edge. She wanted to scream when Darlene sprayed on her deodorant, brushed out her frizzy perm, and sang along with Springsteen's "Pink Cadillac," her shoulders swaying, giving off waves of gardenia cologne. Sometimes Jo slept on a couch in the lounge so she wouldn't hear Darlene breathing in the same room. She'd have to find a place of her own soon, somewhere she could shut a door and be alone.

"And your classes?" His voice blurred. He was using his lunch break to call her, eating a sandwich as they talked.

"Classes are classes." In fact, hers were just like those she'd had in high school. She sat near the back of the room, watching obedient heads bend toward the teacher—Dr. Todd, say—who stood in front of his desk, lecturing. Efficient hands copied down versions of what he had to say about American history. Sometimes a polite laugh lifted from the girls in response to what he intended as a joke, his brows arched in expectation. For her part, Jo concentrated on trying not to bolt from the room. "Hang in there," she urged herself, like her soccer coach, who sang out at the players as they ran wind sprints, "You can do it!" Jo wanted to yell, This has no meaning! None of this is real!

Suppose the teacher could hear her thoughts. Suppose he stopped the class, said, "Fine, then, Miss Hale. Tell us all what *is* real. Tell us what has meaning." What would she say? *Real is what I can touch, what I make myself, anything I learn that isn't for an exam. How I feel is real. Who I am. Whom I love. Love is real.*

"I bet you've got news from the darkroom," Will would say.

She always did. The photo lab was the one place where she could be herself, first in the comforting total dark while she wound her film onto the developing reels, and then in the orangy dim of the safe lights while she made prints. "I'm learning burning and dodging."

"Dodging? Sounds like football."

"It's painting with light. I love it."

"I'm glad. Taking a lot of pictures?"

"Quite a few." A print that she treasured was a shot of one of Will's worn-out running shoes, tipped on its side on the back step where Daisy had left it, the laces like crumpled twists of bright foil in the early morning light, a rime of frost on the cement under it. She'd taken that shot the morning she moved into the dorm, spent time to bracket it to make sure she had a good exposure, although Laura was calling for her to hurry. The underexposed frame was the best—Will's shoe seemed denser, heavier, more substantial even than the house itself in the other shots she took that morning.

"Got to go now, Jo. Surgery. So you're doing all right?"

He meant, Tell me that you are. Lie to me.

"I'm fine."

"I'll get back to you soon."

"Hey, how are you?"

"Neither fair nor foul. Got to go." He timed his calls carefully so that he'd have to hang up quickly. He wouldn't be late for his patients. Will was never late; he was responsible; if he was taking care of you, you could count on him completely. If he were carrying you across a river, for example, he'd never drop you. She imagined him stepping heavily through the tumult of the current, holding her close, her arm around his neck, his arms warm in the cold water which swirled around them.

"Bye, then, Will."

"So long." And always the slightest pause before he hung up, as though he waited to hear if she'd cry out, Don't go! But she didn't.

After she hung up she pressed her forehead against the tiled wall by the phone. Around her she heard the noise of typewriters, several stereos in competition, voices calling, laughter, a forbidden cat mewing, someone playing a guitar. Everyone else was busy, talkative, full of plans or complaints, their own hopes and dreams. All around her the world was urgently in motion. Only she was still, fixed as an old tree. She'd had one moment of fierce affirmation in English, when Sister Catherine read from Shakespeare in her soft, surprisingly passionate voice, ". . . full of sound and fury, signifying nothing." *Nada.* As Darlene liked to say about practically everything, "It's *nada* to me, babe."

What Jo couldn't understand was how content everyone around her seemed to be with this thick blanket of *nada* smothering them. And what if she couldn't learn to go along?

What if she couldn't forget about wanting something real, something with meaning? She'd spend her whole life in the darkroom, hiding—a life in the dark. Impossible love—and everything else was stale, flat, exhausting, a waste of time.

She knew that not even Estelle would have understood her love for Will. But of course Jo never really understood Estelle's love for John Holden, either, especially after Estelle finally brought him up to Highland Park to meet her. That was the summer Jo was sixteen, the last time she saw Estelle.

Jo sat on the steps, arms around her knees, her feet lined up evenly, like a kid in dance class, waiting. And down the street came a dark green Buick convertible, top down, Estelle in dark glasses and a chiffon scarf over her hair, waving. The man beside her had a cigarette in his lips, wore a tan jacket with the collar turned up, aviator shades.

He pulled up to the front walk, and Estelle climbed out. Shy, Jo waited on the steps. In a loose, flowered dress like grandmothers wear, Estelle came up the walk, waving back to John Holden, who stayed in the car finishing his smoke, looking up at the oaks overhead. He had a lot of gray in his hair, but looked younger than Estelle because his face was so thin, his cheekbones and the line of his jaw sharp and shiny. Because now Estelle looked so old.

"Oh, tootsie!" Estelle called as she came. "Look at you! New jeans and new tennis shoes, and you haven't even scrubbed dirt into them yet. And you let your hair grow! Don't it look fine out on your shoulders!"

In one hand she carried a box of candy, in the other something rectangular and brown, like a brick, with a blue ribbon around it. Suspended from a gold chain, her shoulder bag bobbed on her hip.

"Here, give us a smooch!" Estelle set down her presents and caught Jo by her elbows to lift her into her embrace. Her cheeks pleated from the weight she'd lost.

The feel of Estelle's arms and breasts almost made Jo cry, but she got hold of herself. "You smell different," she said against Estelle's cheek.

"Youth Dew. It's *his* choice. I brought you some for your bath. It's a killer, believe you me." She pulled a man's handkerchief from her skirt pocket and blew. "I've already cried my fill, but when I see you the tears just come!"

"You'll stay a while, won't you? Laura's not here."

"We surely will! John, get a move on!"

He climbed languidly out of the Buick and flicked his cigarette butt onto the asphalt. He was taller than he'd seemed in the car, and carried a little potbelly proudly, like a gift. He wasn't good-looking, but Jo thought she understood why women would try to please him—he had that skeptical, conquering look.

"The place needs a new roof." His greeting.

"It needs the works," Estelle agreed. "This here's my baby, Jo." She hugged Jo again, enveloping her in Youth Dew and sweat. "And here's my John!"

"Hi," Jo said over Estelle's shoulder, her hair and Estelle's white scarf brushing her mouth.

John Holden winked, a slow wink that signaled he'd taken a good look at her. And her house, she guessed, because he said, "I been noticing your gutters. I'd have to get up there to see the damage, but it looks like you had a shitty winter."

"John's gone into roofing," Estelle said, squeezing Jo.

He threw his weight onto his right hip and ran his thumbnail between his front teeth. "It's a solid, well-built place, but Estelle here had me expecting a damned palace."

Estelle laughed her good laugh that wobbled her chin. "John, will you fetch that bag of fresh peaches from the car, and the thermos?" To Jo she said, "I thought I'd make us some fresh peach sundaes. We haven't had breakfast yet."

Now Jo was smiling—sundaes for breakfast, that was Estelle's style. She watched John Holden saunter back to his car, a skinny guy with a slight limp and a bald spot barely hidden under carefully combed hair—Estelle's hero. It made Jo sad; she'd thought John Holden might look like Richard Gere, only older, of course, an older Richard Gere.

Estelle switched her shoulder bag behind her, and picked up her presents. "Here's a box of your favorite white chocolate almond bark, and this is for Laura." She handed Jo what she now saw was a heavy loaf of bread. "I took this occupational therapy class and we made these. Bake a loaf of white bread, dry it twenty-four hours in the oven, then shellac it. It's a centerpiece. Laura will love it. You get those peaches from John, while I scout out ice cream from the freezer. I know Laura's got some stashed, right?"

Jo was alone with John Holden. She met him halfway down the walk to take the bag of peaches. He slipped off his shades as he approached her, and she saw his eyes were hooded and weary, as if he'd seen everything and done everything and was searching now for something new.

Handing Jo the paper bag, he said, "Estelle calls you her baby. Hell, you ain't no baby. Where I come from girls your age are engaged. Girls who wear blue jeans like you do are *married.*"

She looked at his hands instead of his face, at the silver and turquoise ring on his index finger and the Indian silver watchband on his wrist, at the curly dark hairs showing beneath the cuff of his pink shirt. "Estelle looks pretty sick," Jo said. "All of a sudden she looks old."

"She's still a good old woman," he said in his husky voice.

"What do you mean?"

He leaned close enough now that she smelled the mints and tobacco on his breath. His skin shone with after-shave and sweat beaded finely on his upper lip, although the morning was still cool. "You know the difference between a *good* old woman and an old *good* woman, don't you?"

She felt herself blushing. He grinned. Then, thank heavens, Estelle was calling for them to come inside, she had the pot on for coffee, and Jo could turn away from John Holden and his casual lechery.

Oh, Estelle, a lifetime of love for him, for a nobody, really, for a greaser who tells dirty jokes to kids. Jo wished she hadn't met him, wished he'd stayed in her imagination as a movie star.

And she remembered how coldly Estelle had summed up Will when she'd first met him: "How much on the ball could a man have who'd settle for Laura?"

No one could understand another's love, that was the truth.

Only Will could understand, and he didn't want to know how she felt about him. *Is that the worst that can happen, Will? That you'll never even know?*

Then on a Thursday evening in early November, when she was so lonely that she'd actually accepted Darlene's invitation to go home with her to South Bend for Thanksgiving weekend, Jo saw Will waiting for her in the lounge when she came out of the cafeteria. He still wore his scrub suit under his coat, so he'd come here from the hospital in a hurry. Her heart sped up: he'd come to tell her he loved her.

"Hello." He put his arm lightly around her shoulders and led her away from the door where the girls were passing.

"Will!" He let her slip her arm around his waist for a moment, then indicated she was to sit beside him on the long sofa under the windows. He turned so their knees touched, and took her hand. Now she saw that he looked both exhausted and distracted, his face pale and circles under his eyes as though he'd lost a lot of sleep several nights in a row. "What's wrong?"

"Nothing for you to worry about. I just thought I should give you some news."

"Laura?" A surge of fear, and to her shame, hope, made blood rush prickling to her face. "Something's happened to her?"

"Laura's all right. She's seeing her psychiatrist, maybe she's even better, I don't know. It's about Trawick."

Jo slumped back against the plastic sofa. "Him! I thought he was out of my life forever."

"He is. I was called down to Emergency for an auto pile-up this afternoon, and I happened to see a chart on Trawick. He was brought in this morning, and he died while they were pumping out his stomach. I guess he took a whole medicine cabinet of prescription drugs, then changed his mind and called the rescue squad. At any rate, when the fire department brought him in he still had vital signs, but he didn't last long. God, he had drugs in his gut that aren't even on the market yet."

First, the shock of it—so near. A man who'd once kissed her was dead. She knew she should feel sorry for crazy Thomas, but she didn't. She was relieved, really, and then ashamed of herself.

What kind of person was she to be pleased by his suicide? "Laura will care more than I do," she said, and wished the words back the instant she'd spoken.

"Maybe. I don't know."

"Does she know about it?"

"Not yet. I came here on my way home. I thought he might have written something to disturb you again."

"No, nothing."

"Sometimes suicides try to blame others."

"He called me for a while, but I wouldn't go to the phone. Then he quit. That's all."

"Good. I was worried for no reason." He took off his glasses and rubbed his eyes, releasing her hand to do so.

"But I'm glad to see you!" She wanted his attention.

He looked at her a moment, then at the clock on the wall beside them. His face was almost gray with fatigue. After all, she thought, he has problems of his own, real ones—the demands of his work, and Laura, with her complicated needs. Wouldn't that be enough to fill his thoughts? Why did she think he dreamed about her as she did about him? She hadn't thought once of what *he* might need, of what real burdens he must carry.

She had imagined and hoped too much. Of course Will loved her. But he wasn't *in love* with her. That was her idea, hers alone. From a single kiss she'd constructed a universe.

Her dreams—he would take her in his arms, they'd drive off to California, leave the past behind. And then what—live happily ever after? Send postcards back to Laura in the hospital, where she was surely headed? A man's whole life can't be left behind—it travels with him.

As she watched Will's somber face, a net of pain formed around her eyes: *See things as they are.* Thomas was a sick man, to be pitied more than feared. I'm a romantic child. And Will? Will is a good man who'd like to save the world but can't even help his wife.

Surprising herself, she stood up. "You were really good to stop, Will. It's better to know about Thomas than not to know. Now I've got to study for a history exam."

"Right now?"

He looked so genuinely disappointed that she said, "In a minute. Shall I get you some coffee from the cafeteria?"

He shook his head. "I should go, too. I've been trying to get home in time to have supper with Laura. Her doctor says that's important." He stood and buttoned his coat. "Jo, how are *you* in all of this?"

But it was only one of his polite questions requiring a polite answer, and she wasn't capable of that game now. Her throat was tight and her chest burned. "I'll walk you to the door," she said. "You'll call soon, won't you?" She knew he'd say yes, and she knew they'd keep the same routine on the phone. And as soon as he left her tonight, she'd go to the darkroom, to her pictures, to the safety of the silence there. Disappear, that's all she could do. And, after all, that's what he wanted from her.

23

On the Sunday after Thanksgiving the temperature dropped to fifteen above zero and the lake began to freeze along the shore. Laura sat on the couch, her legs wrapped in the mohair blanket, the saw-toothed fire the only light in the room. After their light supper of leftover turkey, which she only pretended to eat, not even caring that Will wasn't fooled, he'd said, "Laura, we've got to talk. Really talk." Then his pager beeped and he'd had to go to Emergency. As he left the house he repeated, "When I get home we'll talk."

"I can't take another *talk*," she said. But there was nowhere for her to go. So she waited for him.

She was thinking of a quote she'd copied inside the cover of her ecology notebook when she was in college: "In a cold season seek a minor sun." She'd thought the writer stated a philosophical position, but now she understood better: sheer survival. If you're freezing, seek any heat you can find; and if you're starving, you'll be cold all the time. The warmths she could depend on now were the electric burners on the stove which came up from gray to russet before she moved her hands away, the iron radiators which knocked with steam and hissed it through the pear-shaped valves, hot water, a shot of Will's whiskey held in her mouth, Daisy's heavy warmth, and this blanket of her mother's. Everything else was cold. It was like one of

those sci-fi movies in which the starship veers off course, carrying its doomed crew into the absolute zero of outer space.

She shouldn't be thinking about heat and cold. She should be
planning what to say when Will came back to have his talk with
her. But she couldn't think ahead. There was only *this*. She
pressed her hands under her legs for warmth.

But when she heard Will at the back door, she snapped on
the light at the end of the sofa. It wouldn't be good for Will to
find her sitting in the dark. She'd need her defenses. She ran her
fingers through her hair, and when he came in she managed to
smile. "So you've come back to the scene of the crime," she
said, though that wasn't what she'd intended to say at all.

"How do you feel?" Will asked her. He'd poured himself a
drink and stood in the living room doorway as tense as a
sprinter waiting for the starting gun. He'd practiced his question because he wanted a confrontation. She didn't.

"I'm cold." Surely he could see that. Her teeth chattered, her
lips must be blue. In spite of her goosedown robe, she shook all
the time. "I'm waiting for Jo, actually. A friend of hers is driving
her by to pick up some things."

"She has a key. Let's go upstairs."

But when Jo came by, Will would be interrupted; she'd have
a rest. "Let's wait."

"Then we can talk here. How do you feel?" he repeated. He
wagged his head for emphasis, as he'd said his father used to do.
He enunciated each syllable separately and with equal emphasis, the way he spoke foreign phrases.

He didn't realize that there wasn't any answer to that question. She was a wire made electric with cold and pain, but her
emotions were unplugged. She didn't know why. That was just
how it was now. For answer she drew her robe closer. She
should have gone upstairs to bed again right away after he went
back to the hospital.

It didn't matter to him that she had no reply. He'd asked his
question so he could tell her how *he* felt. She was amazed at how
easy this was for him. He had so many words ready—"disappointed," "fearful," "alarmed," "uneasy," "anxious." They all
had definite meanings for him, as though his feelings were on a

map and he could plant paper flags on important positions: here he was *sorry,* here was *sad,* here was *worried,* here *confused.* Here he was *angry*—but he wouldn't say that, though anger was there, all right, in the center of the map, like a major city flagged by arterial roads: *anger.* He'd always been afraid of anger; he didn't want to lose control. He didn't want to shout and throw things and hit people—she'd heard all his stories about his dad's violent temper. But she could feel Will's anger, smell it—it radiated from him like an animal scent. He spoke to her in simple sentences, but he was full of complicated rage. She should be frightened, but that feeling was gone, too. Nothing was left.

"Don't stand over me," she told him. "Sit down."

"Let's go upstairs."

She wanted her bed. But if he wanted to go upstairs, that meant he wanted to go on talking for a long time. And she was so tired.

He followed her up, waited while she turned on her electric blanket and climbed into her bed. Then he closed the door.

He stood by the dresser in front of her. She watched his mouth, muscles in his face twitching. He didn't know that she wasn't listening to him. The butternut branches were scratching on the window, hickory nuts thudding on the roof. A dog barked and barked down the block, a car ground by on the sidestreet gravel. Beneath it all, the hush of the lake.

After a while he came closer and touched her shoulder. Was he crying? A drop fell onto his hand. He drew it back, wiped it on his pants, and went on talking.

"Please understand," he said several times. His face veered down close to hers—his earnest, intense, English face, with its broad forehead, square chin, unruly shock of brown hair. "I don't know what to do," he said.

Even in bed her skin ached, her bones ached. Her heels and elbows were sharp. She thought of the Indian skeletons Momma and Daddy had shown her on their one vacation out west. *Mesa Verde.* They'd been happy that day—the three of them. Grasshoppers droned, the sun was flat and hot reflecting off the cliffs. In the great fissures in the sides of the mesa were the abandoned dwellings of the tribe that built a culture and then disappeared. They left behind their houses, their pots and baskets, their temples, their graves. The skeletons of their dead. But the people themselves vanished. No one knew why, Momma said. Perhaps it was a change in the water supply, perhaps a crop failure, perhaps a new enemy. No way to know. Only the dead and dying left when the tribe moved on.

Like Will, moving on.

He went to the window and looked out toward the lake. "Hospital. You'll get better." His shoulders knotted, he gripped the windowsill. "Doctors," he said.

The first time in the hospital she'd pretended to go along with their plans, but every night she'd pulled the I.V. from her vein and let the glucose run onto the floor. They'd been angry and eventually she grew tired of them all. She'd wanted to go home, so she ate what they gave her. They praised her as if they were house-breaking a dog—Good girl! Good girl!

"I want to help you," Will said. He drained his glass. In a minute maybe he'd go downstairs for another dose and she could rest. "Help you," but he didn't mean that. Not really. He meant the hospital. And then he'd leave her. Why would he stay? Who *could* love her? Ever, ever, ever.

Mesa Verde: "green table." Momma was proud of her for knowing that. Daddy paid the forest ranger and he gave them a trail map. She ran ahead of Momma and Daddy. The trail led through the pine and piñon from one cave to the next. Numbers were painted on stakes at places of special interest. Guardrails kept visitors back from the edge of the cliffs, but she managed to look over. If you climbed those ladders carved into the orange stone, sometimes you would hang out over space. The guide said that women with papooses strapped to their backs had climbed up those ladders every day to tend the crops on the top of the mesa. Looking up, she was dizzy, so she sat down in Cave 7 to wait for Momma and Daddy.

Then she saw the place where the girl's skeleton had been. The sick girl with the baby.

In a trough of water-hollowed stone, right by the cave entrance facing west, was a marker: "Adolescent female with child. Skeletons on display in museum."

She followed the trail back to the museum. Cases and cases of glass, all numbered. The girl was lying on her side in case number 7, her knees drawn up, her hands under her chin. In the semicircle of her bones, the tiny skeleton of a baby, its knees drawn up, too, its skull resting just under the ribs of the mother. Laura leaned against the glass to look at them. A card said that the girl's head was flattened on the right side. She had been an epileptic and had lain on her right side all her life. She'd died at approximately fifteen years of age—before her child was born.

Perhaps she'd been buried, but Laura guessed the tribe had left her behind alive. When they left the mesa. How could they carry an epileptic, pregnant girl down the cliff? How could they carry her on the trail? There would have been no choice but to leave her behind with a bowl of corn beside her, a gourd filled with water.

"Laura?" He brought the desk chair next to the bed and sat looking down at her.

Maybe she should say, I'm tired. Maybe she should say, Comfort me. He would like soft words from her. He might even want to comfort her. She was afraid to cry—it took too much energy.

She pulled her knees up and rubbed her feet. They were icy, even in wool socks. "Where's the baby?" she asked. "Help me find the baby."

"You're hallucinating." He leaned over her. "Why do you do this to yourself? Why? Why do you do this to me?" Yes, he was crying, and he wagged his head to shake the tears off, crying hard, and he began to shake her, lifted her shoulders from the bed, her hair bouncing against the pillow, her arms flopping, her hands fluttering like broken wings, his face dark with blood. "I'm starving, too! You aren't the only one! I'm starving! Starving to death and I don't know what to do!"

He laid her back down. "Oh, God, I'm so sorry! Did I hurt you? I don't want to hurt you!"

"No." He couldn't hurt her.

He gripped the footboard of the bed.

"You're so angry with me."

It seemed hard for him to get his breath. "Fucking angry at our life! I don't want my life to be like this! I don't want this!"

I don't want you, Laura.

His fists were white on the footboard. "I'm so sick of myself, sick of your being sick. I'm angry at your fucking sickness! I hate it. It owns you, it runs you!" His head shook back and forth. How could he focus his eyes? "It's the only life I've got, Laura!"

Why wasn't she frightened? Shouldn't she at least feel fear?

"You're not listening, Laura!"

Some of the tribe must have chosen to stay behind on the mesa. They would have watched the braver ones climb down the sheer cliffs. They would have watched the tribe walking, growing smaller and smaller toward the horizon until the figures no longer looked like men and women.

From her great distance she laid out the obvious to him. "I'm the one who's screwed up your life."

"Yes! You!" He turned in a spiral of fury, arms raised. "I want you to be well!"

He's walking west along the trail. A woman appears beside him. She's leaving to find food, too. Dust blows up around her legs and her long, purple shadow joins his shadow in the mustard grass of the plains.

She wasn't too dizzy to sit up. "I *see* you, Will."

He came close again, his hands tucked into his armpits—he wanted to make sure he didn't shake her again. "What? What do you see?"

"Someone's with you." The vision was clearer, now. She was beginning to understand it.

His lips went tight, a line. He sat beside her on the bed. "You're having delusions. It's one of the symptoms." He was the doctor again, playing it safe.

But saints had visions when they fasted, and their visions were true. So was hers.

He rubbed his eyes. His face was gray now, the anger bled out of him. "Please, try to understand. I'm going to get you into the hospital tomorrow, whether you agree or not. It's the only way. It's your life, too, Laura."

The woman walking through the dust beside him takes his hand and turns back to look up. Her hair lifts in the wind and she leans against Will's side.

"Will?" She was whispering. Where had her voice gone?

"Do you think you could sleep now?"

"Will?" Maybe he hadn't heard her.

He went to the door. He said, "I'm going to run. I've got to ease my chest somehow. I *have* to run. When I get back I'll come up to see if you're asleep."

The door swung behind him. She saw his hand last.

He took all the air with him. She had to push up higher on her pillows to get a breath. The lamp on her dresser wavered like a candle, the flame trembling on the windowpanes. Some of the oldest ones distorted light. Daddy bought them from another house that was being torn down. He bought the bannister there, too, and some of the doors. He fixed up the house and when he didn't want to live in it any longer he killed himself. He stepped in front of the bus, the driver told the police, "He looked me right in the eye and then he stepped off the curb." They didn't even take him to the station.

And now Thomas. All those drugs. All that rage, and hating women, after all—Jo had intuited that. Sick Thomas. No, she didn't want to be a destroyer like him.

Her hair stuck to her throat, her forehead. How could her face be so hot and wet, her body so cold? She knew the chill, but not the burn in her face. There were some surprises left.

Will said, "It's your life, too." As though she might have thought she had several, like a cat. He was leaving because he wanted his own life. She was wasting hers, and he didn't want any part of that any more.

Then she had to open her mouth wide like a fish. No no no no no no no no no like bubbles coming up through deep water. Her tongue hit the roof of her mouth with faint clicks, like the sound of feet running down a corridor.

She couldn't hold down any more. Something shook her against the bed as Will had shaken her. The room expanded around her and she shrank to a thin core of solid pain. All was gone—her mother, her father, Thomas—all illusion and hope. And now Will.

Oh, please, make it stop.

She'd go to the hospital. She'd get well. She didn't want

death. Will must be healed, too. There must be an end to despair and pain. She must tell him there would be an end.

It was hard to walk steadily, but she reached the window. She touched her reflection. She wouldn't look any different to him, but she was different. Already she was new.

On the stairs, she held the railing tightly. At the couch Jo was stuffing things into her backpack. Poor Jo—Thomas hated her, after all. He'd wanted to punish her for his own failed life.

Jo looked up, startled. "You all right, Laura? You look awfully shaky."

"I'm fine. Just fine."

"You look wobbly."

"I'm a little wobbly. I need to see Will."

"He's running." Jo looked down at the floor. "He said he wanted to be alone. He'll give me a ride to school when he gets back."

Laura took her sheepskin coat out of the closet and pulled it on over her robe. She tugged on her lined boots and dug a pair of Jo's mittens off the shelf.

"Where are you going?"

"I have to tell him something."

"I heard him yelling at you."

"We had a fight. I want to say I'm sorry. It's all going to be okay, believe me. Which way does he go when he runs?"

"The beach, mostly. He runs on the beach."

"In this cold?"

"He likes the beach. But you shouldn't go down there. It's really bitter, Laura."

"I'm okay."

"Listen, you don't look so well—"

But Jo couldn't stop her. At the back door the cold made her breath catch in her throat like a fishbone. She wished she had a hat, but she didn't want to go back inside. She knew enough to start slowly.

When she opened the gate, a cat slipped across the Millets' trash cans. Cecil stepped out of their lighted doorway. He wore his plaid jacket and carried his telescope. "Cecil?"

He waved. "Clear night, no moon!"

"Star-gazing?" Even with the house lights behind him she could barely see him as he walked across his yard to her, but as he came close she made out his white beard and the white hair around his ski cap.

"Should be good viewing from the bluff. It's the best kind of night, black as hell and the wind taking the smog west."

Stars blazed, but under the trees it was black. She didn't need lights. She knew her way through the park with her eyes closed.

"How're you doing? Your husband said you'd had the flu. Pat's going to send over some chicken soup. Jewish penicillin."

He smelled of beer and woodsmoke. "Tell Pat I want her soup more than anything."

"I'll do just that. Where you off to on this cold night?"

"The park. Just for a breath."

"Want to walk with me? I've got a flashlight."

"Which way are you going?"

"To that clearing by the stairs."

Then she'd have to go down the bluff by her old path below the oak. That was the fastest way, anyway. "No thanks. I just want to look at the lake, that's all."

"Watch your step." He turned down the road toward the north end of the park. The yellow circle of light spun at his feet. She was dizzier than she'd thought.

She'd tell Will, "We both have to leave this place of death. We'll have a new life."

She felt her way along the side of the garage and then she was on the lane. She was out of breath and her lungs ached. But it wasn't far to the oak, and then just a short climb down.

As she neared the bluff she heard Jo call, "Laura? Come on back inside, please. Laura?"

It wasn't as hard to run as she thought it would be. Her shoulder brushed a sapling and she stumbled, but her legs were strong.

"Hey, Laura? Come back!"

At the edge of the bluff she called into the wind, "Will!" Her teeth hurt with cold. She couldn't see the lake below, just the sheen of starlight that seemed suspended like a net over the surface of the water. She crouched by the oak and grasped the largest root to lower herself onto the path. Her feet found the rounded stones. Jo was right behind her.

"Laura, don't be dumb!"

But Laura wasn't dumb. She was smarter than she'd ever been in her life. She was more than smart, she was wise.

Then a pain slashed across her chest and down her arms. The pain dragged her hands from the root, and before she could cry out she fell backwards in a cascade of stones.

24

To Will's relief, after Laura died his work was the refuge he needed it to be. It was important to keep busy, very busy. The nurses told him how sorry they were; some of the doctors clasped his shoulders. Then they treated him as they always had. The days went by.

He got home each night after dark—he'd taken to getting his supper at a chophouse in Highwood—and he came into the house without turning on the lights. He liked it that way, the rooms as impersonal as a train station or some other familiar but indifferent place. Laura left him no ghost—dead, she was no more real to him than when she lived. His only ghost was that of himself as a "good" man. He wrung himself with that self-deception. He'd never been such a man, never. What could he have done differently? He could name a thousand things, but not one that he'd had the strength to choose.

And worse, worse, he had wished her dead. As he pounded through the cold that night on the beach, whispering in helpless fury, "Die, then, if that's what you want!" he heard the frightening rip of stones giving way. When he found her on a ledge below the oak he realized that her heart had failed. But he felt as though he'd cursed her.

He walked through the silent house in the dark. Squares from the streetlights shone on the floors and wind hummed in the porch screens. In the distance, the lake creaked in the autumn weather. He sat in the sun-room to watch the oak branches in motion across the sky. He imagined he was on a ship moving slowly out to sea toward some destination not of his choosing. He wasn't afraid, but he was only a passenger. Whatever shore they moved toward was unknown to him. And what good would any plans be?

Then he changed into his gear, and, no matter how cold it was, he took Daisy with him to run through the park and down on the beach. He threw sticks for her and ruffled her fur when the lame old dog retrieved them. The plane lights in the O'Hare approach pattern swept by like slowly falling stars.

In bed, he watched the news on TV. When it was over he switched on his tensor light and read medical journals or paperback novels. He put off sleep as long as possible. Because he often dreamed of Jo.

She was on the edge of a crowd, moving away from him. When he tried to reach her, the crowd moved between them.

Once he dreamed that she was beside him in his bed. He could feel her breath on his shoulders, her slim arm around his waist, her naked breasts on his back. The feel and smell of her went through him like something he'd learned in infancy, an absolute that could not be questioned. A panic to possess her overtook him. All he had to do was turn to her. In his sleep he fought to waken like a drowning man struggling up through deep water, laboring to burst into the air again, and, against all hope and expectation, to be saved.

He phoned her at her dorm twice a week. He kept track; it mustn't be too often. Maybe it was a meaningless discipline, but he marked down the times and the lengths of his calls in his pocket notebook. It reassured him that he could take control over his contact with her.

Dorm noises and static crackled over the lines. He pressed the receiver so tightly to his head that after he hung up his ear was numb. He asked how she was doing. Okay, she said. She wasn't seeing Kit anymore. Her schoolwork was boring, but she was taking good photographs, pictures of things, not portraits—a store window of old felt hats, a porch chair strung with a knotted sash, the pattern of frost on her window. She was seeing one of the nuns, a psychologist, to talk about her grief. So much was lost. So *much*.

In the moment of silence he heard himself swallow. "Good," he said. "Talk to her. What else are you doing?"

She'd met some kids who were okay, not great. She was dating a guy she liked. When she asked him how he was, he said, "Keeping busy."

They didn't talk about Laura, although once Jo blurted, "Do you think she wanted to die?"

He thought he could say yes. But he didn't know. He'd lived with Laura for nine years and hadn't known her needs. She hadn't told him and he hadn't been able to guess. Maybe he hadn't wanted to know. His intentions were lost in the mists. Where he thought he'd been the most clear, he was completely clouded. Before Jo could say anything else, he lied that his beeper was paging him and he'd have to check in.

Then one night she phoned him to ask if she could come to the house and pick up some more of her things. "Tonight?" she asked. He told her tomorrow would be better for him, he wouldn't be on call. He'd pick her up around five and they could have supper together. "It's been a long time," she said.

That night he didn't sleep at all.

The next day was Wednesday, his day off. He canceled his tennis game and instead ran the vacuum, cleaned out the refrigerator, washed all the towels, the sheets, and his laundry. The house was pleasantly quiet and shut in by lightly falling snow. Steam from the dishwasher covered the kitchen windows. He wiped them and gazed out into the backyard where ice coated the pink twigs of the crabapple.

He drove into town and got groceries—steaks, baking potatoes, romaine for a salad, a frozen apple pie. On impulse he stopped at a liquor store and bought a bottle of wine, fruitier than he usually chose and much more expensive. "Having a party?" the clerk asked.

"No, just supper."

"*Some* supper!"

Her parka hood up and her hands deep into her pockets, Jo went ahead of him along the back walk. When he unlocked the back door, Daisy jumped against Jo's legs. She knelt and rubbed her face against the dog's grizzled muzzle.

"You missed me! I won't leave you again for such a long time!" Without turning, she asked, "Has she been eating all right?"

"She's doing well. Her joints bother her, but she still runs with me."

"She smells of fish. When I saw her every day I didn't notice."

He took her parka and hung up their coats. Crouching low and trembling, the dog licked Jo's wrists as she unzipped her boots.

She stood, hands on her hips. She was wearing jeans and a lavender sweater that looked soft as milkweed floss. "The house is so little. Isn't that funny? When I think about this kitchen it seems enormous to me."

"Maybe you've grown." She did look older to him. Her hair was parted on the side, and she'd outlined her eyes with mascara. Her face was blotched from the cold.

"I'll look around and get my bearings."

As she went through the dining and living rooms, she switched on lights. He didn't tell her that he'd grown used to the dark. He heard her upstairs, opening doors. Was she glad to be here? She seemed brittle with nerves. As he was. His hands shook when he took out the steaks, a bowl for salad, the potatoes.

Coming down the back staircase, she paused on the landing. "All that meat? I'm trying to cut calories. Dorm food." She patted her stomach.

He thought she looked wonderful. "How much steak do you want?"

"Half of one of those, and no potato, okay?"

"You're the boss."

She sat down on the stairs and hugged her knees. "Aren't you smoking any more? I didn't see your pipes anywhere, and there's no tobacco smell."

He'd forgotten about his pipes. He threw them all out the night Laura died—punishing himself, he guessed. "I gave it up. Do you care?"

"Everything's *different.*"

He thought her eyes brightened with tears. He wanted to catch her into his arms. "What's up, Jo?"

"I don't know. This is all so unreal. The rooms don't look the same. Mine is as tiny as a closet. Everything is so small and old and dark. When are you going to sell this place?"

"Soon, I suppose. Will you mind?"

"Oh, no! I don't think I want to come here again, either. This part of my life is over, and I'm so glad. The dining room's the worst. I used to stare at the Chinese vases on the buffet and wish I was out of here, someplace else, anyplace else. I don't want to eat in there ever again."

"We'll eat in the kitchen," he said quickly. He should have taken her out somewhere; he was a fool.

"Yes, here in the kitchen. Or on that coffee table by the fireplace."

That pleased him. He hadn't realized how chilled he was, how tight his chest had become. "Right! You fix up the coffee table and I'll lay a fire. That's just what we need. And I want a drink. I got some wine you'll like."

She smiled. "Oh, that's better."

Carrying her glass back and forth with her, she set the coffee table for their meal. He poured himself some whiskey, then built a fire and started the steaks. The aroma of meat and salt made his head swim—he'd forgotten to eat lunch. She stood near him to tear the lettuce. When they went to sit down, she brought the bottle of wine along.

They sat cross-legged on sofa cushions she'd laid on the floor. The wine relaxed her and she talked about school, a job she'd got on the switchboard, a movie she'd seen. He liked that. He was drinking too fast, but he liked that, too—the heat spreading through his chest. The firelight blushed on her face and throat. When she reached for the salt, her warm arm rested against his briefly. He felt as though his whole body was turning from gray to red and then to gold; even his head filled with a golden, radiant heat. He remembered his dream: her warmth against his back, her arm around him, her hand spread on his belly. He watched her over the rim of his glass, her quick changes of expression, her smile.

She took a drink of her wine as though it were water. "So. How are things going for you, Will? I mean, *really.*"

He'd imagined telling her of his guilt, remorse, the limitlessly expanding spaces of the night, his cauterized heart, except where she was concerned. He wished he could tell her that he wasn't sorry to be alone but that a steady, painful ache drummed in his chest because she wasn't with him. "I'm adjusting, I guess. I've always hated that word, but that's how I feel. Like a building settling into its foundation."

She nodded, encouraging him to go on.

What *could* be said? "I'm trying to make some decisions."

"Like what?"

He tried to smile but his lips wouldn't respond. What was wrong with him? Blood seemed to wash through his heart as though a valve had torn. She watched him, her lips downturned. A girl—a kid—looking for reassurance. "Like what the hell to do with this house, for openers."

"What's that mean?"

"When to sell it. What do you think?"

"I guess as soon as you can. You wouldn't move far away, would you?"

"No, of course not. An apartment near here, I guess."

"With a room for me, right?" Reaching for her glass, she knocked it over. Wine pooled on her plate, and he saw that she hadn't touched more than a few bites of her meal.

"Let me get you some milk, toots," he said.

In the kitchen he splashed cold water onto his face and rubbed his eyes hard with a dishtowel. He poured milk to the brim of a large glass and made himself drink a few swallows before he poured again. Take it easy, take it easy. For once in your life, do the right thing. The good thing.

She was hugging her knees and staring at the fire. She drank deeply, handed the glass back to him. She didn't look up. "Will, I did this *thing* today. I turned on the lights in the darkroom. On purpose. The whole lab was filled with the prints I was making. Prints under the enlarger, in the solutions, the bath.

There were some images I liked a lot—a fence covered with snow, some boys running across the field. But I switched on the lights. Not the safe lights, the real ones. I ruined all of it, Will. I just couldn't stand the dark any more. A life in the dark! I knew I was going to ruin all my work and I did it anyway and when I saw what I'd done I didn't care. Wet prints, I dumped them into the waste can. Just walked out."

She was crying. He got down on his knees beside her. He wanted to hold her so he could find comfort for himself. He didn't deserve it. But she did. He put his arms across her shoulders and tucked her head under his chin. Her arms went around his waist and he held her as though he could pull her into the hollow space in the center of his being. Just for a moment. That's all.

A log broke, throwing light across the walls. She sobbed against his chest and he felt warmth spreading there. *Be happy,* he commanded her silently. *You're entitled.*

"It's going to be better," he said against the top of her head. "It's tough now, but it's going to be all right. If you spoiled those pictures, you'll make new ones. You'll make wonderful pictures."

"But the rest of it?"

He felt her breathing steady on his chest. "Everything's okay. You're okay. I'm here. Believe me." He rocked her, slowly, telling himself, Remember this. Remember.

The fire was behind her. He had to close his eyes against its blaze, but even then an orange after-image burned on his sight. In the basement the old furnace groaned; the radiators shushed steam. The wind came up around the house with that low hush that sounded like shallow water slipping over stone. That sounded like the winter lake easing against the shore under its burden of ice.